A HOUSE
CALLED
ASKIVAL

A HOUSE CALLED ASKIVAL

MERRYN GLOVER

**FREIGHT
BOOKS**

First published 2014
This edition published 2015

Freight Books
49-53 Virginia Street
Glasgow, G1 1TS
www.freightbooks.co.uk

The writer acknowledges support from Creative Scotland (formerly Scottish Arts Council) towards the writing of this title.

The lines quoted in chapter 44 are from Emily Brontë's poem *Often rebuked, yet always back returning*.

A CIP catalogue reference for this book is available from the British Library.

ISBN 978-1-910449-25-7
eISBN 978-1-908754-60-8

Typeset by Freight in Garamond Premier Pro
Printed and bound by Hussar, Poland

the publisher acknowledges investment from
Creative Scotland toward the publication of this book

Merryn Glover was born in a former palace in Kathmandu and brought up in South Asia. She went to university in Australia to train in education. Her writing has won awards and been published in anthologies, magazines and newspapers. Also a playwright, her fiction and drama have been broadcast on Radio Scotland and Radio 4. *A House Called Askival* is her first novel. Having returned to live and work in Nepal for four years she now lives in the Highlands of Scotland.

for Alistair, for always believing

Tear down the temple,
Tear down the mosque,
Tear down whatever you can,
But do not tear down the heart
For that is where God lives.

Bulleh Shah
Sufi Poet

ONE

When Ruth finally returned to Mussoorie, it was late August, late monsoon, late in the day. Mist was rolling up from the valley like a brooding spirit, seeping into the hollows between hills, crawling over boulders, drowning trees. From her open window on the bus she felt it slip over her arm, smelling of damp earth and woodsmoke and dread.

Above, the town lay splattered across the ridge like the contents of an upended rubbish bin. It was bigger than before and even more crowded. Buildings shouldered each other along the steep slivers of road – restaurants and trinket shops, grey hovels and multi-storey concrete blocks – all bound together by a tangle of wires, washing lines and battered signs. Below them, on the forested slopes, the colonial bungalows hunkered under their rusting roofs as if trying to shut out the coarseness of the modern age, while Victorian relics, like the bank and the Masonic Lodge, sat forlorn and streaked with damp. Even the newer hotels, with their giant billboards and balcony rooms, seemed tired from the holiday makers and the relentless rain.

She got off the bus at Paramount Picture House, with its sodden film posters peeling off the walls and its broken ticket window. So unchanged, it could have been preserved in formaldehyde, like the specimens in the Bio lab at school squeezed into their watery yellow graves: a shrew, a cobra, a heart. They'd made her skin crawl, as had the cases of beetles stabbed into place, and the stuffed pheasant, gathering dust and losing feathers.

An old coolie approached her with a gnarled hand and an uncertain smile, revealing one brown tooth. At her nod, he stuffed her backpack into his basket and followed her silently up the narrow road through the bazaar. She felt like a fugitive, an exorcised spirit crawling back.

It was unsettling how the place had gone on without her, lending a feeling of callous indifference, betrayal even. So much was just as before: the row of shawl shops, the Tibetan stalls, the Hotel Hill Queen with its five floors built into the cliff. Even the tin shacks at the side of the road were still perched on their stilts like a row of rusting herons that had lost the will to migrate.

But some things were different. The hole-in-the wall booths that used to offer long distance calls now included internet access and mobile top-up; alongside the garish postcards of gods and Bollywood film stars a new pantheon of American celebrities jostled for space; and the old racks of walking-sticks and macramé pot-hangers were replaced with microwaves, televisions and cappuccino machines. Ruth wasn't sure which felt worse: the things that were exactly as she had left them or the ones that had changed.

Godiwala Plastics, half way up the bazaar, was still bristling with the same array of buckets and brooms and soap dishes, but it was the blue basin on the front step that halted her. It was exactly like the one from the foot-washing scene in *The Gospel of Jyoti,* the musical in her last year at school that had begun with such promise but ended in ruin.

On the curve past the Hindu temple the monkeys were ravaging the offerings on the front steps. They squabbled and cuffed each other, shrieked, scampered up the electricity poles and over window frames, leaving rice and flowers spilled across the road and into the gutters. The streets smelled dank. For two months the rain had soaked into the rubbish and dung, the blackened fruit, the roadside mud. The place was swollen with it. Shops sagged, their signboards curling, doors jamming, breathing out mould. Here and there, the damp had loosened a building's grip on the mountainside and swept it right away, leaving a jagged wound and a pile of rubble below. This was the spirit of August, the month when she'd returned to boarding each year after the summer vacation.

Climbing higher and higher up the steep road, she reached the top of the bazaar at Mullingar Hotel, where everyone always rested. The coolie lowered himself onto the steps of a corner store, grunting as he eased the basket strap from his head and tugged off a dirty cap. Ruth dug in her bum bag for her cigarettes and, lighting up, looked across at the Hotel. Why it was called that she didn't know, for it was a slum and always had been. A labyrinth of shacks huddled around the main buildings, some of which now teetered four floors above the precipice. Make-shift stairs and banisters were hammered onto the sloping verandas and the roof was a patchwork of tin sheets fringed with broken guttering, the space above the courtyard webbed with Tibetan prayer flags and washing lines. There was no sign of the Lhasa Café, where she'd bought the joints all those years ago that had been the final proof, if any was needed, that she was to blame.

She looked along the routes that forked at Mullingar. To the west, the road continued up the ridge in a series of tight switch-backs to the *chakkar*, the circular road at the top of the hill. She'd made her way up it many times after a Saturday in the bazaar. To the east, the road levelled out and became Tehri Road, the long ribbon that traversed the Garhwal hills all the way to Tehri city and beyond. She walked along it to the spot where the view opened and she could see Oaklands School. It looked like a scene from a fairy-tale with the red roofs bright as apples in the forest and the neatly swept clearings. Twenty-four years since she'd last seen it.

Now she was forty-one and supposed to be grown up.

She pulled deep on her cigarette, a slight tremor in her hand, and breathed out, the smoke curling around her like cloud.

She'd been expelled.

Expelled.

It sounded like a swift and violent ridding of something venomous; a spitting out of the poison apple – which must have been how the school saw it. But for her, it had been far worse.

Eventually, it had become a self-imposed exile. She'd made no conscious decision to stay away, but as more time had passed and the wounds only deepened, the prospect of return had become impossible.

Until now. Till he was dying and she had to come back.

Ruth flicked her stub onto the muddy road and ground it with her shoe. In clipped sing-song English she gave the coolie directions to Shanti Niwas and pointed up a small path that climbed between the two roads.

'Please take my bag there and tell to them I will come soon, yeh?' she said, and kicked herself that her childhood Hindi lay sleeping like a dog. She wanted to kick *it* – the lazy cur! – hurl stones at it, beat it with sticks till it rose and did her bidding instead of leaving her shackled to this mute gesturing, this silly broken English. But she knew its dormancy was not sloth but neglect; she'd not fed the thing since she left.

Once the coolie had set off, his plastic shoes squeaking, Ruth turned in the opposite direction and took the west road to the top of the hill. She had to see the house, before she lost all courage.

TWO

Shanti Niwas was fragrant with spices. In the kitchen corner, Iqbal fried crushed cardamom pods, mustard seeds and cinnamon in a pan of ghee. His voice rose above the sizzling in the plaintive notes of an Urdu *ghazal,* soaring on the top notes like a great bird, before plunging back to the mellow depths.

What with the singing and the spices and everything else, James couldn't concentrate. At the far end of the room, he sat stooped over a Bible and a print-out of his sermon, shaking his head and clicking his tongue. He rammed his half-moon glasses back up his nose and re-read the opening sentence: 'Is it easier to make a cripple walk or to forgive his sins?' Then he scratched it out, his knobbled fingers pinched red and stained with ink. Above it he scrawled, 'Any idiot can tell when a cripple is healed, but how do we know if a man's sins are forgiven?'

Iqbal hit an especially high note and James threw down his pen. He glared at his friend, but the man's back was turned, the floral bow of his apron bouncing as he ground ginger and chillies on a stone. His whole body rocked with the rhythm, from his buttocks to the bobbing curls at his collar.

James cracked the knuckles of one hand in the palm of the other and swung his head to the door. His daughter's backpack was propped against the frame, where the coolie had set it – he checked his watch – nearly two hours ago. But the little Miss-sahib herself had not come. It was getting dark.

'I think I should go find her,' he said, capping his pen.

'Oh, don't worry, Doctor-ji!' Iqbal wiped the ground spices off the stone with his plump fingers and flicked them into the pan. 'She'll be here any minute now, I'm sure of it.'

He beamed and tipped his head, but James knew he spoke out of hope rather than conviction. Iqbal had been more nervous than him that day, adjusting the furniture, arranging flowers, checking and double-checking the household supplies. He'd even rushed out after lunch for a can of Jubli's Lady Lush deodorant spray and fumigated the place, whipping up a haze of synthetic rose in the bathroom and drenching their shoes. It had sent James into a spasm of coughing and Iqbal into a fit of apology.

He was so, so sorry, he was just trying to make everything nice for her. Perhaps he should throw open all the windows? But then, maybe that would make the house too cold? Should he get the gas heater out of the godown? Or borrow the electric one from the neighbours?

No, no, no. James had put his foot down and an end to Iqbal's feverish preparations. He had already forbidden the tinsel streamers and the banner reading, 'Welcome Home Beauteous Ruth!'

'She would hate all that,' he'd snapped. 'She'd walk straight back out the door and into a hotel.' Iqbal's face had fallen, but he'd agreed to invest his energies in the cooking. It was his forte, his father's legacy, his fate. And, mercifully, its aromas were now vanquishing the last whisps of Lady Lush.

James raked his sermon pages together and stuck them into the Bible. He knew that Iqbal understood his unspoken longing and had made it his own; that he saw both the hope and the helplessness of what lay ahead. He closed the Bible with a thwack, set his reading glasses on top and pushed hard on the armrests of his chair to stand. Iqbal glanced across.

'She's a tough girl, your Ruthie,' he said. 'She'll be just fine, Inshallah. Here, why don't you have a drink or something? Can I get you a juice? Ginger ale? Chai?'

'No, nothing,' said James, and pressed his hands into the small of his back, pushing his hips forward till his spine cracked. 'Most of the time, Ruth is *not* just fine. But by the grace of God, she is still alive.'

'May his Holy Name be praised!' breathed Iqbal.

James grunted and moved to the glass door, rubbing his back. There was a biting between his shoulder blades and his neck was sore. Too long at the desk, bent over his Bible, struggling with words. Why take a man who could barely speak and ask him to preach?

He looked down towards the bazaar where the lights had become smudged halos in the blackening sky. He wished again she had agreed to be met at the bus stop. Or to get a taxi up instead of walking. She'd not been in Mussoorie for such a long time, she might not remember it so well, might not find the house. It used to be a crumbling servants' quarters, ugly as sin. Now it was Shanti Niwas – House of Peace – restored, with shining wood and a Garhwali slate roof, the southern wall a sheet of glass.

But Ruth did not agree to anything, he thought, sliding his hand round to his chest and rubbing the hollow beneath the yoke of his shoulders. She had always been thus. If the family had set out walking, she wanted to go the other way. If they were eating, she wasn't hungry; if sleeping, wide awake. Her mother had called it "spirit". A Spirit of Rebellion, he'd called it and tried to crush it.

He opened the door, straining his eyes in the gloom. It was nearly three years since he'd seen her last – at her sister Hannah's in Tennessee – but so many people and so much bustle, there was no chance to talk. And was there any use? She would not talk anyway, would not open up, would not let him in.

But it was not just her, he knew that. Even when there was an inkling of an opportunity, a moment alone, he never could say anything. He had hoped her mother's death might open a space, but it had not. If anything, Ruth had become more remote, the meetings fewer and further between, her communications shorter, rarer, colder. Most of the time he didn't even know where she was.

Till now. Till he was dying and there was a phone call. Ruth never phoned, but there she was, clear as next door all the way from Glasgow.

'I'm coming.'

'Oh. Good.'

'And I'll stay'.

'No need. Iqbal is here.'

'I'll stay till… whatever.'

'*Accha.*'

And her email had arrived the next day with her travel details: she would be with them on Friday. Iqbal had cheered. James had felt something turn over inside.

As he stood at the open door, the cool night smelling of rain, he felt it again. That deep, unknown, thing, that could be hope or dread.

He knew why she was not here.

He knew where she was.

THREE

Askival had once been his home. That was back in the '40s, when his parents Stanley and Leota Connor had divided their work between the Bareilly Agricultural college in the plains and farming projects in the hills around Mussoorie. When south, they left James in boarding at Oaklands, and when on the hillside, brought him out to stay with them at Askival. During these stretches, he ran the thirty minutes down the steep hill to school each morning, bounding like a mountain deer, and each afternoon plodded the hour back up, a slow mule with his sack of books. But on arrival, his efforts were always rewarded by a hug from the cook and a plate of home baking.

Aziz was the only servant the Connors brought with them from the plains, leaving the rest behind to keep the Bareilly house. For this couple from Iowan farming stock, who had done chores since they could walk and come to India to serve, the very idea of keeping servants was anathema. But India had other ideas. People wanted work and the missionaries must provide it. And so they were compelled to hire a *chowkidar* to patrol the mission compound at night, a *chaprassi* to do odd jobs and deliver *chits,* a *jamadar* to empty the commodes and clean the bathrooms, an *ayah* to care for the infant James, a *chokra* to operate the *punkah* fan in the hot season, a *mali* to tend the garden and pump water from the well, a *khansamma* to shop and cook, and a bearer to serve the meals, wash up and do the housework.

Going to Askival with just one servant was a relief, therefore, especially for Leota, who often felt her chief duty in India had been reduced to the management of household staff. Aziz was not only a superior *khansamma,* but resourceful, cheerful and, most remarkable of all, not too superior to perform the other jobs. As this was also true of Stanley & Leota, they covered the work between them.

And James, as soon as he got out of boarding, was also given a share of the chores. It added to his mixed feelings about being a 'dayski'. While he gained the freedom of wandering the hillside after school and on weekends, he lost the solidarity with those still enduring internment; while he felt the ache of home-sickness dissolve in his mother's embrace, he missed the camaraderie of the neighbouring bunks; and while he escaped the strict regime of the dorm, he became captive again to his father's rule, which was even stricter. All things weighed up, though, the greatest benefit of being out of boarding, was the food. After the stolid fare of the dorm, Aziz' cooking was manna from heaven and James ate like one starved.

On one Saturday in August 1942, James' rapturous eating was shared by his best friend, Paul Verghese. The boys were both ten, skinny and worm-riddled, their hair cut brutally short, knees rough as cheese rind. They polished off Aziz' masala dosas like a pair of locusts, while Leota clucked at James over his belching and his elbows that were either resting on the table or poking out at right angles. Verghese seemed able to keep his neatly by his side, and did not get sauce all over his face. Matters only worsened for James when the mangoes were served. There was, in his opinion and experience, no decorous way of eating a mango; in fact, any effort to do so spoiled the pleasure. On this rare point, he and his father were agreed, and because of it, Leota turned a blind eye.

But Verghese proved them all wrong. While James sucked and slurped – an orange aureole widening around his mouth – Verghese made a series of cuts across his mango till it resembled one of the wooden Chinese puzzles sold in the bazaar. He then drew out the pieces, one at a time, and ate the plump flesh with such precision and delicacy that he was left with no more damage than glistening finger-tips and a sheen on his lips.

'May I lick, Aunty,' he asked Leota, lifting his hands to her.

'Why, sure you can, hon,' she chuckled. 'James here is slobbering all the way down to his elbows, so why not you.'

Verghese slipped each fingertip into his mouth, then licked his lips with a flicker.

'Where'd you learn to cut a mango like that, anyway?' she went on. 'Ammachi teach you?'

He nodded, his brown eyes huge and luminous in his solemn face.

'Well you're gonna have to teach me. That was real special.' Leota grinned and rubbed his bony shoulder. 'Now, you boys go wash and give those mango stones to your beetles.'

'Hooray!' cried James as their faces lit up and Verghese clapped his hands.

Beetle collecting was the foremost passion for Oaklands boys, ignited in one's first weeks in the dorm when older lads paraded their trophies, then fanned by the thrill of catching one's first – ideally in lower kindergarten – then pursued with religious fervour throughout elementary and on into the early years of high school. After age fourteen or so there was only a faithful remnant that carried on, while everyone else gradually converted to the more virile hunting of wild game (if you were lucky enough to have a gun) or, more commonly – but arguably with greater danger – the opposite sex.

For devotees, monsoon was the high point in the beetle calendar, and for those who had eyes to see, the creatures were everywhere. Just the night before at dusk, James and Verghese had slipped quietly along the *chakkar* road from Askival with bamboo poles in their hands and milk powder tins clinking in James' pack. The road that curved through the dark forest on the north side of the mountain was ghostly with mist. It led to the graveyard and was haunted with stories of headless riders and women in white. The boys giggled nervously, skin prickling as they crept towards a lamppost, the bulb a floating blur in the cloud. They could hear the humming of the beetles and saw throngs of them massed on the metal shade and flying around the light in a wildness. The boys lifted their poles and on a whispered *one, two, three* from James, brought them down in a mighty whacking on the lamppost, shrieking and laughing. A cloud of beetles buzzed about the light in panic while others landed on the ground at the boys' feet. James snapped on his torch and crowed at the sight of dozens of helpless creatures on their backs, legs scrabbling in the air.

'Get the tins, Gheesa!' he hissed. Verghese tugged them out of the rucksack and prised off the lids, revealing beds of limp leaves and moss.

'Lots of rhinos,' said James, carefully taking hold of a flailing beetle just behind its head and dropping it into his tin. 'Mean looking critters, *hah*?'

'Yeah, but useless in a fight, man. Hey look! I got a dumpy!' Verghese whooped, holding up a black beast with its curved pincers sprung wide and threatening.

'*Arè yaar*, no fair! Any more, man?' Legend had it that once clamped to your finger, the dumpy stag would never let go, and that a surgeon would have to cut it off – beetle *and* finger. Naturally, they were the desire of every boy's heart.

Once the boys had gathered as many beetles as they could reasonably fit in their tins, they banged the lids back on – with holes made by a geometry compass earlier that day – and tucked them in the pack. The road home was the same, but it had been transformed, graveyards and ghoulish tales forgotten as they clattered along, hitting their bamboo sticks on railings and laughing at their loot.

The next day after the dosa lunch, the boys opened their tins on Askival's south veranda, lifting the lids carefully to knock down any clinging beetles, then dropping in their slimy mango stones. There was nothing the tiny beasts loved more. They would crawl across the stones, feeding on the stringy flesh for days till it finally went off, releasing a sweet-rotten smell every time the tin was opened. Sometimes the fermented flesh seemed to make them drunk and mad and when James stroked their backs, the beetles rose up in fury and waved their legs. He gave them matchsticks, which they broke in half, and some beetles, provoked enough, could even snap a pencil.

As well as keeping his beetles as tortured pets, James had joined the fierce competition to build the largest collection. The technique was simple. He put a wad of cotton in the bottom of a jar, added a few drops of carbon tetrachloride and covered it with a piece of cardboard. He then popped the beetle on top and watched it die. When it hadn't moved for a while, he took it out and stuck it to a board with a pin through its abdomen, taking care to spread the legs and antennae into an impression of the lively vigour it had just lost. Once stiff, he transferred it to his handsome glass-topped wooden case with a neat label giving its common name, such as 'Swear' and its far more impressive Latin name, *xylotropes giddeon,* and the date and location of discovery: 6th August 1939, Fairy Glen. James took tremendous trouble and pleasure in the task and by age ten had accumulated no less than sixty-three varieties of beetle. His science teacher and natural history guru assured him there were over 150,000 worldwide and 1600 in the Himalayas alone. James was aiming for the Oaklands record of 100.

Even more thrilling than keeping beetles for play or display, however, was forcing them to fight. For the younger boys it was these contests that really fuelled the craze. They gathered at recess like a Roman circus around an empty desk, braying and stamping as two winged gladiators duelled to the death. For a long time, the prize fighter was Raymond Clutterbuck's Chinese stag, a menacing black beast, five inches long, with pincers as curved and cruel as a *kirpan.* Having made short work of Elijah Peterson's cherry rhino and ripped Nobby Singh's dung roller to shreds, Raymond was casting about for fresh prey. James had with him that day a female stone carrier with speckled wing-cases and long feelers that arched down her back. He hadn't marked her out for fighting. This was a rare variety and once he'd checked the Latin name with his science teacher, he was putting her in his case.

But Raymond challenged him, setting his stag into the desk and summoning the crowd.

'Fight! Fight! Fight!' they chanted. James felt his cheeks go hot.

'Nah, I'll bring another one tomorrow,' he mumbled.

'Coward,' said Raymond.

'Am not!' James hissed.

'Prove it,' the other boy smirked.

'FIGHT! FIGHT! FIGHT!' the mob shouted.

'I don't have to prove *anything*,' James said, 'but since you're so *desperate*—' and he shook his stone carrier from the box into the empty desk. Raymond ran a pencil down his stag's back and it reared like a demon. Someone jabbed James' stone carrier, making her whip round. Then the pencils prodded and poked till the beetles were forced to run into each other, buzzing madly, pincers snapping. They thrashed about, circling and grappling, backing up, rushing in, till suddenly Raymond's tore off James' feeler. The smaller beetle pulled back, but too late. The stag sunk its pincers into the stone carrier's thorax and as her outer wings flapped helplessly, a thick brown liquid oozed from her side. When she fell limp, Raymond plucked out his champion stag and held it aloft as the crowd cheered.

Fighting tears, James lifted the stone carrier and rested her back in the box. That night he and Verghese buried her under the giant deodar behind Askival. Verghese read the 23rd Psalm and said a long prayer. James said nothing.

Paul Verghese was staying with the Connors that week because his mother was in prison and his father had disappeared. They were not, by most people's reckoning, criminals or low-lifes. Hailing from Kerala, his father, Thampan Verghese, had degrees from two American colleges and was professor of history at Lucknow University. His mother, Mariamma, was a vociferous campaigner against multiple social ills and had set up a school for untouchable girls. They were both Christians from the Malankara Mar Thoma Syrian Church that traced its roots back to AD54 when the disciple Thomas himself (evidently no longer doubting) came to India and planted the faith. It would be hard to imagine a pair more worthy of admiration by the British authorities, yet these very authorities had – just two weeks previous – clapped Mrs Verghese in jail and were hard on the heels of the Professor. The reason was simple: the couple were long-standing activists in the freedom movement and had just stood with Mohandas Gandhi in his Quit India campaign.

Thampan's agitating for liberty in India went right back to his student days in Madras. It was 1919 and the British had brought in their Rowlatt Act, licence to convict suspected "terrorists" without charge, trial or appeal. It incited protest across the country and Gandhi's call for the first national *satyagraha*, the "truth force" by which he intended to bend the will of the British. When troops fired into a street march in Amritsar it was a flame to the touch paper. In the burning and bloodshed that followed, five Europeans were killed and Brigadier General Dyer sent to take charge. He banned gatherings and upon hearing of a large assembly at Jallianwalla Bagh, set forth with his Gurkha and Indian troops. He did not wait to discover that the group was mainly village people come to celebrate the spring festival of *Baisakhi*, nor was he deterred, upon arrival at the enclosed compound, by the sight of many women and children in the crowd. Without threat from them or warning from him, he ordered his troops to fire till their ammunition was exhausted. Then he turned heel and left. Behind him, over a thousand people lay wounded, over four hundred dead.

It was a turning point for India and for Thampan. The twenty-year-old felt his love of the Biblical Exodus story and his love of country converge in a torrent of righteous wrath that swept him to the twin protests of street march and printing press. In this latter campaign he met Mariamma, whose father was the printer. Inky pamphlets on *swadeshi* and the Indian National Congress were soon joined by wedding invitations as Thampan and Mariamma rapidly became a formidable and inseparable pair. All through their post-graduate studies in America, when they shared a single bed and lived off scraps from an Indian restaurant, they remained in close contact with the freedom movement back home, corresponding furiously, raising support and sympathy in America, and sending articles to Gandhi's *Young India* publication. They returned in time to join him on the Salt March of 1930 and were among the 90,000 arrested in the Civil Disobedience actions of that year.

Leota first met Mariamma in the queue for the toilets at the *All-India Christian Conference for the Upliftment of National Women* in Patna in 1937 and the pair struck up a firm friendship. Mariamma followed Leota's recommendation of Oaklands School for her son, as it A) was run by American missionaries rather than the British, and B) had always welcomed Indians. Whenever Mariamma came to Landour she stayed with the Connors at Askival, adding Indian authors to their library and South Indian recipes to Aziz' repertoire. She suspected the books were never touched, but knew the food was consumed with enthusiasm. India, she understood, conquered the foreigner first through the senses, and only later claimed the mind.

In the August of 1942, India's battle to claim its sovereignty from the foreigner's rule reached a new pitch. Gandhi had lost patience with the British for taking India's people and resources for their war whilst dragging their feet over a commitment to freedom. In a fiery speech, he demanded immediate independence and brought the wrath of the British upon his head. Within twenty-four hours, the entire Congress leadership and many supporters were arrested. India responded with greater wrath in a wave of violence, strikes and destruction across the country. Deemed to be the most serious uprising since The Great Mutiny of 1857 (or The First War of Independence, depending on your perspective), Viceroy Linlithgow responded with harsh repression, deploying tens of thousands of troops, making as many arrests and causing a thousand deaths.

When Mariamma and other Lucknow members of the Congress were packed off to prison – with the Professor narrowly escaping – she wrote to the Connors asking them to take Verghese out of boarding in case he became upset about his parents' fate. Leota had wasted no time in rounding up a coolie and collecting the boy and his bags from the dorm. As it happened, he did not appear too fretful on their behalf; his parents had been in and out of prison before and Appachi was very good at hide 'n seek. In fact, any anxiety seemed to evaporate in the excitement of being out of boarding with James. Bedtime at the Connors always involved readings from the likes of *The Jungle Book* and *Huckleberry Finn* and these were thrilling enough to make up for the lengthy Bible passages and prayers that preceded them. Then there were the delights of Aziz' cooking and the fascination of the western possessions at the Connors' house: James' baseball mitt, the National Geographic magazines, the Army Surplus camping gear. Best of all, though, was the freedom to roam the hillside after dark and gather beetles.

Playing with their captives on the veranda that Saturday, sheltering from the steady rain, the boys could hear Aziz humming to himself as he prepared supper in the kitchen behind them.

'James,' Verghese whispered, a little smile forming dimples in his dark cheeks.

'Yah, what?'

'Why don't we stick some beetles into the fruit bowl for Aziz-ji, hah? Just for a little surprise, like?'

James laughed and shook his head.

'You're crazy, man.'

'No, just for fun, yeah, come on. He'll laugh too, I promise.'

'Dad'll kill me.'

'But your Daddy won't know. Aziz-ji would never tell. He'll just give you one play slap on your arm – *tuk* – Verghese demonstrated – 'and that's it. Come on, it'll be so funny, man.'

James was quiet for a moment, teasing a beetle with a long stalk of grass. He listened to Aziz warbling as he pounded and kneaded dough on the kitchen table. He had already told them his plans for supper: Hearty Hamburger Soup with Clover-leaf Rolls followed by fruit salad. James' face took on a lop-sided grin.

The fruit bowl sat on the dining table, fragrant with mangoes, guavas and small, speckled bananas. Stanley and

Leota were in the office, door closed, all sounds hushed by rain. The boys slipped off their tin lids, quickly tucked half a dozen beetles amongst the humps and crevices of the fruit and tip-toed like cartoon villains into James' room. They threw themselves in a tangled heap on the bed, stifling their giggles in the *razai* and clutching their sides in pantomime hilarity. When their merriment had died down they listened at the door. There was nothing but the muffled clatter of Aziz in the kitchen and the occasional shuffle and scrape from the Connors' office, so the boys soon tired and turned back to the room.

'What you wanna do?' James asked.

'I dunno,' Verghese shrugged.

'Tops?' James pointed at a pair sitting on his window-sill.

'Yeah, ok,' said Verghese and started cracking his knuckles.

James tossed him one. 'They're not really sharp enough, though. You got your knife?'

'Yeah, man.' Sitting cross-legged on the floor they got out their pocket knives and whittled at the tips to make them viciously sharp. If your point was lethal enough and your technique good, you could split an opponent's top clean in half. Knives back in pockets they started whipping their tops on the polished concrete floor. James got his to jump onto a tin trunk and then back down, while Verghese managed to spin his top on the palm of his hand for a few seconds till the pain made him drop it. A small red prick of blood rose on his hand like a stigmata and he whooped with pride. Then James turned his top on Verghese's and sent it hurtling under the bed.

'Arè, man, no fair!' cried Verghese as he dived under the bed, with James snickering behind him. He was still underneath, shoving boxes and mouldy canvas bags aside, when they heard a scream and a crash from the dining room.

'My God!' yelped Verghese.

'Shoot,' breathed James, blanched face turning to the door. For the briefest moment they had no idea what had happened, but with the sudden pushing back of chairs in the office and the shouts from Stanley and Leota and the running of feet and the continuing screams, the truth sank home.

Verghese scrabbled out from under the bed, fluff stuck to his hair. 'Quick,' he hissed, under the hullaballoo. 'We have to hide.'

James looked frantically around him.

'The window!' cried Verghese, darting across the room and tugging at the metal latches. But the whole window was warped and rusting with the rains and nothing would give. And it was too late anyway.

There were heavy footsteps in the hall and the door was yanked open.

'James.' Stanley's voice was loaded as a cannon.

Ignoring Verghese cowering by the window, he frog-marched his son to the dining room, pointed to the smashed bowl and the fruit on the floor and asked if James had anything to say to Aziz-ji. The *khansamma* was standing in the kitchen door wringing his hands and shaking his head, tears spilling off his cheeks.

'Is no problem, no problem, sahib,' Aziz pleaded. 'Is nothing hurting.' He bundled his right hand into his apron, but not before James caught sight of his thumb, bleeding and swollen. A crushed dumpy stag lay on the floor.

'*Maf kijiye*,' James whispered to him, his face burning.

Forgive me.

Stanley then took him to the office, closed the door and undid the buckle on his belt. James fumbled with the buttons on his shorts, eyes fixed on the jute matting at his feet, jaw already clenched so tight he knew it would ache for days, though it would be nothing compared to his legs. He lay bent across his father's desk, head turned sideways, face jerking against a musty manila file with the force of the whipping. All through it he could hear Aziz crying in the kitchen. His mother, he knew, would be out the back and walking fast – he never knew where – returning later with lips pressed together and glassy eyes. Of Verghese, he could hear nothing.

When he got back to his bedroom, shuffling slowly, he saw his friend squatting in the corner, arms lashed around his shins, eyes huge and terrified, running with tears. James lowered himself to the bed and lay on his stomach, face to the wall. He heard Verghese creep up beside him, heard his breathing and frantic whispering and felt him tugging on his sleeve. But James did not move or speak. Finally Verghese was called for supper and James lay in the quiet dark, his legs on fire.

A little later there was a soft knock on the door and a seam of light.

'Babu?'

It was Aziz, his voice like a dove's. He slipped in and knelt beside James, a plate and cup in his scratched hands. The thumb was bandaged.

'Sorry, sorry babu,' he murmured, putting the things down on the trunk that served as bedside table. 'So sorry.' He repeated the words in a continual hushing mantra, his head shaking, hand patting James on the shoulder. 'Come,

come, Aziz-ji is bringing supper for you, babu,' he whispered. 'Hamburger Soup by Betty Shirk with Cloverleaf Roll – *Hilda Clutterbuck* Roll, babu! She is baking queen. And I have put this-season extra-fresh guava jelly, by Aziz. Come, come.'

FOUR

Rounding the last bend of the *chakkar*, Ruth glimpsed Askival through the forest, alone on a promontory, attended by trees. Even from a distance she could see the weather-beaten walls, the bleached and rusting sheets of corrugated iron, the decay. She stopped at the gate and studied the house, so quiet and chill.

A bird took off from a branch beside her, sending a strange call into the air and a shower of droplets over her head. The metal gate was locked, so with a quick look over her shoulder, she climbed it and walked up the path, her jeans wetting where they passed through clumps of fern. On either side, the oaks reached out bent limbs to her, shaggy with moss and dripping.

Her last time here, was with Manveer, on the night he died. They stood on the south veranda looking down at the lights of Dehra Dun, a blaze of fallen stars on a black lake. She was cold and he pulled her into the folds of his down jacket, her back against his chest. He smelt of freshly ironed clothes and a grown-up aftershave, though he never shaved. His beard tickled as she rested her head into his neck.

'Manveer,' she whispered.

'Mmm?' He tightened his arms around her, lowering his face so his cheek brushed hers, the folded edge of his turban against her ear.

'Show me your hair.'

Now, as she looked south from the veranda steps, a rising sea of mist swallowed the bazaar and was overcoming the ridge. Shivering in its cool breath, she turned to face the house. The veranda gaped, splintered beams jutting from the plaster like broken teeth, windows staring out at the gloom, empty of glass and blind. She put a foot on the bottom step, but her skin rose in bumps and she pulled back, heading round the outside instead. The walls were bloated and breaking, stone bricks fallen onto the veranda like burst stuffing, woodwork left to rot. Passing the old kitchen she saw a rat scuttle into a hole and from a door further along the stench was like a blow.

That long-ago November night with Manveer, the house smelled of pine and they found a nest in the fireplace. Outside, an octave owl called and they counted the beats between the notes, joining in on the two hoots and laughing. Till the owl fell silent and there were footsteps on the veranda and a crashing door.

She circled the house and now stopped outside a corner room whose windows had once looked east onto the front veranda and north to the snows.

Her father's old bedroom.

Now the north wall had fallen away and the room lay bare to the wind. Ruth wrapped her arms around herself, a hard steel bracelet cutting into her ribs, and turned to the north. A shroud of grey hid the mountains and only a few firs were visible: dark, bedraggled apparitions, dripping cold.

Still unable to go inside, she slipped away down a goat trail through the trees.

FIVE

The trail was the same one James had often used to escape the house when he spotted unwelcome visitors coming up the main path. These included his teachers who pressed him into playing Rummy or Scrabble, visiting preachers who quizzed him about his missionary goals, and Colonel Bunce, who hauled him up for inspection.

On this night in early 1945, James hadn't quite made it down the path before the Colonel spotted him.

'Where are you off to, my lad?' he barked, swinging his stick. 'Come and announce me to your good mother, there's a boy. She has invited the old goat to tea.'

James was forced to usher him inside, hang up the Macintosh that indeed smelled like a goat and call for his mother. Worse, he had to wait in the living room, squirming under the Colonel's gaze, when Leota retreated to check on supper. Stanley was not yet home from work, and Mrs Bunce on a visit to Delhi, so the agony of polite conversation fell to him, thirteen and thick-tongued as he was.

The Colonel declined a seat and stood with legs akimbo, using his stick to prod the sagging ceiling of white-washed burlap.

'Gone a bit soft, don't you think?'

James hung his head.

'Used to be a splendid place, this.' Bunce tucked the stick

under his arm and looked around him. 'You know that? When the dear old Rawleys were here. Persian carpets, lace curtains from Belgium and a grand piano just there.' He swung the stick round and fired an invisible shot into the adjoining room where Stanley's desk now stood, stacked with musty files. 'Not to mention some bloody good furniture from home!' And he hit the leg of a sagging armchair. James flinched. He wished his mother would return from her conference with Aziz in the kitchen.

'One of the oldest houses on the hill,' Bunce said, rubbing his fingers on the wall and sneering at the whitewash that came off on his skin. James tried to excuse himself but the Colonel was just warming up. Leaning an elbow on the mantelpiece, he directed James to a chair with a flick of his stick and went on. 'Built in 1825 by the great Captain McBain – one of the chaps who fought in the Gurkha wars. Do they teach you that history here?'

'A bit,' James lied.

'Too American, that school,' the Colonel muttered, fishing in his jacket for a cigar. 'And too many missionaries.'

James winced.

'Did you know,' Bunce continued, lighting up, 'that early last century, this whole Garhwal area was snaffled by the Nepalis?' He waved his cigar expansively. 'Well, we wrestled it back. Fierce little beggars, though, those Gorkhalis, and it took thousands of our lot and a posse of cannons to squash them. Did it in the end, though.' He sucked on the cigar, his eyes narrowing, then breathed out a long, curling tendril of smoke. 'And then signed them up,' he said, with a twisted smile. 'Better to have that lot fighting for you than against, eh?'

James nodded, the smell making him queasy.

'Be a sport and get me an ashtray, will you?' James couldn't think where one might be, so passed him a used mug. The Colonel raised his brows at the sight of the coffee dregs, sniffed and tapped his cigar. 'Anyway, all the top British officers from the conflict got land up here as rewards and built hunting lodges. The place was wild with game back then, you know! So more and more chaps came and then of course the box-wallas and merchants and before you can say hobson-jobson, you've got a hill station. Very jolly place it was, too. Of course, that was all over on the Mussoorie side.' He stabbed his cigar towards the western ridges. 'This end was very different. Cardiff fellow, Dr Barnabas Jones, set up an army sanatorium here and saddled the place with a Welsh name.' Bunce screwed up his face and dragged out the word. '*Llanddowor*. Good god! No-one could say it without spitting, so it soon became Landour and remains to this day. Then the whole ridge was declared a military cantonment and got rather straight-laced. Mussoorie, on the other hand, was having a gay old time. Hotels and clubs popping up like mushrooms and endless dinner parties and balls. Rather a lot of hi-jinks, too, I gather.' James watched the smirk tugging at the corner of his yellowing moustache. 'You see, Simla was where the Viceroy moved his government for the summer, so one had to behave up there, but in Mussoorie one could let one's hair down. And let it down one certainly did.' He chuckled, gazing out the window. 'It was all rather naughty.'

Then, as if suddenly remembering James was in the room, he blinked at him, tapped his cigar briskly on the mug and set it on the mantel. With a sharp turn, he applied his stick to a tiger skin on the floor and poked some bare patches on the beast's head.

'Your old man?' he asked.

'Yes, sir.'

'Any *shikar* yourself?'

'Just birds.' James felt his cheeks warming. He hoped the Colonel wouldn't poke his silver-black kalij pheasant stuffed in mid-strut on the mantelpiece.

'Birds are for babies, my boy!' the man barked, poking the pheasant. 'You should have seen old Captain Rawley's trophies. The place was bristling with them. Bears, leopards, tigers, ghoral, kakar. Heads and skins everywhere!'

James slid his hand into his armpit.

'Something to aim for, eh?'

The boy nodded, gave a watery smile and dug his nails into his skin.

There had been a deer. A delicate thing with velvet fur and huge eyes. But James had only wounded her leg before she ripped off into the forest. Crying, broken.

SIX

'Lai, lai, la-iiii.' Iqbal's voice filled the open-plan living room at Shanti Niwas. James looked across from his post at the door as Iqbal threw open a tablecloth, smoothed it with his dimpled hands and set a jug of daisies in the middle. *'La, la, la, la, la, la!'* Then he started folding sky-blue napkins into fan shapes. James had forbidden all that frippery at first, when Iqbal had found him, seven years before, clinging to grief and his bare table. But the man was wily. He had started with flowers here and there, dusting off some old vases from the back of a cupboard, and James could not argue. Even Ellen had been allowed flowers. But never had he imagined it would come to this.

He checked his watch again.

'I'd better go find her,' he said, taking down his jacket from the rack in the corner.

'Oh, really?' Iqbal asked, pausing his folding. 'Then I'll come, too, *na.*'

'No.' James held up a hand.

'Ok,' his friend sighed and made an effort at an encouraging smile. 'Take care now, *hah ji?*'

Outside the rain had started. James shook open his umbrella – black cotton with CONNOR painted in large white letters on the panels – and shone his torch onto the wet path.

Once on the *chakkar*, he walked quickly, the rain drumming on the umbrella and flattening his trousers to his legs; it was colder than he'd expected and his jacket felt thin. Squinting down the dark twists of the road, he prayed for Ruth. It was all he had left, though even that was disappearing. In Bible Studies and meetings he rarely prayed aloud anymore and when he did, the words sounded hollow. Alone at the desk in his room, head sunk in his hands, he felt prayers crumble to ash like the burnt end of a mosquito coil.

There had been many times in his life when he had sensed God, felt the Presence like breath, known a quiet leading.

But not now.

Now it was like throwing himself into emptiness; falling, calling, wearing his voice hoarse, but hearing nothing. Even walking the mountain paths, where his spirit was most free, he found himself pleading in vain. There was birdsong and crickets and the sighing of wind through trees, but no God.

This absence had pushed him to Iqbal's side on Friday nights, when his friend touched his nose to the floor and poured song into the void and somehow filled it.

Approaching Morrison Church, where the road divides, James saw her: the small frame in jeans and jacket, hood over her head; the quick stride she'd inherited from Ellen; the hands rammed in pockets.

'Ruth!' he called out. 'Is that you?'

She stopped. Her face was hidden.

He moved into a wavering funnel of light under a lamp, and tilted back his umbrella.

'It's Dad.' Rain blew on his face. 'Came to find you.'

She didn't move.

'I wasn't lost.' Her voice was low, rough, the dragging of stone on stone. She lifted her face and his stomach tightened.

Her mother's fine bones and nose, the full mouth, yet all battened down and hard as steel. Not a flicker in those lovely eyes.

'Ruthie,' he said, her name hurting his throat. He lifted a hand towards her, knobbled and white and getting wet as it hung there. He reached further and touched her arm.

'Good to see you, Piyari.'

She stepped closer, yanked her hands out of her pockets and slipped them round him.

'You too,' she said and gave him a quick pat. He had just enough time to fumble his arm round her shoulders, accidentally pulling her hood off and bumping the umbrella spine against her forehead. His face brushed her hair, a tangle of curls smelling of exhaust fumes and cigarettes. She stepped back.

His hand ran over his mouth and fumbled across his chest. 'Journey ok?'

'Fine,' she said and pulled the hood back up. The rain spattered on it, droplets coursing down her shoulders. 'You shouldn't have come out in this.'

'I'm fine,' said James. 'I was worried about you.'

'Well don't be. I'm fine.'

'Good then. We're all fine. *Chalo!*'

He held the umbrella out to offer her shelter but she ignored it and they moved off, silent except for the squish of her sneakers and the clump of his boots. The rain fell harder, pelting the trees, the umbrella, her back.

Rounding the bend above Shanti Niwas, James pointed at the house.

'That's us,' he said. It shone like a lamp on the dark mountain, light spilling from its windows, blurring in the wet. As they neared the door, the sound of singing rose to them above the rain.

SEVEN

He always sang when he worked, as if the song were an essential ingredient without which the meal would fail, as vital as yeast for the bread or flame for the pot. It was a spell stirred into the food, a prayer for the health and happiness of the diners, a blessing. But on this cold day in 1945, Aziz' voice was a little cracked and jerky. It was not easy to sing whilst butchering a goat.

They had set off from Askival the day before, with their army-surplus rucksacks and tin canteens. James and Stanley had guns in their packs, broken down and wrapped in sleeping bags, while Aziz' bag clattered with primus stove, cooking pots and tins of spice. They took the path straight down the north side of the hill below Askival, a precipitous track that zig-zagged down through rhododendrons and deodars to the Aglar river at the bottom. The forest was deeply quiet but for the crunch of their leather boots and the occasional cry of a barbet, and the three did not break the hush with speech.

When they came out of the trees into a clearing it was dusk and the late November air was chill. Ahead was a cluster of *chaans*, temporary huts for cattle and their keepers in the winter months. Made of rough stone and earth with thatched roofs, they rose from the ground like they had grown there, as much a part of the landscape as the rocks and the scrub. Cracks of light glowed at the doorways and smoke rose in tendrils through the thatch. The people here were well known to the Connors as they were their *dudh-wallas*, the dairymen who delivered buffalo milk each day to Askival and the other houses a thousand feet up on the ridge. They lived constantly on the brink of ruin and were thus top priority in Stanley's agricultural programme. In Hindu classification, they were bottom. Untouchables. Or *Harijans*, as Gandhi had named them. The children of God.

At Stanley's call, the father of the house, Bim, cried out, pulled open the wooden door and drew them in. James was hit by the smells of dung and wet straw and a bitter smoke that stung his eyes. Half of the hut was for the cattle, with just a crumbling wall and a window dividing the space. A buffalo and a cow shuffled and chewed and snorted at the opening, liquid brown eyes surveying James as their hairy ears twitched and long streams of piss gushed onto the straw. Children jumped up and pulled him to the floor, one little boy scrambling into his lap as the others pressed to his sides, giggling and fishing through his pockets for loot. The firelight danced on their faces: chapped cheeks, runnels of snot coursing up and down with their sniffs, hair dry and matted as thorn bushes. None had shoes and the boy wore only a shirt.

As his eyes adjusted to the light, James took in the room. In the floor was an earthen hearth where damp pine twigs spat and hissed over a bed of burning coals. It was not enough to warm the hut, but only to infiltrate it with grey smoke that coiled like ghostly snakes across the thatch and walls. A blackened pot sat on the hearth and Bim's elderly mother lifted the lid to pour tea leaves into the boiling milk. She squatted beside it, an old shawl wrapped around her head, a bidi glowing in her fingers. Her laugh was a phlegmy cackle and revealed a black mouth with two teeth jutting out like tree stumps. Bim sat cross-legged on a straw mat talking with Stanley in a low voice, his gesturing hands throwing shadows on the wall behind. His other buffalo had just died, cutting his milk sales by half, and the hail storm last week had all but destroyed the crop. Aziz knelt on the other side of Stanley, listening with furrowed brow to the flow between Hindi, which he knew, and Garhwali, which he did not. In the corner of the hut, Bim's wife sat on the only bed, paralysed from the waist down, rarely speaking, but always watching, her eyes wild and sad. In another corner there was a dented tin trunk, and behind the fire, some planks balanced on bricks that held a few pots and plates, some greasy milk-powder tins and a brass water jug. Clothes hung from a wire strung across the ceiling, and on the wall was a framed picture of the goddess Laxmi, daubed with rice and tikka powder and garlanded with marigolds that had withered to brown knots. Curvaceous and smiling in her pink sari with gold coins spilling from her palms, she was every bit the goddess of wealth.

Bim's mother poured the tea into three tin tumblers and passed them to the guests, bent double as she shuffled, her hands like claws. When the boy in James' lap asked for some, she cuffed him round the ears and the others laughed.

'You can have some of mine,' James whispered in Hindi as he held the cup by its rim and blew across the top. The tea was too sweet and the milk burnt, but it warmed him and there was enough for all the children to take a noisy slurp.

After the three from Askival had drunk their tea and refused the offer of a meal they rose to take their leave, with much bowing and joining of palms. James peeled the little boy's hands off his own and promised he'd be back, as Stanley pulled two packets of biscuits from his rucksack and gave them to Bim. The children crowed and jumped for them while Bim laughed, holding them high. James stepped out into the cold night, his insides twisting with helplessness.

They spent the night in the vacant *chaan* next to Bim's. One wall had collapsed and the thatch at that end sagged like a hammock, tufts of it spilt across the floor, where weeds had taken root. The wind blew through the hut and into their bones, smelling of dank earth and rotting thatch and making the old door rattle. As Stanley lit two small candle stumps and James swept aside the goat droppings with a twig broom, Aziz unpacked their meagre supper. Cold chapattis, a tin of luncheon meat, three small hard apples and a clutch of his home-made Graham crackers. It was an affront to him to serve such dismal fare, but Stanley had insisted upon it. They would be spending the night at Bim's, he had explained, but, Number One: could not eat with the family as they didn't have enough for themselves, let alone guests, and Number Two: could not possibly sit in the hut next door cooking up their own hot meal as this would be adding insult to injury. Imagine those starving little kids smelling Aziz' curry while their tummies rumbled! Aziz suggested they cook enough for everyone, and Stanley said Yes, but on the second night, when they returned with the kill. It was customary after a hunt to share the meat with the villagers. So Aziz had been forced to accept these terms, but still cringed as he set out the food. His only comfort was the cloth he laid down first, which smelled nice and was printed with flowers.

James slept badly. His sleeping bag was thin and the floor of the hut hard and uneven. Despite crawling into the bag with all of his clothes on, he spent the night clenched with cold, his hands thrust between his thighs, feet like rocks, ears numb. But more than that was the fear. The last few hunting trips he had bungled things. Missed animals completely, or worse still, wounded them. He had seen the disgust in his father's eyes, the way his big hand curled into a fist and then scraped against his bristly chin. Stanley had grown up shooting things. He claimed he couldn't even remember his first rabbit, but their number was legion. And there had been fox and coyote and elk and even bears. His first deer was when he was eleven. James was fourteen and still hadn't shot anything bigger than a bird.

He was woken by his father's hand on his shoulder.

'Come on, Jim-Bob,' he was saying. 'Up now.'

It was utterly dark and cold. James' muscles ached and unfolding himself was like bending metal.

'Chai babu,' said Aziz, appearing from the black with an enamel mug.

'*Shukriya ji*,' he murmured, feeling the warmth seeping through his body.

Stanley had an open Bible on his knees. By torchlight he read aloud the allotted chapter for the morning – the story of Hagar fleeing into the desert with her son Ishmael. Aziz knelt beside him with hands folded in his lap and brows knotted in concentration, bowing his head when Stanley prayed for the Almighty's providence for the day.

After devotions and cold chapattis with peanut butter, they packed their bags and prepared the guns. James pieced together his sleek .318 Westley Richards deer rifle, running his fingers over the polished wooden stock and feeling the power of the thing resting in his hands. His father had bought the gun for his birthday last month from Colonel Bunce who, at seventy, was scaling down his *shikar* exploits, and it was the finest thing James had ever owned. Stanley's gun was an old Remington. It had been passed down through his family for generations, gathering stories as thick and odorous as the grease that he now rubbed across it. Along with the usual tall tales about grizzlies and stampeding bison, there were the legends from the Civil War and the story of his great-grandmother using it to protect runaway slaves.

James didn't know how many of these stories his father believed, but he clearly relished the telling. These were the few times Stanley seemed to loosen up and laugh a little. There would be a spark in his eyes and a dimple would appear in one rough cheek, almost as a sign that here was the chink, the soft spot, the clasp to an inner man who so rarely escaped. And James would sit by, face shining, full of laughter and questions, longing for the moment, if the crack should widen, when he could leap inside.

Head brimming with the gun smells of oiled wood and burnt powder, James pulled on his rucksack and followed Stanley out of the *chaan,* Aziz behind. Outside, the dark was just beginning to soften, but they still needed torches to see the narrow path. They walked in silence, the beam of James' torch playing over his father's heels, the cold air a cloak. The gun was heavy and awkward to carry, his fingers going numb on its icy metal. Slowly, things around began to take shape, a boulder here, a tree there, the hulk of his father's body ahead.

They moved from the path up a tiny goat trail to a patch of scrub where they pushed their rucksacks into the thicket and settled down, screened by the bushes, guns across their knees. Opposite was a rocky cliff, its contours and boulders becoming sharper with the growing light. They sat in silence, waiting and watching, James feeling the cold steal over his body, the tiredness dragging on his eyes. Birds twittered and whistled and the shades of grey around began to blush with colour as if the birds were calling the day into being. Just when James thought he would never move again there was a skittering of small rocks on the cliff. He brought his gun up sharp and felt his father stiffen, though Stanley's rifle remained on his lap. A pair of *ghoral* appeared, moving with light ease, their grey-brown coats almost invisible against the rock, small hooves sure and quick. Then they stopped, as if sensing something, and the front goat turned her head, revealing the white fur at her throat. It was the perfect target.

James' shot rang loud and foreign in the hush of dawn, like a puncture in the sky. The goat fell, the other fled and Stanley roared.

'YES!' he cried, leaping to his feet and shaking his gun in the air. 'He's done it! Thank you GOD, he's done it!'

James felt a dam-burst of joy. He shakily lowered the rifle and looked up at his father, whose face was splitting open. Stanley hauled him to his feet and crushed him in an embrace that was clumsy and smelled of canvas and damp wool. It was the first time they had hugged since James first left for Oaklands, aged four.

At their side, Aziz was dancing. Hooting with glee, he was whirling on the spot, clapping and twisting his hands, and flashing all his pearly teeth in a rapturous grin. He too caught James in a great hug, though it couldn't be more different from Stanley's. Smelling of last night's smoke and the ever-present blend of coconut oil and spice, it felt as easy and warm as a blanket, for Aziz hugged him every day.

Stanley laughed and said they'd better find the beast before the flies did, and the three took up their packs and scrambled down to the base of the cliff. The *ghoral* was lying on the rocks beside a small stream, its legs stuck out at strange angles, its white throat gashed red. They decided to gut it back at Bim's, so Stanley tied the hooves together with vine and lifted it onto James' shoulders. It was a heavy and awkward yoke, but one he had longed to bear. On the steep walk up to the village, Aziz insisted on taking a turn and as James looked up and saw the body lying across his shoulders it reminded him of the picture in his children's Bible of Jesus carrying the lost sheep.

Except the Good Shepherd's creature had just been saved.

Long before they reached Bim's village, the children spotted them and came pelting down the path, yelling. They jumped to touch the *ghoral* and flung their arms around James when they learned it was his, but their speed and their cries had another source. A leopard had killed Bim's last buffalo.

Back in the village, Stanley sat on the front step of the hut as Bim told him the story and wept. He had taken the buffalo up to a high field early that morning and left it to graze, but when he returned, it was dead, the leopard's mark clear on its throat. The man wiped the tears with the back of his hand and shook his head, his body slumped, voice a high-pitched, nasal lament.

In front of them, Aziz and James butchered the goat, a

crowd of children gathering around, quarrelling over the scraps. The sounds of knives hacking through bone were punctuated by snatches of Aziz' song, which was little more than a sorrowful repeated phrase, like a wail of wind down a pipe. It cut into James, along with Bim's cries and the mingled smells of soil and blood and excrement and the sight of the goat's severed head at his side, with her glassy stare and poking tongue. He turned from her face and sunk his cold fingers into the warm wet of her belly and drew out the intestines. The boy who had sat in his lap seized them with a yelp and ran his hand down their slippery length shooting faeces at his sister. His grandmother scolded him and confiscated the entrails, adding them to a platter already loaded with the dark, glistening pieces of kidney, heart and liver. She would also keep the hooves, the skin, the head, the bladder and the bones. Everything was precious.

When the butchering was done and a cat and two dogs were licking the scraps off the ground, Aziz began chopping vegetables as Bim took Stanley and James up to see the buffalo. She was lying in a field beside a stretch of forest, her eyes bulging as if caught in that first fit of terror, her torn throat a mass of flies. They stood in silence at her side. From the village they could hear the dogs fighting and more distant, the repeated *whoop whoop whoop* of a river mill.

'Leave it here,' said Stanley at last. 'The leopard will come back tonight to eat and we'll deal with it.' Bim lifted his hands in a gesture of assent and hopelessness. James was transfixed by those hands. Their skin was cross-hatched with a thousand lines, each a seam of dirt; the palms were calloused as the buffalo's hide, yet marked by unhealed cuts and the swelling of splinters; all the fingernails were broken, some black, one missing. Bim's life was written across his hands, but it was like a fortune told backwards: the story of his past so deeply inscribed that it was impossible to see a future.

The three of them built a *machan* in the nearest tree, a make-shift platform on which to sit and watch, and then Bim led them back to his *chaan*. It was only mid-afternoon, but the sky was growing dark and an icy wind rose from the gully. The trees on the opposite slope were waving their branches like shipwrecked passengers and the air smelled metallic. As clouds massed overhead there was a rumble of thunder and the first spitting of rain. Hard as arrows, it pelted through their clothes, and as they started running, it turned to hail. Lashed with ever bigger stones, they fell wet and breathless into the door of the hut, the ground behind turning white, the last shreds of the crop flattened into the mud.

Inside, the air was thick with smoke and the aromas of curry. Aziz was kneeling by a pot on the stove and delivering swift instructions to Bim's mother and one of the older girls. On the bed, the younger children sat like crows and watched, firelight in their hungry eyes. Their mother did not appear to have moved since the day before, but she was smiling.

Bim poured out home-brewed liquor from an urn in the corner and tried to press it on his guests. All refused with pained apologies till he finally shrugged and gave some to his mother and his wife. Then he sat nursing his own dirty glass between his knees, sipping and talking and pushing away the tears that kept running down his face.

'What have I done?' he asked, over and over again. 'How have I angered the gods? What must I do to appease them? How will we live?'

James shifted in his damp jeans and wished his father would say or do something that would help. There seemed to be little.

At last the meal was ready and they all fell upon the food in relief. The children were like vultures and their grandmother barked at them to slow down, but they ignored her. James ate slowly, complimenting Aziz on his cooking but struggling to enjoy it.

When they were finished, he and Stanley re-assembled their guns, letting the children stroke and hold them before they loaded the ammunition and stooped to head out the door. The storm had passed but the night was still cold and banks of cloud hid the stars. They crunched across the ghostly carpet of hail and up through the fields to the forest. The buffalo lay like a dark boulder, one silhouetted horn rising in salute. They climbed onto the *machan* and sat in silence. James wriggled his toes in his shoes and pushed his hands into his armpits, feeling the bumping of his heart. Stanley barely moved. It was a long wait. The night deepened, the clouds slid away and a weak moon rose above the ridge.

Just when James had grown so stiff and cold he thought he would die, there was a low growl behind them. His hair stood on end. He took up his gun. They heard the leopard growl again as it moved right under the platform and over to the buffalo. It was hard to see it in the darkness, little more than a shape of deeper black sliding through the shadows. A few feet away, it turned and went back into the forest. James tried not to make the slightest move, controlling his breath so as not to hiss. Twice more the leopard came out, once circling the buffalo, but each time slipping back into the trees. Finally it moved to her side and sniffed around the bloodied neck.

James could just make out the line of its body, but could not tell if it was crouching or lying. Then they heard it growl again and the sound of tearing flesh as it savaged the buffalo's throat.

James' guts turned to water. He felt Stanley raise his gun and did the same. They waited, their eyes boring into the dark, seeking out the leopard's shape, searching and probing. If they missed, the startled beast could easily leap to their platform, ravenous and enraged, a rippling cannon of teeth and claws. James heard the click of Stanley's safety catch and the holding of breath.

Therewasashotandawildscreamandtheleopardflewtowards them and James fired and Stanley fired again and the scream died.

They held still. All was silent.

James was panting, the sweat pouring down his sides, hands starting to shake. At last Stanley moved.

'I think we got him,' he whispered, and James was shocked to hear a tremor in his voice. They turned on their torches and shone them on the ground below. The leopard lay at the foot of the tree, long and sleek, as if caught mid-bound.

The shots woke the sleepers in the *chaans*, and they came running, Aziz with a flashlight and Bim with a flaming torch, a couple of children scampering beside. At the sight of the fallen leopard Bim danced and sang, his breath high with spirits and sorrow, his face lifted to the moon.

The next night, as James lay back in his bed at Askival, he was woken by the cry of a leopard in the forest. It was far down the slope below the house, a distant, chilling howl that seemed to rise out of death itself. Then another voice joined, and another and another, and they rose in pitch and fury, getting higher and closer, till the trees around the house were ringing with their unearthly screams.

EIGHT

To Ruth, arriving at Shanti Niwas in the dark and rain with her father, the singing inside sounded like an angel. But when she walked through the door it stopped, and it was the smell of the cooking that caught her like an ambush.

In the centre of this swirling, seductive aroma was a plump man in a floral apron, laughing. He wiped his hands and held them out to her, damp and stained yellow with turmeric. His grip was excited and squeezing and left her own hands smelling of garlic. Everything about him shone. The glossy black curls that bounced with the nodding of his head, his creamy skin, slick with sweat and oil, the white teeth, the Gandhi glasses, the eyes brimming with light.

Iqbal.

James stood smiling from one to the other.

And now, with her bag across his shoulders like a sack of grain, the incongruous man was ushering her up to his bedroom. Most pleased to have vacated it for her, he hoped she would approve. She did not, and fought the arrangement fiercely on the landing, but he merely laughed at her protests and refused to give way.

'I will be at bliss on the camp bed in Doctor-ji's room,' he beamed. 'And the Rani Ruthie cannot sleep on the sofa!' He wagged his finger.

'Yes I can! I've slept on a lot worse.' She stood with her back to his closed bedroom door, arms folded across her chest.

'So have I, *beti*, but is no need when a comfortable bed is there.' And he reached round her to take hold of the handle, his breath smelling of cloves. She blocked his arm.

'I will not put you out of your bedroom.'

'Come, ' he appealed. 'I have scrubbed my hands to the bone for you. Do me this kindness.'

She looked from his soft hands to his eyes, brown and warm. They reminded her of that dark sugar syrup she used to pour on pancakes. What was it called? *Gur.* Yes! A word of Hindi, at last. She felt it hum in her head as she met his gaze: dark and sweet, a lure for flies. Then she sighed and let him pass. Iqbal flashed an enormous smile and flung open the door like a ring master.

She stared. Iqbal set down her pack and bowed deeply.

'I am trusting your happy comfort here,' he said and stood erect, gazing about him with satisfaction. The walls were a crowded scrapbook of pictures, posters, calendars and photos, the floor an archipelago of rag-rugs, the bed teetering with cushions. Every surface was bedecked with lace and shiny fabrics, and on top of these, Iqbal had martialled a mind-boggling array of ornaments: Chinese fans, bowls of marbles, cuddly toys, fake flowers, shell sculptures, wooden trinkets and a plastic Scotsman with bagpipes. On the desk, a set of lacquered Kashmiri boxes bristled with pens and assorted stationery and beside them stood a vase of marigolds, their sharp smell fighting with the clamorous notes of a cheap deodorant. A large window above the desk looked south to the plains, though by now it was dark and raining and merely bounced back Ruth's reflection. She looked lost and shabby next to this radiant man in his florid world. He grinned and waved. She forced a smile and yanked the curtains shut.

'You will be performing your toilet,' he said, gave a little bow and swept out of the room.

If smelling Iqbal's food had caught her in the seductions of memory, eating it was surrender to the moment. The meal was a gift: fluffy rice topped by a golden river of daal; a mound of *sag* with buttery chunks of *paneer*; a ladle-full of steaming mutton curry and a hot chapatti, fresh from the *tawa*. Iqbal served them with small flourishes and fragments of song, and Ruth found herself laughing and caught a glow in her father's hawk eyes.

Throughout the meal, Iqbal beamed at her like she was his own child, plying her with extra helpings and questions.

'Did you manage to eat that rubbish they gave you on the plane?'

'Oh yes. I always eat it. Every last cracker.'

'You must have been so, so hungry! Here, have some more *gosht*.' And he dolloped the mutton on her plate as if trying to compensate for years of inadequate rations.

'Oh thanks. No, I wasn't that hungry. Just the habit of a life time. I can't leave food.'

'Never allowed to,' James said.

'Say that again. If you didn't eat something on the plane, Mom would wrap it in a napkin and you'd get it for your next meal.'

'Waste not want not!' chimed Iqbal, lifting a finger.

Ruth tore her chapatti in half and scooped up a piece of slippery mutton. She shot a look at James.

'Oh yes,' she said, dragging her words. 'We never wasted anything.'

Pencils had been used till they were stumps and pages from old notebooks folded into medicine packets for the pharmacy. Clothes were patched and repaired, old sweaters re-knitted as socks. Food was never thrown out, not even a grain of rice. And as for time, it was most sacred of all and never to be wasted on idle pleasures.

But the wanting? That never ceased. Ruth had felt it like an ache in the air around them. Her mother's eyes drawn to shop windows, fingers stroking a bolt of silk. Hannah straining for approval, and gaining approval, yet straining still. Ruth's own miserable longing to be at the centre of their hearts, for once. But more than all of them, James. Wanting only to serve God, he always claimed, to take up his cross. And yet no matter how hard he served and how far he dragged that damn thing – dragging them behind – it never seemed enough. Always that hunger in his eyes, that bent back, the troubled hands. Always the wanting, and never getting.

Like me, Ruth thought. She was not what he had wanted, right from birth – she was convinced of it – because after big sister Hannah, she should have been a boy. They'd even received A Word when Ellen became pregnant. The Lord to Abraham: 'Your wife will have a son.' Perfect. But when a girl emerged, red-faced and howling, it was clear their appropriation of prophecy had rather let them down. Or Ruth had. One way or the other, it set the precedent.

After supper, Iqbal refused Ruth's help in clearing up and they argued again, good-naturedly, while James' mouth curled into a half smile and he muttered something about an unstoppable force and an immovable object. Iqbal won, again. All grinning and *gur* eyes, damn him. But Ruth extracted a promise that she could help from the next day.

'*Accha, accha.*' He tilted his head from side to side and sent her off with a mug of chai, its spiced smell rising like a genie. She put it on the coffee table and got out her cigarettes, glancing at James on the sofa, gangly legs crossed at the ankles, hands tucked in his armpits, eyes closed. He looked asleep but she felt his alertness, the tuning of his ears, the waiting. At the sink, Iqbal hummed as he washed the dishes, his tune light and folksy and vaguely familiar. She stepped out the door and huddled under the narrow eaves, the rain against her legs.

I don't get it, she thought, as the lighter flared. Who the hell is this guy and what's he doing here? When she'd tried a few casual questions over dinner, Iqbal had been evasive.

'Oh, I'm just the fat fellow in the films,' he'd said. 'How do you say—? Comic belief?'

'Relief,' said James.

'Ah yes!' He laughed. 'I'm that one. Wheeled on when the story gets too sad.' And he winked at James. Ruth followed his gaze but her father gave nothing away.

'But,' she probed, slicing into her sticky gulab jamun. 'Do you work?'

'Not so well,' he said, rubbing his hip and grinning. 'Rusting a bit, you know, and losing some marbles.'

She sighed. 'Are you retired?'

'Oh no! Doctor-ji is retired, Ruthie, and he goes to meetings every day, writes reports, plants trees, clears rubbish and visits the villages. Is very hard work and I am avoiding for long as possible, Inshallah.'

'But—!' Ruth huffed with an exasperated half-laugh.

James wiped his mouth on a napkin and spoke. 'Iqbal *was* down at Oaklands three days a week teaching Indian Music and a cookery class.'

'Really—?'

'What he doesn't want to tell you is that he has taken leave so he can look after me. It is against my wishes.'

'Oh,' said Ruth, and swallowed a lump of gulab jamun.

Iqbal tilted his head and eyebrows, a helpless little shrug, a diminished smile. Rain shattered on the stone terrace outside.

'I'm... here,' she offered, slowly. James turned his gaze on her, a pale blue searchlight; it made her tighten.

Iqbal jumped up and started gathering dishes. 'But you are not here to be house-maid,' he said, voice bouncy as a ball.

No.

Cigarette finished, she took up the cane chair opposite her father and pulled a kashmiri shawl round her shoulders. Iqbal's tune was slower now, sadder. *A friend*, James had said. Yet he waited on them hand and foot, second-guessing their needs, fussing and spoiling, just like a devoted servant, or a doting mother. Though Ellen, she thought bitterly, had not been allowed the spoiling.

Warming her hands on the mug, Ruth sipped her chai and looked around the room, struggling to remember the old servants' quarters it once was. Grey concrete, streaked with damp and hung with ragged washing. Scabby children in the dirt at the front, chickens pecking, a broken chair. James had said the servants were moved to a smart, new block about five years ago and this would have been pulled down, had he not bought it. He'd hired unemployed Garhwali labourers to re-build it with strong stone walls and a tiled roof. Inside was all white and wood and glass. Ruth was surprised by its beauty. James had scorned beauty in all things but nature; only God could create beauty. Man's efforts were vain, illusory and decadent.

Yet on the wall behind James there was a painting: a bluish shape against a background like sun-burned rock. Gradually she recognised the shape was a woman with her eyes closed and face lifted, as if for a kiss. The more Ruth looked at it, the more it gave.

Her gaze dropped to James, his head resting against the wall, fine white hair falling over his forehead and down to the caterpillar eyebrows. Shadows pooled in the hollows of his face and there was a scattering of dandruff on the shoulders of his sweater, a brown thing with patched elbows and sagging sides that hung on him like a dust sheet. He'd always been lean, but when she'd held him so briefly at their greeting on the road, the jutting of his ribs had shocked her.

Like that day in Tennessee when she was seventeen and had walked into his bedroom. It was just a few weeks after they'd left India and the morning of Hannah's wedding. He was curled up on his side, back to her, in nothing but underpants. His ribs were convulsing like the poles of a wind-blown tent, and there was a sound she'd never heard before. A strange, almost silent hacking; the beating of breath; the rise and fall of sobs. In it she recognised a loss greater than her own, and a source deeper than she understood, and though she felt a tearing rush of love, she could not reach for him. She slipped out, frightened and alone.

Outside, the rain had softened into a dripping dark. From the bazaar a voice rose, like a song of lament. Iqbal laid a handful of cutlery on the counter and James' eyes jerked open, roving from him to Ruth.

'Time for prayer,' James said.

She stared at him. That was the call from the mosque. Time for *Muslim* prayer. He waved his hand at her.

'You've had a long journey, Ruthie. You get some rest.' She hesitated, but he seemed impatient.

'Ok,' she murmured and with a slurping draught, downed the last of her chai and stood up, pulling the shawl around her.

'Thank you, Iqbal. I've really missed good Indian *khana*.' Another word! Hindi returning, of its own volition, as if some of the curry had slipped down to the old dog and revived it. Just two words so far – no more than whimpers, really – but Hindi, nevertheless. Tiny acts of salvage, of reclamation.

'A happy day!' Iqbal smiled, untying his apron. 'Our Ruthie has come home. We have killed the fatted calf.'

'This isn't—!'

'Home is where the family is!' he interrupted, gesturing to James.

'Of course,' she murmured and turned to the stairs. 'Night Dad.' She leaned over the edge of the sofa and kissed him lightly on the top of the head. His arms flew up like a startled bird and grabbed her, but she pulled back. Then she wished she hadn't seen his face: so briefly lit and then dark.

'Night Ruth.' His arms dropped and she felt an ache in her breastbone.

As she climbed the stairs she saw Iqbal unfolding a prayer

mat and a white skull cap. She froze. *He was Muslim?* She looked at James, who was opening a scuffed, taped-together Bible, thick with papers.

In Iqbal's room she stood behind the door and listened. The low murmur of James' voice gave way to Iqbal singing, but this time a strange and haunting tune that stirred feelings she could not name. After a few minutes the song died, but the feelings remained, lifted and wheeling like a flock of birds.

She shook her head and turned to examine his pictures. Bollywood actresses shimmied beside Alpine meadows; gleaming cars parked themselves around a framed Arabic text; on a hospital fund-raising calendar, a man held up his leprosy-mutilated stumps, and everywhere, teddy bear and kitten greeting cards nuzzled amongst a vast array of snapshots. Many of the photos were of westerners, often standing with Iqbal, and mainly missionaries, judging by appearances. Several of them were women, grey-haired and determined. 'Women outnumber men on the mission field thirteen to one,' Grandma Leota used to say. 'The men are just scared.' Ruth was never sure if their fears centred on the mission field or the women.

In one picture, Iqbal was sitting on a stage beside a sitar and tabla with a group of people, all relaxed and laughing. They looked like musicians and dancers and one man was laughing so hard his eyes were hidden. Ruth was sure she knew the face but couldn't place him.

Then she saw a picture of Hannah & Derek and her stomach clenched. There they were, in the back garden of their Tennessee home, arms bursting with their seven children, mostly red-heads like Derek, all clean-scrubbed and looking so happy and healthy and home-schooled that Ruth wanted to spit. And was at once ashamed. It was not their fault and, in truth, she loved them. And yet hated that smug Blessed-by-the-Lord! look stamped all over the picture, and the fact that not one of them was hers.

But when had Iqbal met them? She realised again how little she knew. How little she'd wanted to know. Or at least, that had been the message she'd given off, all these years, like a skunk's fierce smell.

She searched for a picture of herself, but when she couldn't find one, felt a pang of hurt and then scorn. Why would Iqbal have her picture? She'd never even acknowledged his existence. Hannah probably sent birthday cards and knitted socks.

Snorting, she started to undress, but felt suddenly exposed. She was an impostor in this man's den, humming with his presence and the spirits of all he had gathered here. It made her skin shrivel, the missionaries, the actresses and the man with the leprous mitts all watching as she tugged her t-shirt off and unclipped her bra, craning to see her pull down her jeans. Hannah and Derek, of all people! She turned her back on the faces, only to see herself in the mirror on the wardrobe door, naked now but for her underpants and her jewellery. She allowed herself a long, cruel stare. It was a map of loss. Her breasts hung tired and uneven on a torso that was too scrawny for the swell of hips and thighs. The once-taut stomach was slackened, having not pulled itself together after grief. She hadn't shaved for weeks and the growth on shins and armpits was a ragged black. Everywhere the slight coarsening of texture, the tide marks of age, the scars.

She leaned close to read a card that was sticky-taped onto

one corner of the mirror. It was handwritten in a curly script:

Just as fragrance is in the flower,
and reflection is in the mirror,
in just the same way,
God is within you.
– Sikh saying –

Manveer had been Sikh. Though when his poor parents had come for his body, there would have been little sign of it. She shivered, her skin risen in bumps, feet like ice, and yanked on a fresh t-shirt. Dumping the bed cushions onto the floor – satin, frilly, embroidered – she was determined that all this would have to change tomorrow. There was something unbearably intimate about sleeping here surrounded by every expression of Iqbal's taste and affections, as if she was curling up in his mind. Tossing aside a small, ancient teddy bear, she peeled back the *razai* and saw the one thing that was not his.

Pink polka-dot sheets.

Did he know their heritage? How they'd gone with her into boarding, age six, and remained till she left. On that last day, her mother had ripped them off her bed, as if the sheets themselves had been the scene of desecration. They must have been left in India when their family stumbled back to America that bitter November of '84. Ellen had first bought those sheets from a Sears catalogue on furlough, persuading James that it wasn't luxury but frugality to buy things that would last.

They had outlasted Ellen.

Might outlast us all at this rate, thought Ruth, as she crawled in. Turning in the cool sheets, she suspected the sofa would have been more comfortable; the bed had a thin mattress on a hard base and a pillow that did not give under her head. And the sheets smelled of mothballs.

It was the smell of boarding school. The smell of everything she owned at the beginning of every semester, when she unpacked her things from the tin trunk that had been left in the attic at school. Crushed flannelette nighties, corduroys with patched knees, old sweaters and polka-dot sheets. In the early years, kneeling on the cold floor, she'd tried to fold her clothes properly but ended up with messy bundles and a rising panic. What if she was scolded and made to do it again and not given any cake at Tea?

The trunk she'd brought from Kanpur was always better. Things lifted from it still smelled of life, of home: clothes washed in Surf and dried in the sun, peanut butter cookies, Mom's soft scent, Dad's coffee. Ruth would press her face into the Kanpur things and inhale, the ache in her chest tightening like a metal band. But the home smells soon died under the weight of the naphthalene that invaded her cupboard like a bad spirit and lingered over it for weeks. It was also the smell of the boys' toilets if you were walking past when a door swung open, and the smell that sunk like a rock in your stomach as you pulled on your missionary barrel clothes and the other girls snickered, and the smell of the night when you lay in bed and felt cracks forming inside you and the seeping of tears.

In her dream, the bell was ringing and Ruth was supposed to line up for school, but was far away on a narrow path of the hillside. Dad was in front, carrying her bag, and Mom was behind and they were all going to Kanpur. But then Ruth realised she was alone and knew she had done something wrong but didn't know what and wanted to say sorry, but couldn't go fast enough with her bumping, dragging bag. She had to get to the road before they got on the bus! The faster she ran, the more her things fell out and that was another wrong thing so she had to keep finding them – jeans, a teddy bear, baby clothes – but some tumbled down the *khud* and were out of reach and Iqbal came by singing. Then she was at school with everyone standing in line but she was naked and Hannah was the teacher and Ruth had forgotten her bag and forgotten Mom and Dad. So she ran again, and finally, she was on the *chakkar* walking to the house. The house at the end of the longest walk in the world, round so many twists and bends in the mountain that you thought you would never reach it. But it was always there, reeking with grief. And she knew Manveer was there and tried to run but her legs would not move at all, like the air had turned to *gur,* and she tried to call, but the sound would not come till she pushed so hard it was like a groan from the grave but it was too late. He had gone.

She woke up drenched in sweat and tears, her chest heaving with sobs, hands gripping the *razai* that was pulled up around her head. Then she realised that her bed was completely soaked, her nightie clinging to her, the wetness still warm on her legs. She lay in the dark for the longest time. The dorm was quiet, except for the breathing from the bunk nearest her. Then someone rolled over and made lip-smacking noises. It was Sita. Somewhere else a snort, a cough. Way off, she could hear the faint ticking of the Kozy Korner clock that hung just outside Miss Joshi's door.

She could try to change the sheets in the dark, but then she remembered that her clean ones weren't back from the *dhobi* yet and the mattress was wet. Perhaps she could lay her towel over the wet spot? But then it would still soak through and she'd have to dry her face with a sour towel in the morning. She wished for Hannah, but Hannah was in the Dispensary with a tummy bug. Even more, she wished for Mom, but Mom was in Kanpur, asleep in the dusty house in the corner of the hospital compound, far, far away.

Carefully, quietly, Ruth peeled back the *razai* and climbed down the bunk, her wet nightie clinging to her legs. In the dark she couldn't find her slippers, so walked barefoot on the cold concrete floor, out of the Grade 1-2 cubicle and down the dorm to Kozy Korner. She stood for a while outside Miss Joshi's door, once again going over her options, but there didn't seem to be any.

She knocked, *very* softly. There was no sound from within. Her feet were going numb on the floor, her legs stinging and itchy now where the urine was drying. She knocked again, a little louder. Still nothing. Finally, taking a big breath, she rapped firmly, several times.

At last, a sound from within. A rustling.

'Who's there?' Miss Joshi's voice was muffled by sleep and doors.

'Ruth.' She was trying not to be too loud as the Grade 1-2 cubicle was just feet away and like all the cubes, only had cupboards for walls. The whole dorm was one long room and you could hear everything from Kozy Korner at one end to the Grade 6 cube at the other.

'What is it?' The voice was irritated now and no longer muffled.

'I... um,' Ruth imagined the whole dorm awake now and

lying with their ears pricked. 'I've got a problem.'

There was a huff, a creaking of the bed and a rummaging around. Ruth heard the inner door of Miss Joshi's apartment opening and a switch snapping on. Light shot under the main door and over Ruth's icy toes. She heard Miss Joshi's footsteps across the room, the jingling of keys turning in the lock and the door yanking open. Silhouetted in the light, Miss Joshi's hair rose around her head in a frazzled mane, as if she had spent the night tearing at it. Her face was dark.

'What?' she demanded.

'I had an accident,' whispered Ruth.

'What sort of accident?' Miss Joshi snorted, as if she couldn't possibly imagine.

Ruth dropped her head, gripping one hand in the other. 'I wet my bed,' she mumbled.

'Good God! Do you think I want to know about that in the middle of the night?'

Ruth was stumped.

'Do you?!' Miss Joshi demanded.

'No,' breathed Ruth, feeling her chest caving in.

'And what do you think I'm supposed to do about it, hm? Turn all the lights on and wake everybody up so we can change your sheets?' Miss Joshi was reaching the pitch she employed for the dinner queue. She did not sound very worried about waking everybody up. 'Is that what you think, huh?'

Ruth shook her head, tears turning the light at Miss Joshi's feet to a blur. Though she bit hard on her lip she couldn't stop the stinging in her nose or the wobbling of her breath.

'Now go back to bed and we'll fix it in the morning,' Miss Joshi said, beginning to turn away.

'But, my bed...' and Ruth broke, clutching her arms around herself as she crumpled into sobs.

'Oh God,' Miss Joshi hissed. She wavered, then leaned over and put a hand on Ruth's shoulder. Her voice was softer. '*Cha, cha, cha* now darling. Stop that now.'

But Ruth's crying had engulfed her and she could no more stop it than turn the tide. Miss Joshi bent awkwardly over her, a great bird in her fringed shawl, and wrapped her arms around Ruth's heaving shoulders. Ruth could feel her long nails as she patted her head and back.

'Shush now, *beti*, shush now,' she clucked. 'We'll think of something.'

What Miss Joshi thought of was to rinse Ruth down with a couple of mugs of cold water – there was no hot at this time of night, but the icky-icky had to be removed – and to put her back to bed lying on top of her *razai* with another one as a cover, a spare she'd found in a cupboard.

'Don't forget to strip your bed in the morning,' Miss Joshi whispered, pointing a dark talon at the polka dot sheets. Then she clutched Ruth's head in her hands and planted a wet smacking kiss on her forehead.

'Sleep well now, darling.' Her breath was a curdling of stale tea and garlic.

Ruth listened to the sound of her rubber chappals slip-slapping back to her apartment, then rubbed her forehead and curled into a tight ball. She was naked and still cold from the dousing. The top *razai* was scratchy in places as though things had been spilled on it and dried like scabs. It smelled of mothballs.

NINE

James watched from his window at Askival as the Colonel and his wife came up the path, their labelled black umbrellas – BUNCE 1 and BUNCE 2 – bobbing above their ponchos. It was September 1947, monsoon and nearly dark. Mrs Bunce carried a torch, while the Colonel strode in front, striking and swinging his walking stick like a parade master's baton.

He propped it against a pillar on the veranda and stood billowing his umbrella in and out, gusting raindrops before him. James heard the squeal of the screen door and saw his mother stepping forward with out-flung arms.

'Welcome, welcome!' Leota cried and helped Mrs Bunce with her poncho. 'My, but if the heavens haven't opened today and spilled themselves! Come on in and get dry.'

James moved to his bedroom door and peered through a slit to the hallway where Mrs Bunce was pressing her powdered cheek to his mother's rough one.

'Lovely to see you, Leota, dear,' she gushed, all scent and tinkling pearls.

'Indeed!' said the Colonel as he snapped his heels and bent to kiss her hand. Leota cackled and led them through to the living room, James slipping in behind. On a clear day, the French windows offered views across the Dehra Dun valley to the Siwalik Hills and sometimes a glimpse of the plains beyond. But tonight there was just cloud and rain. A leak in the roof pinged drops into a *dekchi* on the floor and a small puddle was forming on a windowsill. James felt the dampness of the air and remembered the Colonel's tales of the good old Rawley's roaring fires and hot chocolates shot with whisky. Now an iron *chula* squatted in front of the fireplace, rumbling and spitting and giving off an acrid smell as its wet wood struggled to burn.

Stanley appeared in the archway from his office and gave both guests a solemn nod and a handshake. James had never seen him kiss any woman – not even Leota – and was glad of it. He attempted to take the same approach, but found himself crushed against Mrs Bunce's bosom as she planted a lipsticky peck. Fighting the urge to wipe his cheek, he took the Colonel's out-thrust hand and was relieved to see no sign of the stick. After supper, he would show Bunce the newly mounted buck's head on his bedroom wall.

'Evening, James!' Bunce barked. 'Good day at school?'

'Yes, sir.' He tried to find a place for his hands. At fifteen, he had become less and less at home in his own body as it kept outgrowing his clothes and his control. He was like a creature trapped, struggling not so much to get out of the cage as to master it. At last the adults settled into the fraying armchairs and he could sit down, hunkering back into his seat, hands tucked round his sides, feet sticking out like boats.

'How are things, Colonel?' asked Leota as she moved amongst them with a tray of orange squash.

'Bloody awful.' He knocked back his drink like a vodka and banged the glass down.

James shot a look at his father.

'Just terrible,' murmured Mrs Bunce, looking into her

squash and shaking her head.

'Why ever?' asked Leota. 'What's happened?'

'I'm afraid the whole country's gone mad,' said Bunce. 'Well, both countries, to be precise. It's a bloody disaster.'

Stanley cleared his throat. 'Things are getting worse?'

'Well, all the Mohammedans are trying to get into their Promised Land and all the Hindus and Sikhs are trying to come the other way, and they're rather colliding in the middle. Not a pretty sight, I can assure you.'

He took peanuts from a bowl near him and tossed them one by one into his mouth.

Mrs Bunce sighed. 'We knew partition was never going to work,' she said, as if she herself had reluctantly allowed it. 'Just like independence, really.'

'They've only had it for three weeks.' Stanley looked at her across his massive hands, fingertips pressed together. 'It's a little early to judge, don't you think?'

James slid his gaze from his father to the Bunces and back. Stanley never moderated his words for the sake of diplomacy. To the contrary, he seemed to regard it his God-given calling to wield the Sword of Truth whenever he caught a whiff of falsehood, half-truth or lame argument. James had felt its cut many times and had learnt extreme caution in the choosing of words. It had made him slow of speech, stuttering, strangled. Most often he sheltered in silence.

'Supper ready, Memsahib,' announced Aziz, appearing in the archway between dining and living rooms, his apron a well-scrubbed white and tied neatly in a bow. It was his custom, whenever there was company, to discard the grease-splattered apron he'd worn for cooking, and to don a clean one for serving the meal. It matched his pearly teeth and the starched cap that sat at a jaunty angle on his black curls. The apron had also been used to wipe his glasses just prior to his entrance so that they, like everything else about him, shone. He smiled broadly as he stepped to one side with a small bow and a sweeping gesture towards the table. He had done his best with the few resources available. A slightly greying bed sheet served as table cloth, the cutlery was miss-matched but vigorously polished and he'd folded an assortment of napkins in the Delhi-restaurant style, though he had never been to Delhi. In the middle he'd set a vase of dahlias from the garden and on either side, a pair of candles flickered cheerfully in brass holders.

The Memsahib herself was uninterested in such ceremony, but Aziz had persuaded her to indulge his passion for it on special occasions. He also knew it would be every bit the expectation of Colonel Sahib and his wife, and although Memsahib Leota never did anything to impress anyone – least of all snooty Britishers – she let Aziz have his fancy table so long as no-one expected *her* to fuss with airs and graces.

As the party moved through to the dining room, Aziz stopped James with an arm around his shoulders.

'Hungry, babu?' he asked, eyes twinkling.

'*Bahot* hungry, ji!' James flushed and returned a lopsided smile.

'*Accha, accha, bahot accha!*' Aziz slapped him on the belly. 'I have yum yum *khana* for you. Sit, sit!' This had been their pre-supper exchange since James was a child but tonight Aziz sensed his discomfort. He saw the smirk on the Colonel's face and the frown on Stanley's and slipped back into the kitchen.

Behind the door he listened through the rain as the

scraping of chairs fell silent and the blessing began. It used to be an unbearable moment as his perfectly timed dishes cooled in the long minutes of Stanley's prayer, but he had learnt to allow for the delay and to detect in the Sahib's cadences the final canter to the end. He had also learnt to adapt his planning when Stanley was away and Leota gave the blessing. Hers was always the same and always short:

'For what we are about to receive, may the Lord make us truly thankful.'

On such occasions, Aziz was indeed thankful. However, he did admire the Sahib's religious fervour and believed that rising to the demands of the situation was – along with artful table dressing – one of the many skills a good *khansamma* must possess.

As everyone murmured the Amen he lifted his tray of soup and after an appropriate pause for the party to drape Delhi-folded napkins across laps, he pushed through the swinging door.

'Tomato Chowder!' he announced, lowering the tray to the sideboard. 'Recipe of Mrs Wilhemina Klinkingbeard.'

'Who?' asked Bunce. 'Do we know her?'

'No,' said Leota.

'American Ladies Club of Lahore,' said Aziz, setting bowls of soup before each diner.

'Eh?'

'Somebody knew her and put her recipe in the book,' explained Leota

'What book?' asked Bunce.

'The Landour Community Cookbook, darling,' said Mrs Bunce, resting a hand on his arm. 'It's what our *khansamma* uses all the time. Everybody up here does. Leota was the editor, weren't you, dear?'

'I guess,' said Leota with a tip of her head.

The Book, as Aziz knew well, was the culinary bible of all hillside memsahibs and their cooks, providing tips on everything from baking at altitude to substitutes for cornstarch. His Memsahib had put it together fifteen years before with a bevy of missionary ladies who all spent their summers on the hillside and congregated at the Landour Community Centre to swap paperbacks, children's clothes and recipes. Aziz was steadily working his way through The Book with Leota, memorising each dish, as he could not read. His dream was to have one of his own creations included in the next edition, and to this end he committed many hours of diligent practice.

'Boston Brown Bread!' he fluted, moving behind the diners, offering slabs of the thick loaf. 'By Mrs Marjorie Humphwell.'

'Thank-you, Aziz-ji,' said Leota. 'It smells great.' She gave him a toothy smile, her face creasing into a map of contours and ridges in which the blue of her eyes almost vanished. Aziz bobbed his head, patted James on the back and disappeared through the door.

The boy took up a large spoonful of soup and slurped. He felt his mother's kick. Opposite him, Mrs Bunce was making delicate scoops into the outer side of her bowl and slipping the soup through her lips without a sound. The Colonel matched her. James watched his father, who being out of range of Leota's foot and authority, tore his bread in half and dipped. Mrs Bunce's eyebrows shot up. James suppressed a smile as Stanley pushed the soggy wad into his mouth.

'So, Dick' he said, chewing. He had always refused to use

the Colonel's rank. 'We've heard rumours. Give us the facts.'

The Colonel dabbed at his moustache with his napkin.

'Well there are thousands – millions I shouldn't think – trailing across the desert to get to the other side. Jinnah's told the Mohammedans that they haven't got a future in India and likewise, the Hindus and Sikhs on his patch are trying to get out.'

'But what about their homes, their farms?' asked Leota. 'Are they leaving everything?'

'They can't take the land with them, can they?' Bunce buttered his Boston Brown Bread with vigorous strokes and cut it into triangles.

'But do they all wanna leave, or are they being forced off?' asked Stanley.

'No edicts from on high, if that's what you mean,' replied Bunce. 'But, seemingly, as soon as they got wind of partition, people thought the farms and businesses in Pakistan should automatically belong to the Mohammedans and the ones in India to Hindus and Sikhs, so they started attacking the owners if they were the wrong lot. So, forced off, yes, but by their neighbours.' He took a bite of bread, chewed with a snapping action of the jaw and swallowed. 'And I'm sorry to say, it's all got rather bloody.'

James felt his bread stick in his throat. He looked at his mother. Her spoon was suspended half way between her bowl and her open mouth. Stanley's bread, wedged in his calloused fingers, was dripping tomato red onto the cloth.

'What do you mean?' he asked.

'Oh, everything you could imagine and worse. Setting fire to homes with families still inside, hacking people to death with knives, clubs, sticks – their own blighted fingernails, if they have to.'

There was silence. Outside, a low growl of thunder, like the beginnings of a rock-slide. The kitchen door swung open and Aziz appeared, his smile dimming at the sight of the unfinished soup.

'Enough, Memsahib, or I come back?'

Leota looked questioningly around the table but no one wanted more.

'Ah – yeah. No. We've had enough, thank you, ji,' she said.

'That was *lovely* soup, Leota,' Mrs Bunce cooed. '*You* must have taught him that.'

'Well... aha,' Leota replied, and wiped her mouth. Aziz cleared the bowls and swept out.

A scurry of wind rattled the windows and the rain thrummed. A candle sputtered. James felt the hardness of the chair against his bones.

Stanley spoke first. 'There had already been so much trouble but we hoped independence might–'

'Sadly, not. The violence is worse than ever and it's swept across the country. Mainly in the north, of course, and the Punjab is undoubtedly the most desperate. I've just come up from Amritsar, and I kid you not—'

'Chicken Fried Walnut!' declared Aziz, entering with a steaming tray. 'Leonard Peterson. First Prize!' He laid it in the centre of the table.

'First Prize?' asked Bunce, peering down at the dish of crumbed joints garnished with tomato rosettes and fronds of carrot.

'The school hobby show,' said Leota, distractedly.

'1931,' confirmed Aziz, holding up a finger. 'Every hobby show prize winner making in Book.'

'Oh, I see,' said Bunce.

'Beside with Oven Roast Potato and Spinach Greens!' Aziz set the vegetables on the table and beamed at everyone, confident that whatever had gone wrong with his Tomato Chowder would not be repeated with the main course. This one was Never Fail.

'*Shukriya*, Aziz-ji,' Leota said, as he backed out with an incline of the head. 'Margaret, please help yourself to some chicken.'

For a few blessed moments they managed to keep the conversation to exclamations over the food and complaints about the weather, but not for long. Stanley was impatient.

'So what are you all doing about it?' he asked.

'Not a great deal we can do, really.' Bunce sawed into his chicken. 'It's got terribly out of control. Never seen anything like it. I tell you, I served in both the wars and nothing I witnessed there was as bad as this. Nothing.'

'Really?' asked Leota, her sun-damaged face puckered, brows like bunched knitting. She hadn't managed much of her chicken. 'Do you mean ...?' Her voice trailed off.

'I mean everything,' said the Colonel, putting down his knife and fork. 'Everything. Do you know, that on the day they celebrated independence, hordes of Sikh thugs went mad in a Mohammedan ghetto in Amritsar? Slaughtered every male and stripped the women. Raped them, dragged them to the courts of the Golden Temple, then cut their throats.'

There was no sound but the rain.

'Dickie!' breathed Mrs Bunce.

James felt a coldness flooding his stomach. He looked at Leota. Her hand was pressed to her mouth, eyes round as buttons. His father's face was fixed on the Colonel, gaze narrow and knifing. From the kitchen came the sound of Aziz stacking dishes.

'I have never met a Sikh who would do such a thing,' said Stanley. 'Never.'

'Well I've recently met hundreds,' the Colonel replied. 'I was called to the Temple. I saw the women.' His jaw had tightened and a vein was pulsing above it.

'Mercy,' Leota murmured, shaking her head as if trying to wake herself from a nightmare.

With a squeal of hinges, the kitchen door swung open again and Aziz stepped in, face radiant, but immediately crushed.

'What is wrong, Memsahib?' he cried in Hindi. 'Is it no good?'

'Oh... no, Aziz-ji. It is very good, but we are... not so hungry tonight.'

She looked around the table. Everyone was shaking their heads, putting hands up in front of their plates – no more.

'Maybe a bug is going around?' she murmured, dropping a hand to her stomach. '*Maf kijiye.*' Forgive us.

Aziz pressed his lips together and began removing the plates, loudly scraping leftovers from one to the other. He strode back through the kitchen door, head high.

James took a sip from his glass of squash. Mrs Bunce was smoothing her napkin on her lap, the Colonel straightening cutlery. Outside the rain fell harder. They could hear it rushing down the tin gutters, spattering on the edges of the veranda, drumming the earth. From the living room came the fumings of the *chula* and the steady drip, drip, drip into the *dekchi*.

'If it's any consolation,' said the Colonel, as if it was incumbent upon him to save the evening. 'It's not just the Sikhs. The Hindus and Mohammedans have been just as bad.'

'That is no consolation,' said Stanley.

'Quite.' The Colonel brushed his moustache and arched his brows.

Aziz appeared again, not with his former brio, but managing a brave smile. He was at a loss to explain the failure of his cooking tonight. Normally it generated waves of good cheer, laughter, animated conversation and abundant praise. He glowed in it, lapped it up, loved nothing more.

But tonight something had gone desperately wrong and he could not fathom what. Nor, indeed, could he imagine a worse occasion for such a disaster. This was the night for which he had been preparing for weeks; the night when the class of guest would be just right and the Memsahib would allow three courses and the bed sheet cloth; the night of his triumph. For what he now carried aloft from the kitchen was nothing less than the pinnacle of his culinary achievement, the result of long practice in the alchemy of egg whites and sugar, and the dish for which he held out greatest hope of earning his name in The Book.

'Mogul Mango Meringue Pie!' he announced, as if ushering in an awesome personage. 'By Aziz Mohammed Hashim!' He set before Leota a giant white confection with a stiff dome and teetering minarets. The stunned silence he took to be awe.

'I am entering for next hobby show,' he beamed, offering the pie slide and knife with a flourish.

'Splendid,' said the Colonel at last, and there was a helpful *ooh* from Mrs Bunce. James made a sound half way between a hum and a grunt and Leota took the utensils, lifting her drained face to Aziz.

'Thank you, ji,' she said, quietly. 'It looks...'

But Aziz never heard, for there was a whip-crack of lightning, thunder like a battering ram and a zap from above as the lights went out. Everything happened at once. Mrs Bunce squealed, James knocked over his glass, the Colonel shouted *Good Lord!*, the glass rolled, Leota gasped *Mercy!*, the glass smashed on the floor and Stanley said *Arè?*

'Aziz is saving! Aziz is saving!' the cook cried, rushing to the kitchen.

'Watch the glass!' yelled Leota.

There was a furious rummaging and crashing from within and Leota jumped up with a candle from the table.

'You okay, ji?' she asked through the kitchen door.

'*Theek hai, theek hai,*' he called. 'Helping the light!' He hurried through with a clutch of candles and matches.

'Will somebody sweep that glass?' said Stanley.

'Oh dear,' murmured Mrs Bunce. Another flash of lightning blanched the sky, capturing them all for a moment in awkward pose: white, frozen, eyes and mouths wide like a badly timed photograph. Then the dark again.

'James!' said Leota, lighting another candle. 'Get the broom.'

'Aziz is doing!' the cook cried as he pushed James back in his seat and disappeared again into the cavern of the kitchen, shielding a stuttering candle flame with his hand.

At last, when the glass was swept, everyone back in their seats and the table ablaze with a small forest of candles, Aziz gestured again towards his meringue Taj Mahal, bowed gracefully and slipped out.

The pie trembled as Leota sliced. A minaret toppled. When she tried to get a piece onto a plate, it flopped, shooting a slippery wedge of mango onto the tablecloth. The Colonel chuckled. Leota squeezed a tight smile, kept cutting, plundering, dividing onto plates.

'He's frightfully good, your *khansamma*, isn't he?' said Mrs Bunce, taking a nibble.

'The best,' Leota replied, fiercely. She knew Aziz would be lurking behind the kitchen door, straining to hear.

James forced himself to bite a piece of pie; it was sticky, clagging his teeth and hard to swallow. Down the table, Stanley had not touched his. In the candle-light, his heavy brows threw wild, tufted shadows up his forehead. He studied the dark soup stain on the cloth beside his plate, rubbing it with a finger.

'And when they leave their homes... to get to the other side... are they makin it?' he asked.

The Colonel tilted his head and finished his mouthful, jaw snapping. 'Some are, yes, certainly. There are hundreds and thousands of them, you know. Great long columns – miles long – walking with all their clap-trap on their heads. And some are getting there, yes. Refugee camps are springing up on both sides.'

James poked at the white crests of meringue on his plate, glistening in the flickering light.

'And the others?' asked Stanley.

Bunce shrugged. 'End of the road.'

The storm threw rain against the window like a fist of

gravel. Leota shook her head. Mrs Bunce put a hand over hers.

'I know,' she breathed. 'It's just awful.'

'But what about buses, trains?' pressed Stanley. 'Why are they all walkin?'

'They're not. There are plenty of buses and trains. Packed to the gunnels.' The Colonel drew his napkin across his forehead, where a sheen of sweat had appeared. 'But that's even worse.'

'How?' asked Stanley.

'You haven't heard, then,' said Bunce.

'I'm asking,' Stanley growled. James shifted in his chair. Bunce stiffened.

'On the day of so-called freedom, a train rolls into Amritsar from Pakistan. Station packed with Sikhs and Hindus waiting for relatives from the other side. There's the driver in the engine, but the windows of the carriages are empty. Open the doors and see why.' Bunce paused to scratch his eyebrow with his little finger. Everyone watched him. 'All on the floor. Dead.'

Leota closed her eyes and lowered her face into her hand.

'Dickie...' Mrs Bunce warned.

'I'm sorry, dear, but they asked for the facts.'

'Yes, but—' and she cocked her head towards James. He flushed and looked down, fiddled with his hands.

'They were all killed?' asked Stanley, incredulous.

'Would have been better if they were. But no, there were survivors. A woman lying in her husband's blood. A boy on a luggage rack. A baby with no ears.'

Something in Leota broke. There was a shuddering sound and a gasp. With one hand clawed over her eyes and the other gripping her mouth, she started to sob.

'Oh Leota,' cried Mrs Bunce, and put a hand on her

shoulder. 'Now Dickie, that's enough!'

'No,' said Stanley, slowly, firmly. 'We need to hear.'

And it seemed the Colonel needed to tell, as if some dark current within him had been unstoppered and he had neither power nor will to staunch it. He lit up a cigar and in a low, flat voice, through coils of smoke, told the tales of horror from across the country: the demonic mobs, the gutters of Lahore running with Hindu blood, the railway platforms lined with Sikhs holding their curved knives, waiting for the next Muslim train.

James hunched in his chair, skin crawling, hands clammy. Bunce's words and the sound of his mother's cries had awakened in him a primal terror, as if a curtain that had shielded him was torn and he could feel evil breathing at his back. Worse, he had always thought that curtain was a wall, a rock of certainty, a belief about the world on which he leaned. Now it was gone and what lay beyond was an abyss of unimaginable darkness.

India had always been his home and he had seen much. A dead man on the road, shimmering with flies. Uncountable beggar children in filthy scraps. A woman burned and hairless, because her dowry was not enough. But none of it – nothing he'd ever witnessed, heard or read – was as terrible as what Bunce now described.

He longed to howl, to scream, to weep like the rains, but he did not make a sound. Stanley was there, and though the boy's eyes stung and his throat burned and his chest was tight as a drawn bow, he would not crack in front of his father. He would hold it all in, pack it down, heave boulders on top and little suspect the damage within.

No one remembered Aziz, pressed behind the kitchen door. When they finally got up from the table and the Bunces took their leave, the Muslim *khansamma* slipped quietly into the empty dining room. Napkins lay in crumpled heaps. The candles were burnt stumps, wax dribbled across the table. At Stanley's end, the bed sheet was blotted with soup, and at James's with orange squash. Beside Bunce's place there was an ashtray and the butt of his cigar. On every plate, slices of Mogul Mango Meringue Pie sat, collapsed and barely touched. With shaking hands, Aziz carried them through to the kitchen and slid them into the bin.

TEN

At the top of the graveyard path, Ruth ground her cigarette into the soil and started down the mossy steps behind James. He turned, nearly bumping her, and lifted the cigarette butt into a cotton bag hanging across his chest. It already held an old chips packet, half a shoe and several bits of plastic. Her cheeks burned and she mumbled an apology.

The Landour Cemetery was on the northern side of the mountain, half-way between Morrison Church and Askival on the back *chakkar*. The slope here was a cathedral of trees: deodars, pines, Himalayan cypress, rhododendron, horse chestnut and oak. She used to play in the graveyard, years ago. Capture the Flag, Hide and Seek, Flashlight Beckon. They would come for cast parties and class nights out, small flocks of teenagers running over the gravestones giggling, diving behind tree trunks, squealing when someone leapt out or grabbed from the dark.

Huddled round small campfires they told the obligatory ghost stories. The headless woman who followed you on the road. Old Colonel Bunce's grave that smelled of cigars. The bastard child buried alone in the forest, crying at night. Ruth's best friend Sita was horribly good at it. Her huge eyes bulged white in the moonlight as Ruth's skin rose in reptile bumps.

There were also the illicit forays from the dorm when they crept up the mountain like fugitives, contraband smuggled under their clothes. It was here, leaning against a stone angel, that Ruth had smoked her first cigarette, gasping at the sting in her throat, yet resolving to master the art. In truth, it had mastered her, holding her captive to its slow poison, so that she'd never been able to quit and had many times slid into a ravenous chain smoking. She hated how it lingered on her breath and stained her teeth, how it would never leave her. The first hash had also been here, bought from the Lhasa Café at Mullingar by her then-boyfriend, who had squatted beside her in a crumbling tomb rolling the joint by candlelight. The son of an Australian diplomat, he was three years older, failing at school, but excelling at the addictive arts. Ruth was fifteen and her reputation already in shreds, her parents despairing.

But when she'd come to the graveyard alone – always by day – she was a different person and it was a changed place. Light filtered between the great trees, wildflowers speckled the grass, birds sang. At those times the gravestones were no longer dark hiding places, but windows into vanished lives, speaking not of horror, but of loss. The oldest were British soldiers and East India Company folk lying quietly amongst wives and infants, hopelessly far from home. Ruth had gathered flowers and laid them on the silent stones, whispering the beautiful names. *Barnabas Llewellyn Jones, Maribelle Constance Winshaft, Eliza Rose McBain.* She never imagined one would be her mother's.

The funeral had happened without her as she'd been sailing across the Atlantic and no one knew where she was. Since school she'd always lived that way, often wandering and out of touch, always vague about her plans. There were occasional postcards and emails, but she let months go by with no news at all. Hannah berated her for it in vain and her parents had given up pleading.

But when her mother died, all her bitterness had lashed back at her. The harbour master met her on the pier at Plymouth with a furrowed face and a printed message. Ruth showed no emotion, but drank herself into a stupor that night in The Gull and Goose and woke in a strange bed with a strange man. She slipped out before morning to the seafront and stood in the wind, weeping.

When Ruth was very small her mother bathed the girls in a tin tub in the bathroom at Kanpur. She would lift them out, wrap them in towels, and rub them down singing silly songs as she went. *Head, shoulders, knees and toes... Two little eyes for Jesus... This little piggy went to the bazaar...* No little piggies in India ate roast beef. They got curry or chapattis or laddus. Ellen would powder her girls with talc, button them into soft nightdresses and brush their hair. Ruth always wailed through this bit, as her curls were tangled, but her mother would distract her with pretty ribbons and clips. Then they took turns to sit in her lap for stories, Ellen reading from *Little House on the Prairie* and *Children's Bible Favourites*. Ruth burrowed her head under her mother's chin and breathed the smells of Ellen's day: the dried sweat, the fading perfume, the bread, and that soft whiff that was only on her mother's skin and had the power to heal. Then they sang a quiet song, like *Jesus Keep Me in the Cross*, and said a very quiet prayer. *Now I lay me down to sleep, I pray the Lord my soul to keep.* Sometimes Ruth was already asleep by then, rocked by the lull of her mother's voice, cheek against her heart. *If I die before I wake, I pray the Lord my soul to take.*

James stopped at the foot of a black grave. All around, the giant deodars stood watch, their trunks laced with ferns, breath cool and sighing. Ruth moved slowly to his side, hands thrust deep in her jacket pockets. The stone was polished marble, engraved in gold.

To live is Christ,
to die is gain.
Ellen Louise Goldman Connor
1931 – 2001

A scattering of dry pine needles lay across the marble. There were no flowers. Neither said anything for a long time. Grey fingers of mist were curling round the trees and taking hold of their ankles.

'Iqbal helped me choose that,' James said, pointing a scrawny hand at the inscription.

'He was here then?'

'Arrived a few weeks after the funeral.'

'Oh.' She wanted to ask why, where from, what for, but there was an ache growing inside her chest as the other questions she had never asked welled up. She dug her fingers into her palms and took a breath.

'Was it quick?'

'I think so.' His hand moved to his chest. Ruth could see every liver spot and hair on the translucent skin and how his veins pushed up, blue-grey and forking, like the tributaries of swollen rivers.

'Where were you?'

James didn't answer for a moment. His fingers opened and closed on the pilling wool of his sweater.

'Working at the hospital.' A bird called. The mist hung about them, listening. 'Got home quite late. She was on the floor.'

Ruth felt her nose stinging.

'Must have been in the middle of baking. Oven on, a pie burning, dropped dishes lying around.'

There was a sigh in the deodars above them, a trembling of ferns.

Ruth pictured her mother, collapsed and twisted with flour in her hair. Then James finding her. She felt a snapping inside and the rising of tears. Turning quickly away, she caught sight of wild orchids growing on the *khud* side and through blurred eyes tugged at them, pulling out lumps of moss and earth with their roots. Face hidden, she dusted off the soil and laid the flowers on the gravestone.

'There's no need,' he said. 'She's not here, you know.'

'But I am!' she spat.

'Oh *Piyari!*' James startled. 'Oh – come now...'

But she was gone.

He took a few steps after her, then stopped and watched her crashing up through the forest. Crying, broken.

He knew if he pursued, she would run further away.

Had it always been like this?

He saw her sitting on her bed, about four years old. Spanked and banished from the table for refusing to eat. He'd gone in to make peace. There she was, elfin face white as stone, bloodless lips pressed together, arms buckled across her chest. He knelt and put his hands on her knees. She flinched.

'*Piyari...*' he began softly. *Beloved.* She glared at his hands.

'Look at me,' he said, hating the edge in his voice.

Her gaze slid up. Grey-green eyes, flashing and hard. Like scales.

The mist was thick around him now and murmuring rain. He shivered, pushed his hands into his armpits and looked back at Ellen's headstone. When she died it was like all the burdens of his life had poured down upon him. A stoning of the spirit. He had stood alone at her grave and wished to be dead.

In truth he was not alone. The funeral was attended by hundreds, but for all their hymn-singing, kind words and cups of tea, they were as good as the gravestones to him. On the phone, Hannah had cried, but couldn't come because she was about to give birth. And Ruth. Well, Ruth was, as always, unreachable. He had endured it with a bitten lip for so many years, but when it came to her mother's death, he had bellowed. Not at Ruth, though he wished to. Nor at Hannah, for she already knew. Nor, indeed, at anyone who had anything to do with it.

At someone else, entirely.

ELEVEN

It was three weeks after Ellen had died, and James could not get the Landour Community Cookbook to sit flat. Every time he lifted his hand, the page turned by itself and he lost the recipe. Because the book was so old, many of its stained pages had been taped together, and while some of the tape had lost its stick, other bits were newer and tenacious. Like this bit, which sat in such a way that the pages tugged and would not lie open. He yanked the straying page back, slapped his hand on the central margin and rubbed hard.

'Stay!' he barked.

Tuna Hash by Patty Lutz. It didn't look difficult. He could peel a potato, beat an egg, open a tin of tuna. But tonight he could not do it without rage. The potatoes smelled like the soles of his hiking boots and were so small and gritty they lost half their weight in peeling. As he tried to grate them, one slipped and bounced right away so that he sliced a shred of skin instead. A smear of blood shone on the grater. When he went to find a bandaid he realised he didn't know where they were kept, so pressed a wad of toilet paper against the cut and returned to the recipe. Baking Powder. Where was that? A left-handed rummage in the cupboard produced an empty box.

Ellen would not have allowed this. She had noted down whenever a household item was running low; she had kept lists. Of everything. He was still finding them.

Must Read
The Cloud of Unknowing
Les Misérables
Christ of the Indian Road
The Four Quartets

She had suggested they read the same things and talk about them, but he had maintained that novels were a waste of time. When she explained she wasn't thinking of novels alone, but poetry also and spiritual writings, he replied that the Holy Scriptures were more than sufficient. It silenced her.

Just as Stanley had always silenced him.

Projects
Plant out flower pots
Baby quilt for Hannah
Cookbook introduction

There had been many projects and plans over the years. Especially when the girls were at Oaklands. She said she liked to keep her hands busy, but he knew she was just trying to fill the gulf. That if her hands were occupied they might forget the two small bodies they longed to tend; the bathing – from soft faces to dusty feet – the braiding of hair, the blessing of foreheads in quiet sleep. But the hands did not forget. They ached with the memory and at night in her dreams she would sometimes grasp him and cry out, as if she were drowning.

Her last project had been the updated edition of the Cookbook. Leota had intended one, all those years ago, but it had been swept aside in the aftermath of the tragedy, like everything else. Fifty years later, when James and Ellen left the hospital in Kanpur and settled in Landour, Ellen came across a dusty file of Leota's notes and recipes in a mission godown behind Morrison Church and got excited. She gathered a small team of editors for regular meetings in the Community Centre, and roamed the hillside collecting recipes from the motley crew of residents. There was the Dutch vegan woman with a shaved head and expertise on bean sprouts, the Anglo-Indian Brigadier who could name the joints of a wild boar (if only one was still allowed to shoot the damn things!), the fourth-generation *khansamma* from Goa bringing coconuts and a Portuguese twist, and the ancient spinsters, Dorothy and Iris Winshaft, who had never been to England but preserved the legend of it, as passed on by their mother, like a pickled egg. Their eyes misted over when they recalled Mummy's Devilled Fowl and Celery Fritters, not to mention her Macaronie a la Teddie and – oh! – her Roly-Poly Pudding. The Book was unfinished when Ellen died.

Along with her neatly labelled lists, she always had several small scraps of paper lying around which James knew to be her daily, scribbled, on-the-spot, Must Remember notes. They turned up in the pockets of her cardigans, in her Bible, on pin boards.

phone Hill Queen
get Vicks
Bible Study prep
Paul Verghese for supper
write Ruth

Despite Ruth's rare and unsatisfactory replies, Ellen had continued to write to her and Hannah every Sunday afternoon. Tucking two sheets of blue airmail paper and two sheets of carbon under a page of her diary, she recorded the events of the week. It was cheerful, homey stuff. New paediatrician at the hospital, wonderful music this morning at Hindustani church, the dog roses in flower. No mention of James' dark days or her own quiet struggle.

When she had finished, she took the first airmail sheet and wrote at the top, 'Dear Hannah and Derek'. As the years went on, she added Miriam, Elijah, Caleb, Noah, Damaris, Zachariah and, finally, Jethro. 'Such beautiful names,' she would say, and James could hear the yearning in her voice. She only saw them once every three years on furlough and almost ate them alive with her hungry eyes. On another sheet of paper she answered any letters they had sent, of which there was always at least one. Hannah wrote regularly and had her brood organised on a "Write to Gramma and Grampa" rota.

At the top of the second carbon copy, paler and a little smudged, Ellen wrote 'Dear Ruth'. At the bottom, she paused. James would watch her trying to think what to say, sitting at her little fold-down secretaire in the corner of the living room, staring into the garden. She generally settled for something uncontroversial. 'It's great that you're exploring again.' 'Hannah said you're helping out at a women's refuge.' Or a veiled hint: 'Hope this gets to you, as we're not sure of your address right now.' She had learnt not to ask for more. Expect little and you won't be disappointed.

That was the theory, anyway.

By the time she died, most people around her were using

email, but it was not for Ellen. She wanted the paper her loved ones had held, the handwriting, the enclosed photographs, the sticky artwork. She kept them all, the sacred bundles of her daughters' letters, tied with ribbon and tucked into labelled shoeboxes. They dated back to the girls' first weeks at Oaklands, when they could barely write and most of the page was taken up with a drawing.

In the early years, she'd felt the welling of tears at each letter's arrival, even when the news was good and they seemed happy enough. But if ever they spoke of illness, or missing home, or crying in their beds at night – which Ruth so often did – Ellen's tears spilled down her face and into the crevices of her neck. Sometimes she begged James to let her go to them. Always he refused. The girls were just fine and would turn out the better for it. And how could she abandon the streams of impoverished mothers on the maternity ward just because she was missing her own girls? Was she placing herself and her own family above the needs of others? Above the calling of God? All the great mothers of the Bible gave up their children. The mothers of Moses, Samuel, Jesus. Indeed, the great fathers also. Think of Abraham. Think of The Heavenly Father Himself! It was the ultimate sacrifice and surely the sign of a godly parent and the highest love. And if the Father knew when each sparrow fell to the ground, would he not also care for their daughters?

So Ellen learnt to staunch her tears, to write cheery letters, to smile and wave bravely at each farewell. She never knew the wells of James' unshed tears, the depths and darkness of those wells, or the great stone that lay across them.

When he discovered the empty box of baking powder, James crushed it in his fist and threw it, along with the soggy grey mass of potato, into the bin. The Landour Community Cookbook he hurled at the wall and for supper he had fried eggs. Again.

He washed up in scalding water, splattering Ellen's old apron and letting his hands swell and flame an angry red. His eyes stung, throat burned. Leaving the dishes on the drainer, slippery with soap scum, he carried a cup of coffee to the living room. It had grown dark, but he did not bother to turn on a light. Setting the coffee on a table beside him, he sank onto the tired sofa, his head falling to his hands. It was soundless, at first. Just a juddering of the ribs and choppy breath, but then it rose till he was shaking and flooded with tears. His sobs pushed him deep into the seat, dragging his shoulders, bending him double as their beating got louder. Louder and faster. Not just in him but beyond him, where it was also a rattling and a voice.

He held his sobs. The beating went on.

There was someone at the front door.

His breath rushed out on a gasp and he looked around him in the dark room.

Pound, pound, rattle, rattle.

'Sahib!' the voice called.

James froze. The voice. His hands clenched the crumpled fabric of the apron, heart raced. *That* voice.

Impossible. The man was dead.

'Doctor-sahib!'

But it *was* his voice. James got up and made for the back door, legs shaking. He would slip out through the garden and down the hill, escape this madness, run out into the night and never come back. Just as Aziz had done.

But in the dark he kicked over the small table and there was a crash as his coffee hit the floor.

'Sahib?'

James turned slowly towards the voice, his breathing heavy, body tense. At last, lifting the apron to the mess of his face, he wiped his eyes and squeezed the dripping end of his nose and made his way to the door. With shaking hands he drew back the bolts. Top, middle, bottom. Three hard scrapes of metal against metal, like the cocking of a rifle.

TWELVE

It was Iqbal. With a tray of tea and toast. Ruth stood blinking at him, still muddled by sleep, a shawl clutched around her.

'*Chotta hazri*!' he beamed.

'What?'

'Little breakfast,' and he slipped past her to lay down the tray. 'You can have in bed, if you like.'

She scratched her head. 'Um... What time is it?'

'Six-thirty, *beti*.'

'Oh god.'

His face fell. 'Too early? I am mistaking. I wait three days – but you are not overcoming the jet lag?'

'No, no, you're fine. I just wasn't expecting... Thanks. But you don't have to—'

'Pleasure is mine, *beti*!' He smiled again.

'Please don't call me that.'

His eyes and mouth went round, anxious.

'I just...,' she said. 'They remind me of someone... Not so nice.'

His eyes narrowed, head nodding slowly.

'*Accha*,' he said and brought a dimpled finger to his mouth. 'Not uttering again.'

'Thanks.'

They stood in fragile silence. Ruth felt acutely conscious of her bare legs sticking out under the fringed shawl. Pasty white legs, prickly black hairs. As if suddenly aware of them also, Iqbal bowed his head and scuttled out.

Ruth added *chotta hazri* to her list of Things to be Changed.

It was one small victory she did achieve, though she lost the larger battle over the sleeping arrangements. Iqbal insisted he was up before dawn every day and would cause her no end of disturbance if she was sleeping on the sofa. It sounded like he would do it on purpose. However, when she hid all the tea towels and waved the last one at him like a flag, he was forced to honour his promise that she could help in the kitchen.

'I'm using this and you're not having it,' she crowed. He stared at her, nostrils flared, eyes sparking. Then his face softened.

'I surrender,' he sighed, bowing deeply and gesturing to the wet dishes.

James, who was watching from the table, shook his head, lips tugged into a small, crooked smile. For a long time he had tried to help as well, but Iqbal's protests had triumphed. 'Doctor-ji is paying all the bills – the food even! – and not charging the rent, so he must leave the house-keeperly things to Iqbal. Is the fair thing, only.' James was deeply uncomfortable with Iqbal performing the duties of a servant, but the man had insisted he was not: 'I am friend, only,' he'd said. 'A brother. Like wife even!' and he'd winked. James had thrown up his hands in defeat.

But Ruth was not easily defeated. Along with washing up, she pestered to learn Iqbal's cooking. He was most happy to teach her! The *desi khana* – the Indian food –however, was all in his head and she had to scribble down his tangled instructions as they went along. Half of it was delivered in song, the other half in riddles.

Garam, garam, garam masala,
Dhaniya, zira rakhiye!
Khana rani ke liye,
Bahot mazedaar chayiye!

It was exasperating, but Iqbal would just chuckle.

'You have to learn by heart, Rani Ruthie,' he chimed, holding up a finger. 'There's no other way.'

The western recipes were easier, as they all came out of the Landour Community Cookbook. Ruth went quiet when she first saw the book with the faded green cover lying on the kitchen bench. It was a week after her arrival and Iqbal had promised baking. The book was battered, with a broken spine, and speckled with grease and yellow-brown stains. She turned the pages gently. Some were held together with sticky-tape, others torn. Everywhere, her mother's neat, small handwriting.

Delicious! Or, *Too much sugar.* Or, *Re-heats well.*

Next to a recipe for Chocolate Brownies she saw Hannah's round hand: *First prize at Hobby Show!* and a host of smiley faces. There were several recipes by Grandma Leota: Ham Scrapple, Good Plain Butter Cake for the Hills. And a couple of pages had dog-eared corners: Omelette, Macaroni Cheese, Tuna Hash.

'The Doctor-ji's,' Iqbal explained. 'Easy peasy.'

'God!' Ruth snorted. 'Dad cooking?'

'Only when needed. Three weeks. Then Iqbal is doing.'

Ruth studied his face. She wanted to ask why he had come but it felt impertinent so she turned back to the book. Next to a recipe for Never Fail Wacky Crazy Cake she saw her own teenaged writing. Large, florid script: *Failed!!!!!*

The exclamation marks continued to the edge of the page. It had been for her mother's birthday and Hannah was already graduated and back in the States. In the kitchen in Kanpur, Ruth and James had pored over the recipe together while Ellen was at a Ladies' Meeting. They had argued over which oil to use and whether to check the cake half way or not. In the end neither checked it at all and Ellen came home to the smell of burning and a thick, black tar on her best cake tin. It was a long time before Ruth tried baking again.

Iqbal tapped a recipe for Cinnamon Buns. 'Everybody is liking these.'

'Oh, yeah. By Mave Fishbacker. She was my friend's Mom! Let's make em!'

He tipped his head.

By eleven o'clock the pastries were arranged on a floral plate in all their plump, sticky glory. Ruth sat cross-legged in her chair, sinking her teeth into a warm bun. Things melted inside her. It was the taste of Sunday afternoon Bible Club. Never mind the singing and the sermons, you went for the Tea: the steaming hot mugs and the platters of home baking. Even Sita went to Bible Club. The hosts knew fine well that the way to these boarders' souls was through their stomachs. They were the Fishbackers, who lived at Fir Tree Bank round the hill beyond Sisters Bazaar, and were another missionary institution with several generations on both sides. Came to India with the Aryans, they used to joke. Mr Fishbacker was away in the plains most of the time, but when he came up to Landour he played the piano in honkey-tonk style and shouted 'Hallelujah!' Mrs Fishbacker held Bible studies and baked. They both dressed much the same way as their pioneering forebears and the furniture in their rabbit-warren house was shabby. They were other-worldly, unswerving, kind. Their daughter Dorcas was in Ruth's class, but wasn't a close friend. Dorcas was boring.

Ruth helped herself to another bun. The smells of cinnamon and risen bread filled the room and seemed to bring a loosening to James. His hands were lifted, voice stronger than usual, eyes bright. He was arguing with his old friend and sparring partner, the Reverend Paul Verghese.

'There needs to be some way of getting people to talk,' insisted James.

'You can't talk to thugs.' Verghese tapped the newspaper on the table between them. There was violence in Orissa. Militant Hindus burning churches, attacking Christians. 'Their only language is blood.'

'But we are called to be peacemakers,' James appealed, spreading his hands.

'You can't have peace without justice, James!'

'Nor without forgiveness.'

'Forgiveness is not enough. People need liberation. You cannot ask them to go on forgiving and forgiving if nothing will change.'

'Seventy times seven, Paul.'

'So you're telling them to shut up and suffer it.'

'Not at all. But forgiveness changes things.'

'People, yes, but not systems. And *that* is why we must fight.'

'Paul, Paul, we can't *fight* for peace. Your theology!'

'*You* challenge my theology?' retorted the Reverend. He was not long retired from a life's tenure as Principal of

Covenant Bible College, Lucknow. There were a dozen books to his name and as many letters after it. James laughed softly.

'I know, I know. I'm just a retired doctor and part-time rubbish-picker. What do I know?'

'You know when you've lost an argument, and that's a good thing.' Verghese flashed him a grin and winked at Ruth. Opposite James' unkempt clothes and shaggy head, the small man looked polished and buffed as a piece of palace furniture. His Brylcremed hair was combed into an unmoving black cap that matched his rectangular moustache and the thick rims of his glasses. Inside the stiff folds of his suit he sat upright like a cardboard cut-out, shoes clamped together and so shiny they reflected the room. After every delicate bite of cinnamon bun he returned it to the plate, rubbed his fingertips to remove the sugar and dabbed at his lips with a napkin.

Ruth smiled. It was just like his son, another class-mate of hers, and the most fastidious person she'd ever met.

'How's Thomas?' she asked.

A cloud passed across the Reverend's face. He wiped his mouth again, brushing out the corners of his moustache. James looked down at his hands.

'Thomas has given himself over to the iniquities of the flesh,' said Verghese and looked Ruth straight in the eye. Her mouth was full of bun.

'Oh,' she managed. 'I'm sorry.'

She wasn't in the slightest. She was electrified. Thomas? Of all people! He was always going to be an evangelist. Save India. Maybe the world. She wanted to ask to which particular iniquities of the flesh he had succumbed, but resisted.

The Reverend's eyes needled her, as if she might possess

some information that would explain the tragedy. She was, after all, equally ruined. But she offered nothing and busied herself with brushing sugar off her t-shirt and licking her fingers. James turned to her and when she met his gaze, her chin jutting out, she was caught off-guard by his tenderness. She blushed and stood up.

'Time to go, ji!' she called out to Iqbal, who was checking kitchen cupboards and scribbling on a list.

'*Hah-ji, Sani-Rani*,' he sing-songed. He had said nothing during the other men's debate but Ruth had heard little whistles and clicks and seen him shaking his head. Now he gathered the list and a bundle of bags and tucked them into a backpack. They were off to Mussoorie bazaar for food shopping and Ruth's first lesson in tip-top ingredient selection. That was the excuse, anyway.

At the fork in front of Morrison Church she hesitated.

'Shall we take the back road?' she asked.

'Certainly! The flora is most beautiful on the northern side. Doctor-ji knows the name of each and every plant and is introducing me.'

Ruth smiled as she imagined Iqbal shaking hands with a maidenhair, exchanging pleasantries with a tree, getting chummy with a clump of moss. Sure enough, the whole way along the back *chakkar* he pointed out ferns and flowers, picking some and pressing them into her hands. Shield fern, violets, lily-of-the-valley, bracken, peacock flowers, soft dryad fern, reindeer orchids and wild ginger. She breathed in the damp, woodsy smells and wondered again why this man was in her father's life.

'Iqbal-ji,' she ventured, trying to sound casual.

'*Rani-ji!*' He was bubbling with bonhomie.

'How did you and Dad meet?'

She caught a flicker of consternation on his face. 'Oh, our brotherlyhood is going long time back.'

'You were never around when I was growing up.'

'Oh, no. My family had shifted to Pakistan that time.'

'But you came back.'

'Yes.' They were passing through the graveyard and he stopped, laying his hand on his breast. 'The blessing of God be upon your saintly mother,' he murmured. Ruth couldn't think what to say. 'Are you wishing to make visitation?' he asked, gesturing down the path.

'No. I've been with Dad.'

'Enough then,' said Iqbal, as they walked on. 'She is not there anyway. She is with Jesus.'

'You don't believe that.'

'And how does Miss-sahib Ruth know what I believe? You only met me this one week.'

'I know you're a Muslim.'

'There are Muslims and there are Muslims.'

'And?'

'I am Muslim with a small "m".' He smiled and held up a finger.

'Moderate?'

'No.'

'Middle-of-the-road?'

'No.'

'Mild?'

'No.'

She made a horsy huff. Iqbal chuckled. 'Give up?'

'Have to.'

'Mystery!'

'Huh?'

'It's a mystery what this old fool believes!'

Then he laughed, a round rich sound like the swelling beat of a tabla. It washed over her in a wave and she laughed with him and realised that in the last week she'd seen her father laughing more than she ever remembered.

Yet at the same time, she'd seen something else.

A longing in his eyes when he looked at Ruth; an appeal.

They arrived at the far end of the ridge where the road bends back round the southern side of the hill. On the promontory ahead lay Askival.

THIRTEEN

It was the middle of September 1947 and the rains were dragging on. Monsoon was once again playing her cruel trick, that annual metamorphosis from bride of promise to bitter wife. Every year when she arrives, veiled in silver rain and fresh as a flower, she is greeted with jubilation. Grown men dance in the streets, women laugh, children run naked in the swirling water. She is a blessing, a relief from the unbearable heat, a cure for the cracked earth. And how abundant are the fruit of her loins! Crops rise like armies in the fields, trees hang heavy with foliage, vines run rampant over wall and courtyard.

But then she sours, becomes a disease. She floods the place with her brown swill and eats away at the heart of things; pelts people on their way to work, soaks them to the bone and flushes their filth down the streets. In the hills, she infects the houses till they go swollen and speckled, reeking of damp, furniture sagging. Bed sheets never quite feel dry and clothes carry a constant smell of wood smoke from the *dhobis* hanging them up in fire-lit rooms. At the bottom of wardrobes, shoes sprout a whitish fuzz and in kitchen cupboards, mould stealthily conquers the food. Even the people take on a sodden, fishgrey look as they appear through the mist, rain-spattered clothes clinging to their legs, skin cold.

It was just such a person who came up the path of Askival that wet afternoon, his shalwar legs rolled to the knees, chappals flapping through the mud. Carrying James' hiking back pack and the Memsahib's black umbrella (CONNOR 2), Aziz was returning from the bazaar with the shopping. He walked round to the back of the house, propped the umbrella on the veranda and pushed through the screen door to the kitchen, where the Memsahib was checking a tray of kidney beans for worms. She was peering at them through the grey light from the window, the power having failed again.

Sahib had left the hillside a week before. Two days after Colonel and Mrs Bunce's visit, he and a party of medical missionaries had travelled down to the plains to help in the refugee camps. Aziz had overheard these plans over the wasteland of that supper and when he had finished clearing up, he'd slipped out to the servants' quarters and into the warmth of his bed where Salima and the baby lay sleeping. But he had barely slept, and when he did it was only to enter dreams that left him sweating and crying out.

The night before Stanley's journey, Aziz had made him a packed lunch of army-surplus-Spam sandwiches, a banana and two peanut butter cookies and filled a water bottle from the filter. He'd watched as Stanley lifted his gun out of its box, hesitated, and then returned it. In the days after he'd gone, Aziz begged the Memsahib to explain all she knew, but she was cautious. It was her way to make no fuss, but he could read the map of her face: the contours of worry, the drooping of eyelids from broken sleep, the stretched greyness of her skin. He knew she had not heard from the Sahib since he'd left, though this was to be expected. Few letters were reaching Mussoorie, and a telegram would only be used in emergency. Aziz had asked the Memsahib about their plans. His every move was determined by theirs, and although this had once brought security, it now filled him with unease. He worried they did not understand the forces at work around them in this country that they loved but did not fathom. These two countries, now. The Connors believed, they hoped, they had faith that God would provide and goodness prevail. But if it didn't (and He didn't), they could leave. They were Americans. They had passports, money, choices, multiple futures, whereas he – and his family – had one: them.

But despite his anxious probing the Memsahib had given nothing away.

'We don't know the next step, Aziz-ji, but the Lord does.' She spoke in Hindi, the norm for their conversations. 'And all things work together for good for those that love Him.'

Aziz wondered if the promise included him. He loved Allah. Was that the same? Well, in truth, he worshipped Allah in submission and fear. Did that mean love? He knew Allah to be good and merciful but did not know if that would help him in the here and now, or just in Paradise. Would he and his family be safe if the missionaries were gone? What work could he get? No one else would want his Walnut Fried Chicken and Peanut Butter Cookies. There was no point turning to his parents for support. They were poor as dust and already relied on a meagre share of his monthly earnings. And Salima's people were of no use. She'd been illegitimate and kicked from birth. The day Aziz married her, she'd begged him never to return her to that cursed village. He had promised and prided himself on the life he gave her: a clean and comfortable room in the servants' quarters, food and clothes enough and his own devotion. In turn she had given him the delights of her body and the unsurpassed joy of a son. But now he churned with worry for them. All but his love was under threat.

In the week since Sahib had gone, he had felt fear tightening round him like a snake. By the time he arrived back from the bazaar that afternoon, he was out of breath and his heart thumping.

'Memsahib,' he said and lowered the backpack, water dripping off him onto the floor. 'They are all talking in the bazaar. The Punjabis have come. They will kill us!' He pulled off his wet, fogged glasses and rubbed them on his kameez. The Memsahib looked at him, steadily. He could not stop the trembling in his hands as he pushed his spectacles back up his nose.

'That's not good talk, Aziz-ji,' she said. 'It just breeds panic and there's no call for that. Did you get the stuff?'

'Memsahib, it is true! Some Sikhs have already moved into Mullingar Hotel and one Muslim family there was pushed out. Traders are leaving town already. I saw them going.'

'Well, I think they're being a bit hasty and there's certainly no need for you to worry. You're perfectly safe up here. Now, where's that mutton?' She reached for the pack. 'We're needing it for tonight's supper.'

'Yes, Memsahib, but there won't be any more.' He was sweating as he helped her pull open the flap and undo the drawstring. 'All the butchers are going. They told me.'

'Well now,' she muttered and pulled newspaper-wrapped parcels out of the bag.

'And all the cake-wallas, jam-wallas, sweet-wallas, Memsahib!' He passed two jars and a tin to her. 'All Muslim. All going.'

'We'll just have to do without, then,' she replied, inspecting the labels on the jars and setting them firmly on the bench. Her mouth was tight.

Aziz stood by the empty backpack and looked at her. On the tray at her elbow some of the kidney beans were moving.

By six-thirty, he had everything ready for supper and was just waiting for James to return from school. He was off collecting ferns and beetles with Paul Verghese and the Natural History Society. Aziz could never see the point. The garden was thick with ferns, the house with bugs. If James simply sieved the flour he would find plenty of weevils for his studies, and should he venture into the kitchen early morning, he might even be greeted by a scorpion, tail high.

Aziz checked his Mutton Stew (recipe of Mrs Meribelle Winshaft) and ran a fork through the rice. He added a tin pitcher of water to the neatly laid table and looked through to the living room where the Memsahib was unravelling an old knitted sweater by the light of a kerosene lamp. A radio beside her was talking like the Colonel Sahib. It was too fast and crackly for Aziz to understand, but he read much from her body as she sat upright, pushed forward in her chair, reading glasses askew on the end of her nose, eyebrows low and scrunched. She kept shaking her head and sucking in her breath, a wet hiss across her teeth. All the while, her large mottled hands yanked at the wool, the sweater disintegrating on her lap.

There was a crashing at the door.

'Mom!' James shouted as he came down the hall.

'What in mercy—?' cried the Memsahib, jumping from

her chair, wool tumbling to the floor. James appeared at the living room door, sweaty and rumpled, his torch still on.

'There's a house on fire on Mullingar hill! I saw it. Just below the Hotel. People were running everywhere, shouting, screaming.'

His wild gesturing made the beam from his torch dance across the room. It hit Aziz in the eyes and he squeezed them shut. Behind the closed lids he pictured the house on the hill, the flames, the black flicker of bodies trying to escape.

Just below the Hotel.

All the houses there – on the steep, rocky, eastern slope of Mullingar Hill – belonged to Muslims.

The next morning, as he was making the porridge for breakfast, Aziz heard Bunce Sahib at the door and slipped into the hallway.

'Been a bit of unpleasantness,' the Colonel was saying to the Memsahib, 'and I've taken the decision to get the lot of them out.' Behind him, Aziz could see two Gurkha soldiers, still and erect, uniforms neat, chins sliced by helmet straps.

'The Nawab of Rampur is an old friend and a good chap. He's got a pile down the other end of the bazaar – used to be Wildflower Hall, you know? Rampur House, now. Well he's given that as a refuge till we get everybody bussed back home.'

'Mercy!' The Memsahib shook her head. 'I never thought Mussoorie would be troubled.'

'Just a matter of time, eh,' said the Colonel. "I've bumped into a few gangs of thugs already. "Any Musselman?" they ask. "Any shikar?" Like they're off on some bloody hunting trip. Appalling!"

Aziz felt a cold sweat break out on his palms. James, still in his pyjamas on that Saturday morning, had come out of his bedroom and stood listening, one hand across his heart, the other twitching at his side.

The Colonel's voice was brisk. 'Then last night they burned down that boarding house where the Pathan labourers live, so enough's enough, I say.'

'Never, never,' the Memsahib murmured, hand on her mouth. Aziz felt sure they must hear the thumping in his chest.

'I've brought these chaps up from Dehra Dun,' the Colonel Sahib went on, with a jerk of his head to the Gurkhas. 'Stationed them all through the bazaar. Got some of them rounding up the Mohammedans and escorting them down to Rampur House. This pair'll take your lot.'

'Well, thank you, Colonel,' the Memsahib said and turned, stopping at the sight of Aziz at the end of the hallway. For a long moment he held her gaze, then dropped his head and slipped back to the kitchen. He wiped his hands on his apron, hung it on the hook behind the door and ran to his quarters.

The Memsahib followed with bags and helped him pack as Salima sat cross-legged on the floor nursing the baby. When the child dropped off the breast, mouth soft and dribbling, eyes closed, she pressed his warm, heavy weight to her back and tied him on with a shawl.

'We'll walk with you to Rampur House,' said the Memsahib, 'to help you carry your *samaan*.'

'There is no point, Memsahib,' said Aziz, shaking his head, eyes glistening behind his glasses. 'We must only take what we can carry between us, because that's all we can do at the other end.' He did not know where the other end was. It seemed

Pakistan was the only safe place for them now, but they knew no-one there.

'But cooking things and food,' the Memsahib pressed. 'There will be nothing at Rampur. Let us carry those for you and you can leave them behind if you have to.'

Aziz lifted his hands in surrender.

They walked down the mountain together in the pouring rain, a small troop of ants clinging to giant crumbs. Aziz had a duffel in one hand and in the other a bedding roll wrapped in canvas, bouncing against his leg with every stride. He wore an army surplus rain mac of Stanley's that swamped him in wet, flapping folds and the smell of kerosene. Under Leota's waxed poncho, Salima carried the baby on her back and several string bags of clothes, the legs of her shalwar plastered to her shins. James had his hiking pack and an umbrella while the Memsahib struggled with another umbrella and a clinking bundle of pots and utensils. The Gurkhas walked in silence at the front and rear, bayonets resting on their shoulders, faces still as slate as rain coursed off the brims of their helmets.

As they passed Mullingar Hotel, they saw the burnt ruins of the houses and breathed the bitter air, thick with the smells of soaked ash and smoke. They were joined by others in the bazaar, all clutching children and possessions, some lugging metal trunks between them, others with rolled-up carpets on their heads. All were bent under the rain, clothes wet against their bodies, make-shift rain shields slipping from their backs. One man carried two chickens by their feet, the birds squawking and flapping, while another tried to lead a stubborn goat. Every few hundred yards a pair of Gurkhas stood, armed and silent. Here and there, a ransacked house, broken windows, a looted shop. At the tiny bangle stall of the Muslim *churiwalla* they saw only smashed glass. A thousand fragments of light and colour broken in the mud, beaten by rain.

But Aziz also recognised unexpected faces in the exodus. The Jain proprietor of Busy Best Stores was accompanying his Muslim neighbours and the Hindu man from Baba Sweets was holding an umbrella over an elderly couple. Mrs Chatterji of the Antique Shop – another Hindu – walked with a large family, carrying their small daughter in her arms as her sari got splattered by mud, and there too was Mr Godiwala, the Parsi Plastics man, with his arm around a bearded friend. On the bend near the bus stop, he saw Mr Harbinder Singh, owner of Paramount Picture House, his tall turbaned frame pulled down by two heavy bags, back soaked, as he walked with a young Muslim couple. He was the only Sikh they saw that day and Aziz did not dare to meet his eye.

FOURTEEN

30th September 1947
Kurukshetra

Dear Leota and James,

It is dark now and late and my candle half burnt. Though tired and sore eager to sleep, I must write this now as Thampan Verghese is travelling to Mussoorie tomorrow and can take it to you. How do I tell what I have seen in these past two weeks? A part of me does not wish to attempt it, for anything I say is like suggesting that a grain of sand is the desert, or one small lick of flame the entire furnace of hell. And yet the burden of it grows heavier in me each day and I must lay some of it down in writing. I do regret if easing my load serves only to increase yours, but I know you will be anxious to hear how we are. Please have no fear for my safety, or that of our brothers and sisters in the Lord. By God's grace we are all protected and in good health. 'We are troubled on every side, yet not distressed; we are perplexed, but not in despair.'

I will begin at the day I left you. We all met up at Mullingar Hotel at 5am and there were about thirty of us – all the folks on the hillside with medical training that could be spared, plus myself as team co-ordinator and General Dog's Body. We walked down to Kingcraig and by God's mercy a bus was waiting there and it got us to Dehra Dun in time. But that was where the trouble started. The train was already full, so we had to fit in wherever we could and I ended up standing the whole way. By the end, we had people on the roof and hanging from the windows and perched on the buffers and every bit of running board or doorstep. It was hot and humid, of course, and as more bodies got pushed together there were rivers of sweat running down us and a stench rising up that was full strong enough to knock you out. And I tell you, I dearly wish I had been knocked out before I witnessed the next thing.

The train was crawling down the tracks and at every station the men had weapons. At one of these, a small band of Sikhs and Hindus made their way down the platform pulling open the compartment doors and demanding the Muslims be handed out. At our door they caught sight of an old fellow with a beard hunkered down in a corner. He was furiously denying he was Muslim, but the others in the compartment dragged him forward. I guess they had no choice, what with guns and knives in their faces. I called out that he was old and to leave him be, but they paid me no heed. On the platform they yanked down his pyjamas to reveal he was circumcised and took up such a howling you would not think it human. I will not relate what they did next but can only say it was the most terrible thing I have witnessed and I still pray to our Father to release me from the image of it.

I don't think I really believed old Bunce's report until that moment. Now I believe it all, and worse. If ever I needed proof of a world in the grip of Sin, I have seen it.

We finally arrived at Kurukshetra at dawn, where a truck took us to the camp. There are already tens of thousands of refugees here, mainly Hindus who have come across from

Pakistan, but Sikhs also. They arrive in droves every day, some off the trains, some in buses or the backs of trucks, some on bullock carts and horse drawn wagons piled high with possessions. Many come on foot, already ragged and sick, carrying their few belongings, their children, their old parents. Some weep that they have left loved ones on the way because they could no longer carry them, or because they had died. Many women have given birth on the road – often prematurely – only to pick up the baby and walk on. Some are abandoned by their families as soon as labour overcomes them and they deliver alone. Some have arrived with a dead infant in their arms.

And it is not just the poor, but everyone. I have met lawyers and landowners and wealthy business men, scientists and professors. What they have in common is their loss. Some do not know if any family members are alive. In this land where folks are surrounded by family from birth, to be left alone is almost worse than death.

I cannot begin to record all the stories I have heard. A school teacher from Lahore told of his life-long Muslim neighbours arriving in the dead of night with knives. A young man fled his burning village, but is still haunted by the screams of his family who died in the flames. Countless women have been seized and raped – even girls as young as five – and when I hear the seething desire for revenge I confess I feel it too. And yet I know that these horrors have been inflicted by both sides and that the rising waves of retaliation are serving only to destroy them. Every face is full of misery and hopelessness and a sorrow that we may never comprehend. The words that return to me time and again are those of our Lord's: 'When ye

therefore shall see the Abomination of Desolation ... woe unto
them that are with child, and to them that give suck in those days!'

Of the many refugee camps across both countries, I believe
Kurukshetra is the largest. It is constructed of row after row
of make-shift tents that stretch on forever across this dirty
field. When I say "tent" I refer to a mean strip of cloth thrown
over a string held up with two sticks. It affords only a bit of
shelter from the worst glare of the sun, but does not keep
out the mud or the flies or the dogs or the rain. For so long
the plains were gasping with thirst as monsoon was late, but
now it has come, it has brought troubles of its own. Filth and
disease are swirling around the feet of all these homeless folks
and babies are crawling in it. Nothing can get dry, or clean or
healed. Nearly every one of these thousands of people is sick or
wounded and the team is overwhelmed. I tell you, at times like
this, I wish the Lord had equipped me to be a doctor instead
of a farmer, but He has placed me here to dig pit latrines and
plant vegetable gardens and build new wards and what all, so I
must accept His Wisdom and His Call.

Before we arrived, there were already half a dozen medical
centres in operation and we are setting up more. Each one sees
over a thousand patients daily. Smallpox, typhoid and cholera
are rife, along with the usual dysentery and tuberculosis, and
with the inadequate sanitation, the diseases are spreading fast.
Today, Dr Hilda Clutterbuck vaccinated nearly 2000 people
for cholera with one kidney basin of alcohol, two steel needles
and one syringe. Her glasses became so smeared by flies that
the health assistant had to clean them for her, as she would
not stop working. Many of the doctors here are refugees
themselves, but joining the work seems to help them cope.

Also, the effort of the Indian Christian Council has made a big difference. They offered their services to the government very early on and have called on medical missionaries and Indian believers across the north. Thampan has been one of the main leaders in this and he is praying that, apart from aiding the destitute, it might persuade the government to protect religious freedom in the new constitution. There are many forces that oppose it. I do believe this is our opportunity to show the saving love of our Lord Jesus Christ and I pray many will respond to His grace. It is this hope that sustains me, as our days are long and we fall to our sleeping mats at night exhausted. There is very little food, just one chapatti and tea in the morning and not much more in the evening. I try not to remember our Aziz' fine cooking, but when hunger is gnawing at me, I find I am missing him sorely! Please pass my greetings to him and Salima.

Our team prays together each morning, and though we are tired, it is this half hour in His presence that gives us strength. It is sobering, too, to realise that only in the face of such a crisis have the different Christian groups come together. We are all here: Presbyterians, Mennonites, Baptists, Episcopalians, Methodists, Catholics and Pentecostals. European and American missionaries working alongside our Indian brothers and sisters and, indeed, working under their leadership. This is the Saviour's hour.

Do you know, this place is an ancient battle ground in Hindu mythology? Thampan explained it to me. According to the Mahabharata, it is named after King Kuru who was the ancestor of both the Kauravas and the Pandavas who fought their war right here all those thousands of years ago. And it was here, in that battle, that Krishna was the charioteer for King Arjuna and preached to him about love and duty. And it was that teaching that became the Bhagavad Gita – The Song of Love – that I am told is Gandhi's favourite Scripture. What on earth can he be thinking, now, I wonder?

These last few days I have felt at the heart of darkness. We took a truck along one of the routes of the refugee caravans to pick up the birthing mothers and anyone too weak and sick to keep going. People are heading in both directions along these roads and sometimes they have turned on each other. Everywhere around us dogs and flies were swarming over the carcasses and vultures falling in flocks. I saw a young man too weak to fight them off his wounds and in another place, birds so gorged they could not fly. We had to check bodies lying on the ground for signs of life, and when I moved one slain woman, I found a child was curled beneath her, bone thin but breathing. She was light as rags in my arms and her head flopped like a stone. By the time I got her back to the truck, she had died.

My Dear Ones, my candle has burnt and I am finishing this in the dark. Forgive the horror of what I have told. I hoped it would bring me some release, but I fear it has not and that the distress I have caused you is in vain. Forgive me and pray. I thank our Father that you are safe at Askival. I cannot imagine these troubles extending so far, but in whatever circumstance, I know that you, Leota, will be wise, and I admonish you, James, to be brave.

I commit you both, and dear Aziz and family, into our Lord's Providence.

In His Name,
Stanley

FIFTEEN

At the gate to Askival they fell silent and stood looking at the house.

'Have you seen it?' asked Ruth.

'Oh yes.' Iqbal's voice was quiet. 'But I am not coming for some time.'

There was a gurning in the grey sky and the first splatters of rain.

'Come on,' she said and clambered over the gate, still holding her wildflowers. Iqbal followed, struggling with his plump frame and long shalwar kameez.

Ruth waited for him on the south veranda, standing before the gaping hole that was once a French window, the very spot where Manveer had kissed her. When Iqbal gestured for her to go first, she gripped her posy and stepped into the room. The ceiling was sagging and had leaked rain across the floor, soaking a pile of charred wood, some flaps of newspaper and the crusting remains of a picnic.

She laid the flowers on the mantel piece and moved slowly through the house, Iqbal following. Rubble and litter spilled across the rooms, and everywhere the peeling walls were mottled with black. Most bore graffiti: Hindi, English and the universal language of crude art. The door to one room was jammed shut, while the next opened onto a mess of shit and flies.

Back in the living room, she pushed at the damp rubbish with her foot.

'It's horrible. This was such a lovely place.'

'Even in your time?' Iqbal walked through the archway to the former dining room where an old sheet lay rotting in a corner.

'Well it was beginning to crumble, but it still had... beauty.' She looked around, then followed him. 'Certainly none of this trash. Hardly anyone came here. Just birds and mice.'

'And you.'

'Yeah. I felt a sort of bond cause it had been Dad's place. And it always seemed lonely. Everyone called it the Haunted House.'

Outside, the rain was swelling, plashing on the leaves, stirring the smells of earth and grass.

'Why?'

'There were so many stories, you know.'

'Such as?'

She was silent for a moment. 'The Irish girl who eloped here with her Indian lover.' Her eyes slid to Iqbal. Had James told him about Manveer? His face gave nothing. 'Way back in East India Company days. Her family had him killed and she threw herself off the *khud* behind the house. They say on certain nights when the wind is high you can hear her screaming.'

'Ah, romance!'

'Ill-fated romance.'

'They so often are,' Iqbal smiled. Ruth bent to pick up a piece of broken cornice from the floor.

'Do you speak from experience?' she asked softly, not looking at him.

'No, no. I had arranged marriage. Skip romance and straight to the arguments!' He slapped one hand against the other and laughed.

'That's a shame.'

'Yes,' he said simply. 'We are divorced.'

'Oh.' She squatted and laid the cornice down. She wanted to know more without giving more but it didn't seem possible. Hugging her arms around her knees she surveyed the room.

'You know what really gets me? That this place isn't loved anymore.'

'How do you know?'

'Well you wouldn't let it fall apart like this, would you? If it was mine...' Her voice trailed off.

'Sometimes we love, but cannot do what is needed.'

Ruth shook her head. The room smelt of piss.

'Grandma said it was the most beautiful, elegant house. Before their time, of course. They couldn't afford anything fancy, but way back it had a grand piano and lace curtains and the garden was a mass of flowers. It's a crime to be abandoned like this.'

'Are you knowing why?'

'She thought there were water problems. After they left in '47, other missionaries lived here for a while but it fell into disuse.'

'Is very strange,' said Iqbal.

'Yeah. I heard that bad things kept happening here. People got sick, had nightmares... felt this terrible grief.'

'Did you feel it?'

She paused.

'Not then. It was sad, and a bit spooky at night, but...'

She looked over to a window and beyond where the rain was sweeping across the veranda. 'I loved it.'

'Your father also.'

'Well, you'd think so, but he never came. Said it was private property and we shouldn't trespass.'

'But you did.'

'Oh yes,' she said, standing up. 'I did a lot of things I shouldn't.'

Iqbal folded his hands across the swell of his stomach. 'Then you are like us all.'

'The main thing we have in common, isn't it? What defines our humanity?' She laughed bitterly. 'Sin.'

'No, no, Ruthie!' His face was struck with alarm. 'We are being made by God—'

'Sorry, don't believe in him.'

'*Loved* by God!'

She took a breath to argue but saw the urgency in his eyes and let the breath out on a tired sigh. 'Sorry.'

Iqbal's mouth hung ajar for a moment, brows up. Then his face eased and he spread his hands. 'I understand.'

She turned suddenly to her pack on the floor. 'Listen, I can't stand this mess; let's do something.' And she pulled out a handful of plastic bags and started shoving fistfuls of rubbish into them. Iqbal chuckled.

'So like Doctor-ji!' He knelt beside her and took a bag. 'He is helping one excellent clean-up programme: FRESH. Fight Rubbish Everyone and Save the Hillside! He is being so proud of you.'

'I don't think so,' Ruth murmured and used a piece of newspaper to scoop up something black and furred with mould.

'Yes, yes,' Iqbal insisted. 'He is telling me you are always helping to others. Making the gardens for city kids, serving in soup kitchens, giving the shelter for homeless.'

'Oh, only a bit,' she said, embarrassed. True, she had felt compelled to work for the underdogs and the neglected, but was never sure if it was motivated by true compassion or the need to redeem herself. Either way, she never learnt boundaries and got too involved and sometimes burnt. Then she would move on and feel ashamed for not sticking at things, not committing.

When all their bags were full and stacked by the French door she looked round at the cleared floor. 'God that feels good. The rest of the place is still a dump, but it's a start.'

Iqbal tipped his head. 'Excellent start.'

'I wish I'd seen it when it was first built. Grandma said it was a Scottish guy, in the raj days. Called it after a mountain on the island of Rum, where he came from. You know I've climbed that mountain.'

'Was it beautiful?'

'No.' She pointed to the downpour outside. 'Covered in fog and pishing rain!' They laughed.

'Actually, one of the ghost stories might have been about him,' she said, remembering Sita telling it, on the lawn right outside this room. It was one of Mr Haskell's class parties and they were huddled round a fire, squeezing in close as the night got colder and the tales more chilling. 'There was this British family here who had a Hindu cook. He'd been with them for years and his wife was ayah to the children. But during the Indian mutiny he poisoned them.'

'No!' Iqbal breathed. 'Terrible! What happened to the cook?'

'I don't know, but the ghosts of the family still haunt the place, they say.' She walked across to the window, looking south where the rain sheeted over the ridge below, veiling the bazaar.

'At least is not lonely,' Iqbal said. 'All of them, plus the young elopees.' He pushed open the cracked wooden door into the kitchen. 'And a few others.'

'A lot of tragic things happened,' Ruth said.

'I know.'

She turned sharply, but he had disappeared.

'What do you know?' she asked, following him into the kitchen.

'Did you ever hear the one...' It sounded like the start of a joke, but his face was solemn as death. 'About the American missionaries and their Muslim cook?' He turned the tap over the stone sink. There was an empty hiss.

SIXTEEN

Two nights after Aziz and Salima had moved into the refugee camp at Rampur House, James sat on the floor of his bedroom at Askival. He lifted the Westley Richards to his shoulder and squinted down the sights at the head on the wall. 'Gotcha!' he breathed and grinned, remembering the thrill of shooting the thing last June. Out on the back hills with Stanley, they'd spent a whole day without getting anything. Then just before heading home, James spotted the black buck in a gully, drinking from a stream. As he crept closer, the creature lifted its head, eyes bright, listening. James got it right in the heart.

'You're a man, now, son,' Stanley had said, hand heavy on his shoulder.

The buck was stuffed and mounted by the taxidermist in the bazaar and now hung in James' bedroom above the fireplace, flanked by his framed collections of beetles and butterflies. James lowered the gun and stared into the beast's glassy eyes. It stared back, nostrils flared, antlers bristling, its unblinking gaze one of imperious outrage. There had been no opportunity to show it to Colonel Bunce yet, what with the partition troubles and all, but James hoped for one soon. He was confident of a military clap on the back and a 'Jolly good show!'

Outside, the September night clung about the house like a washerwoman's skirts. The dripping from the trees was gradually giving way to the scratching of cicadas, while far off in the forest a barbet struck three pure notes. Askival, on its promontory at the western end of the ridge, floated like a lamp on a dark and hushed sea.

The quiet was broken by a sudden beating of footsteps on the path outside, a cry and a crash as a body flung itself against the front door.

'Memsahib! Memsahib!' a voice screamed, fists pounding.

James dropped his gun and ran for the door, meeting Leota half way down the hall.

'Who in heaven's—?!' she cried.

'Let me in Memsahib!' The voice was possessed. 'Aziz, Memsahib! Aziz!'

Leota pushed back the heavy bolts on the door – top, middle, bottom – and pulled it open. A man fell into her arms.

'Aziz!' she cried, but he whirled around and slammed the door shut again.

'Lock all the doors, lock all the doors!' he begged, pushing at the bolts with shaking hands.

'Aziz, Aziz!' Leota raised her voice over his panic. 'James will do that. Now you just come in and tell what's happened!' She tried to lead him towards the living room, but he ran to the store cupboard at the end of the hall, yanked open the door and pushed his way in, shoving aside boxes, tennis rackets and hiking boots.

'They will find me!' he sobbed. 'Lock the doors, lock the doors!'

'Go James,' said Leota, with a swift wave of her hand as she went after Aziz.

James took off through the house, knowing full well that

it was tightly locked. Stanley had left Mussoorie with strict instructions that Leota lock every door and window at dusk and check them again before she went to bed. His instructions to James were to be the man of the house, to look after his mother and to read three chapters of the Bible each morning. 'No Bible, no breakfast,' was his fond maxim.

Now rushing from door to door, James strained to understand Aziz' crazed outpouring. 'The Punjabis! The Sikhs!' he heard, then a tumble of words punctuated by sobs and an anguished wringing like an engine under strain.

Leota's voice was low and firm. 'Which Sikhs? Where?'

More garbled words in a high-pitched crescendo. 'They tried to kill me!' he squealed. James felt his guts go cold and a sudden prickling in his eyes. He was checking the bolts in the last room when he heard his mother call out.

'James! Get some warm water and clean rags!'

'Ok!'

'And some Dettol!'

He ran to the kitchen and grabbed at things, scalding his fingers as he poured hot water from the Thermos flask, then struggling through to the hall, rags and Dettol under his arm, water slopping over the sides of the basin. Aziz was sitting half inside the store cupboard with his legs outstretched to Leota, feet covered in blood.

'Take that through to your room, then help me with him,' Leota said.

When they got Aziz onto the bed, he huddled into a corner of it, whimpering, his feet tucked under him. James saw a smear of blood across his *razai*.

'Now, you just put your feet in here, ji, and I'll clean you up,' said Leota, on her knees beside the bed, swilling a capful of Dettol into the water. It smelled of washed floors in hospitals.

Aziz shook his head. 'No, Memsahib. I will do.'

'Oh nonsense, now,' she replied, in her firmest tones. 'I was a farm girl before I became a Memsahib, remember? I've cleaned up a lot worse than this.' But both she and James knew his distress was not about her hands in all that blood and dirt but the taboo of her touching his feet.

'Shall I do it?' offered James, trying to hide the shaking of his voice and hands.

'No, you get some sweet tea and cake. Come now, Aziz-ji, your feet in here.' Leota's voice now could not be disobeyed. James watched as Aziz, face messed with dirt and tears, miserably lowered his feet into the cloudy white swirl. He winced at the sting of Dettol, fresh tears squeezing from his eyes.

'You just hush now, ji, everything's all right,' Leota murmured as she gently washed his feet. 'Hush now, hush now.'

When James returned with the tea and one of Aziz' own home-baked chocolate chip muffins, the man had stopped crying, though he still trembled. Leota was pressing his feet dry with a towel, clucking and shaking her head.

'What happened?' mumbled James to his mother.

'The Sikhs! The Sikhs, *babu*!' Aziz replied, pointing at the window, where the curtains were drawn. 'They tried to kill me! *Hai-a!* Just like that, they tried to hack me to bits!'

Leota spoke quietly. 'It seems Aziz stumbled upon a group of Punjabi refugees and got a fright.'

'A hunting party!' Aziz cut in. 'Just above Mullingar they

jumped out with knives! *Aaaaiiii babu*, they tried to kill me – but I ran faster and I got away! My chappals fell off and my feet got cut.'

'Did they follow you?' asked James, kneeling beside him.

'Yes, yes! Some way they followed, but I ran so fast, *babu*, I ran so fast, I could not hear anymore. I don't know where they are.'

'Well I'm sure they won't find you here, Aziz,' Leota said, resting his feet on the towel. 'We're much too far away from the bazaar and too high up. And anyway, it's pitch black out there. Don't you worry, you're perfectly safe.'

Aziz' face crumpled again and he dropped his face into his hands, great sobs welling up through his body.

'Now, now,' Leota said, reaching up to pat his arm with her chunky hand. James awkwardly stroked Aziz' other arm.

'Why did you leave Rampur House, anyhow?' Leota asked.

'My glasses, Memsahib,' Aziz cried, gesturing to his wet face. 'I broke them and I must be leaving spares here.'

'*Arè*, Aziz!' Leota scolded. 'Such foolishness for a pair of glasses!'

'But Memsahib, I am lost without them.'

'And you nearly lost your life *for* them,' she retorted, standing up with the bowl of bloodied water. 'Now, I'll clean up this stuff and then we'll look for your spares. I could have sworn we packed those, but we'll look anyhow.'

'I am doing, Memsahib!' he cried, pointing to the basin and trying to stand up, but buckling under the pain of his feet.

'No, no,' she said, briskly. 'You just sit there and have some tea and cake. James, you get him some TP so he can blow his nose. And wrap him up good, he's still shaking.'

'Yes, Mom,' he replied and passed the roll of toilet paper from his bedside table to Aziz. The sniffling man mopped his eyes and nose as James draped a musty blanket around his shoulders. Then he took Aziz' wet wad of toilet paper, tossed it into the bin and pressed the mug of tea into his hands.

'Come, eat something, ji,' he murmured, remembering the many times Aziz had said those same words to him when James had fussed over his food as a child. The cook had sung silly songs and made the *brinjal* dance on the end of a fork, or the *alu* do battle with the *gobi* until James had creased with laughter and found himself eating just to please the man. But this was not the time for dancing muffins, far less ones that fought, so James merely perched the plate on Aziz' lap and whispered again, 'Eat, eat.'

But in the pause that followed, they heard a sound that made eating impossible.

The sound of running feet on the path outside. Many feet. And shouting. James jumped to the window and peered out between the curtains.

SEVENTEEN

Ruth leaned against the door and folded her arms. Iqbal still had a hand on the tap, face half hidden.

'Dad's family and their cook, you mean?'

'Yes.' He turned the tap off.

'Dad wouldn't talk about it, but Grandma did. It was her best story. Used to tell it in a half whisper with these wild eyes and her head shaking. But said we mustn't mention it to Dad, cause it made him upset. He adored that guy.'

'What did she tell?'

'Seemingly the cook got caught up in the troubles after independence and was chased by a mob of Sikhs all the way up here.'

'*Accha.*'

'The cook ended up shooting one of them, here on the front veranda. Grandma saw the whole thing.'

Iqbal was silent. Behind him, the rain was softening, trickling down a beam that hung like a broken bone from the veranda roof.

'And then?' he asked.

'They killed him.'

Iqbal's mouth puckered slowly. He nodded, then looked out the window, searching the horizon.

'Has stopped raining,' he said at last and pushed open the door onto the veranda. The screen mesh was long gone. Ruth followed him and, squatting with her back to the house, lit up a cigarette and drew deeply. Iqbal leaned against a pillar, polished his glasses on his shalwar and held them up to the light.

'He was my father,' he said and put the glasses back on.

She froze. He turned to her with a bitter-sweet smile.

'Oh god,' she whispered, smoke curling out on her breath. Her throat felt dry. 'I never knew.'

He gave the slightest nod.

'Dad never talked about it. He's never even explained who you are.'

'Is painful for him.'

'My god! It's much worse for you. Don't you feel angry?'

'For what?'

'Well – goddam all of it! Angry at the thugs who killed your father? Angry at religion for causing all this violence? Angry at Dad's family that they didn't protect yours?'

He lifted his hands in submission. 'The thugs, well they sinned, but they were also having sin against them. They lost everything, refugees, you know, such violence to their people. God be their judge.'

'God's the problem. None of the violence would have happened if it wasn't for religion.'

'No, I'm not thinking this. God and religion is not the same. Sometimes opposite. And religion is not making people good or bad. People are making good or bad religion.'

Ruth sucked on her cigarette and blew out hard. 'And good people can make very bad religion, believe you me.'

'How can good people make such mistakes?'

Ruth paused. 'Hell if I know.' She stubbed her cigarette

fiercely on the concrete floor and stood up. 'What about Dad's family? Surely they could have done better to protect your father?'

'They tried. Sheltered him that night placing themselves in danger. Your grandmother tried to make peace – so brave! And your father... he tried to help, also. A brave boy. And then they helped my mother and me flee to Pakistan. They arranged work with the missionaries that side and gave pension till death. They are also paying my education – more than my father could have dreamed – and your father is now giving me home. I am blessed.'

Ruth gazed at him. 'God, you sound like the Dalai Lama,' she snorted and turned towards her daypack against the wall. 'Wish I could be that chilled.'

'Is not chilling you need, Rani Ruthie, is warming.'

She felt a sudden crawling of her flesh and shot him a narrow look. Was he hitting on her, the sleazy bastard? No. His face was sincere, hands folded together. It startled her. She had spent most of her life stirring male desire, usually on purpose. From as early as kindergarten, boys had giggled around her, left notes on her chair and teased each other in her presence. She soon learned the effect she had on them and loved the power of it. She could change things, make things happen, turn heads and hearts. The older she got the more she employed it, until it became something not of her own bidding but a force quite out of her control, that she was powerless to stop. Perversely, it had begun to control her, to change her, to turn *her* head and heart till she no longer knew what dark god she served.

But it had no effect on Iqbal. He looked at her with frank interest, but as though he saw right through her body to the being within; like the tired sexual aura that hung about her was invisible to him. In his gaze she was a child, and Ruth was surprised at the relief it brought. After years of fighting off anyone's attempts to look after her, she found herself suddenly grateful for the sense of shelter in this man's presence. She was not expecting it – this being disarmed – and felt strangely vulnerable and safe at the same time.

Warming, he had said. You need warming.

'Yeah, well good luck,' she grunted.

'No luck, no fate,' he replied, smiling. 'Just the mercy of God.'

Part way down the road towards the bazaar, Iqbal stopped and placed his hand over his breast.

'Are you all right?' asked Ruth.

He nodded, pressed his hands together and touched his fingertips to his forehead.

'This is the spot where my father gave his life, may he rest in peace.'

Ruth stared. There was nothing but the rough-cast concrete road, a stone wall and the steep drop beyond. Rhododendron trees grew up from the *khud*, their hairy trunks heavy with moss and fern.

'He is buried in the Muslim graveyard down by the stream, below the school servants,' Iqbal said.

'Do you visit?'

'Once. But he is not there.'

At the top of Mullingar Hill Ruth paused outside Farooqi Tailors and ran her fingers over an embroidered shalwar kameez hanging at the front.

'I had so many clothes made by these guys.'

'Then I am following your steps,' beamed Iqbal. 'I too patronise this *darzi*. They are good at flattering one large paunch.' He seized his stomach with both hands and wobbled it up and down.

Inside the tiny shop, a young man was bent over a treadle machine in the corner, as an older man sat cross-legged on a platform, marking fabric with blue chalk. They nodded and gave salaam to Iqbal, but their eyes slid to Ruth. Suddenly the older man's face creased into a wide, gap-toothed smile and he stood up, pressing his chalky hands together and shaking his head in wonder.

'Welcome home, Ruth,' he said, his voice thin and cracked as his skin.

She gave a salaam and a smile.

'I make you something?' He waved his hand to the shop as if to a vast emporium. 'Jacket? Pant? Ball gown?'

'No thank you,' Ruth said. '*Nahi chahiye.*' More Hindi. That phrase with which she had fended off hordes of market traders and railway vendors. *Not needed. Not needed.*

Dancing costume?' And he grinned again, performing a small, grotesque caricature of a dance move.

'*Nahi, nahi, nahi*,' she said, struggling to keep up her smile. 'I have plenty. Salaam!' And she turned quickly and kept walking down the hill. She could hear Iqbal say something and the men chuckling, then he caught her at the bend.

'Doctor-ji says you are dancing with top company in Scotland.'

'Was,' said Ruth, and stopped at a *churiwalli* squeezed into a corner of a crumbling building. She ran her fingers over the tightly packed bangles, their bright colours and gilt trim brazen in the shabby street. 'It's not a top company. It's an experimental dance theatre group with a reputation for breaking boundaries. But I don't dance anymore.'

'Why not?'

'Oh, I got tired of it and left.' She didn't tell him she had become pregnant and this time chosen to keep the child, even though the father did not want it. She'd had a scan and seen the baby's moon head and his waving fists and her life opening. But at six months, when her belly and her heart were swelling around him like ripening fruit, he had died.

The funeral was small and desolate and she had named him David. Beloved.

She had not told James or Hannah.

The bangle seller was a thin woman with a toddler at her breast. She pushed him off and leaned forward to Ruth, her wet nipple pointing like a finger.

'You like?'

The toddler squealed and clutched at the breast. Ruth withdrew her hand.

'Come now!' cried Iqbal. 'The Rani Ruthie must have bangles! I will purchase for you.'

'Don't be silly,' she muttered, but saw his disappointment. 'Look, I'll get them myself, but you can help me choose.'

'To match your eyes,' he said, tapping a set that were parrot green and speckled with gold.

'Shit, they're not that colour!' she laughed but stuck out her arm, already circled by a steel band. The *churiwalli* took hold of her wrist and tried pushing on a set of bangles, but they jammed just above the knuckles. The woman clicked her tongue and began kneading and crushing Ruth's hand as she squeezed the bangles forward. The flesh on either side bulged white and red and three bangles snapped. More bone-bending, more bangles, more breaks. The child started screaming and kicking his mother; Ruth yanked her hand back, pulled money from her bag and thrust it at the woman.

'*Nahi chahiye,*' she said, turning swiftly to go, her hand throbbing, skin hatched with tiny red scratches. The last time she'd worn glass bangles she'd smashed them all in one go and the cuts had gone up her arms.

'Doctor-ji said you did Indian dance at school.'

'Yes. Did he also tell you he didn't approve?'

'He said you were very gifted. Beautiful dancer.'

Ruth was silent for a moment. 'Well, he never told me that,' she muttered. She had always felt the bitter irony that the one thing she'd excelled at was the very thing they would not celebrate. 'He and Mom tried to stop me.'

'No, no. He is telling me they were in the two minds, but good Reverend Verghese is persuading them to permit.'

'Yes, but reluctantly, and they hardly ever saw me perform.'

'Such shame,' Iqbal sighed. 'You must join the dancing at Oaklands.'

She nearly choked on her harsh laugh. 'I'm telling you, I don't dance anymore. Ever.'

The dancing at Oaklands. At one time she'd been at the heart of it, spinning in her Garwhali skirts, feet slapping the floor with Kathak rhythms as ankle bells rang, her lithe body tipping and balancing like a long-legged bird in the rigour of Bharatnatyam. She could still feel the pulse of it, still hear the tabla and her teacher's *dha dhin dhin dha* and still remember the steps. But she did not speak of it.

They passed the gurudwara where a handful of Sikhs were removing their shoes as a repetitive singing spilled from the temple door. At Mr Bhasin's shop just beyond, Iqbal inspected the vegetables, squeezing, sniffing and running his fingers over the skins. He chatted with the dignified Sikh grocer, exclaiming over the size of the paw paw and the price of tomatoes, all the while expounding for Ruth his planned menu for the week and his dismay at James' diminishing appetite.

'Tell me, Ruthie,' he said. 'What were his favourite things? We have to tempt him!'

Ruth scrunched her eyes, summoning memories of childhood dining tables. She saw her father eating, often with his hands, though it was a custom Ellen only adopted when cutlery was unavailable. Their main meal had been Indian food at lunch time, prepared by the ayah or *khansamma*, and in the evening it was plain fare: bread, eggs, maybe soup. Ellen delighted in cooking but because James insisted on a frugal table, her art was in bringing richness to the simple: the fluffiest scrambled eggs, broths that warmed the heart, bread of heaven. Whatever was put before him, James ate with quiet appreciation. Ruth had never known him to complain about food or to refuse it. He received it as a gift, whether stale crackers or a wedding feast, always thanking God at the start of the meal and the cook at the end. But had there been any dish that he particularly favoured? Anything that made his face light up?

'Mangoes!' she said, at last. 'He adored them.'

'Ah yes. This I am knowing! We are both beloved of the kingly fruit. Are you a lover also?'

Ruth smiled. 'I haven't had a really good mango in years.'

'Then mountains of mangoes for us!' Iqbal declared. 'Three kg, Bhasin-ji.' With a tilt of his lavender turban, the Sikh piled the fruit onto his metal scales and Iqbal beamed at Ruth. 'We will have fresh and cooked, mixed up and alone. We are finding every variation on mango theme and setting before the Doctor-ji!'

'Good,' she said, and felt the prickling of tears.

In Shangri-La Handicrafts Haven, she twisted a scarf around her neck and looked into the mirror. There were shadows under her eyes, grey half-moons that told more than she wished. Next to them, the stud in her nose and the row of silver hoops up her ears were jarring.

'Beautiful madam,' the shopkeeper declared. 'This is silk-wool mix, madam, from Kashmir.'

Iqbal nodded keenly. 'But you must try pretty colours! This grey is not for you.'

'Neither is that pink,' said Ruth, warding off the wildly patterned fuchsia that Iqbal proffered. She could imagine it somewhere in his vivid bedroom, but not on her. He sighed and stroked the other shawls unfurled across the counter. Ruth drew out a black one.

'You will take one for your boyfriend?' he asked.

'Haven't got one.' Ruth draped the black shawl over her head.

'Doctor-ji is thinking.'

'He's got no idea.'

'Then you should tell him.'

'Why?'

She could feel him looking at her, but kept her gaze on the mirror.

His voice was soft. 'Because no-one is loving you more.'

Her eyes fell to the tasselled ends of the shawl in her scratched hand.

He spoke again, quietly, urgently. 'And there is still time.'

They stopped at Mrs Chatterji's Antique Shop under the Clock Tower, where a satellite dish jutted from the wall and a goat bleated at the door. Inside, the gloomy cavern was crammed to the ceiling with the debris of the raj: china plates, snuff boxes and umbrella stands slumbering together under layers of dust. The first time Ruth had been here she must have been about seven and remembered playing with a prayer mat while her father stared at a mounted buck's head on the wall.

Today, the light was a jaundiced yellow, the air heavy with incense. The stock had not changed – most of it barely moved – and the woman with a gaunt face and stringy hair sitting hunched in the corner was unmistakeably the daughter of the first proprietor. She had a hairball dog in her lap and a nasty cough.

'That is antique,' she said about everything Ruth touched. 'Very expensive.'

The buck's head was gone and in its place hung a Mogul-style painting. Three be-jewelled men rode on camels across the desert, a domed city in the distance, a star above.

'Looks like a Christmas card,' said Ruth, a little scornfully.

'Journey of the Magi,' wheezed Miss Chatterji, pronouncing it "Maggie" like the packet noodles. 'This is silk, Madame, not card. Very famous painting. Everyone is wanting.'

'I am thinking the Maggis were Sufi,' said Iqbal.

'Really?'

'Yes. Muslim mystics – like the dervishes, *na?* Whirling.' He circled a finger in the air, hips swishing.

'Yes, but the Magi who visited Jesus were around before the Muslims.'

'Ah, but the roots of Sufi are also before the Muslims.'

'Muslims with a small "m", eh?'

A rolling, drumbeat laugh. 'Yes, yes!'

'Cool,' she smiled wryly and looked back at the painting. 'I love the camels best. All that high-stepping, haughty stuff. Wonderful.'

'Very expensive,' came Miss Chatterji's thin voice, through a phlegmy spasm of coughs. The dog shook itself, an animated wig with a tinkling bell. 'But I can give discount.'

'No thanks,' said Ruth.

'Are you knowing why the camel is proud?' asked Iqbal, a dimple forming in his cheek.

'No.'

'Because of the Beautiful Names of God.'

'Oh?'

'There are one hundred divine names and Allah – may His Name be praised – revealed 99 to his prophet Mohammed – may peace be upon him. But the last one he is telling only to the camel.'

Ruth grinned. 'I like that.'

'True story,' said Iqbal, with a tilt of his head.

She laughed.

In the afternoon the rain returned and they took shelter in

Baba's Sweet Shop, settling onto benches at opposite sides of a laminate table, their bags and parcels pressed around their feet. Ruth had bought a stiff broom, a basin and a bottle of Dettol at Godiwala Plastics, whilst Iqbal's prize purchase was a glow-in-the-dark crucifix from Miss Chatterji's. He thought the Doctor-ji might like it. Ruth did not tell him otherwise or that she'd known the original owner.

When a dark-skinned waiter with a withered foot had taken their order, Ruth picked up a newspaper on the table and scanned a feature on staying healthy and happy through Ramadan.

'Hey, aren't you supposed to be fasting?' she asked.

Iqbal smiled sheepishly. 'I'm not a very good Muslim.'

'Doesn't bother me,' she shrugged. 'I'm not a very good anything.'

'This is not true, Rani! You are good at many things.'

'Nothing that matters, Iqbal.'

'What matters?'

She folded the newspaper and pushed it away. 'I wish I knew.'

They were quiet for a moment.

'You are coming here,' he said. 'It matters very much.'

She wondered if Iqbal believed she'd come simply to provide comfort at James' final hour, or if he knew more?

'So,' he asked, when their sweets arrived. 'You will go back to Glasgow?'

'I don't know.' She picked up a jalebi.

'Doctor-ji thought you were at last happy.'

She laughed softly and took a bite, a squirt of sugar syrup hitting her chin. 'Whatever that means,' she murmured.

Iqbal raised an eyebrow.

'There's nothing to keep me there,' she said.

'Where will you go?'

'I have no idea.' She looked over his shoulder to the street outside. A giant bull was standing in the road on a diagonal, blocking traffic. As the rain poured over him, bleeding the puja powder on his forehead, the driver of a stuck car started honking his horn and shouting. The bull didn't budge but flicked his tail and let out a golden stream of piss.

At the top of Mullingar Hill they paused for breath. The rain was spent, clouds snagged on the slopes like fluffs of cotton from a beaten *razai*. Ruth pointed across to the tumble of Mullingar Hotel.

'Is the Lhasa Café still there?'

'I am not hearing, no,' said Iqbal. 'You were frequenting?'

'Ah... yeah,' she said. 'Great momos.' She didn't mention the illegal fare that the sallow-faced owner had sold quietly alongside his steamed dumplings and chow-chow. She'd been introduced to it by the Australian boyfriend who took her into the back room on Saturdays for a joint, where they'd blown the smoke out the windows and giggled throatily as they ran their hands over each other's thighs. She'd returned many times and always had a little supply tucked into her sock drawer or the inner pocket of her handbag.

'Many Tibetans are still abiding,' Iqbal said, 'but not running café, I think.'

'Right.'

She and Iqbal stood looking at Mullingar: school children straggling home in navy uniforms and ribbons, a motorbike careening past, three old men squatting with *bidis*. There was the sound of hammering on metal and the burning scream of an angle-grinder.

'That is Malik's blacksmith,' said Iqbal. 'On the very site of Captain Young's original stable.'

'Who?'

'You are not knowing? This man was first resident in Mussoorie and Mullingar is first house. His hunting lodge, only. Maybe he was friends with your Scotland Sahib from Askival.'

'Yeah maybe.'

'Captain Young is very *bara* Sahib. He is starting the Gurkhas, even. These Nepali wallas gave him such a thrashing he signed them up!' Iqbal clapped his hands together and laughed.

'Huh. I never knew that. So the old bit at the back was his house?'

'Yes, yes. And courtyard was potato garden. He is hailing from Ireland, you see.'

'Oh, right. I always wondered where the name was from. But why the Hotel bit?'

'Mullingar has been many things. Hunting lodge, orphanage, hotel. In war time it was hospital also.'

'What a history. Somebody needs to look after that place.'

She turned and started walking up the path. Oaklands lay on the opposite ridge, laced with mist.

'Are you looking round the school yet?' Iqbal asked, following her.

'No.'

'Why not?' He sounded astonished.

'Haven't got round to it.'

'You must see! So much is changed! Really fancy now.'

There was a pause. The path was narrow and covered with litter, the entire slope serving as a rubbish dump for the houses above.

'Yeah, I will. Sometime.'

'And you might be bumping with old school friends.'

'Oh?'

'There is one fine boy – Kashi Narayan. He is excellent artist and coming time to time for projects.'

'Yeah, I remember him. Kinda sad, strange kid.'

'No, no. Is very happy fellow. Always laughing.'

'God, that's a change.'

'Oh yes. I was working with him on big dance and music show one time. He is full of the joys.'

EIGHTEEN

Ruth hadn't known Kashi very well until *The Gospel of Jyoti* in their senior year. It was the kind of production that brought strangers together and tore friends apart. It was how she fell in love with Manveer and how she lost him.

Manveer had started at Oaklands in the seventh grade, but she'd paid him no attention at the time and he'd done nothing to gain it. They occupied different territory. Whilst he dwelt quietly on the social margins, she was firmly centre stage, talkative, pretty and colourful as the fringed scarves she wore. That was in the days when her bright plumage still hid her wounds and she could fool everyone that she was doing just fine. She had fooled herself.

Indeed, it was a bravura performance, gaining applause from parents, teachers and the missionary community at large. And an essential one, though at the beginning she didn't know it. She let the side down by weeping openly when she was first left in the dorm, aged six, and went on to cry every night till mouldy stains mushroomed on her pillow and her room-mates hissed at her to shut up. And she bubbled more at meal times, and when teachers rebuked her, and when the other girls were mean, which seemed like every day.

True, it was not all bad. She hurled herself into the skipping and hopscotch, could rattle off the hand-clapping rhymes at high velocity and was a whiz at jacks. Tea in the afternoon was always accompanied by a square of cake or a handful of *namkin* and some teachers were kind and some girls friendly, at least some of the time. But none of it compensated for the ceaseless ache of homesickness that ran like a cold stream through her life, sometimes low and quiet, but easily rising and too often flooding.

In the second grade she tried to run away. She had rehearsed the route in her mind countless times: walk all the way through the bazaar to Paramount Picture House, get a bus to Dehra Dun, get a train to Kanpur, get a rickshaw home. Her pulse quickened as she imagined herself rounding the corner at the hospital gates and being swept into her mother's arms. But in the event she only got as far as the turning beyond the school when a truck sprayed her with filthy brown water. She ran back to the dorm, a mess of mud and tears, and was scolded, stripped, dressed in her pyjamas and made to sit alone through supper.

That night in bed she cried again and prayed for her mother to come. She was a passionate believer, though her faith was a potent cocktail of love and fear – a thing her elders would have deemed entirely appropriate. *The fear of the Lord is the beginning of wisdom.* But it was not making her wise. Just anxious. On the one hand, she loved the Lord Jesus when he appeared in soft blue robes with children on his lap and sheep across his shoulders. She pictured herself nestled against him when he told his stories, or helping him hand out the multiplying loaves, or dancing and whooping like a mad thing when he raised the centurion's daughter.

But several of the Oaklands teachers were at pains to remind her that He was Coming Back to Judge and she had better Be Ready. No More Mr Nice Guy. Worse still, He would deliberately time his arrival for the moment everyone was least expecting Him, just to catch them all out. Ruth's mind boggled. The chances of Him turning up while she was singing a hymn or reading the Bible where hopelessly slim. She sweated at the thought of all the other things she might be up to when He swept in. It put her in mind of the times she lifted rocks and watched the tiny critters beneath scrambling about in panic. Justifiable panic, as it happened, because she usually stomped on them. What would Jesus the Judge do?

When Mrs Cornfoot took evening Devotions, she was clear: He would decide who went to Heaven or Hell. Though she had a few misty-eyed things to say about Heaven, it was her descriptions of Hell that were especially vivid and Ruth would sit with arms clenched around her nightie-clad knees, eyes watering with fear. The vital thing, it seemed, was to make sure you had said The Sinner's Prayer and asked Jesus into your heart. Then you were Saved and everything would be ok. This was a momentous and life-changing act and one should record it in the front of one's Bible and notify one's parents. (Perhaps for evidence, should there be any dispute on The Last Day.) Desperate that there be no doubt whatsoever, Ruth said the prayer fervently, wrote it down (in CAPITAL LETTERS, UNDERLINED) and wrote to her parents immediately, who duly rejoiced.

But she was plagued with doubts. Mrs Cornfoot had also said, in another Devotions, that God's ears are closed to the prayers of sinners. Then he can't have heard Ruth's prayer. And it can't have worked. She was too ashamed to admit this to any of the adults (who had somehow got around this logical impossibility) so she huddled under her covers at night and said it again, and again as quickly as possible, and again and again and again, desperately hoping that somehow, for even the slightest moment, she might no longer be classed a sinner or that God might experience a temporary reprieve in his deafness. She was never sure if it worked.

But she still believed. In God and his Providence; in her parents; in faith itself. After the initial devastation of boarding school, she came to accept that it was the necessary sacrifice for the Lord's work because without it, Mom and Dad couldn't run the hospital in Kanpur and preach the Gospel in its wards and corridors. This service to God was the purpose of life and nothing – not even family – should be placed above it. She sincerely believed this, and by enduring the homesickness she and Hannah were doing their part, taking up their own crosses. And she wanted to do that. She loved the Lord Jesus and wanted to obey him and give her life for him as he had given his for her. It made her feel significant, gave meaning to the pain. Hers was not vain suffering, but purposeful, and Ruth could not help casting herself amongst the martyrs, the drama of her life helping her to bear it.

For a time, anyway. Until the drama became a sham to her and she could no longer stand her role in it nor have any faith in the script.

But back in the seventh grade (when Manveer first slipped quietly onto the scene, stage left, as it were, and Ruth barely noticed), she still believed and was still behaving herself. More or less. Trying, at any rate. She spoke politely to the staff, never swore (out loud) and followed Hannah up the hill on Sunday mornings to Morrison Church, still wearing a dress for the occasion.

But the strain was beginning to show. She was caught messing about in Study Hall once too often and made to sit alone. Her jumbled wardrobe, crammed with clothes and a mish-mash of possessions, always failed Cupboard Check, so she was confined to the dorm on Friday afternoons to tidy it. Worst of all, Hannah spotted her holding hands with a boy on Film Night and wrote home about it. In a reply from Ellen, which was neatly carbon-copied to Mrs Cornfoot, Ruth was banned from films for the rest of the semester and warned that if she could not keep her hands to herself then no doubt the dorm mother could find useful employment for them.

Indeed she could. Mrs Cornfoot thrust a square of sandpaper into the offending hands and sent Ruth to scrub off the graffiti in the Upper Dorm toilets. As Ruth worked, she cursed Oaklands and her parents with equal measure, not realising that with the scouring away of crudities on the cubicle walls there was an equal and opposite erasing of an inner text.

It was one she had never consciously questioned, instilled as it was from the cradle and reinforced by daily repetition. A text that was not just The Word, but also all the other words that rode along with it, like bus passengers clinging to the roof. A text by which all things were understood and measured, all things bound and loosed, all things named and known. It was also a text by which Ruth found herself increasingly accused and rarely acquitted.

Her parents claimed to take their Bible literally, but were selective in application. Although the Scriptures didn't mention boyfriends and dating, these were forbidden. And though the text did permit drinking and dancing, the Connors did not. This latter was particularly painful for Ruth. As a baby she'd started bouncing whenever she heard music, as a toddler she'd skipped and spun round till she was dizzy, and as a little girl had pinned scarves over her hair and performed the dances from weddings and festivals. Her parents had watched all of this with tender amusement and not refused the folk dancing in PE. Nor had they minded the early years of her Indian dance when it was just village lasses in full skirts chasing their goats. But it was disco that was definitely out. And jazz, and tap, and aerobics, and creative movement, and anything involving hip swinging or tight clothes. For Ruth, however, who longed to attend the discos that were the new privilege of seventh grade and to choreograph splashy items for the High School Talent Show, these bans were a great trial. And a test of faith. She was starting to see the discrepancies in her parents' Biblical code and it was eroding her own.

Along with dancing, for example, there was the scorn of jewellery, that had some basis in the Apostle Paul, but the Connors chose to ignore the prohibition, from the same pen, of women braiding their hair. Hannah's braids, in fact, were so long she could sit on them. They hung like glossy twists of treacle down her straight back, tasselled ends bouncing off her buttocks as she walked. Ruth's hair, on the other hand, was too curly and only got to her shoulder blades before growing out, like tumbleweed, so in the eighth grade she cut it into a layered cascade of curls and stretched a sparkly headband across her forehead like Jane Fonda. It was the envy of the dorm and the wounding of her parents.

But she had not cut off all her ties. She still believed and in this she was not alone. Oaklands was brimming with Belief. At least a third of the students were the children of missionaries like her – Mish Kids, they were called – though having Christian parents from Overseas was about all they had in common. Ruth certainly had little to share with Dorcas Fishbacker whose folks were Canadian Mennonite and even stricter than the Connors. Dorcas wasn't allowed to wear trousers or go to *any* social activities, in fact, wasn't even allowed to stay in boarding because of the potentially corrupting influences (like Ruth). Mrs Fishbacker, whose greying braids were always neatly pinned under a headscarf, stayed on the hillside year round while Mr Fishbacker came and went from whatever it was he did in the plains. Ruth wasn't sure, but it seemed to involve large trunk loads of Bible tracts. Dorcas called it Full Time Ministry, which distinguished it from what the Connors did, which was Ministry on the Side, as if it was a garnish or a blob of sauce, the main dish of their medical work clearly not counting.

Ruth met Dorcas' superiority with her own barbed pity. 'You mean, you can't even go to the Valentine's Party?'

But she couldn't help noticing that, despite all her restrictions, Dorcas was happy. Smugly so. After all, she had the trump card: her parents. Sacrificing jeans and films was nothing to the loss of home. While Ruth and the others insisted on regaling her with tales of midnight feasts and shared wardrobes, Ruth knew whose lot she preferred.

At the opposite end of the missionary spectrum lurked Ben Lacey from the World Alight Mission. He wore a skull necklace, listened to the Doors and filled the margins of his notebooks with violent cartoons. Ruth couldn't wait to see his parents, but when they arrived at the end of the semester they were disappointing. Mr Lacey wore polyester trousers and Mrs Lacey was fat. But it made Ben's deviance all the more fascinating, so when his sweaty hand crept towards hers through the first reel of *Fiddler on the Roof* she did not ram her hand into a pocket but let it rest – available, delectable – on her knee, welcoming him with fingers wide. She never found out what Ben believed.

Oaklands was also roost to a sizeable flock of Asian Christians, although many kept their heads down and their wings folded. It was years, for instance, before Ruth realised that Matthew Sugitharaja from Sri Lanka was Methodist and knew more hymns by heart than her. Or that Lydia Lalvunga from Mizoram came from a whole tribe of Baptists. Frankincense from Calcutta, on the other hand, nailed her colours to the dorm wall on the first day of grade three in the form of a glow-in-the-dark crucifix. It terrified everyone except for Sita, who stirred it into her dark and bubbling pot of horror stories. And then there was Thomas Verghese, Syrian Orthodox and claiming a religious heritage back to the first century. Thin and possessed of an electric energy, he cherished the prophecy – delivered at his christening – that he would one day be India's answer to Billy Graham. It proved not to be the answer anyone was expecting, but at that time, at least, they all still believed.

In various things. Though nominally a Christian school, well over half the students were not. "Non-Christians" they were called, though the likes of Thomas and the Fishbackers preferred the term "the lost." To themselves they were Hindus, Muslims, Buddhists, Sikhs, a handful of Jains and Zoroastrians, some Jews and one Ba'hai. Plus, of course, the "nothings" who apparently didn't believe in anything.

'How can you believe in *nothing?*' Ruth asked Aulis Nikulainen after a Religious Education class where the Finnish boy had confessed to his parlous state. They were in the echoing racket of the school dining room eating a lunch of stale white rolls and runny mince.

'It's better than believing in something that's not there!' he retorted and stalked off to the disposal hatch with his half-finished tray.

And then there was Kashi Narayan. With an Austrian hippy-turned-Buddhist nun for a mother and an Indian guru-turned-tour operator for a father – now divorced – he had been brought up in profound religious confusion. He did seem lost. Not so much that he'd gone astray, but more that he'd been abandoned: dropped in the wilderness of boarding school without map or compass while his mother turned prayer beads in a monastery in Dharamshala and his father ushered wealthy foreigners around temples. For Kashi, the fact that anything was possible meant that nothing was sure.

The school is a Melting Pot of religion and culture! Principal Withers always claimed. *No – a Fruit Salad!* advanced Chaplain Park. *We live closely together but keep our distinct identities!* Ruth pondered the images as she gnawed on her roll and decided that either way the outlook was grim. Fondue or fruit, you got eaten.

Or was Oaklands more a blend of the two? She imagined the fruit salad left out in the sun, everything oozing into everything else. Chunks of banana going brown in the heat, orange segments sweating, mangoes slimy and soft.

The truth was, life in the dorm wasn't like any of that. None of the softness of ripe fruit or melting cheese, but something infinitely more feral. It was a jungle of wild, exotic plants. Beautiful, rare, strange. Some that stung, or shot out, or devoured you, others that intertwined and grew together in hopeless entanglements.

Some that did both.

Like Sita. She was Ruth's best friend and the first person she'd met when Dad dropped her off in Lower Dorm at age six. In Fruit Salad terms, she was Hindu, but as a plant, much harder to classify. She told jokes and fabulous stories. Terrifying stories. Her series on the Vampire Clown had left Ruth in the grip of horror for months. But you could forgive her that because if you were afraid at night she always welcomed you into her bed. And most of the time she shared the treasures of her Candy Cupboard. Her Dad was in the Indian Foreign Service and sent Foreign Candy. Ruth craved it and traded with Mom's peanut-butter fudge, but it wasn't as strong a currency as Reese's Pieces and M&Ms, and Sita drove hard bargains. There were times when she wouldn't let Ruth have anything at all because she was mad at Ruth because Ruth had spoken to Frankincense and Frankincense was being mean to Sita and Sita thought Ruth was supposed to be *her* best friend. At these times Sita unwrapped her Hersheys bar slowly, with maximum rustling, and ate it, even more slowly, in front of Ruth. If she was really mad, she'd share it with everyone else. Even Frankincense.

Thus for Ruth, the business of boarding school was survival, conducted in the extremes of intimacy and isolation, where she was never alone but dogged by loneliness, exposed to all but never revealed, surrounded but abandoned. The great casualty was trust. In others, and in love. By the ninth grade, even her trust in the family faith was beginning to falter, though at the time it felt more like gain than loss. Hannah had graduated and gone to her deeply conservative Christian college in the States, taking her restraining influence with her. Ruth missed her more than she would admit, but she relished the lack of surveillance. The possibility of being her own person was appearing like a seductive light on the horizon. That person was starting to swear (when no staff were around), to smoke hash (in the graveyard and the back room of the Lhasa Café at Mullingar Hotel) and to join the trend of scornfully denouncing anything cheap and poor quality as 'mission' (choosing to ignore the slight pang every time she said it).

That person, however, was still not allowed to attend school dances and the nights alone in the dorm were dull beyond bearing. On one of these she lay on her bed (pink polka dot sheets) blowing enormous gum bubbles and listening to the Devil's Music on Sita's tape player. The crashing of ACDC and KISS alternated with the soulful crooning of Air Supply and Bread and she sang along to them all with equal gum-snapping and gusto. She knew she should be doing homework, but it bored her and since she could never compete with Hannah's A Honour Roll precedent, she'd long since decided to wallow in the below-average depths. She pretended she didn't care. Just like she pretended she didn't care about the dismay in her father's eyes or the anxiety in her mother's. Indeed, if Pretending was on her report card, she would be getting straight As.

Through the wall she could hear Mrs Cornfoot bumping around in her apartment, the smell of her pickled onions seeping into the dorm like the tentacles of an invisible octopus. Ruth could tell from the sounds that Mrs Cornfoot was running a bath and knew from experience that this would take some time. She would not emerge, damp and warm as a steamed pudding, till 10.30, just to check all the girls were back from the dance. It was now only eight. Sita and some of the other girls were sneaking up to the graveyard to meet Ben Lacey and his cronies. There would be joints and beer. Maybe more.

Slipping out was easy. Mrs Cornfoot was singing along to her praise tapes as she sloshed about in the tin tub and didn't hear the main door creak open and click shut. But what Ruth hadn't bargained on was the cleansing effect on the lady's soul. At the very moment the girl was disappearing up the shadowy path behind the building, her dorm mother was being moved to tears by The Bethel Trio's trembling rendition of *What a Friend We Have in Jesus*. It convicted her about young Ruthie Connor. There was no doubt the little scallywag was way outta line and causing everyone no end a worry and what'll-we-do, but maybe what the poor girl needed was not punishment but a little plain old-fashioned love.

Mrs Cornfoot lumbered out of her bath, towelled down and donned her quilted robe. Humming, she put together a tray of two hot chocolates, some home-baked coconut cookies and a small vase of dog roses. To get out of her apartment she had to put the tray on the floor, open the door, pick up the tray, walk through, put it back on the floor, close the door and bend to pick up the tray again. It was no mean feat for an overweight woman with osteoporosis and asthma. The exercise had to be repeated at the door into Upper Dorm –

down, up, open, down, up, through the door, down, up, close, down, up, on – so by the time she shuffled into Ruth's empty room with her rattling tray, she was sweating and a bit out of breath.

It was the end of plain old fashioned love.

Ruth was gated for the rest of the semester, denied pocket money and made to pick hardened chewing gum off the bottom of beds. Mrs Cornfoot sent a graphic report to the Connors and when Ellen's reply arrived – neatly carbon copied to her daughter – Ruth took the family photo by her bed and smashed it.

And so it was, that by the time she got to the twelfth grade and Manveer moved from his bit-part to the role of romantic hero (or tragic victim, as it transpired), the stage was well set for Ruth and her world to fall apart.

NINETEEN

For most of high school, Manveer had been serious and studious, a bit square, with heavy-rimmed glasses and plaid shirts tucked neatly into his corduroys. He hung out with a clutch of other Indian boys with similar academic focus and dress sense, and Ruth never had two words to say to them. But in the summer holidays before his senior year, he'd gone to Canada – where his parents had newly settled – and returned transformed. He wore contact lenses and Levi jeans and was impressively tall, an effect enhanced by replacing the boyish *patka* cloth on his head with a full turban. Though his voice had broken some years before it suddenly seemed darker and richer. Or perhaps Ruth was just listening for the first time.

Because Manveer had joined the choir. At Oaklands everyone had to take at least one year of an 'aesthetics' subject and this invariably presented a challenge to those students – mainly boys – who did not feel aesthetically inclined. It was particularly acute for those boys – mainly Indian – who were marked out by their families for careers in business, computing or hotel management and for whom aesthetics seemed at best irrelevant and at worst, a threat to the Grade Point Average. Choir was considered the soft option and the least likely to dent the GPA.

Ruth was in it because she liked singing and had a crush on the teacher. Like her, Mr Haskell had been born and brought up in India by missionary parents, attending Oaklands in the sixties. Tall and reedy, he had waist-length hair in a pony tail, always wore kurta pyjama and favoured sitting on the floor. When directing choir, he perched on the piano stool with one leg tucked under him like a guru, the other on the pedal.

In today's class, however, Ruth was finding it hard to sing. It was the first day of semester and she was tired from her journey from Kanpur and weighed down by the spirit of August. It was the same every year, returning to cold dorms shrouded in cloud and feeling the familiar sadness seeping into her like damp. To make matters worse, she had left home on bad terms. Dad had read aloud a letter from Principal Withers warning that any further deviances on her part would result in expulsion. Mom had sat beside him, hands folded in her lap, eyes searching Ruth for a sign of contrition. There was none. Not that she lacked it, but that it was so choked by the competing emotions of anger and hurt it couldn't find voice.

Nor could her singing that day, so she was glad when Mr Haskell's attention turned to the boys. Listening to the basses, he looked up from the piano in surprise.

'Who's that?' he asked. There was embarrassed confusion in the back row.

'Yeah, who farted?' hissed Abishek, a short plump boy with bright eyes. A titter of giggles and elbow nudging.

'That big voice,' said Mr Haskell. 'Somebody sounds amazing. Who is it?'

A rush of *not me, it was you, no way, yeah you, not me* from the basses till Dorcas Fishbacker settled it.

'It's Manveer.'

'No way, man!'

'Yeah, you're right behind me. I can hear you clear as day. It's definitely Manveer, Mr Haskell.'

The boy flushed and slapped his music over his face while the others slapped his back and whistled.

'Veeru, yaar, you're it, you're it!!'

'Get stuffed.'

'*And* you farted,' said Abishek.

'Well, well, well,' said Mr Haskell, folding his arms, a soft smile playing on his face. '*Man-veer.*' He breathed the name like it was a new idea.

Ruth looked from him to the boy, who couldn't help grinning through his embarrassment. His eyes met hers for a moment and she smiled back, noticing for the first time how long and thick his lashes were. Nice teeth, too. She turned again to the front as Mr Haskell was clapping his hands and calling for attention.

'Ok, guys. Before we finish up I wanna tell you about a production I'm taking to Delhi for Activity Week. It's called *The Gospel of Jyoti* and it's the life of Jesus in an Indian setting.'

Ruth's ears pricked up. This sounded better than a sweaty hike or a tour of duty in an orphanage.

'I've written it all myself,' he went on, 'and like, man, I've been working on it for years – but now I think it's ready to roll. It's gonna have Indian music and dance and a really cool set and oh – you wouldn't believe – *everything!*'

The class grinned at him and nodded, eyes alight and Ruth felt her pulse quicken. Mr Haskell's enthusiasm was infectious, his productions always gaining an eager following, inspiring the shyest youths to lift their voices, the ugliest ducklings to spread wings. She hadn't joined one so far, reserving her

acting skills for the pretence that was her life, but she knew
Mr Haskell well. He was one of the advisors to her class, with
Ruth and Sita in his group, and was legendary for his parties
where they made cheese fondue and wore bed sheet togas, had
campfires under the stars and played Murder in the Dark at
the Haunted House.

And on Fridays, he helped Chaplain and Mrs Park run
a Discipleship Group that met at 6am and drew a small
gathering of yawning teenagers. Ruth liked to think she was
immune to discipling but still went for the french toast and
the opportunity to sit beside Mr Haskell and impress him
with her harmonies. Also, deep down, it was harder to give
up on the Christian tribe than she had thought, and even
harder to contemplate them giving up on her. Mr Haskell
and the Parks prayed for her – they said as much – and the
knowledge gave her a strange brew of feelings. She was sure
there was more than pious concern in his eyes when they so
frequently lingered on her, but any offerings of attention and
care – however mixed the motives – were to be welcomed.
At the same time, she was wary about the subtle pressure to
surrender; to confess her waywardness and come back to the
fold. So to hide her confusion, and just in case anyone thought
she might be capitulating, behind his back she made fun of
Mr Haskell's hand gestures and the breathless passion of his
prayers.

That passion was now focused on his production and
the hands were flying. Mr Das, the Indian Music Teacher,
had helped with the score, he said, and Mrs Banwarilal,
Indian Dance Teacher, would choreograph. (Good news
for Ruth, who was one of her star pupils, a feat she only

narrowly achieved in the face of her parents' opposition to the tight sari blouses, rippling hips and Hindu themes.) The art department would do backdrops and Mrs Park and her home-ec classes were helping with costumes.

'All I need now is YOU!' he cried, throwing his arms wide. Ruth was sure he looked straight at her before swinging his gaze around the room. 'It's gonna be hard work, so don't audition unless you're prepared to give it all you've got. But if you do, I can promise you an experience you will never forget.'

His eyes returned to her and she smiled back, her heart racing now. This was it. Her chance. Though the thought was barely conscious, she sensed an opening. If her parents would let her take part, if they would only come and see her dance – in a *Christian* show – it could change everything.

As they squeezed out of the doors at the end of class, Ruth noticed Mr Haskell stopping Manveer and talking earnestly, an arm around his shoulders. The boy smiled and flushed and muttered something in reply before walking down the corridor, the other boys banging him on the back and whistling.

'O-ho, Veeru!! He wants you man, he wants you bad!'

'Are you gonna be Jesus, man?'

'No way, man, Jesus was blonde.'

'But Indian setting, yaar.'

'Hey, you could play Samson!'

'Samson's in the old testament, you dickhead!'

'Details, details, this is gonna be Bollywood Bible, shitface, anything goes.'

'Shut up,' Manveer said and veered off into the Physics Lab. Ruth watched him go.

TWENTY

When James was fourteen (over a year before the troubles of partition), he joined the choir for a better view of Miss Lawrence's bosom. She'd arrived at the school in February and the effect in the boys' hostel was like a match to kerosene. Things were bad enough with fifty males in a confined space bristling with testosterone and tall tales, but the arrival of a woman who looked and walked and spoke like a film star was too much. She was Anglo-Indian and had dark wavy hair that swung around her face and brushed her neck. Astonishingly, she wore lipstick and perfume and high heels – the very things James had learnt marked a woman as a non-Christian! – and her dresses, though simple enough in post-war austerity, somehow slid alluringly over her generous curves. It was these curves that were the focus of much fantasy and fevered critique in the dorm. Perhaps it was the tilt of the heels, or that intoxicating mixture of naive and knowing sensuousness, or just Nature's abundant gifts, but Miss Lawrence had a way of moving that made her hips and thighs and breasts *roll*. Especially when she directed the choir. All that swinging and sweeping and swishing. It was glorious and though James' singing voice was decidedly below average, his vision had never been better.

But it was under serious threat if he believed the Hostel Housemaster on the subject of 'self-abuse'. At this rate he would be blind, mad and deaf by the time he graduated. It was hard for James to believe that something so intensely pleasurable could be abuse, but it was undoubtedly sinful. Why else would he lie there, a sticky towel pressed between his legs, feeling a wave of shame wash over him as the waves of pleasure receded. And yet he could not help it. Every day his body flared when Miss Lawrence bounced up from the piano, or when he noticed the tightening of a girl's blouse, or when he just lay in bed at night trying desperately to think of anything else.

But his mortification was complete when the magazine was found. It was 1946, and through most of the war British soldiers had been stationed in Mussoorie for furloughs, bringing their tins of luncheon meat, their cigarettes and whisky and their reading material. Most of this did not require much vocabulary or, indeed, much imagination. Though the Tommies had moved on, some of their literature had found its way into the Oaklands senior boys' hostel where it fuelled a vigorous black market, with such valuables as Swiss chocolate and toilet paper being feverishly swapped for the increasingly tatty magazines. James had long fought the temptation, but when Verghese secured a copy of *Private Patsy* (in exchange for two essays and a week of math homework) he was undone.

The Housemaster found it under James' mattress and embarked upon a swift and decisive raid of the dorm. All illicit material was publicly burned and all guilty parties publicly shamed. Their punishment included daily cleaning of the toilets, a month of cold showers and complete loss of pocket money. James was also stripped of his posts as Class President, National Honour Society Treasurer and Bible Club hander-outer-of-hymn books. He was humiliated and crushed. But all of this he could have borne and recovered from, in time.

What was unbearable was Stanley's letter.

James read and re-read it, hunched over on his bunk with his face burning, and wondered if there was anything he could ever do to redeem himself.

TWENTY-ONE

Ruth went back to Oaklands alone. She did not take the quickest route, straight down the mountain on the path below Shanti Niwas, for that way was still impossible for her. Instead, she took the long way round, walking east on the *chakkar* road past Sisters Bazaar, through the quiet forest at the back of the hill to the eastern end of the ridge. From there she could see Flag Hill, with its tangle of Tibetan prayer flags on the summit, and the steep slope down to the Aglar valley. Beyond was a vast landscape of bulky hills like slumbering giants with shaggy heads of forest and small villages tucked in the curves of hip and arm. Ruth felt an intense longing to rise out of herself and soar across that world to where the invisible snows touched the sky.

There was a rushing in the trees that made her jump. A troop of langurs were springing through the branches, their long limbs a silvery grey, faces black. One turned his eyes on her, bright and fierce, and she caught a hiss through teeth before he swung away. She remembered those monkeys, but had forgotten their name.

Turning back she took the path that curved around the southern side of the hill, weaving through the trees till she came out at Lookout Rock and paused. Below her, the dorm buildings were encircled by cloud and the top of Witches Hill floated like a dark island. The air was a cool breath on her cheek, heavy with the smells of earth, leaf and rain. It brought a dull ache and the memory of the Bible Club hike when the high school kids took the elementary ones for a picnic to the Hill. She'd been nine and revelled in the games of Capture the Flag and Kick the Can and the hand-clapping choruses. But they'd got back to the dorm late and she'd dumped her little backpack and run to supper. She only found it again a week later, but by then her water bottle had leaked and a banana was squashed and the cheese powder from her sandwich had slithered everywhere. This mess was all over her Bible. A white leather-bound King James edition with gold edges and a red ribbon marker, it had a name plate inscribed to her in Grandma Leota's strong hand. It was now ruined. Distraught and frightened, Ruth hid it in a rubbish bin and cried herself to sleep.

But Mrs Cornfoot found it the next day and held it up at Devotions demanding to know who had done such a terrible thing to God's Word and how dare they put it in the trash? Ruth felt panic flood her as the dorm mother turned to the nameplate, but the words were obliterated by mouldy banana and Mrs Cornfoot hissed and shook her head and said no-one would get Candy Cupboard until the perpetrator owned up. Sita knew it was Ruth's and impaled her with fierce eyes. Trembling, Ruth raised her hand and confessed, but before she could explain how it had happened, Mrs Cornfoot hauled her up the front and said how sad and angry God must be that His Word was treated with such contempt and how ashamed her Mom and Dad would be. Ruth was crying, with one hand over her snotty face, the other arm still caught in Mrs Cornfoot's painful grip. Her letter home that week was a torrent of apology and despair

Please don't be angry and ashamed with me. I didn't mean it and I'm so sad I spoiled Grandma's special Bible and Mrs Cornfoot said I can't love Grandma or my Bible or God very much if that's how I treat the Word and I'm crying every night and I can't even read Psalms or Jesus Promises to comfort me. Please can't you visit this semester, Mommy? It's too long to wait till Christmas and if this goes on your daughter will be dead of sorrow.

Ellen's reply had been gentle and reassuring. They understood it was an accident and Ruth could have another Bible and she was not to worry about sorrow. It did not cause death, but built character. Mommy couldn't come now but they were looking forward to a special time at Christmas.

Ruth took out a cigarette and lit up.

Last night, Iqbal had wagged his finger at her.

'You should stop this smoking,' he'd said. 'It is ruining your tongue. You cannot taste properly and see how good is the food.'

'Tastes fine to me.'

'Because that is all you are knowing! Is like black and white to colour, bird in the book to singing in the tree!'

She sucked on her cigarette and blew a series of smoke rings. Everyone else warned her about lung disease and early death. Only Iqbal seemed more worried about the sensitivity of her palate.

Iqbal.

She still did not understand why he had come. By all accounts, his life in Pakistan had been full and content, his job there teaching Urdu to missionaries better than a couple of days with the brats at Oaklands. He claimed it was to give condolences to James on Ellen's death. Ruth was suspicious. It was a long way for a man you didn't remember. And why stay?

And what was this strange business of Friday prayers? Iqbal had invited her to join them a week after her arrival, but she'd sat stiff and wary in the corner. Then James had read from the Bible: *I will sing to the Lord, for he has been good to me.* She had felt bitterness rise in her like bile; her face stony, arms tight across her ribs, eyes burning. Iqbal had glanced at her and the shock on his face made her snap. She'd leapt from her chair like a cat – right in the middle of the passage – and shot up the stairs. He'd jumped to his feet and flung out his hands. *Ruthie! Are you sick?!* Upstairs she had thrown herself on the bed and pressed her hands over her ears. She'd never tried to explain, let alone apologise.

There was a long history of that.

She let out a long, noisy breath. Cigarette half finished, she crushed it into a small tin she now carried and pushed it into the back pocket of her jeans. Her mouth was gritty, smoke lingering in her nose. She waited for the smells of the earth to return.

In the stillness there was a tiny movement at her side, a beetle on the rock. Its back glinted blue-green like an oil slick as it lumbered over the crevices. There had been one like that along with dozens of others in the glass case in the bio lab, with pins through their guts and long Latin names. At the bottom of the case, another name: James Adoniram Connor.

He had shown them to her when she was about seven, on one of his rare visits from Kanpur. Lifting her onto a lab bench so she could see, his fingertip had scrolled along the glass as the beautiful, strange words rose from his tongue like an ancient prayer.

Dorcas anteus, batocera rubus, hemisodorcus nepalensis, hoplosternus shillongensis...

Such beautiful names. So much better than the English ones she could read herself: Chinese Cow, Dumpy Stag, Rhino Dung Roller.

'I got them all when I was at school here,' he said. 'Started when I was four. Anybody can get fifty beetles, but a hundred is a real challenge.'

'How many did you get?' She tugged on a stray curl above her ear as she pondered the glossy backs, the articulated legs, the pincers.

'Ninety-nine.' He grinned. 'Can you believe it?'

'Are you still hunting?'

He shrugged. 'Oh, just keeping an eye out, you know. But I think maybe that last one'll find me.'

She pictured a beetle with walking stick and binoculars, scanning the horizon, searching for him, taking a swig from a metal canteen, pressing on. She wished they would meet and she might witness it. But then – her father would suffocate that last beetle and impale him on a board! She burst into tears and James swept her off the bench in confusion.

'*Piyari! Piyari!* What's wrong? What happened?'

She never could explain.

Squatting on Lookout Rock, she reached out a finger and laid it in front of the beetle, holding her breath as it crawled on. Slowly, she lifted it to her face.

'What's your name, little one? Mmmm?'

Its feelers waved, tiny feet clung, wing cases opening and closing.

'Might you be the 100th beetle?'

A flash of wings and it was gone.

She chose a Sunday afternoon to return to Oaklands because it would be empty and that was what she needed. Beside the gate was a long flight of steps that led to a terrace beside the high school building and another higher up from where you entered Benson Hall. Had she walked up those steps to Chapel twenty-four years ago with Manveer, instead of steering him to the Haunted House, how different everything would be. For a start, he would be alive. Did that mean she was to blame after all?

The steps were steep and slippery with moss and she walked slowly, her hand on the cold metal rail, still wet from rain. On the lower terrace she peered into classroom windows. The library was bigger, brighter; lots of computers. There was a room filled with maps of the world and posters of people in national costume, dancing, eating, laughing. Social Studies? she wondered. RE?

Her most memorable Religious Education course had been taught by Chaplain Park in a multi-purpose room with no posters and a persistent smell of musty jute matting. It was called *Search for a Meaningful Existence* but rather than arriving at one, it was a survey of humanity's many and varied attempts. It had given Ruth her first taste of that uneasy feeling she later recognised as doubt: the possibility that the rock beneath you was sand, or simply not there at all; that sand shifts and rocks can be thrown; that many are the gods and many the godless.

She remembered that awful day when Kashi was giving his presentation on Eastern Pantheistic Monism and his hair fell over his eyes and his warty hands shook as he held his sheet of notes. And then he unveiled a painting he'd done, pulling an old towel off a canvas which he propped on the front desk. The picture was a red orb pulsing in a limitless blue sky and he began explaining how it depicted Brahman – the cosmos – and Atman – the soul – being One.

'One… giant tomato,' whispered Abishek. There was a sputtering of laughter around him; Mr Park scowled. Kashi's face darkened and he licked his lips, but kept going.

'God is everything,' he said, his dirty finger waving in a circle around the centre of his painting. 'God is the cosmos. God is all that exists and nothing exists that is not God.'

Another voice hissed from the back: 'No, I think it's a blob of ketchup. He's just spilled his lunch.' More giggles – from Ruth, also – and Mr Park stood up, his chair scraping, and strode to the back of the room. He laid heavy hands on the shoulders of two boys.

'Go on, Kashi,' he said, voice weighted with warning.

'All is One,' whispered Kashi. 'There is no you, or me.' His hand fell to his side; he took a breath. 'No good. No evil.' Draping the towel back over the painting, he returned to his seat, tears in his eyes.

Ruth felt her skin go cold and turned away from the window. She looked across to the garden at the far end of the terrace. It always used to be a little overgrown, unkempt: grass pushing up through the gravel and a few clumps of straggling marigolds. You could sometimes persuade teachers to take you there for a class in the sunshine and then everyone would loll about chewing on grass stalks and not listening.

Now it had been restored. Small shrubs grew from paving that included broken china and hundreds of fragments of smashed bangles, bright shards of colour and light like peacock feathers and rainbows. There were also tiles of fired clay with children's hand prints and words like *love, freedom* and *hope*. At the centre rose a small tree with bright green leaves and hundreds of tight buds waiting to open, a strange thing, Ruth thought for September. A slate at the threshold read: *Oaklands Peace Garden, Celebrating 60 Years of Independence, Aug 2007.* A year ago. Underneath, a signature like a rune: KN.

TWENTY-TWO

Late March 1947 was Evangelism Week at Oaklands. The students had been organised into teams to tackle the various tasks associated with this annual event. Some had painted large banners with verses such as 'Jesus is Lord!' and 'No One Comes to the Father but by Me' and these were hung from the balconies around the quad and plastered along the corridors of the High School building. Senior Choir, under the tutelage of the luscious Miss Lawrence, had polished their suite of hymns and the Drama Club had put together a play on the life of William Carey, first Baptist missionary to India. James was in both performances, indeed was throwing himself into all aspects of the week with urgency as he was still trying to restore his reputation after the fiasco with *Private Patsy* the previous year.

The guest speaker for the campaign was the Reverend Enoch Peterson, a senior Mennonite missionary with a long history in India and an equally long beard. He had started growing it on the ship to Calcutta and combed it daily, reciting The Lord's Prayer in Bengali as he did. A moustache, however, had never been allowed to sprout and his upper lip was as soft and sensitive as a petal. A deeply scholarly man and beloved of the Bible, the Reverend Peterson believed he could not preach his own Scripture to Hindus unless he was prepared to listen to theirs, so had spent much time discoursing with Brahmin priests and scholars. 'You have not truly understood another religion until you are tempted to convert,' he taught. And had he felt tempted? Well, that was to be the subject of his talks at Oaklands: *Seeking the Unknown God*. The first night was tantalizingly – and controversially – titled *Christ the Sadhu*.

But there was a problem. Another spiritual teacher was in town that same night, holding a meeting in the bazaar: India's Holiest of Holy Men, the Great Soul Himself, Gandhi-ji. News of this visit was creating a stir amongst the students, especially the Indians. Verghese and James carried their polite request to the Principal's office at 8am on the Monday. Could interested persons please go? No. The Principal was very clear: all Oaklands students were expected to attend Reverend Peterson's talk or stay in the dorm doing homework. If anyone was discovered in the bazaar there would be no mercy.

Verghese strode out of his office with James scampering to keep up.

'That,' said Verghese, stabbing a finger towards the Principal's door, 'tells you everything you need to know about why India must have her freedom! How dare he tell me – an Indian, with *Christian* parents fighting for liberation – that some foreigner's message is more important than my own country's prophet!'

'Well...' fumbled James. 'He's not saying—'

'The arrogance of you all!'

'Me?'

'You American missionaries are no better than the British. You think you can come here and tell Indians how to live. Even in the church, for godssake! We've had Christians here for a lot longer than America or Europe, yet you think you bring Jesus like some big new idea!'

'Gheesa... hey, man... no.'

Verghese turned and strode off, James at his heels again.

'Please!' called James. 'Don't take it out on me, man. I'm not like that.'

'Yes you are,' Verghese fumed. 'You've never said it, but you think it. You can't help it. It's in everything you missionaries do. You're better than us, higher up, further on and you're here to give hand-outs to the poor Indians because we're too stupid and backward and heathen to do it for ourselves.'

'No way!' James felt heat rising up his neck. 'That is *not* it at all.'

'Well why are you here, then?'

James stared at him. 'Maybe,' he started slowly, through his teeth, 'because you *could* do it for yourselves but you *haven't*.'

Verghese spat.

Assembly that morning was brimming with evangelistic fervour and James had to join the choir on stage for *To Be a Pilgrim* but felt so sick he could only mouth the words. He couldn't see Verghese anywhere and couldn't concentrate on Reverend Peterson's opening address. Through the day he tried to sit next to Verghese in class and at lunch, but his friend either moved to another seat or refused to look at him. Finally, in their last period Biology lesson, James could no longer bear it and decided to risk everything. As they waited in stony silence for their dissection frog to die, he scribbled a note and pushed it across the bench. Verghese flicked it to the floor, but James picked it up and pressed it open in front of him. Verghese gave it a cursory glance and looked away. Then he turned back, slowly, and read it again. His face was unmoved at first, but then he looked up at James, his eyes piercing, questioning. James nodded. Verghese broke into a huge grin, tipped his head and gave a low whistle.

'All right, man,' he whispered. 'You're ok.'

Gandhi's prayer meeting was in a field near Paramount Picture House where the road split, one branch wending down towards Dehra Dun, the other running along the ridge to the Mall and the Savoy Hotel. Oaklands students rarely went that far in the bazaar where the spirit of a fading raj still lingered like a dowager at the ball. There were still fancy-dress parties at the Savoy, but muted by the recent war and the coming independence, and the music drifting from the bandstand outside the library was more wistful. No more Land of Hope and Glory but a lot of Abide With Me. And though most of the promenading couples on the Mall were still British, they felt privileged if they were joined by the dashing Mr Nehru in his home-spun and topi and his impeccable civil disobedience.

A whole hour before the meeting, the field was already teeming. People were milling about, piling off rickshaws, standing around in knots, buying food, chasing children, calling and chattering. James and Verghese pushed their way through the crowd to a space at one side, but as more and more people arrived they were jostled and crushed till James found himself wedged between a clutch of young nuns and a large man with a verdant moustache. Verghese was right behind, hands on James' arms, chin pressing into his shoulder, his voice a low, intense murmur as he explained how the wheels of independence were turning unstoppably now, but how his parents feared the country would break apart before it could break free.

At last there was a flurry of excitement from the back, then a hush as Gandhi appeared, lean and upright, with a small group of women surrounding him. They helped him onto the dais at the front, setting his notebook in front of him and his spittoon to one side. He sat cross-legged in his home-spun white dhoti, wrinkled and bony, hands pressed together in Namaste. His face was a beacon, a wide smile creasing his cheeks and revealing his few jutting teeth and a radiant warmth. He inspected his large pocket watch then set it beside his notebook.

'That's the only bit of modern technology he owns,' whispered Verghese. 'He is passionate about time. Every second belongs to God and should be lived for God.'

A large man in white kurta pyjama started playing chords and little runs of notes on a harmonium. There was something rippling and generous about him, the way his big soft stomach quivered and his oily hair fell in ringlets to his shoulders, his plump fingers slipping easily across the keys. The other hand pumped the bellows of the harmonium as he lifted his shiny face, closed his eyes and began to sing.

'Jodi tor đak shune keü na ashe tôbe êkla chôlo re...'

The audience echoed back. '*Êkla chôlo, êkla chôlo, êkla chôlo, êkla chôlo re.*'

'By Tagore, you know,' hissed Verghese. 'One of Gandhi-ji's favourites. Amma and Appa sung it with him on the Salt March.' He joined in till the end, his tuneless voice right at James' ear, his breath on his cheek.

'It's in Bengali,' he said at the end. 'You know what it means?'

James shook his head.

'*If they don't answer your call, walk alone, if they're afraid and cower in silence facing the wall, open your mind and speak out alone.*'

He would have continued, but a hush fell over the crowd as Gandhi began to speak. His talk that night was of his conviction that *ahimsa* – non-violence – was the only right way for India to win its freedom and the unity of its religions.

'Non-violence implies love, compassion, forgiveness. If I am a follower of *ahimsa*, I must love my enemy. The practice of *ahimsa* calls forth the greatest courage.'

James' Hindi was fluent but it was the language of kids and the bazaar and not sophisticated enough for Gandhi's discourse, so Verghese gave a whispered translation.

'Poverty is the worst form of violence and to forgive and accept injustice is cowardice. One must be the change one wishes to see in the world.' Beside James, the large man with the moustache was swaying his head in agreement and James could smell the paan he was chewing and the oil in his hair.

'Those whom God has made one, man will never be able to divide.' Gandhi went on. 'For I believe with my whole soul that the God of the Koran is also the God of the Gita, and that we are all, no matter by what name designated, children of the same God.'

James' head was spinning. He kept hearing things that sounded like Jesus, but in the next breath things that didn't. There were readings from Sufi poets and Jain prophets, quotes from the Bible and chants to the Buddha. He felt excited and disturbed, and just when his confusion was at its peak, Gandhi announced the next hymn: *When I Survey The Wondrous*

Cross. The nuns at James' right elbow sang lustily and Verghese was as loud and tuneless in English as in Bengali, but James struggled to join in and struggled to know why.

Finally Gandhi called the meeting to prayer. It was an ancient invocation, long and rhythmic, rising and falling in a river of words that James did not understand. He was filled with unease. Surely it was a Hindu prayer, to a Hindu god? He felt he should not be a part of it, should not give his assent or murmur amen. Guilt twisted inside him as he thought of the Reverend Peterson's talk, at this very moment. In his desperation to make amends with Verghese, he had risked being discovered, and his parents being informed, and another letter from Stanley. Everything he had worked to restore would come crashing down again, and worse. For what could be a greater outrage than spurning Evangelism Week for a prayer meeting in another religion? This muddle of religions! He started to sweat. By being here was he betraying his faith, his family, his God? His eyes snapped open. He had to separate himself from this heathen prayer!

He watched Gandhi. His eyes were closed, his face puckered with the intensity of his words, head shaking softly from side to side and folded hands bobbing slightly, as if in constant pleading. Sometimes his voice caught or trembled and his breath was uneven, wavering. He looked like a man carrying his entire people on his back and breaking under the strain. James felt a sudden urge to stand beside the old man and to hold up his praying hands, like the Israelites held the arms of Moses at the Red Sea. It was a feeling so unexpected and intense and conflicting that he couldn't name it. Something like longing, or heartbreak. Or love.

It was after nine o'clock when they got back to the dorm, panting, their sides splitting with cramp. They slipped in through the servants' entrance and up the back stairs and were still out of breath as they rounded the corner into the main corridor. Right in front of them were the Housemaster and the Reverend Peterson.

TWENTY-THREE

The Prodigal was still a long way off when the Father saw him, dropped his plough and ran to him – but tripped on the bottom step, went flapping and hopping into the front row of tin chairs and landed in the laps of Ruth and the other Loose Women. There were cheers, claps, howls of laughter and a rising *ow, ow, ow!* from Thomas Verghese (alias the Father) as he tried to gather his limbs and his dignity from the cackling girls.

'Hey, that's your son's part!' called Abishek, pointing to Kashi (the Prodigal) who was at the far end of the aisle, staggering towards home. 'Those are Kashi's babes, man. Hands off!' Kashi pulled a hopeful grin.

'Ow,' Thomas wailed. 'I didn't touch anything, I promise.'

'Are you all right?' Ruth asked, giggling, as she helped him get up.

'Yeah, yeah, just a broken leg and wounded pride, no big deal. *Arè, arè,*' he moaned, rubbing his bashed shin. 'You guys ok? So sorry.'

'Yeah, fine,' said Dorcas, straightening her skirt over her knees.

'No, it was a pleasure, baba,' smiled Sita, a twinkle in her large, liquid eyes.

'Ok, ok, everyone,' Mr Haskell interrupted, coming down the aisle from where he'd been watching in the back row, his kurta pyjama flapping with his stride. 'That's enough now. You ok, Thomas?'

'Yeah, yeah, I'm fine, Boss. Sorry about that.'

'*Koi bat nahi* – doesn't matter. Right – let's take that again, ok? Ladies, we'll just get to the end of the scene and then go from the top, yeah?'

The girls nodded. Their contribution today was minimal – just a bit of carousing with the Prodigal when he was in party mode.

Now he turned to the Father and put his arm around his shoulders.

'That's coming along great, Thomas, but that moment when you look up and see him, I want you to really think about that. You haven't heard from him in years – just rumours about wild living. You're heartbroken. For all you know he could be dead. But all of a sudden – there he is! He's alive!'

Thomas puckered his lips and nodded. They all looked at Kashi. His mud-coloured hair fell in a tumble over his face and down his dirty neck. His clothes were too big and unwashed, fingernails black, one tooth splintered. It was not costume; it was just Kashi, who also smelled like the bottom of a *dhobi* bag, had cat breath and didn't speak clearly. He was forever joining things – basketball teams, hiking trips, productions – but never making friends.

Mr Haskell jabbed his pencil in the air. 'Hallelujah – he's *home*. I want to see that.'

'Ok, Boss,' said Thomas. He limped up onto the stage as Kashi returned to the back of the hall, Mr Haskell to his seat and the girls to comparing their hair. They spoke in whispers, huddled together, as Mr Haskell hated talking in rehearsal and had been known to throw his script on the floor and yell at people.

'Have you ever cut yours, Dorcas?' Ruth asked, fingering the other girl's long braids.

'Just trims now and then,' she said. 'I want to grow it till it touches the ground.'

'Why?' asked Sita. 'Aren't you going to step on it?'

'I'll loop it up or something.'

Ruth grinned. 'Yeah, what about Princess Leia hoops over your ears.' And she wound the braids into fat wads. They giggled, except for Dorcas whose face went pink as she drew her braids back and smoothed them behind her shoulders.

'I wish I had your hair for this part,' Ruth said.

'Yeah,' said Sita. 'How are you going to dry Jesu's feet with that little tuft of curls? You'll tickle him to death!'

It was Dorcas' turn for a merry giggle and Ruth's to blush.

'*Nahi, nahi.* I'm going to have a wig, you pakora. Mr Haskell's getting one in Delhi.'

'No, I've got a better idea,' winked Sita, whose own hair was a thick black bob that shone like polished wood. 'Psst, Veer!'

The boy was sitting with Abishek on the other side of the aisle doing his chemistry homework and waiting for his appearance as the Prodigal's elder brother. He looked up at them and smiled and Ruth wondered whether the eagerness in his eyes was for her or for Sita. No chance it was for Dorcas.

'Come here,' hissed Sita. He put down his books, glanced back to where Mr Haskell was deep in discussion with Kashi/ Prodigal and slipped across to them, squatting in front of Ruth who was in the middle. She could detect a sophisticated after-shave, and something about the smell and the way his steel *kara* curved over the dark hair of his wrist gave her the slightest shiver.

'What?' he asked.

'Ruthie needs some serious hair for Maya Magdalen. Can't you just lend her some for the production, yaar?'

Manveer grinned. 'I'd love to, babe,' he said, looking at Ruth. 'But—' And he ran his finger across his throat.

'What – your Dad?' asked Ruth.

'Oh everybody,' he chuckled. 'Dad, Mom, grandparents, aunties, cousins, the bus driver, my dentist even. They'd all pile in.'

'Even in Canada?' asked Dorcas.

'Oh they're worse there, man! My Mom and Dad weren't that strict here, but now – my god – you should see them. At the gurudwara all the time, all their friends are Sikhs and Mom won't cook anything but Punjabi *khana*. It's such a drag.'

'But they don't mind you doing this?' asked Ruth, pointing to the stage where the Father and Prodigal were now embracing.

Manveer shrugged. 'No. They were cool about it. Don't ask me why. What about yours, Sita?'

'Oh, fine. They're so busy arguing about north India versus south India they haven't got time to worry about Christianity. And they know converting's the last thing I'd do, anyway, so they're not fussed.'

'Right on, sister!' said Manveer and they hi-fived.

'You bet!' added Ruth, raising her hands so they could both slap them. 'You stick to your culture and don't let anybody shove stuff at you.'

'Amen!' said Sita.

Dorcas' face went pink again and she looked down at her hands, fiddling with the ric-rac on her blouse.

'You guys got off easy,' Ruth said. 'My Mom and Dad

nearly banned me.'

'No way, really?' asked Manveer. 'But it's all about Jesus!'

'Yeah, I know, that's what I argued, but they have this *thing* about dancing.'

'Oh, is that why you're never at the discos?' asked Manveer.

'Right. Those are totally out, but they don't like my Indian stuff either. Too many gods and love stories. But Thomas' Dad finally talked em into it. Good old Rev Verghese.' She didn't add that her parents' reservations about the production had been far outweighed by their relief that she might, at last, be doing something constructive with her time, a sentiment they had expressed in no uncertain terms in their letter on the subject.

'Yeah, my parents weren't too sure either,' said Dorcas, 'especially about the Indian setting. They thought it might look Hindu, but they got a Word that God was going to use this show mightily so that's why I'm in it.'

Sita wrinkled her nose. 'Mightily for *what?*'

'For spreading the Gospel of Christ.'

Ruth cringed at Dorcas' evangelistic bluntness, but at the same time admired her courage.

'But what's the big deal?' Sita said. 'Jesus is one of the Hindu gods, anyway.'

'He is not a Hindu God!' flashed Dorcas.

'Hindus are happy to have him, so why not?'

'Jesus said he was the ONLY way.'

'Yeah, but that's just in the Bible. There are other books where he said other stuff.'

'Yeah,' said Manveer. 'I heard about one where he didn't actually die on the cross, but came to Kashmir and was like some kind of sadhu. He's actually buried up there. They have photos of his grave.'

'No way, that's cool,' said Ruth.

'It's crud,' said Dorcas. Her face was pomegranate now and her eyes sparking. 'Total CRUD!'

'How do you know?' demanded Sita. 'It's possible.'

'No way is it possible! The Bible is the ONLY word of truth on Jesus and it says clearly he died, was buried, rose again and then ascended into heaven—'

'Heaven – Kashmir – same thing,' said Sita and they laughed. All but Dorcas who spun out of her seat and half-ran towards the side exit of the hall. Ruth caught a glimpse of her crumpling face just before the door slammed.

There was a horrible silence for two seconds and then Mr Haskell threw his script on the floor.

'WHAT IS GOING ON?!' he yelled. 'How dare you make that racket in my rehearsal!'

The three froze, eyes down.

'Who was that?! Who slammed that door?'

Manveer, Sita and Ruth slid their gaze from one to the other.

'Was it Dorcas?' Mr Haskell demanded.

Ruth looked up at him and spoke, just above a whisper. 'She went to the bathroom ages ago. I think that was the wind.'

He impaled her with his eyes. She held his stare. Finally he shook himself, sighed and picked up his script.

'I thought this show was God's gift to me,' he muttered, riffling through the pages of the folder. 'But sometimes I wonder...'

TWENTY-FOUR

When James and Verghese walked right into the Housemaster and the Reverend Peterson after Gandhi's prayer meeting, James thought his life was as good as finished. He couldn't even begin to speak. Verghese struck up a babble of excuses, but the Housemaster held up his hand.

'Reverend Peterson has something to say,' he said, his voice dark. 'But before he does, is there anything you need to say to him?'

James hung his head and mumbled a sorry. To his horror, Verghese only straightened.

'Reverend,' Verghese began, in a piping tone, 'I sincerely apologise for not attending your talk, which was, in point of fact, a subject of great interest to me. I can assure you, however, that our absence was in no way an act of disrespect to you but an answer to a higher call.' He took a breath to continue but was interrupted.

'I agree,' said Reverend Peterson.

The boys gaped.

'Pardon, sir?' said Verghese.

'I agree with you,' the old man repeated, his eyes twinkling now and two dimples appearing in the soft cheeks either side of the beard. 'I was dismayed when I discovered – too late alas – that Gandhi-ji was holding a meeting in town tonight. I would have loved to be there. In fact, I would have cancelled my talk and insisted we all go. Much more important than an old wheezer like me. You've got me here all week and you can have me anytime. But the Mahatma! That is very special and his message is what young men like you need to hear, *hey na?*'

He clapped Verghese on the shoulder, who, for once, was speechless.

'Now,' said the Housemaster, in a tone rather firmer than the Reverend's. 'You both know you broke serious rules by going against the Principal and sneaking off campus. However, Reverend Peterson has pleaded with us both to be lenient. I have asked him, therefore, to devise your punishment.'

He turned to Reverend Peterson.

'I could think of nothing worse, boys,' the Reverend said, 'than making you listen to my talks for the rest of the week.' He beamed. 'But to soften the blow, I'd like you to join me at Tea each day to argue with me. It's always good to hear from teenagers while they still know everything.'

And he winked. James looked up into the smiling eyes and wanted to hug the man. All he did was mumble, 'Thank you, Reverend.'

'And boys,' the man continued, almost as an aside. 'Your fine Housemaster has agreed with me that, in this instance, a letter home won't be necessary.'

TWENTY-FIVE

It was a Sunday evening in late October, and the night before *The Gospel of Jyoti* cast travelled to Delhi. The rest of the school had already left on their Activity Week expeditions so the campus was strangely quiet and there was no High School Chapel. Instead, the *Gospel* group gathered in the boys' hostel common room for their own service. Mr Haskell had filled the room with candles and flowers and arranged cushions in a circle. There was Indian music playing and in the middle of the floor a chalk mandala of a cross. At its heart was a wheel, that could have been Gandhi's spinning wheel, or the Tibetan wheel of life, or the wheel at the centre of the Indian flag. Ruth found it hard to tear her eyes from it; the more she looked, the more she saw. There were flowers and birds woven into the design and vivid colours that glowed in the candle-light. She wondered who had drawn it and how they could have given so much for just one night. The next day the sweeper would come and slosh over it with his mop.

Just as the service started Kashi slipped in, hovering at the edge of the room looking for a free space. At first no-one moved until, across the room, Dorcas squeezed up and patted the cushion beside her. Kashi shuffled round the back of the circle, dropped into an awkward cross-legged sit with knees and elbows jutting out, and kept his head down. His hair was matted and his clothes grubby, streaks and smudges all across his sweatshirt and jeans. Ruth wondered why he couldn't even make an effort for church.

They sang songs from the show and favourite choruses and read passages from the gospels. At one point they held hands and said the Lord's Prayer in their own language and she realised it was the first time she had heard Sita speak Telegu. She squeezed her hand and Sita squeezed back. Then they sang *When I Survey the Wondrous Cross* and Ruth remembered being very small on her mother's lap as she sang it, pressed so close she could feel the vibrations in her chest. At the end, Mr Haskell took a towel and a basin of water and kneeling beside Thomas Verghese, washed his feet. Thomas did the same for Pema beside him, and she for Ruth and she for Sita and so on.

Till it got to Kashi. As Dorcas turned to him with the basin of water, he cringed under his cowl of lank hair and pulled his feet away. They were bundled in ripped running shoes, with laces snapped and re-tied and patches sewn on by the *mochi*. The threads around one patch had come loose and a dirty sock bulged through.

Dorcas waited, but he shook his head. He pointed to the next person and wouldn't meet her eye. She looked to Mr Haskell who gestured her to move on. Shuffling on her knees, the water sloshing a bit, she got to Nazira and smiled with relief when the girl slipped off her sandals.

After the service, as they milled around and drank cocoa, Ruth saw Mr Haskell take the basin back to Kashi, who had not moved from his cushion. He put a hand on the boy's shoulder and was saying something. Kashi shook his head again. Mr Haskell waited. At last, the boy tugged at his laces and slowly pulled off his shoes and socks. Even in the candlelight, Ruth could see the filthy nails and the warts. Mr Haskell drew the feet into the basin, poured handfuls of water over them, rubbed and kneaded them and lifted them onto the towel in his lap. He dried them softly and set them back on the floor.

It was only then that Ruth realised the smears on Kashi's clothes were chalk. All the colours of the mandala; all the colours of the birds and the flowers and the cross. She felt something knife through her. A feeling so intense and sudden and strange she couldn't name it. Something like longing, or heartbreak. Or love.

TWENTY-SIX

The next day, the whole *Gospel* circus travelled to Delhi in a chartered bus, roof groaning with set and sound equipment, body bursting with excitement. They sang most of the songs from the show along with *Ten Green Bottles* and *Jesus Love is Bubbling Over* (in four-part-round plus harmonies). Their palms were sore from clapping, their bums from the bouncing over the pot-holed road and their throats from laughter and raucous song. Mr Haskell eventually put a stop to it.

'You guys'll ruin your voices,' he sighed, but he was smiling.

Once down the mountain, the bus passed through endless flat fields broken by dusty villages and towns and the occasional strip of forest, ringing with crickets. If they lifted their windows they were buffeted by a warm, gritty wind, so they only opened a crack and sweltered in the vehicle's inner scents: the heady blend of slapped on fragrance and souring sweat, cherry lip gloss and vinyl seats, bubble gum and hot metal. As the day wore on, they slid against each other, bodies pressed together in the intimacy born of shared dorms, shared showers and shared beds. Some fell asleep, flopped and dribbling, while the couples hunkered down behind sweatshirts to make out.

Ruth's latest boyfriend had graduated and gone to Germany in the summer, so she sat next to Sita, who'd never had a boyfriend. She was choosy, she claimed. Ruth was not choosy and though she still wrote impassioned letters to the recently departed boyfriend, her eyes were roving.

Most of the time they roved towards Manveer. He was next to Abishek, across the aisle and one seat up, with earphones on. His thigh bounced along to the music and the fingers of his left hand drummed on the armrest. Every fold and crease of his red turban was immaculate, pressed flat as if the whole thing had been ironed in place, and she wondered how long it took him to wrap it. Around the edges of the turban his hair spread like undergrowth, down the back of his neck, across his throat and along the line of his chin where it thickened into a beard. There were even tiny veins of hair that ran over his temples and became the dark ridges of his eyebrows. She wondered how he looked with his hair down. Would it make him any less masculine? And would he grow it long enough to step on it? She pictured him with Princess Leia hoops over his ears and smiled to herself.

'What?' demanded Sita.

'What what?'

'What are you laughing at?'

'I'm not laughing.'

'Something's funny. What is it?'

'Nothing.'

'Nothing my ass.'

'Yeah, your ass is pretty funny.'

Sita whacked her with a paperback. 'Witch,' she said.

Ruth hit her with a magazine. 'Bastard.'

'Hey! No fair. I never said "bitch," I said "witch".'

'Ok then.' Ruth hit her again. 'Wastard.'

Their laughter made Abishek turn to them, grinning. Manveer pulled off his earphones and twisted round.

'Hey!' said Abishek. 'Can you guys shut up? I can't get to sleep.'

'You're not sleeping, you half-wit. You're eating,' retorted Sita.

'Yeah, give us some,' said Ruth. 'I'm starving.'

'Here.' Manveer passed across a bar of Amul chocolate. 'Have mine.' His fingers touched hers.

'Thanks, sweetie. You saved my life.'

'Anytime, babe.' He winked.

For the rest of the bus journey she savoured that chocolate, the feel of his fingers and his wink She curled them together like a jalebi, warm and delicious, and cradled them in the seat of her stomach where they sizzled and melted and spread out from her lap to her thighs.

It was evening when the bus arrived in Delhi and spilled its bellyful of teenagers onto the pavement outside the Unity Guesthouse on Shivaji Marg. Though the end of October, the air felt warm to the hill-dwellers and wrapped about them like greasy towels. It smelled of exhaust and hot rubber, stale cooking fat and a million bodies crushed together in the mortar of the city. Along the broken pavement a man came limping, one leg swollen to bursting and covered in open sores. The teenagers parted to let him through, his slow hobble watched from downcast eyes, their hands jammed in pockets. As they turned into the guesthouse gate they were caught by the fragrance of the *rat ki rani* that grew in a wild tumble over the archway. Its small pale blossoms glowed in the softening dark.

The Guesthouse was run by Kip, a tall, horse-like woman with cropped white hair and a toothy grin. She threw her hands open in welcome.

'Ruthie Connor!' Her eyes were shining. Ruth had known Kip all her life – just "Kip' to everyone, no "Miss," "Aunty," surname or "ji" – and always felt enormously liked by the woman. Somehow, she sensed she never had to do anything to win Kip's affection, nor could she do anything to lose it. Kip had a way with those big, knuckled hands, too, opening them wide as if to say, 'Well look who's here! Ain't this the best?' without expecting anything of you. Ruth hugged her and was caught up in her lean strength and a smell like split wood.

'When are your Mom and Dad coming?'

'Saturday.'

'Wonderful! Bet they wouldn't miss it for the world. I'm real excited myself. Got tickets for Friday night.'

'Great.'

Kip held Ruth at arm's length for a moment, her keen eyes missing nothing.

'Look at this beautiful young woman. Can't believe we're going to see you in a show.'

Ruth flushed and gave a lop-sided smile.

She lay on her lumpy mattress that night and listened to the sounds of Delhi. Traffic buzzed and whined like a hive of mechanical bees, a radio nearby played film music, the neighbours clattered their pots, a dog barked. It sounded like Kanpur. The Connors' house there was at the edge of the hospital compound and behind it, over the high wall, was a busy corner of the city where life did not stop for the night. Whenever Ruth returned from a semester at Oaklands she spent the first few nights taking forever to fall asleep as the noises invaded her head, and when she finally drifted off she would be woken with a start by a blaring truck horn or the roar of a metal shutter. But she welcomed the sounds because they told her she was home. Whatever noise broke her dreams in the morning and whatever time it was, she could just roll over and go back to sleep. No bell, no queue for the showers, no trudge up the hill to school with a heavy bag of books. No boarding.

But most of the time there were no parents either. By the time she got up, James and Ellen were already at the hospital. Apart from their four weeks of annual leave, and Ellen's summer month in Mussoorie, they both worked full time, year round. In fact, James rarely took all his allowance and there were some years when he had no vacation at all. There were always mission colleagues away, staffing crises, more work than workers. When the girls were small, Ellen had dropped back to part time, sharing their care with an ayah, but once they were both at Oaklands, she resumed her full schedule. On the girls' long vacations, there were various arrangements. Sometimes it was an ayah again, or sometimes their days were spent with other missionary families, or latterly, once they were old enough, they were left to themselves. This had suited Hannah just fine, who played her clarinet, read books and put together photo albums, but was a trial for Ruth. She craved places to go, things to do and, above all, people. It was especially excruciating when Hannah left for college in the States and Ruth, from fourteen, was alone.

She nagged her parents to let her explore the city, but on that point – as on so many – they were resolute. A young western girl out on her own in India was asking for trouble. They suggested she go with some of the young ladies from church, or the off-duty nurses. She tried it a few times, but always found it uncomfortable. She was like a trophy to them. They paraded her through the bazaar on their arms, fussing over her, showing her off, giving her the best seat, the first drink, the last word. They giggled as they questioned her about school, 'Do you sit next to the boys in class?' 'Have you ever had a beau?' 'Do they let you have fashion?'

There was something about these outings with them that was strangely unsettling. They were fascinated with her and yet in their company, she could not be herself. It made her feel guilty. When she was little she had played with her Indian friends – some of these very ones – and it had been easy then. At five they were not so different. They all wore dresses, ate peanuts and played skipping games in the dust. But once she had gone off to her "Amrican" boarding school and started wearing jeans and listening to pop music, she had moved into a different world. And though she returned to Kanpur every vacation, slipping back into shalwar kameez and Hindi, each time she felt more a visitor, a foreigner, an interloper, even.

She watched her parents negotiate their worlds. Her mother came from a cultured New York family but had embraced India with the same unflinching determination as she had her faith and her husband. Ruth knew that from Ellen's first week in India, she had adopted the sari and forsaken western dress. It was almost shocking to see her change into a skirt for their flight back to the States each furlough and Ruth cringed at the sight of the pale legs with their spidery black hairs. She wasn't sure where her mother looked more out of place: in India where she was white or in the churches "back home" where the other women bristled with make-up, shoulder-pads and big hair.

But Ellen's donning of the sari was only the beginning of her grafting onto India. She learned Hindi with vigour, spending hours with language teachers and amused neighbours, filling notebooks with verb-ending charts and lists of vocabulary, and sticking devanagiri words onto furniture around the house. On Saturdays she went into the bazaar to learn the names of vegetables and the etiquette of bargaining and on Sundays sat cross-legged in the small, crowded Hindustani church, clapping and singing, then furrowing her brow through the long, sweat-dripping hour of the sermon. And on every day, without exception, she opened her door to the many who called: beggars, colleagues, fruit wallas, *razai* beaters, drug addicts, knife-sharpeners, homeless women and holy men. Ellen had embraced India, and in return, it had devoured her.

Whereas Dad, Ruth thought, was as good as Indian anyway. He slipped in and out of Hindi with the ease of blinking. Sometimes he seemed to forget which language he spoke. His palate was thoroughly local, preferring all things to be flavoursome, strong and aromatic: curries stinging hot, coffee milky and laced with sugar, fruit so ripe it oozed. But deeper than all these things, he was bonded to the place in a way that Ruth could not claim. His feet didn't so much walk on the ground as rise out of it.

Why was it different for her? Like James, she'd been born and raised here (apart from those excruciating furloughs in the States when she was finally the right colour but wrong in every other way.) They rolled around every fourth year, but in James' time it had been every six. He'd hardly spent any of his childhood in America, when she added it up. A year when he was three, which he said he didn't remember, another at ten, which he remembered all too vividly as he didn't know how to play American football and became the class punch bag, and then not again till he was sixteen, when his family moved back and he finished school and went to college. He seemed to love India like his life depended on it. Like it was his life. But it wasn't an easy, relaxed love, full of laughter, like Kip's. He named it God's Call, but to Ruth it seemed more a bondage, as if he had long ago sworn some blood tie from which he could never be released.

From her bed in the Delhi guesthouse, she lifted her hand till it was silhouetted against the window. Yes, she loved it too. Her fingers spread and curled into claws. And she hated it. She had watched her parents consumed by the place and had tried to shout louder than the Indians and be a bigger problem than the patients and a harder task than running a hospital. But none of it seemed to push her up the pecking order. Her mother despaired, her father disciplined, but they did not deviate. On the scale of needs, India always won.

Floating on the edge of sleep, she heard coughing from the end of the room. It was Nazira, who played Mary the Mother of Christ (alias Ma) but also unrolled her prayer mat beside her bed morning and evening and performed *namaaz*. Her mother was a very strict Muslim, but her father seemed more liberal and had given his blessing to the production. They were coming all the way from Islamabad to see it.

Ruth imagined her own parents coming. Mom might just wear one of her special saris that only came out for extremely important occasions like Christmas or Indian Independence Day. (Otherwise, she wore hospital blue.) Dad would probably be in his black *shirvani*, his wavy hair still damp, hand on his breast as he talked to somebody. Maybe Reverend Verghese. She felt a delicious shiver as she pictured them sitting in the auditorium and the lights going down. Complete blackout and then the first notes on the sitar and Ruth lighting a *dia*. Centre stage. *The Gospel of Jyoti*. The Good News of Light. They would love it. They had to, because it was about Jesus and what's more Ruth – *their* Ruthie – was honouring God.

And she was a damn good dancer.

She went over each scene as she had done countless times: her parents in concentrated attention, then a look of surprise, a gasp here, a laugh there, a glance at each other with smiling eyes. They were being wooed and won. She was sure they would adore the parable of the Good Untouchable and the Song of the Suffering Servant, which was so, so cool. And what about the Resurrection? That would slay them. And the curtain call! The thunderous, thunderous, thunderous applause. Mom and Dad leaping to their feet, hands beating together like bhangra sticks. A rising wave, a standing ovation. And she, Ruth, bowing. Centre-stage. Holding hands with the others and bowing and beaming and bowing.

Then backstage. Mom and Dad bursting through the doors, faces alight with astonishment, pride, delight, LOVE. Mom would be first, probably, throwing her arms wide. 'Ruthie!' or 'Honey!' she might peal as she engulfed Ruth in her arms. And how hard and close she would squeeze. And then Dad – maybe shaking his head, grinning, waiting – ready with his big embrace. Yes, and there would be tears in Ruth's eyes, and in Mom's eyes, and, maybe, just maybe, in Dad's eyes.

TWENTY-SEVEN

James sat at the desk in his bedroom at Shanti Niwas typing on a laptop. The window before him looked out onto shifting ranges of cloud and he could feel the cool air through the glass. At his back, the room was bare, almost void of possessions save a small bookcase stuffed with Bible commentaries, field guides and medical texts. A narrow bed with old blankets jutted from one corner, Iqbal's camp cot from the other, and a worn scrap of rug lay between. The windowsill held a random and dusty gathering of bits: binoculars, dried and crumbling ferns, loose change, keys and the glow-in-the-dark crucifix Iqbal had given him. The room smelled of mouldy shoes and old books, of unwashed laundry and coffee. It had a temporary, hiking hut feel to it, as though James had never properly unpacked, or was just passing through.

To his right, his King James Bible lay open at Luke's gospel, its thin pages dense with underlining and margin notes. To his left, a commentary, and spread across the remaining space, the pages of his sermon, cross-hatched, blotted and annotated.

'Who can forgive sins?' he typed. 'Is it only the one who has been sinned against? But what if that person has died? What if your sin *caused* his death? He cannot forgive from beyond the grave!'

He had a sudden thought and flipped back in his Bible to the Psalms. Yes, it was there: King David, after causing the death of Bathsheba's husband. His song of remorse to God:

'Against you, *you only*, have I sinned.'

'And so,' James' knobbled fingers tapped the keys. 'Is it only God we sin against and therefore only He who can forgive us?'

But, David had unquestionably wronged Uriah. Would he not desire his forgiveness? Or even Bathsheba's? But you cannot be forgiven by a dead man, because he is gone. Can you be forgiven by a member of his family? Or is it an outrage to forgive on behalf of someone else?

God does.

He took a swig of coffee, cold now and too sweet, and felt a faint wave of nausea. It was his daily companion now, as was the encroaching weakness, and the sour taste in his mouth. No one knew the hour or the day, but he suspected it to be soon. Outside, the cloud was curling and turning on itself, waves of silent cold billowing over the house, blotting it like the soaked cotton he once used for killing beetles.

And what, he wondered, if you receive the forgiveness of God and the forgiveness of the wronged, yet still carry guilt? What if you realise that your sins have rippled out to encompass many, indeed all around you: the sins of the fathers visited on the children and the children's children. Do you seek them out, one by one, and beg forgiveness? And what if they do not forgive? What if even one does not forgive? Do you stand unforgiven?

His hand slipped across the frayed wool of his sweater, rubbing on his sternum. And what if all, even God, have granted forgiveness yet you cannot forgive yourself? For the damage has been done and you know not how to repair it; indeed your very struggle to atone has only deepened the spoil, and the heart's hunger remains.

TWENTY-EIGHT

When the *Gospel* party arrived at the Krishna Theatre the next morning, a sleepy chowkidar at the gate wouldn't let them in. Said there was no booking. Ruth felt the warmth of the sun and a faint prickling of sweat on the back of her neck as Mr Haskell dug in his bag for the paperwork. The man looked over it for a moment, swatted a fly, then handed it back with a shrug. No one had told him, he said and leaned back in his seat, chewing on his paan. Mr Das stepped up and appealed gently in Hindi, his yellow palms outstretched. The man gave a dismissive wave and gazed off down the road. At that, Mrs Banwarilal pushed forward and fired a volley of words at him, voice flailing, hands chopping like kitchen knives. Ruth couldn't follow all of it, but enough to understand the man was a shame and a disgrace to his employer, his country and his mother. Lashed into submission, he muttered something through his stained teeth and slithered off the stool with the keys.

Inside, the theatre was dark and smelled of back alleyways. The chowkidar unlocked the door to the AV booth and switched on some stuttering lights. The walls were stained and the theatre seats shabby, some broken right off. Tendrils of spider web dangled from the lamps and the stage was gritty underfoot, the air tasting of dust. The chowkidar stood at the back and scratched his crotch.

'It's ok,' said Mr Haskell, sounding like he was trying to

keep breathing. 'We're going to clean this place up... and tonight, we fill it with Light!'

'Amen!' shouted Thomas.

The chowkidar claimed he didn't have the key to the sweeper's cupboard, so Mr Haskell sent a small party out to buy cleaning materials. Ruth wasn't allowed to go. A letter from her parents, endorsed by Principal Withers, had insisted she be under the strictest supervision throughout her time in Delhi. So she sloped off to the toilets to smoke. It was filthier here than in the theatre, so she puffed quickly and tried not to breathe through her nose. In the slit of light from the window she studied the graffiti: multi-lingual and graphic. At least here she couldn't find her own name. It appeared now and again on the toilet walls at Oaklands usually with words like *slut* or *fuck off.* Sita assured her it was just because Ruth was pretty and had boyfriends and the bitches were jealous. But it always stung and Ruth could never understand why people invested effort in hatred.

Once the shoppers returned, the cast and crew worked for the rest of the morning with mops and brooms and buckets and cloths, whipping up clouds of dirt and chasing it down, splashing dettol into basins and sprinkling it about, wringing rags and tipping swill. To begin with, they groaned and huffed and urged Mr Haskell to demand his money back, but by late morning they had settled into a rhythm of work and were finding a secret pleasure in the restoration.

*   *   *   *   *

That same day, the 31st of October, 1984, a large Sikh man sat listening to his radio in the accounts office of the Kanpur Christian Hospital. A stout, unflappable man with regal bearing and a rich voice, Gurpreet Singh was the hospital's longest-standing employee. James often sat with him at lunch and listened to the stories of his glorious Sikh heritage, though slightly exasperated that the line between history and myth was so hopelessly blurred. Eventually he enjoyed the tales more when he accepted that in Gurpreet's mind no such line existed, and whilst James wanted to know what *really happened,* Gurpreet wanted to tell what *mattered.*

Now in his fifties, Gurpreet had worked at the mission hospital since he was a boy, progressing from Junior Peon to First Mimeograph Operator through Admissions Department Clerical Assistant to his final promotion as Senior Bookkeeper. His girth had grown with his status, so that now he was in possession of the hospital's finest paunch, carried on a frame so towering and strong that he appeared not so much fat as architectural. He took pride in his job, being punctual, meticulous and incorruptible. Though these attributes won much respect from the other staff, they were eclipsed by his singing voice and startlingly fluid dancing. His versions of Bollywood hits, complete with glittering costumes and tasselled turbans, were the undisputed highlights of the annual Independence Day celebrations.

On this morning, however, as he sat wedged behind his small desk, singing along to the Hindi film music, his crooning was interrupted by a news report on All India Radio. He listened, perfectly still, and when the music returned, he slowly switched it off and rose from his desk. His massive legs felt empty.

*   *   *   *   *

Rehearsal had only just started when Mrs Banwarilal went out to buy the lunches, and by the time she got back the cast were sprawled on the stage, weary from their cleaning and already bored with technical cues. Down-stage left, the girls sat comparing the henna on their hands which Sita had done for them, claiming expertise after countless family weddings. Ruth studied her palms, their white, foreign skin so colonised by India. Flowers, paisley shapes, swirls and dots coiled across her hands like a map of a mythical world. It was a branding, a tribal tattoo that marked her as one of them, yet she knew she was not. Nor did she feel American, despite her passport. Of that she was certain, and proud. But she didn't quite know to whom she belonged, feeling always different and rarely content to be herself. Whoever that was. The mantle of the rebel that had fallen so easily on her shoulders had become too heavy to shed and she had forgotten what was under it, finding it easier to fulfil grim expectations than to struggle free. Until now, when her part in the *Gospel of Jyoti* was offering a different role and a chance to reveal, in performance, a truer self.

Centre stage, Thomas Verghese (alias Jesu) was lounging at the foot of the banyan tree from which he was about to be hung, while behind him, Kashi (the Prodigal) was adjusting the back hangings on which he'd painted scenes of village life – a mud hut, a well, a skinny cow. He still wasn't making many friends but his artwork was winning grudging respect. Meanwhile Manveer, who played the Beloved Disciple (Jaya) as well as the Prodigal's brother and the Thankful Leper, was at the top of a ladder focusing a lamp. Ruth had watched him through the morning, flirted, laughed at all his jokes and found an excuse to touch his neck when she straightened his collar. This in turn had given him the opportunity to take her hands and inspect the henna. He had cradled them gently, tracing their patterns with his fingers and finally, with a soft whistle, declared them beautiful.

'Have you got that?' Mr Haskell called up to the AV booth at the back of the theatre. 'I want complete black out and then the centre spot coming up slowly on Jesu on the tree.'

'Ok,' called the voice from above. 'Got it.'

'Right,' Mr Haskell murmured, flipping pages in his script. Ruth yawned and stretched out her legs in front of her, propping herself up on her elbows. Mrs Banwarilal, who had put the box of lunches on a front seat, sidled up to his elbow.

'Roger.'

'Yeah?' he said, not looking up.

'I need to speak with you.' Her voice was a little strained.

'Oh... right,' he said. 'Now?'

'Right now.'

Mr Haskell dumped the script on the nearest chair and clapped his hands to stop the chattering that had broken out amongst the cast.

'Ok, everyone,' he called. 'Time for lunch. Girls – could you pass these round please? Don't anyone leave the theatre, we're starting up in twenty minutes. Got a lot to get through.' And he ran his hand across his untidy ponytail and turned to Mrs Banwarilal.

The girls pulled brown paper sacks out of the boxes at the front of the stage and started passing them round. Ruth noticed with annoyance that Sita gave one to Manveer. In fact, she was handing out to all the boys.

At the foot of the stage, Mrs Banwarilal was speaking in a low, urgent voice, her hands flapping like the wings of a wounded bird. Mr Haskell listened, shaking his head, again and again. Then he walked across to Mr Das, who was eating a samosa and brushing crumbs off his waistcoat. When the old man heard, he lowered the samosa and his head. Mr Haskell turned to the stage and clapped his hands again. His face was grey.

'Ah... everybody?' he said. 'I got some bad news. Mrs Gandhi was shot this morning.'

*   *   *   *   *

James called a meeting of all Sikh staff, releasing them for the day and inviting them to move their families into the hospital compound. Gurpreet Singh nodded solemnly from the back of the room but said he would stay at home as his elderly mother was too frail to be moved. Other families came, their possessions in bundles and bags, clutched in straining fingers, balanced on heads. In the already full hospital accommodation, space was found, Hindus, Muslims and Christians squeezing up for their Sikh colleagues. James and Ellen absorbed two households and sent the canteen staff out to buy as much food as possible.

*   *   *   *   *

As the *Gospel* bus slipped through Delhi late that afternoon, Ruth felt a snake of fear rising inside her. She had never seen the streets of an Indian city so quiet. Shops were shut, there were few vehicles on the road and people were scuttling to get inside, heads down. It was an edgy quiet, the drawing back of a tidal wave, a sling-shot.

Rounding the corner into Safdarjung Road, they saw a shouting mob swarming up a side alley.

'Oh, my god,' said Sita.

Ruth clenched her hands inside the pockets of her sweatshirt, heart thumping. Others in the bus gasped, whimpered, gripped each other. The driver swore and slammed on the accelerator. Speeding on, they passed more clots of men forming in the streets, smashed shop windows, and the acrid sting of burning tyres. It was the smell of violence. As they stopped at a traffic light, the engine growling impatiently, a group of men ran at the bus wielding sticks, raving and demon-eyed. The driver shot a look up and down the intersecting road and roared off through the red light just as the first blows banged off the metal flank. Sita sucked in her breath and Ruth grabbed her arm. The driver gained speed the rest of the way, running more red lights, blasting his horn and sometimes careering down side roads till he finally stopped with a scream of brakes outside the guesthouse. Everyone was thrown forward, Ruth's head slamming against the seat in front. Biting back tears she snatched her bag and joined the scrum of teenagers pushing out of the bus and through the compound gates.

They spent the rest of the evening in the common room huddled in front of the small black-and-white television, arms around each other, faces pale and pinched. Ruth and Sita were on cushions on the floor, propped against the knees of the girls behind. As Brahmin priests chanted prayers and people wept, foreign reporters began to leak the news that would run like fire along the nation's short fuse. She had been shot whilst walking across her garden. (*She is gone! She is gone!* Men shouted, their faces contorted, wet with weeping, hands beating their own bodies.) Shot by her bodyguards. (*Blood for blood!* The crowd screamed.) Who were Sikhs. (*Kill them! Kill them!* A mob with clubs, iron staves, frothing mouths. The newly sworn-in Prime Minister, Rajiv Gandhi – the son of the dead – was appealing for calm.)

'It's because of the Golden Temple,' said Manveer.

'Yeah, man,' said Abishek. 'But that was inevitable.'

'You think she did the right thing? Slaughtering them all? In our holiest shrine?'

'No way, yaar, no way. I didn't say that. Just that it was going to blow up at some point.'

'You bet, man.'

Ruth looked at Manveer, hunched on the couch just behind her. His eyes held a fierce glitter, his bearded jaw thrust forward.

'Explain what happened at the Temple,' she said softly.

'Back in June, don't you remember?' said Sita.

'A bit.' Ruth felt foolish.

'Operation Blue Star,' Manveer explained. 'She shut down the whole of the Punjab and sent four thousand troops to attack the temple. Killed hundreds of people and destroyed even the holy heart of it. All these ancient scriptures and precious things – *sacred* things – turned to ash!'

'Because Bhindranwale had turned it into his military headquarters!' said Abishek. 'He had a huge stash of weapons there and was running a training camp, forgodsake.'

'For what?' asked Ruth.

'For Sikh independence!' said Sita, irritation in her voice. 'The Khalistan movement, you know?'

Ruth had heard of it, vaguely.

'Yeah,' Manveer cut in, stabbing the arm of the couch. 'But that temple was full of innocent people as well. She picked a festival day and there were thousands of pilgrims inside.'

Abishek spread his hands. 'A lot of those pilgrims never wanted their holy shrine used as an army base and never wanted separation from India.'

'Exactly. So why'd she have to plough in and kill them?' His eyes were branding irons.

'They were given time to leave.'

'Oh yeah? Why so many dead at the end, then? You're really backing that bitch, aren't you?'

'No way, man, cool it. I hated her too, and Blue Star was wrong and all that, I agree, but so was Bhindranwale.'

'Yeah, because she put him there! Thought she could use him to take power from her main enemies in the Punjab, but he got bigger than she'd planned. So she had to destroy the monster she'd made.'

Abishek gestured assent. 'I know it. You're right, man.' He glanced back at the fire-breathing mob on the television. 'Looks like it didn't work.'

Manveer's lip curled and he gave a curt nod, a slight bouncing starting up in his thigh.

'Do you have relatives in Delhi?' Ruth asked softly. He shook his head.

'No. Punjab.'

He looked at her for a moment, then back at the screen. She wished she could rest a hand on him, but Sita was in the way.

Behind him, through the door, Ruth could see Mr Haskell sitting in the front hall making frantic phone calls, sometimes in English, sometimes Hindi, always ending with banging down the receiver and scratching his hair. It was starting to look like the tail of a flea-bitten horse. At some point he shut himself in his room and did not re-appear.

Gradually, a few calls came in from anxious parents who had tracked down the guesthouse number and Kip urged everyone else to phone home. It was after eight when Ruth's turn came. No answer. It seemed late for Mom and Dad to be at the hospital.

'Maybe they're at a meeting or something,' offered Kip.

Ruth shrugged. She knew they had the guesthouse number as they always stayed here when they came to Delhi. They could have phoned. She tried again, listened to the dial tone ring out, then lowered the receiver softly into its cradle and slipped back into the common room.

That night as she lay again on her lumpy mattress the sounds of Delhi were changed. Though there was still the sugary whine of a love song on someone's radio and the clattering of pots and the council of dogs, further out the mechanical bees were subdued and the larger clamour of the city muted. And further still, and deeper down, beyond the earshot and worst imaginings of Oaklands teenagers, were the sounds of a nation breaking apart, once again. Foundation plates shifting; old scars opening like fissures in the rock; people falling through and being sucked down into the furnaces of hate, like sacrifices to a demonic god.

*   *   *   *   *

In Kanpur, casualties were beginning to arrive at the hospital: a group of men attacked by a Hindu mob, with dirt in their bloodied wounds and fury in their faces; a woman, clutching the shreds of her shalwar, so badly raped she could not walk; an old man, wild-eyed and weeping, his burnt grandson in his arms. More and more came, the trickle becoming a dark flow of both the injured and the afraid. The hospital took them all. It was nearly midnight when James and Ellen got home, weary in bone and spirit. The house smelled of bodies and fried onions. Turning on the light in their room they saw an old man and several children in their bed. The sleeping faces scrunched against the brightness, but no eyes opened. Ellen moved to the bed.

'No,' said James.

'Honey!' she hissed. 'I'm tired and we have to work tomorrow. They don't.'

'We've got sleeping bags. We'll find somewhere else.'

She pressed her eyes shut, shook her head.

He reached out a hand to her shoulder. 'We can't move them – where would they go?'

She pushed past him out the door, snapping off the light. He felt his way after her in the dark.

On the floor of their office the hard jute matting dug into their sides and smelled of mildew. They remembered Ruth and the *Gospel* group in Delhi that week, with Kip at the Unity Guesthouse. Ellen would phone in the morning.

*   *   *   *   *

At breakfast Mr Haskell was wearing the same clothes as yesterday and it looked like he had slept in them, or perhaps not slept at all. His face was as grey and blotchy as the porridge Kip set before him. He didn't touch it. Thirteen days of official mourning, he said. No entertainment allowed. No show. There were gasps and groans; Ruth felt it like a kick. She watched Mr Haskell's chin crumple as he pushed back his chair with a scrape and strode out of the room. Mrs Banwarilal was left to field questions. She was in a crisp sari, her long, black hair wound into an elegant bun, face bright with lipstick and a nose-ring.

'Don't *worry*, darlings,' she said, lifting braceletted hands. 'Everything's going to be just *fine*.' Though it plainly wasn't. Delhi was erupting and they would have to stay put till the police said it was safe to travel. Mr Das had a second cousin in the force who would keep them informed. In the meantime, there was to be no leaving the compound, no girls in boys' rooms and vice versa, and no eating without permission. Food would be short.

Ruth went and cried in the shower, unable to believe it. There was something unbearably cruel about the dream having come this far, so close and vivid she could almost touch it, only to be snatched away at the last minute. She came out to a message from Kip. Mom had phoned and was glad to know they were all ok. She and Dad were real busy at the hospital. Lotsa love.

'Did she say if they're still coming to see me?'

'I said you'd call back when you knew the plans.'

Yes, the plans! There was hope. There was still a performance back at Oaklands at the end of Activity Week.

It didn't compare with three nights at the Krishna Theatre in Delhi, but it was all she had now. She would phone them back and ask if they'd come up to Oaklands to see the show and spend some time with her. Kip had said they wouldn't miss it for the world.

Ruth tried phoning several times, but the home number rang out and the hospital switchboard was jammed. She slammed down the receiver after her third attempt. How could they expect to provide a medical service if no-one could get through?! She tried to fill the time playing board games with the others but there were more fights than usual and when she amassed a fortune in Monopoly, Sita rallied everyone against her till she crashed. As they all crowed in triumph, Ruth threw down the dice and said, 'Stuff it up your arse!' and stormed out.

Running up the outside stairs of the house, her nose was stung by the smell of burning and once on the roof she could see smoke stacks rising like black, snaking fingers across the city. There was distant shouting and the sounds of smashing and banging and what might have been gun fire. Despite her parents' keen interest in the nation's political twists and turns, she had never paid much attention, so there was a great deal about this crisis she did not fathom, a fact that Sita seemed intent on exposing. She wanted her parents, their reassurance, their presence, their dowdy, stolid ways.

When it was clear no-one was coming after her, she slipped back inside and was relieved to see Monopoly packed away and a small group returned to the television, Sita beside Manveer on the couch, Abishek on the floor with a newspaper. Ruth found a chair. The reporting on Delhi came and went and was suspiciously selective, focusing on grieving crowds and mourners filing past Mrs Gandhi's bier. But there were also brief glimpses of vengeance. Mobs had begun ransacking Sikh homes the night before and there were scenes of gutted houses and people weeping.

Mr Das pointed at the television. 'My cousin is telling me these thugs are taking the electoral roll and finding the Sikh homes that way.'

Manveer sucked in his breath.

'Shit,' said Sita.

'Hey, listen to this.' Abishek tapped the paper. 'You know the President got back yesterday? Well, I quote: *On the journey from the airport, the President's motorcade was stoned.* I love it! At least somebody's having a good time.'

'Not funny, man,' Manveer muttered.

'No, sorry.'

'Why would the crowd do that?' asked Ruth.

'Because the President's Sikh, of course!' said Sita. 'Didn't you know that? Zai Singh.'

'Oh, yeah, of course...'

So, the President was Sikh, the bodyguards that shot Mrs Gandhi were Sikh, and – Ruth had discovered – the army chief that led the attack on the Golden Temple was also Sikh. She did not understand.

In the late afternoon, Kip put her head round the door and asked if anybody wanted to bake anything. She had spent much of the day trying to catch the news herself, in between making multiple phone calls and checking over supplies with Mohan, the cook, but a house full of teenagers needed direction and Mr Haskell, who had not appeared since breakfast, was not providing it. Ruth could see the strain in her eyes, but also her determined positivity in the face of crisis. It was what Grandma Leota called *missionary spirit* and a quality that had always evaded Ruth.

She followed Dorcas into the kitchen, trying to smile as Sita joined them. Kip took down the Landour Community Cookbook, dating back to her days running the Fairview Guesthouse in Landour many moons before. It was where Ellen usually stayed when she visited, which wasn't very often, in Ruth's opinion, though more than James who rarely came. The rooms at Fairview were cramped, with mis-matched furnishings and cold bathrooms where spiders leapt out of tooth mugs, but the sense of reprieve for Ruth was profound. In the early years, anyway. Since Hannah had gone back to the States, however, she had found her mother's visits made her squirm. Despite longing for her to come, she would invariably discover how much Ellen annoyed her, with her reading aloud from missionary newsletters and her scuffed running shoes under her sari. And all her questions.

'How about Easy Cookies, girls?' asked Kip. 'Betty Shirk's recipe. She was some woman, I tell ya. Could feed five thousand with a couple a crusts and a tin of tuna.' She ran her calloused finger down the page. 'This is good. You only need condensed milk, peanut butter and cornflakes, and I think we're in luck.'

The girls nodded eagerly.

'Oh yeah,' said Dorcas. 'I've made those with Mom. They're real easy.'

'Great,' said Sita, 'cause I've never baked before.'

'You haven't?!' cried Dorcas, as if Sita had just admitted leprosy.

'Well I bet you guys have never made *idli*,' she retorted.

They hadn't.

'Hey, I've tried,' said Kip with a smile. 'But I couldn't match the Cochin Café down the road, so I just go there.'

'I hate *idli*,' said Dorcas. 'Tastes like papier mache.'

'Well if you can't stomach the food you shouldn't be in this country,' said Sita.

'I like *most* Indian food, Sita, and anyway, *idli's* from the south and I never go there.'

'Why not?! What's wrong with the south?'

'There's nothing wrong—'

'Come on, guys,' Ruth cut in, 'let's just make the cookies, ok?'

Kip handed her the book and winked. 'I gotta go and sort some stuff, but Mohan'll help you.' The *khansamma*, who had appeared at that moment through the back door, tipped his head to the girls.

'Right,' said Sita, snatching the cookbook. 'Mohan!' Without looking at the man, she read out in swift Hindi all the ingredients and utensils and commanded him, in imperious tones, to fetch them, and quickly. Ruth stood by, embarrassed, as Mohan did as he was told. Dorcas went to help him.

Sita flicked through the book disdainfully. 'Any Indian food in here?' she demanded. 'Any Indian cooks?'

Ruth balanced her tray on one hand and knocked on the door. No answer. She knocked again and waited. Something like a groan came from the room. She pushed the door a crack and peered in. It was dark, the curtains drawn, air thick with the smell of socks and sweat and unknown male things. She slipped in, pushing the door shut with her foot.

Mr Haskell was a heap in the bed, his face buried. She knelt down by him and set the tray on the floor as there was no room on his bedside table. It was a mess of scrunched toilet paper, a wallet spilling coins, glasses, pills, books, pens, plectrums and a clotted hanky.

'Mr Haskell?'

Silence.

'I brought you a coffee and something to eat,' she said softly.

No movement or sound.

'Condensed milk cookies. We made them this morning.'

He drew his head out from the sheet. It caught her breath. Framed by the wild tangle of hair, his face was puffed and even in the dim light she could see the red scratches and the eyelids so swollen that he peered at her through slits.

'Are you ok?' she whispered.

'I'm cursed.' His voice was a rasp. 'Everything I touch falls apart. My final show at college... the leading lady broke her leg and we had to cancel. Then the school where I taught first was so bad they shut it down – one week before my production. And so much more... oh, god, you wouldn't believe. My life has been such a mess, but then... I got back to faith, I got the job here, I thought I could start again. *The Gospel of Jyoti* was the sign of God's blessing... and my thank offering. I've been working on it for years, Ruthie, years! Now this...'

The tortured face caved in, mouth trembling, eyes squeezing shut as tears coursed down the scratched cheeks. Ruth lifted a hand to his shoulder.

'Oh, Mr Haskell...' she breathed. 'I'm sorry.'

He was crying hard now. 'I wanted... to tell this story... I wanted... to share... my Lord and his—' There was an eruption of sobs that overwhelmed him for a minute. And then he gasped: 'His... *love.*' And he wept like a child.

Ruth couldn't think what to say, so stroked the heaving back. His hand shot out from under the covers and grabbed hers, pulling it to his face. She felt the hot tears, the wet flesh, the chapped lips kissing her palm. She started to withdraw but he pulled hard, dragging her down to him and clutching the back of her head. Burying his slippery face in her neck, he kissed her fiercely, sobbing and kissing, over and over. For a moment she struggled, but then felt the wave of panic become excitement and she turned her face so his mouth found hers and their kissing was hard and wild and deep.

The sound of footsteps broke them apart and Ruth jumped up and turned to the door. The footsteps moved on and after a moment of paralysis, she shot out of the room.

In the common room that evening where the television droned on, she slipped quietly onto the sofa beside Manveer. Shaken by her encounter with Mr Haskell, she could only hope it would never be repeated, noticed or mentioned. Sita, however, had already asked, with a piercing look and arched brow, if Mr Haskell had enjoyed his cornflake cookies. Ruth had shrugged, mumbled *dunno* and changed the subject.

On the neighbouring sofa, cross-legged in his shawl and holey socks, Mr Das was providing a running commentary on the unfolding events, generally disputing the meagre information on the official broadcasts.

'The city is spiralling out of control,' he warned. As if in agreement, the television announcer declared an indefinite curfew from 6pm that night. 'The army should be called,' Mr Das said, wagging a finger.

'Yeah, but the army is mostly Sikh,' said Manveer bitterly. 'Why do you think they haven't been called, huh?'

Mr Das shook his head, over and over.

'It is *too* bad, it is *too* bad,' he wheezed. 'There will be no end, no end.'

* * * * *

That day in Kanpur a bus-load was brought in. The driver and several passengers were Sikh and a mob had dragged them out, doused them with petrol and set them on fire. Even the women. Even the children. James walked down the row of charred bodies in the hospital hallway, checking for life, a faint pulse, a breath. He felt a tightening in his chest like a metal fist.

Again, he and Ellen worked deep into the night, running with trolleys to theatre, putting up drips, tending burns. They gave blood that minutes later was threading its way into the boy with no feet, the old man bludgeoned, the woman stoned almost to death. They barely ate that day, thankfully slurping the cups of hot, sweet chai that nurses pushed into their hands.

At home, two plates of food had been left in the kitchen and their bedroom vacated, but their sleep was broken by the sounds of coughing, snoring and babies crying.

And for James, the memories and the nightmares.

* * * * *

On the Friday morning Abishek persuaded Mrs Banwarilal to let them go to the Taj Palace Hotel, just a few minutes' walk away.

'We'll be fine Mrs B,' he cajoled. 'Much safer than all holed up in here. The hormones are erupting like a blocked toilet. Can't you smell it?'

'Oh Abi,' she giggled. 'That's gross!'

'Or maybe it's just my socks, but, no, seriously – somebody's gonna get violent, or go insane, or proposition the cook. It's desperate. It'll be on your head, Mrs B, on your conscience for life, you'll never forgive yourself, you'll—'

'Shut up, you great buffoon and get out. On you go. All of you. You're driving me mad.' She lifted her jingling wrists in defeat. 'Just be back in time for supper.'

So they went. They'd seen fragments on TV, but not a fraction of the truth. Ruth certainly knew nothing of what was happening in Kanpur. And perhaps, what they did know, they couldn't face. Certainly, they were helpless before it and removed, so all in their own way, for their own reasons, turned from the nightmare and slipped into a dream. The Taj Palace Hotel was an oasis of cool air and clean floors where piano music drifted through potted palms and cutlery chimed softly in the restaurant. In the courtyard garden, fountains tinkled and bougainvillea fell in lush curtains around the glittering pool. It was a mirage of peace.

On the other side of the city, the poorest Sikh ghetto of Trilokpuri was engulfed in fumes and fire. Mobs moved from house to house kicking down doors and slaughtering any Sikhs they found. If they could not break in, they cut holes in the roof, poured kerosene down and threw in their flaming torches. Some Sikh men in the city tried to disguise themselves by cutting their hair and shaving their beards; others found their hair hacked off for them and their beards burnt. Some Sikh mothers tried to disguise their identity by dressing their sons as daughters; others found themselves trapped as men threw burning tyres over them – both mother and child – while policemen stood by watching. Some Sikh families found refuge with their Hindu neighbours; others found their neighbours at the door with knives. And once again, like ghosts rising from a brutal and unfinished past, trains began rolling into the city stations bearing corpses.

Back in the illusion of the Taj Palace, the Oaklands teenagers took a dip in the hotel swimming pool and worried about body hair and inadequate bulges. At lunch time they piled their plates at the salad bar and sipped iced lemonade, and in the long afternoon the boys played arcade games as the girls drifted to the beauty salon. Ruth borrowed money from Nazira and got her first manicure, her hands taking on a whole new life under gleaming nails, blood-red and false.

TWENTY-NINE

Twenty-four years later, her short nails were chipped and her fingers finely veined with dirt. She had cleared Askival of its rubbish and swept and scrubbed it, inside and out. The work had been deeply satisfying, especially the visions that came to her of what it could become. She didn't know who owned it or how to protect it, but she dreamed of a space clean and beautiful, full of light. And people. A mixed cast of imagined characters entered her rooms, usually unbidden. Whenever Manveer appeared, the house returned to that November night when it was dark and they had clung to each other in the cold. But if she held the bright Askival in her mind, Iqbal always came bustling through and then she would find her father sitting by a window and her sister gathering children like chicks on the lawn and finally, her mother. At a writing desk, or baking, or holding flowers. Once, she was holding a new-born. The image of Ellen was fragile and wavering and whenever she lifted her face, she disappeared.

Ruth kept working, ignoring the damage that was beyond her power: the lost sheets of roofing, the collapsed walls. Her hands were rough now and her back stiff but the task compelled her. On this damp September afternoon she carried a backpack heavy with whitewash, bucket and brushes. She and Iqbal were on their way home from the bazaar and stopping at Hillside Hospital to meet James, who wanted to show her around. In the foyer, she put down her pack and studied the framed photograph on the wall. Her mother, straight-backed and gazing off to the right, was wearing her customary sari and her customary smile. It was how most people remembered her. Serene, unwrinkled, purposeful. Ruth had other memories.

'A great beauty,' said Iqbal, from behind.

'Yes,' she murmured and dropped her gaze to a table stacked with paperback books bearing bright green covers. 'Oh my god – I don't believe it. The Landour Community Cookbook, 2nd Edition!'

'Oh yes, excellent project.'

Ruth opened one. 'Edited by Dr Ellen Connor. I never knew about that.'

'Yes, yes. She is working on this before she passed to heaven. They are selling for hospital funds.'

'My god, that's amazing.' Ruth took a copy to the receptionist and dug in her bag for her wallet.

'You are the Connor-jis daughter?' the receptionist asked shyly, taking Ruth's money.

'Yes.'

'Both your parents are revered here as gods.' The young woman smiled. 'You must be very proud of them.'

'One has to be,' said Ruth, picking up the book. 'Thanks.' She turned and walked to the waiting area opposite where Iqbal stood, eyebrows raised. The receptionist watched Ruth as she studied a rack of leaflets in the corner. Some of them were health messages, written in Hindi and English: *"Stop Aids!" "TB? Take your medicine!" "When You've Had Two, That Will Do"*.

'Send that one to Hannah,' she snorted, showing it to Iqbal.

'Your sister has one great love of life. She cannot resist creating more.'

'You don't have to prove it by having seven kids.'

'How are you proving?'

She floundered for an answer. 'Well I... Iqbal, to be honest, I don't think I love life. I just live it.'

'Is tough without love,' he murmured.

'I didn't say I didn't have love! Just that... I don't love *life*. Not my life, anyway.' She sighed, and stuffed the leaflet back in the rack.

Along with the health messages there were a set of dusty religious tracts. Jesus in his flowing hair and robes with outspread arms: *'Come unto me all ye that labour and are heavy laden.'* A cross spilling light into a pool of darkness: *'Break the power of SIN.'* A pair of folded hands: *'Our Father'.*

'There was a permanent display of these in our dining room in Kanpur,' she said, tapping them. 'Mom would never miss an opportunity to save the lost.'

'Doctor-ji is not using?'

'Yeah, he did a bit, but never much of a talker, so it was normally Mom that handled the propaganda.'

'When I am arriving, there are no tracts.'

'Oh really? Huh... maybe Dad cleared them out after Mom died.'

'No. Nothing was cleared. Even her toothbrush was still sitting. I am helping with all that sad thing.'

'Oh,' said Ruth.

'Are you knowing these?' Iqbal asked, showing her a tract.

'The Four Spiritual Laws? Oh yes, they were drummed into me for the first seventeen years of my life, Iqbal, along with

god-knows how many memory verses, but I have dedicated myself ever since to systematically forgetting the lot.'

'I will test,' said Iqbal, opening it and beckoning. 'Tell to me.'

'Groan... Let's see...' She squinted into space. 'Number One: *All have sinned and fallen short of the glory of God.*'

'Incorrect.'

'What?! That's definitely right.'

'Is very true thing, Rani Ruthie, but is Law Number Two. What is One?'

She stared at him, drawing a blank. 'I could have sworn...'

'Your forgetting is very successful.' He tipped his head.

'Let me see that,' she said, snatching the leaflet, but before she had time to look, a large lady in a green sari swept into the foyer.

'Ruthie!' she crowed, throwing open her arms. It was Mrs Puri, the hospital administrator and long-standing friend of the family. Ruth allowed herself to be swathed in big arms and a cascade of silk, the shelf of Mrs Puri's bosom pressing against her. Her breath smelled of paan.

'Oh, sweetie,' cooed the lady, stepping back and holding Ruth at arm's length. 'You haven't changed a bit. Still beautiful as ever. But not quite so naughty, na?' She tweaked her nose. 'Sooo good to see you!'

'You too,' Ruth said, through her teeth, shoving the tract into her pocket.

'Darling, we're all so glad you came. Your Daddy misses his girls so much, I just know it. Of course, he's got good old Iqbal here, but it's not the same.'

'Iqbal does a better job than I could,' said Ruth. 'Certainly cooks better.'

'Oh!' Mrs Puri clasped a hand to her breast and rolled her eyes. 'Iqbal's cooking is without compare. Nectar for the *gods*! But he's not a nice, cuddly daughter, is he, and that's just what your Daddy needs right now.'

Ruth grunted. Iqbal winked at her. Mrs Puri grasped Ruth's arm in her red-nailed hand. 'Darling, have you seen the new Dr Ellen Connor Maternity Suite?'

'Yes,' Ruth lied.

'Oh! So much money poured in after her passing, so many people wanting to remember her, so many stories of lives saved! From Kanpur, and here, and all over the world. She is the mother of thousands!'

'Dad showed me the letters,' said Ruth. The box had remained on the living room floor, unopened.

'Your mother, Ruthie, was a damn good obstetrician. None to match her,' said Mrs Puri. Then, in a conspiratorial tone, 'But I know her secret. She told me once.' Ruth and Iqbal leaned in. 'Before every single birth, she placed her hands on the mother's body…' She allowed a dramatic pause, red nails fanned, 'and *prayed*.' Another pause, then Mrs Puri slapped her hands together as if playing the trump card and let forth a honking laugh. 'How's that, *na*? Brilliant!'

Iqbal joined the laughter. Ruth raised her brows and pulled a strained smile.

'I must go now, sweetie,' Mrs Puri sighed, pinching Ruth's cheek. 'I've got a meeting but, listen, don't you be sad, huh? Whatever will be will be.' And she swished out, a solid, flightless bird with a fluttering tail.

Ruth met Iqbal's merry face with a scolding glare and turned to examine a painting on the wall. It was an Indian scene: people gathered around a stone pool, their bodies bent, heads bowed. Some reached towards the pool, yearning, while others sat, defeated. In the foreground stood a holy man with ragged hair and lungi, his back to the viewer. With muscled arms raised and hands unfurled, he was looking down at an old man on the ground, naked and blind. The holy man's body was dark, but the scene before him lay bathed in light, as if emanating from his hidden face.

The picture held her gaze, tugged on her. At the bottom, the same signature she'd seen at the Oaklands Peace Garden. KN.

'Doctor-ji is little delayed,' said Iqbal. 'Shall I get some tea and snacks from the canteen.'

'No thanks, I remember their food.'

'You were here?'

'When I was eight. Tonsillitis.'

Ruth had lain in the grip of fever, her head throbbing, her throat so raw each swallow was fire. The walls had bent over her and the flowers on the curtains begun to spin and her bed to tilt and she'd been forced to grip the sheets not to slide out. She'd prayed for her parents to come and thought there was an answer in the approaching footsteps, but it was not them, so she'd prayed harder. All day, every day, footsteps had come and gone and each time her heart had leapt at the hope of seeing them, like a fish hurling itself upstream. Irrational, wild, ridiculous hope.

A young man with a white coat and stethoscope walked in, his face alight.

'Salaam Iqbal-ji!'

The men clasped hands and banged each other on the back.

'Lakshman! Salaam!'

'You must be Ruth.' he said, extending his hand.

'Yes,' she said. His grip was strong, his smile warm.

'Oh, it is a joy to meet you. Any daughter of the Connor Doctors is always welcome here.'

'Lakshman is one of their students from Kanpur,' Iqbal explained. 'He's working in Mussoorie for – how much – two years now?'

'Nearly three, in fact, but it's flown.' Then suddenly his face became serious and he leaned closer to Ruth. 'I am so sorry about your father's illness. We are praying desperately for his healing.'

'Thanks,' she mumbled.

'He has given his life for India,' Lakshman continued. 'We are begging God to let us keep him a little bit longer. He's been so fit! – walking out to all those villages – and teaching in here, or all over the hillside clearing rubbish and planting trees. We can't believe his time has come.'

'He is believing,' said Iqbal, softly.

'Yes,' said Lakshman, and breathed out a sigh. 'I think he welcomes it. He has run the race and is longing to go home. We just can't bear to lose him, eh?' He looked at Ruth with such tender sadness that it floored her. She felt a sting at the back of her nose, and unable to speak, turned and walked out the door.

It wasn't till she was half way up the path to Shanti Niwas that she realised she still had the tract in her pocket. The First Spiritual Law: *God loves you and has a plan for your life.* Ruth ripped it to shreds and threw it down the *khud*. She immediately had a vision of James on one of his FRESH missions, scrambling over the hillside, hessian sack in hand, stooping to pick up the pieces.

THIRTY

It was Saturday morning, the third day of waiting at the Unity Guesthouse and the day of Mrs Gandhi's cremation. Entire Sikh communities lay gutted: homes and property destroyed, over two thousand people murdered and tens of thousands fleeing to refugee camps. The army had finally been summoned to help and the violence was beginning to ebb. They and the police would be thick upon the streets for the funeral procession and control would be tight. Mr Das had got word from his second cousin in the force that it would be safe to leave that evening. Ruth called home as soon as she heard and nearly whooped when the phone was answered, not detecting the strain in her father's voice.

She was tripping over herself with relief and urgency. 'Everything's ok here. Can you come up to see the show next week? Please?'

'What?' He sounded far away.

'You know – *The Gospel of Jyoti!* All the performances here were cancelled so we've only got one now, back at Oaklands. You have to come! It's amazing.'

There was a pause, then his voice. Like a whip.

'What in God's name—? Your *show?* No, of course we can't come up to see your show! Have you no idea? *No* idea what is happening around you? Ruth?' He was terrible, incandescent, like she'd yanked open the door of a furnace. 'Are you *that* selfish?!'

She fled to the roof of the house and huddled in a corner, barely breathing, stinging with the rebuke and the exploding of her dream.

Her silly, selfish, *stupid* dream.

The school party set off at sunset as a dusty orange pall gathered over the city, the air heavy with smoke and incense. Driving through the barren streets they saw gaping houses and overturned trucks, still smouldering. Here and there were charred bodies. Sometimes they could make out the remains of a turban, crisp and flaking on a blackened head, but even when they could not, they knew all the dead were Sikhs.

Except for Mrs Gandhi, of course, whose body was also burnt that day.

Mr Haskell, looking tired and older and avoiding Ruth, had put the white kids by the windows, and when he ran out of white ones, moved on to the half-white, like Kashi. The idea was to make it look like a bus full of foreigners, which was why Ibrahim from Somalia was an exception to the colour scheme and given a front window seat. Notions of foreignness were complex at Oaklands. Most of the white kids were brought up in Asia, or other places not of their citizenship. Many, like Ruth, were born in India. On the other hand, half of the "Indians" had passports from Canada, Europe and the US with accents to match. There were quite a few with mixed parentage and homes in several continents. It was hard for most of them to say where they were 'from' but at Oaklands this growing up between worlds was not a lack of identity, but integral to it. And as much as they might have protested the idea – Ruth especially – the school itself had become home.

Manveer, the only Sikh on board, was put on the back seat in a row of girls. Ruth and Sita commandeered the spaces either side of him while Abishek whistled and said Manveer was exploiting national crisis for personal gain.

'Shut it, Abishek,' Sita said.

'Yeah, that's not funny,' Dorcas added.

'Don't worry,' said Manveer. 'I'll just beat him up back in the dorm.'

'Oh, you wish, babu! You wish!' crowed Abishek. 'This guy can't even squash a cockroach.'

'Least he doesn't look like one,' said Sita.

'Ow-ow-ow-OW!' Abishek howled, shaking one hand as if badly burnt.

'Cut down, yaar!' grinned Manveer.

'Cut down *bad*!' Abishek vouched, with a defeated shake of the head and a crooked grin. Ruth tried to smile, but the events of the past few days were taking their toll. Manveer looked at her keenly, his dark eyes searching and gentle.

'You ok?' he whispered.

'Yeah,' she mumbled, and stared at her hands. The nails mocked her.

As they pulled out of Delhi, the great Doab plain stretched around them, flat and patched with fields, the ground turning cool and bloodless as the low sun drew all colour into itself. Ruth could see dark figures walking along the field edges towards the muted glow of village lights. It was the same scene she gazed out on from a train window every time she travelled back to Oaklands after a vacation. Mom and Dad would take her from Kanpur to Lucknow and then hand her over to the party of Mish Kid travellers from Varanasi, Calcutta and even Nepal. They would meet up in the high-ceilinged waiting room at Lucknow Station where fans turned slowly and a man in khaki swished a filthy mop from side to side. The handful of adult chaperones would count heads and bags while Ruth and the other girls squealed and hugged each other and scanned for signs of new clothes. If someone had been "home"on furlough they were the envy of the rest with their new jeans, Nike running shoes and permed hair.

The goodbyes were brisk and matter-of-fact. Dad would pat her on the head and say a short prayer. Mom would squeeze tight, but let go quickly and smile so brightly that Ruth could only smile back and wave. Then they were gone.

On the train there was always happy chatter and hi-jinks. They bought steaming sweet chai from the platform wallas and had competitions hurling the conical clay cups at pylons. They ate samosas and puris, glistening with hot oil, and passed round bananas and peanuts and bottles of warm Limca. They told jokes, played cards, swapped comics and chewed gum and at bed-time squirmed into their canvas *bistars* on the bunks and whispered and giggled. In her early years, when the train was rattling through the dark and everyone was quiet, Ruth would move her face to the window and stare into the blackness. Only then would she cry. Silently. No one ever knew, not even Hannah on her bunk above. And by the time Hannah had left Oaklands and Ruth was fourteen, she had stopped crying on trains. Almost stopped altogether.

The bus rumbled and rocked, setting the tinsel and pom-poms at the front window swinging. Ruth felt the warmth of Manveer's arm and thigh next to hers and glanced up at his face.

He was staring straight ahead.

Then he stiffened.

Out of the black, further along the road there was a sprinkling of lights. As the bus sped closer, the lights waved and brightened, moved out into the road and blocked it.

The driver swivelled his head round. 'Hide him!' he shouted and pressed on the brakes. Everyone whirled round in their seats. Mr Haskell jumped up.

'Manveer!' he shouted. 'Get down!' Manveer had already dived under the seat as Ruth and the others were yanking shawls over their knees.

The bus slowed to a halt, the chug of its engine drowned by the shouting of men. There was a banging on the door and a tightening of the air as Mr Haskell opened it a crack.

'Let us on! We are after the Sikhs!' a man bawled. Ruth felt a shock down her body.

'There are none here,' Mr Haskell replied in Hindi, his voice brittle. There were yells from the mob and the man pushed on the door.

'No Sikhs on this bus,' said the driver, with a dismissive wave of his hand.

'We are a school group,' Mr Haskell went on. 'Just kids. Foreign kids.'

The foreign kids stared bug-eyed at the men, who had sticks and sickles and rusty blades. The Indian kids slunk down in their seats. The driver revved his engine, the men hesitated and Mr Haskell shut the door. The bus took off.

Once the black had completely swallowed them again and the headlights stretched out into empty road, Mr Haskell moved down the bus and without looking at Ruth, knelt and lifted her shawl.

'It's ok, Manveer,' he said, though his voice was still strained. 'You can come out now.'

Manveer crawled out and dusted himself off. 'That was a close one, Mr Haskell,' he said, trying to laugh.

'Yeah, I know,' the teacher nodded. 'But don't worry. We're not going to let anything happen to you.'

Manveer sat down again between Ruth and Sita.

'Mr Haskell?' came a girl's voice from half way up the bus. 'Yes?'

'I think we should pray.' It was Dorcas.

Mr Haskell stood without saying anything for a moment. As he held onto the seats around him, his body jerked and swayed with the motion of the bus. Both Mrs Banwarilal and Mr Das nodded vigorously.

'A-huh, Dorcas,' Mr Haskell said slowly. 'I'm sure a lot of people have been praying already.'

'Yeah, but, I mean, out loud,' she pressed.

Mrs Banwarilal piped up. 'Yes, yes. I think that is a very good idea. Please pray.'

'Right,' said Mr Haskell and ran his hand through his hair, dislodging a chunk from the ponytail. 'Ok, Dorcas. You go ahead.'

Ruth looked at Manveer but he had already closed his eyes and bowed his head.

'Dear Lord,' Dorcas began, her voice thin and faint under the roar of the bus. 'Please be with us now. Please keep us safe...'

Manveer slipped his hand over Ruth's. When Dorcas finished there was nothing but the noise of the bus, the growl of its engine, the bouncing and squeaking of its old joints.

Then another voice began. It was Thomas Verghese.

'Oh Holy God, Our Father,' he began. Ruth tensed. He was known for long prayers that pushed out the boundaries of ecclesiastical discourse. 'In thine infinite grace and mercy thou hast ordained the days of our lives and even the very hairs upon our miserable heads. Thou hast always granted solace in times of tribulation and protection from the vicissitudes of the evil one.' There was a blast on the bus horn. Thomas waited then raised his voice. 'On this dark night of the soul, we cry out to thee. Forgive us our iniquities. Judge us not harshly, and though we be deserving of eternal damnation, in our distress we beseech thee to extend thy mercy and spare us from the grave.'

There were a few *amens*. Mr Das clicked his tongue appreciatively.

After quiet, a voice came from near the middle of the bus. It was Kashi. No one had ever heard him pray.

'Dear God,' he said, his rough voice breaking as he spoke. Then a silence that made people wonder if he'd finished. Or perhaps was crying. But at last he continued. 'We need you.' Then another silence. And finally, 'Amen.'

The bus heaved on. No one else spoke for a moment till there was an *amen* from Shamim, the devout Muslim boy who had surprised everyone by joining the production and cheerfully playing the disciple Peter (alias Pawan). Then a cascade of *amens* around the bus. Ruth heard Manveer whisper it and she squeezed his hand. He squeezed back and stroked her thumb with his own.

Then there was a prayer from Abishek (Judas), who was Hindu, and Nina, (Woman at the Well) who was Zoroastrian, and Pema, (Martha, Roman Guard and Second Pharisee) who was Tibetan Buddhist, all interspersed with the Christian kids (assorted disciples, guards, lepers and Sadducees). Ruth was even contemplating praying herself, when there was a further blast on the horn and a volley of curses from the driver. Up ahead another swarm of lights was filling the road.

There was a sharp hiss from Manveer as he squeezed her hand, then scrambled down under the seat. The girls yanked again at their shawls, Sita swearing, Ruth starting to shake. This time the men were drunk or perhaps just delirious with rage. They howled and drummed their fists on the sides of the bus and banged open the door. Mr Haskell tried to block them but they shoved him aside and piled up the steps. They were heaving, sweating beasts, dishevelled and roaring, sticks and knives in their hands.

'Where are the Sikhs!' they shouted. 'Any Sikhs here? We will kill them!' Flaming torches lit their faces and licked the ceiling of the bus. Ruth could see streaks of dirt and grease on their faces, missing teeth, scratches.

'No Sikhs here,' insisted Mr Haskell, voice loud but wobbly, as he tried to pull one of the men back from the aisle. The man was big, with a thrusting stomach and a face flecked with blood. He swiped at Mr Haskell like a mosquito and began pushing his way down the bus.

'I will check,' he said, running his eyes over the students and banging his stick against each metal seat. As he moved closer, Ruth could see rings of sweat at his armpits and a long, dark stain down the front of his kurta. She wedged her hands under her buttocks to hide their shaking but could do nothing about the pounding in her chest. When he got to her he stopped, the bulk of him blocking the aisle, a giant hand gripping the seat in front. One of his bulging eyes lolled to one side, while the other fixed her with a lewd stare, his mouth half-open and strung with spit. As he leaned close, reeking of alcohol and sour skin, she felt sick with fear. His face inches from hers, teeth rotten, breath coming in heavy rasps, he took his stick and began lifting the shawl across her knees.

Just then a shout came from further up the bus and he swung round. Ruth breathed out and shoved the shawl back down. A weedy man was pointing at Mrs Banwarilal.

'You!' he shouted. 'You're *sadarni*!'

'I am not!' she said. 'I'm Hindu.'

'No, she's Sikh,' said the man with the stick, starting to move back up the bus. 'Look at her hair.' Her shiny tresses were today woven into a long, muscled braid that fell half way down her back.

'I am not! I swear it!' she cried, but the men were closing in.

'Leave her,' Mr Haskell shouted, trying to push his way past the men.

'Get her!' one shouted, and the stick man grabbed her arm.

'No!' screamed Mrs Banwarilal.

There was a crashing blast from the horn.

'STOP IT!' The driver jumped up on his gear box. The men turned to him in surprise. He was laughing. 'Stop it, friends! I'm your Hindu brother.' They cheered. 'Do you think I would let Sikhs ride on my bus?'

'If you did we'd kill you!' a man shouted, shaking his sickle.

'Of course! But there's no need,' the driver said, spreading his hands genially. 'Do you not believe that if there were any Sikhs on my bus, I would have killed them at once and thrown their bodies to the jackals?'

The mob crowed with delight.

'Their eyeballs to the birds!' a man squealed.

'Bones to the dogs!' cried the bus driver.

'Balls to the rats!' called another.

More cheering. The driver laughed and swayed his head. The men shook their torches and weapons in the air and trumpeted, *'Khoon ka badla khoon!'* *'Blood for blood!'* the driver echoed. The men clapped him on the back and shook his hand as they filed off the bus, chuckling and cheering. The one with the stick grabbed his head and kissed the top of it, leaving dark smears on his temples. As the bus started up, the mob drummed their fists on the side and called out praise to God.

Mrs Banwarilal was crying, and Dorcas moved to sit beside her, putting an arm around her shoulders. Ruth's shaking had taken over her whole body and tears stung her eyes as she knelt in the aisle and reached in to Manveer. He gripped her hands and she bent forward, pressing her face into his fingers. Sita twisted round in her window seat trying to see him and fumbled underneath till she found a shoulder. They patted and stroked him, murmuring softly in the cramped space as Mr Haskell came down the bus. There was little to say and his assurances sounded lame; Manveer refused to come out till the bus stopped for a toilet break. The girls squatted in the dust on one side of the road while the boys lined up on the other, a herd of them standing close around Manveer as he relieved himself into the dark. Back on the bus he sat next to Ruth again. She dusted some fluff off his turban and once the bus lights were switched off, took his hand.

Everyone was silent. It was like fear had sucked half the air out of the place and breathing was difficult, chests tight. Old Mr Das, sitting half way along, finished the last of his paan and leaned over the boy next to him to open the window. There was a sudden blast of cold, a loud spitting and then the window slammed shut. Clearing his throat, he began to sing.

'*It is dark now, my God, my God. How dark and cold now, Father God.*' It was the Song of the Cross, which Jesu begins and the others join. '*All alone now, Man of God, Save yourself, oh Son of God.*'

But no one joined Mr Das. Some watched him, a grey shadow in the dark bus. Others kept staring out the window. Others were asleep, or pretending to be. Mr Haskell sat on his front row seat, head in his hands. Ruth leaned against Manveer, resting on his shoulder, wishing to curl up inside him. Mr Das sang on, stopping once to cough and clear his throat, but starting again in his wavering voice.

'*All is lost now, Son of God, It is finished; where is your God?*'

THIRTY-ONE

James and Ruth walked across the foyer to Benson Hall, his stick tapping on the polished concrete, her running shoes squeaking. It was the Hall where she had rehearsed *Gospel* but never had an audience, where her seat was empty that last Chapel service, and where she and Manveer should have graduated with their class in a parade of saris and speeches and embracing – but hadn't. The great double doors stood wide and today a drama group was working on the stage with a young black woman.

'She's very good,' said James, with a wag of his head. 'She directed Othello in the summer. Set it during the British raj with Othello as a Muslim prince.' He clicked his tongue. 'Just wonderful.'

He smiled at Ruth but she only murmured *hmmm* and turned to look at the Senior Art paintings on the foyer wall. They were all in traditional Indian styles: Mogul scenes, Tibetan iconography, village art. One was luminous in its beauty: a face with eyes closed and a high, porcelain brow. The mouth was delicate, the eyes curved in the exquisite lines of the Buddha in meditation, the hair a flaming red.

'That's an amazing painting,' she said, moving closer. In the hair, she saw an eagle, an ox, a lion and a winged man. 'Done by a student?' She peered at the signature in the top corner. KN.

'He was in your class,' said James. 'Kashi Narayan. He

comes back now and then to work with the kids. Made a Peace Garden with them last year. Do you remember him?'

Ruth nodded.

'A very gifted artist,' he went on. 'That painting at home, you know? The woman in the desert. That's his.'

'Oh,' Ruth said, remembering the red orb in RE class and her own snickering.

'It's called Hagar's Kiss. Your mother chose it.'

James had asked her last night to make this trip with him. She had nodded but not looked up from slicing her mango. Iqbal was beside her at the kitchen bench grinding cinnamon.

'Oh yes!' he'd cried. 'Excellent plan!' As if it was news to him. In fact, it had been his idea, pressed on James so frequently and with such confidence that James had finally swallowed his fears and put it to Ruth. Iqbal was now humming as if the whole thing was settled, but James knew it was not. It would take a lot more than Iqbal's wiles to win that girl. He searched her face, but she gave nothing away. In fact, it was the kind of face that took everything – all the light from the room, the notes of Iqbal's song, the smell of spices – and stole it. The kind of face you wanted to slap.

'I've got to run a few errands,' he said, trying to sound casual. 'Thought you might like to look around.'

'Yeah, sure,' she breezed, tossing the mango stone into a plastic bucket and washing her hands.

'So much has changed. You wouldn't believe.' And he turned his gaze back to the pages of his sermon.

It wasn't going to work. He knew it already, but what else could he try? Ellen's grave had proved a disaster, as had

Hillside Hospital, and Askival was impossible. He knew she went – once even with Iqbal – and was trying to clean it up, though he could not fathom why. The place was crumbling and restoration would take more than one woman and her whitewash. But, they could not even speak of it, far less go together. Something twisted inside him, just below his diaphragm. She thought Askival was all hers: the memories, the downfall, the haunting.

And so, visiting Oaklands was his only hope. He prayed it would open spaces between them and they could make peace, but he knew that simply being there together did not take them to the same territory. It was a place they had both inhabited but an experience that was worlds apart. He acknowledged he didn't know the full truth of her life there, but neither did he trust her account of it. Hers was a history increasingly re-written over time and in conflict with the testimony of others. Yet she wielded this botched text like a legal document: a statement of the crimes against her for which she demanded harsh sentence. For which, he felt, she had already exacted years of punishment, casting himself and her mother to an emotional exile that meant Ellen died in grief. It still brought flashes of anger.

And yet – he rested his inky hands on his notes – it was true. She had been damaged. The death of that boy seemed to break something in her that never mended. He could understand grief, but not the scale of hers; from what he'd heard, she'd barely known him. And surely she could see the damage she'd caused to others was far greater, and for all her protesting, it was clear she was at fault. Perhaps that was it. Shame. The insidious destroyer. Though she held the outsides of herself together, he knew that within everything was a pile of splintered shards and from time to time you could see the sharp corners poking through and the seeping, weeping sadness of it all. And that confronted James with his own shame. For however great her guilt, and however much she slanted her story and even lied, at its heart was a terrible truth and in the dock a guilty man. He had failed her. All because of an older shame. And worst of all, he had been forced to watch Ellen punished for his guilt. It was the story of his life.

He longed to make right his wrong, to tend her wounds and flood her with healing, to reconcile her to himself and, even more, to the memory of her mother, but he could find no way to bridge the gulf. He looked back at her, studying a recipe in the Landour Community Cookbook, elfin chin thrust forward, finger curling around a tendril of hair. It made him ache. Her determination, her delicacy; under all that defiance, so fragile. He wished he had understood that long ago. Right from the start.

Turning back to the scribbled and scratched text of his sermon he made another margin note. *Faith.* The paralysed man was brought by his friends. Did he persuade them or did they persuade him? He could not have gone without them. And it was *their* faith that healed him, said Jesus.

Could James' faith heal Ruth? Could it restore her own faith? For that was his deepest prayer.

She had returned to Mussoorie. And not just at the eleventh hour to say an obligatory good-bye, but with a few months to spare. Knowing that she was not, in any technical sense, *needed,* she had still come. In that decision James had felt more hope than anything he'd seen in the past twenty-four years. But how battered that hope was now. How faint. Just enough to ask for this visit to the school. It might open a door, help him to speak, or her to speak. But how tied their tongues, and how poor.

They moved on down the big hallway. Most of the doors were closed, breathing out the thick hush of busy classrooms: pages turning, pens scratching, murmured discussions, teachers' voices lifted above the hum. But the door to the bio lab stood open and they slipped inside; it was gleaming, all white and stainless steel. Gone were the ancient wooden worktops carved with initials, the cracked ceramic sinks, the crowded shelves.

'Shit!' Ruth said. James winced. 'Where is everything?' There were no specimens in formaldehyde, no cases of beetles, no moulting silver-black kalij pheasant.

'There was a fire.'

'But your collections?' He had donated his butterflies, too, his pressed wildflowers, his ferns.

'Everything destroyed.'

'Oh my god... that's terrible.'

'Worse things happen.'

'I know but....' A hand moved to her stomach. 'All your precious things.'

There was silence. He looked away. When he had left his collections at the school in the December of 1947, it was a mere speck of dust in the landslide of loss. The nation's. His own. He wanted to tell her that story, but couldn't begin.

At the bottom of the stairs, they studied the notice boards

that ran the length of the main corridor. A large chart set out the fixtures for the Table Tennis tournament and there was a sign-up sheet for a shopping trip to Delhi, which was full, and another for cleaning the servants' quarters, which had two names. Ruth ran her eye down the list for the Honour Roll.

'Look at those,' she murmured.

'What?' James leaned in.

'The beautiful names.' Her finger slipped down the sheet. 'Sasafras Irani, Rolf Pleitgen, Wungram Shishak, Eldred Zachariah, Madoka Kumashiro, Jemima Rastogi, LeLe Aung, Cleopatra Matovu, Tensing Wangyal, Ambareen Sahoo, Meghal Jatakia, Delilah Rabbany, Song Han Lee.'

James nodded. 'Not many places in the world you get names like that side-by-side in class, eating together, sharing dorms.'

Sharing pain, Ruth thought. Swilling around together in the Melting Pot, the Fruit Salad, the Jungle.

She pointed to a poster about a series of films celebrating Independence. *Freedom: Captured on Film.*

'Looks interesting,' she said. 'Have you gone to any of those?'

'No,' said James, rubbing his ear. 'I'm not into movies.'

'I know, but I thought you might be interested, having witnessed it all.'

James dug into his trouser pocket and drew out a crumpled hanky. He blew his nose and stuffed it back.

'No.'

She snorted softly. He had never told any of his partition stories. Always got edgy, changed the subject or simply wouldn't speak. After years of turning her back on India, she now wanted to know it again, to understand.

There was a loud ringing just above their heads and the thunder of chairs and desks pushed back, a gathering storm of feet. Doors were yanked open and students poured out, rivers of them spilling along hallways, up and down stairs, around corners.

They were mainly Asian, with black and brown hair and skins in every tone from the chocolate of south India to the jasmine of Korea. Here and there was an African face, or a European, a blonde head, a flash of ginger. Some had arms looped casually around each other, a group were laughing, one boy sang.

Beautiful faces with beautiful names.

It did not look like a jungle, or pain.

The bell overhead rang again and the last trickle of students slithered into classrooms as doors closed.

'There are hardly any westerners now,' she said.

'No, not so many western missionaries in South Asia.'

'I see.' Thank god, she thought.

'In my time,' he said, 'it was nearly all white kids. Mainly American missionaries, a few from other places and just a handful of Indians, like Paul Verghese.'

'So, the missionary era's kind of over then, is it?'

'Oh no. Plenty of these are mish kids, but their parents are Asian.'

'Really?'

'Yes. There are more missionaries in the world now than ever before, but you wouldn't recognise them.'

'Dear me,' she muttered. 'That's a bit frightening.' She had long ago signed up to the popular charges against the missionary endeavour: missionaries destroyed cultures, imposed western beliefs on the rest of the world, exploited poverty to further their spiritual ends. This swelling of the ranks by Asian Christians was unsettling.

In the Quad they wove their way through the games of tag and skipping to the stairs in the corner. James made slow progress, gripping the banister and breathing hard, a small thread of spit swinging from his mouth. Ruth wiped it with a tissue, realising it was the first gesture of physical care she had given to either of her parents.

At the top of the stairs they stepped into Lower Dorm, except it was no longer a dorm. In place of the cupboards and bunks and cold concrete, a sprung wooden floor gleamed in the sunlight. Where Kozy Korner had been was now a thick red rug bearing a harmonium, a pair of tabla and a sitar.

'Indian dance studio,' James said.

The door to Miss Joshi's apartment opened and a young woman in jeans and bare feet walked through. Her face, framed by a short pixie cut, was open and lovely, a tiny diamond glittering in her nose.

'Hello,' she said. 'Can I help you?' Then she frowned. 'Ruthie Connor?! Is it you?' She skipped across the room and clasped her hands. 'I'm Neetu! Neetu Banwarilal, remember?'

With peels of laughter, she embraced Ruth and told how she'd followed her mother's footsteps, but how Mrs Banwarilal had died two years before.

'She was still choreographing to the end. Her last project was with Kashi Narayan – remember him? Iqbal was singing in it too, and lots of kids dancing. All about creation. Such a wonderful thing!'

'Sounds it.'

'But what do you think of this place?' Neetu waved her delicate hand across the studio.

'Incredible. Such a change from Lower Dorm.'

'Yeah? I was never in boarding. What was it like?'

'Depends who you ask,' said Ruth. 'I hated it.'

James shifted on his stick.

'Oh,' Neetu said softly, shooting a look at him. 'I think it's a lot better now. The dorms are very bright and homey and the kids are really happy.'

'How nice for them,' said Ruth and walked over to one of the windows. It looked out to the eastern ranges that faded to smudges on the horizon. A lammergeyer vulture hung above them, motionless, its wingspan wide on the air. In grade two she had lain on her bunk beside this window and wished she could fly.

The greeting from Neetu was echoed many times by a handful of ageing teachers, grey-haired secretaries and long-serving employees, whose faces lit at the sight of her. She was known, remembered and contrary to her belief, welcomed. Some even said, 'Welcome home.' It un-nerved her.

As they walked down the winding path from the school to the residences, a watery sunlight filtered through the trees and the air carried notes of pine and moss. James pointed his stick at a clump of ferns, bedraggled and yellowing.

'That means monsoon is nearly over,' he said.

She was silent. There was no sound but their footsteps and the tapping of his stick.

'You were happy, too, Ruthie,' he said, at last, so quietly it was almost a whisper. 'Some of the time. You were.'

'How would you know?'

'Hannah said so, and your teachers.'

'They would say that.'

'But they knew you, they cared about you. Mrs Banwarilal, the Parks, Mr Haskell.'

That last name shot her. She was galled he would cite the very man whose lie had seen her expelled in unbearable distress and – worse – blamed for Manveer's death. But they had always believed him over her.

She almost spoke but stifled it.

At the boys' residence they found the young dorm parent up a ladder repairing a basketball net. Winston, from Assam, was proud of his patch and happy to show them around. The whole residence was recently refurbished and the room they entered had new fitted bunks, cheerful curtains and rugs. James smiled as he looked around him.

'Boy, it sure is different,' he said shaking his head, one hand resting on his chest.

'When were you here?' asked Winston.

'At Oaklands? Oh, on and off from 1936 till I guess... December 47. Four to sixteen. My folks worked in Bareilly, but they were on the hillside a lot too, so I was out of boarding half the time.'

'Wow,' said Winston. 'Not many kids are here for that long any more. And we don't take them in boarding till third grade, anyway.'

'That's good,' said James. 'Four is a little young.' And he walked to the large window that looked west over the bazaar.

Ruth examined the posters of rock stars and motorbikes.

'What was it like back then?' asked Winston.

'Oh, it was good,' said James. 'And bad. I was homesick at first. Cried a lot.' He glanced at Ruth but she did not look back.

'Yeah, I'm sure,' said Winston. 'No luxuries is those days, eh?'

'No, no, not at all.' Though it was not the spartan facilities that had caused pain. It was the older boys taunting him for his wonky teeth and his wet bed. Every night they'd stolen his teddy bear and tossed it round the dorm till he was a whirling dervish of fury and snot and tears. Until one of his fists finally hit a nose and there was a jet of blood and a howl. It was a rite of passage and no-one took his teddy bear again. But instead of feeling triumphant he had lain in bed stroking the bear's ear and wondering what his mother would think.

All he said to Winston was, 'No, no luxuries. Just one *chula* in the common room and no heat in the dorms.'

'Really? These guys all have their own heater.'

'And we had bucket baths. Showers when you got to senior hostel, but sometimes they were cold.'

'No!'

He didn't explain this was for punishment, like when *Private Patsy* was discovered. Even Ellen never heard about that.

'Twice a week – Wednesday and Saturday,' he said.

'No way. These boys get hot showers every day. They can pick morning, afternoon or evening.'

'Like a hotel!'

'Yeah, and they think I'm room service.'

'What's the food like now?' asked James.

'Well the kids always complain, of course, but I think it's pretty good. They have a choice – either an Indian meal or something Western.'

'Do they know how lucky they are?' asked James.

'I keep telling them, but maybe we should get you in to do devotions one night, Dr Connor.'

'I'd like that.'

'Are devotions still compulsory or do the kids get a choice about that too?' asked Ruth, speaking for the first time.

'Up to eighth grade they're still compulsory,' said Winston.

'No way. You mean you still make all these Hindu and Muslim and Buddhist kids sit through Christian indoctrination every night? I thought the place had moved on a bit.'

Winston shrugged. 'It's still a Christian school. The parents know the deal.'

'No, they don't. They think their kids will just have to sit through a few boring talks. What they don't realise is that an army of evangelical teachers and pupils are on a hunt for their souls.'

James gripped his stick.

'That's a little harsh,' Winston said.

'You can't deny it! I remember it well. Feverishly praying for all the non-Christians. "The lost" we called them. Some of the poor bastards were so miserable and homesick they'd come along to any Bible study as long as there was home-baking and a caring Mrs Somebody to talk to. And once you were there you couldn't withstand the pressure for long. Everybody singing and looking at you meaningfully, raising hands, calling on the love of Jesus. You didn't stand a chance.'

'Sounds like you escaped,' observed Winston.

Her stare was cold.

'I was thrown out,' she said.

THIRTY-TWO

It was James who first dropped Ruth off at school. The task fell to him because Ellen couldn't face it, though the girls never knew. He had brought her and Hannah on the overnight train from Kanpur, then the bus from Dehra Dun and finally the long trudge through the bazaar with a trail of coolies. In Long Dorm he saw their trunks installed in their cubicles and struggled through a polite conversation with Miss Joshi.

At last it was time to go. He nodded dutifully at the chattering dorm mother and, with a hand fumbling the handkerchief in his pocket, turned to look at the girls. They were sitting cross-legged in the Kozy Korner playing dolls with Sita. The new little friend wore her hair in bunches tied with incongruous pink ribbons that matched her frilly dress. Miss Joshi had pointed out her bed right next to Ruth's. They were both in Grade 1, both six years old, though Sita, having arrived the day before, established her authority on all subjects, including the care of dolls. At that moment she was stripping Ruth's doll and giving instructions on bathing, while ten-year old Hannah rummaged in a shoebox for its pyjamas. Ruth was rocking Sita's doll to sleep.

James called them, his voice steady. 'Hannah, Ruthie. It's time now.'

Ruth was too busy. 'Shhh!' she hissed, pressing a finger against her lips.

Hannah dropped the pyjamas and ran to him, throwing her arms around his waist and pressing her face into his woollen sweater. He patted the top of her head and looked across to Ruth, who was kissing her doll.

'Dad's gotta go now, *Piyari*.'

For a moment she seemed not to have heard, but then suddenly shoved the doll between a pair of cushions and scampered across, throwing her arms around both father and sister. James bent forward and rubbed their backs, smelling the mingling of shampoo and exhaust fumes in their hair. There was a slight ache in his throat. He swallowed and straightened up.

'Goodbye, my good girls,' he said, a hand on each shoulder.

'Where are you going?' Ruth asked.

The question shocked him. 'Home. To Mommy.'

She looked puzzled.

'But aren't you staying with us?'

'No. Daddy's going back to the hospital.'

'Why?'

'Because...' he stammered, 'it's what I do. It's my work.'

Ruth gazed at him. 'I want to go, too.'

He couldn't believe it. They'd been over this so many times. How could she still not understand? Hannah came to his rescue.

'No, Ruthie. We're staying here at school and we'll go home at vacation.'

'But who's going to look after us?' asked Ruth, genuinely baffled.

'I am!' fluted Miss Joshi, beaming down at her a little too brightly. 'We're going to have a super time!' Her eyes were ringed with so much kohl they were like twin bruises in her oily face.

Ruth studied her for a moment, then turned back to her father. 'When's vacation? Is it the weekend?'

James felt panic rising inside him. Hannah had never been like this. 'Not the weekend, *Piyari,* but not too long. Mom's gonna come up and visit you in a couple months.'

Her face quivered. 'I want Mommy now.'

'But Ruthie, Mommy's not here—'

'I want to go home!' she wailed and hurled herself at James. He felt sweat breaking across his neck and armpits.

'Oh–ho,' he murmured huskily, patting her back. 'Oh-ho now...'

Hannah wrapped herself around Ruth from behind and said *shh-shh-shh.* Miss Joshi clicked her tongue and, from the other side of the room, Sita stared.

James disentangled himself and pulled a wadded hanky from his pocket.

'Now, now, that's enough now,' he said sternly and dabbed at Ruth's wet face. 'You need to be good and make Mom and Dad proud.' She still shuddered with sobs. 'Make Jesus proud.'

This brought on a fresh flood of tears.

'Daddy has to go now or he'll miss the bus.' His voice was snappy and he hated it. He gave the hanky to Hannah and put a hand on her smooth, shiny hair, his other on Ruth's tangle of curls.

'Remember, girls, the Lord Jesus is always with you.'

He had been meaning to pray over them, but could feel a crack opening up inside him and everything beginning to slide towards it. Quickly he dropped a rough kiss on each face – Hannah's soft and still, Ruth's a wet mess – and pulled back before her out-flung arms could catch him.

'Bye, now!' he called as he pushed out the door, just aware of Hannah hugging Ruth, and Ruth starting to scream.

He ran down the stairs of Lower Dorm and wanted to keep running for a long time, but his coolie was waiting with his bag in the Quad, and he had to stop and breathe and hide the crack that was widening inside. He rubbed his hand over his chest and gave a small tilt of his head. The coolie tilted in return and stood up, shouldering the bedroll.

They walked out the school gate and down the road, the monsoon mist a cold breath through the trees. The faint sound of bells and clopping hooves grew louder as a party of *dudh-wallas* appeared, large milk cans clinking on the saddles and a ripe smell of donkey, dung and sour clothes filling the air. James and the coolie walked west towards the bruised sky and the first lights of the bazaar, past the sprawling untidiness of Mullingar, with its lines of washing like seaweed on the hull of a ship, and all the way down to the bus stand at Paramount Picture House. From there, the bus zig-zagged three thousand feet down the mountain, blasting its horn and swaying at every bend, finally disgorging its green-gilled passengers a hundred metres from the railway station. It was night now, and the light bulbs on the road-side stalls glowed under their speckling of grease and dirt.

In the second-class compartment that James was sharing with a Tibetan lama and a family from Meerut, he laid out his bedding roll on the top bunk, put his wash kit and frayed hand-towel on top and took out his Bible. The lama nodded to him and smiled, his fingers sliding over prayer beads, his burgundy and saffron robes falling to a pair of Adidas running shoes. The mother and grandmother of the Meerut family were organising dinner, opening aluminium tiffin carriers and instructing the others on where to sit and what to hold. Each carrier was a stack of three round tins that opened to reveal rice, chapattis and an array of curries. The mother offered food to the lama, who lifted a hand in refusal and blessing, and then to James, who thanked them but already had chai in a clay cup and a bag of samosas. He offered these in turn, but they too declined with much smiling and tilting of heads and exclamations at his Hindi. He thanked them, then turned his attention to his Bible. The Meerut father, however, was expansive and not deterred by James reading. Eager to practice his English, he asked after his good name and his citizenship. Normally James gave himself with full attention to these encounters, but found this time he struggled through the customary conversation about his work as a doctor in Kanpur, his childhood in India, whether he was married and how many issues he had. Naturally the man wanted to know where these fine daughters were being educated, and when James explained that he had just left them at Oaklands, the man from Meerut puffed his cheeks and blew out, spit trembling on his lips.

'Oh, Doctor-sahib. You are very lucky to afford such a school for your children. And they are so lucky, likewise. Lucky, lucky, lucky,' he murmured, wagging his head.

Lucky James nodded and dropped his gaze to the Bible. The Gospel of Luke, underlined verses: *'I tell you the truth,'* *Jesus said to them, 'no one who has left home or wife or brothers* *or parents or children for the sake of the kingdom of God will fail* *to receive many times as much in this age and, in the age to come,* *eternal life.'*

There was a chug from under the train, a hiss of steam and a jerk that threw them forward. The whistle blew, late passengers scuttled for doors and coolies followed with teetering trunks. For two minutes all was shouting and shoving and the smells of soot and bodies till the brakes wheezed, the whistle's haunting cry rang again and the train pulled out of Dehra Dun. James looked up at the mountain. Its outline was hidden against the black sky so that the lights of Mussoorie lay scattered across it like a range of lower stars.

He knew that one shone for Hannah and Ruth. Closing his eyes, he pressed his hand over his mouth and gave his body to the rocking of the train.

THIRTY-THREE

He stood on the platform at Bareilly Station in 1937 and felt his hand sweating inside his mother's. It was early March but already the sky was like a sheet of beaten tin, the air thick. They both wore wide-brimmed *topis* but it didn't stop James squinting as he looked down the shimmering tracks. He was five and waiting for the Doon Express to take him back to Oaklands for his second year in boarding. This time last year, the whole thing had been an adventure and he'd nearly wet his shorts with excitement as he'd joined the Calcutta Herd on the train and waved a wild goodbye to his parents.

But now he knew where he was going.

The station was a churning sea of life. Women in limp saris clutched children and cloth bundles and bickered while their men folk went for tickets or cigarettes or a newspaper twist of peanuts. Thin, rangy coolies wove through the crowd with trunks and cases balanced on their turbans, as dogs trotted amongst them, sniffing, ravaging small piles of rubbish and spraying urine on pillars. Vendors moved up and down calling out in ceaseless sing-song tones. *Paan, bidi, cigarette!* The tobacconist – teeth and fingers stained red from betel nut – had his wares arranged in a large tray suspended from his neck and the smell was a mingling of fresh green leaves, hot chilli and smoke. James watched the chai-walla push past with his gleaming samovar and a teetering stack of earthen cups on a cart. When he served the tea it was with a magician's skill, first filling a cup from the copper tap, then adding a splash of milk and two spoons of sticky grey sugar, and finally mixing the lot by pouring the tea backwards and forwards between two cups, gradually drawing them further and further apart till the tea flowed in a rippling brown arc. Behind him came a water seller with a bloated goat skin slung across his back, its head gone, legs sticking out as if in shock. *Hindu jal! Hindu jal!* he cried, and stopped for a man squatting near James. The goat's neck served as spout and the water poured in a clear stream down the drinker's throat, his Adam's apple bobbing, nothing spilling or touching his lips. Further down the platform another vendor with a goat skin was hawking *Muslim jal.* James' Christian jal, boiled and cooled, was in the tin canteen at his hip.

There was a hollow ache in his stomach and the smell of the puris sizzling in hot oil nearby made him feel sick. His father appeared, sweat spreading at the armpits of his shirt, grey trousers held firm by his thick belt. He smiled at James from under his topi and held out a stick of sugar cane.

'There you are, son,' he said. James took the cane with his free hand.

'Thank you,' he whispered, mouth dry as leaves.

There was a distant wail of horn and the platform heaved. Coolies without luggage leapt forward, mothers grabbed stray children and men barked orders. The train appeared, a great chugging beast spewing smoke and steam, horn shrieking as it slowed down in a hiss of brakes. Before it had even stopped, the coolies were upon it, like trappers with a wild animal, leaping up its flanks, gripping on bars and handles. Doors were flung open and at each compartment there was a colliding of bodies as people tried to get out and others in, some resorting to windows, others to scrambling over their neighbours. James felt his mother tug on his hand as she started striding down the platform.

'Which bogey is it?' she called over her shoulder. Stanley was helping the coolie lift James' trunk and bedding roll onto his head.

'G!' he shouted and came after them. The train did not stop for long, which was an absurdity since Bareilly was a big station and the same train would loiter for long, unexplained stretches in the middle of the night at empty platforms where there was nothing but sleeping beggars and flies crawling over a single bulb.

A rotund man with half-moon glasses jumped out of a third class compartment and waved. It was Bishop Lutz from Calcutta, who had drawn the short straw and was the designated chaperone for the Calcutta Herd, which included his three wild sons. Leota broke into a run and James' legs pumped furiously to keep up, his hand almost slipping from hers. Several grinning faces appeared at the window as the Oaklands kids looked to see who was joining them. One boy was firing hard popcorn kernels at stray dogs, while another was calling to the cigarette walla. James recognised Raymond Clutterbuck with his red hair and mean laugh. Stanley arrived with the coolie trotting behind and James' bed roll and tin trunk were passed through the door and added to the pile of luggage in the centre of the compartment. The train whistle blew in a long, sickening wail and James felt a flood of panic. He gripped his mother's hand.

'Goodbye JimBob,' she said, with determined cheer and

knocked playfully on the top of his topi. 'Have fun.'

He bit his lip, but it was useless. His face was already crumpling, eyes spilling over. Stanley scowled at him from under his topi.

'Time to get on, son,' he said, voice a little gruff.

James shook his head wildly.

'No... no... no,' he gasped, tears running down his face now. 'Please...?' He saw his mother's face change, just for an instant, like a curtain dropping and revealing a naked grief he should not have seen. But then the curtain snapped back and the vigorous cheer returned. She even laughed.

Stanley did not. His face was turning red. The whistle screamed again.

'No son of mine cries like a baby. Now get on the train.' And he yanked James from his mother's side and half-pushed him into the compartment. There was a hiss of brakes, a great clanking and a jerk as the train began to roll. James looked out through the blur of tears at his mother's waving hand and fixed smile and at his father, one hand on a hip the other lifted, whether in blessing or banishment James never knew.

THIRTY-FOUR

In Shanti Niwas, Ruth opened the battered shoe box on the coffee table and untied the ribbon. The letter on top was the first she had sent home at the end of her first week in boarding. Aged six, she was not able to write much and the page was dominated by a drawing of a princess. Above it, in thick lead pencil, she had scrawled, 'dir MomndaD hauUryu iAmfYn' Underneath the picture, the word 'rUTh' was almost obliterated by a storm of hug and kiss signs. The whole thing was rather smudged. On the outside, Miss Joshi had written, 'Ruth is settling in very nicely.'

She put the letter down on the table and picked up the next one. Near her, in the kitchen area, Iqbal was humming as he chopped vegetables for pakoras. James had gone for his weekly Bible Study at Paul Verghese's house, Firclump, and had refused an escort, despite his bent hobbling, now with two sticks.

A pale light filtered into the room from a sun beginning to emerge at the end of monsoon. It was like a delicate queen recovering from flu, appearing on her balcony, still wrapped in blankets of cloud, raising a limp hand and a smile for her subjects, but with little strength.

In the cool, Ruth crossed her legs on the sofa and tucked them under her shawl. The letters were much the same for the first few weeks: a large picture – usually princess, bride or fairy – a few illegible words and an occasional cover sentence from Miss Joshi, who had inspected the inside. 'Ruth is getting better at dressing herself.' 'Ruth is learning to eat up all her food.'

The week Miss Joshi's inspections ceased, however, the golden-haired heroine was crying. Her enormous tears flew to the far corners of the page and the writing beneath said, 'i HAT it hir!!!!!!!!' Miss Joshi had written on the outside, 'Ruth is a delight in the dorm.'

Folding the letter, she remembered her first night in boarding. After James had gone and the bearer rang the dinner bell, the twenty Lower Dorm girls ran to the sinks and shoved their hands under sputtering blasts of cold water. Hannah helped Ruth, trying to get her to use soap, though Ruth could see that no-one else did. Sita was one of the quickest and shouted, 'Last one's a smelly pig!' as she shot down the stairs at the front of the pack. Hannah and Ruth were the last and arrived to a howling of *Smelly pigs! Smelly pigs! Oink, oink, ha, ha!* till Miss Joshi appeared, swishing in her socks and chappals, and clapping her hands for silence.

After grace, they filed across the dinner hall to the servery where a row of bearers in white jackets and topis stood behind stainless-steel vats of food. Hannah gave a plastic tray to Ruth and meekly held out her own to the first bearer. Dinner that night was Meat and Potatoes, a greasy concoction of mutton bits floating in a soupish gravy with chunks of vegetable. That was slopped into the main compartment and a spade-full of mashed potato thwacked beside it. Then into one of the corner slots of the tray went some long-boiled cabbage and into another a wobbling slice of iridescent jelly.

'*Thora, thora*!' the girls cried. *Just a little bit, just a little bit!* Everything that hit the tray had to be eaten and the scraped dish inspected by Miss Joshi before it could be pushed into the washing-up hatch.

'This is yummy, *na*?' said Sita, shovelling forkfuls into her mouth.

Ruth rested her head on her hand and stared at the food.

'Come on, Ruth,' Hannah cajoled. 'You have to eat it or you'll get bawled out.'

Long after everyone else had gone upstairs, Ruth was still sitting at the table with Miss Joshi beside her. The dorm mother had gone beyond gentle encouragements: 'Come on, sweetie,' and lies: 'It's delicious,' and threats: 'You won't get any Candy Cupboard on Sunday,' to sharpening her final weapon: 'I'll have to write to Mummy and Daddy and tell them you've not been a very good little girl. They won't be at all happy about that, now will they?' Blackmail usually worked where all else failed, but so far it was just producing twin trails of tears down Ruth's dirty face.

Iqbal poured oil into his *kadai* and turned on the gas, his eyes slipping to Ruth. He saw her smile over some of the early letters, and then go quiet. Some she held onto for a long time, before adding them to the growing pile on the table. As she read, she tugged on a curl of hair just above her right ear. He dropped balls of battered pakora into the hot oil and checked his *dekchi* of spiced chai. As he cooked he sang an Urdu *ghazal* by Faiz.

'*Why have you tattooed yourself with these wounds?*'

His voice rose and swelled and dropped and trembled, his

cheeks quivering, lips soft. Lifting the freshly cooked pakoras onto a plate, he poured some chai into a mug and carried them over to Ruth. She was lying down on the sofa, the shawl up over her mouth, tears dripping off the end of her nose.

Iqbal nudged some of the letters aside to make space for the mug and plate.

'*Lahore pakore,*' he said, '*aur garam chai.*'

Ruth didn't move. Iqbal returned to the kitchen corner and sang on as he added more pakoras to the *kadai*.

'*When the night has passed,*
A hundred new roads will blossom.
You must steady your heart,
For it has to break many, many times.'

He had nearly finished frying them all when Ruth sat up and spoke, her gaze fixed beyond the window.

'Iqbal?'

'Yes.'

'Have you seen these letters?'

'Of course not. Your father is not showing me your private things.'

She was quiet for a while, then picked up the chai and sipped it.

'I want you to read them,' she said.

Iqbal poured his own chai and leaned back against the kitchen bench, looking at her. She turned to him, her face wobbly and blotched, eyes a bright wet green.

'So you will know my story.'

'Yes. Of course.' He slurped his chai. 'In exchange for one thing.'

'What?'

'You read the letters about your mother.' He pointed to the box in the corner of the living room that she had not opened. 'The ones sent to Doctor-ji after she is going home.'

THIRTY-FIVE

The bus crept into Mussoorie in the grey dawn of Sunday morning. Nearly everyone was asleep, flopped against windows, bags, each other. They began waking on the rutted bumps of New Road, feeling stiff and cold but at once flushed with relief at the sight of the school. Ruth wiped her mouth with the back of a chapped hand, hoping Manveer hadn't noticed her dribbling. He opened his eyes and smiled at her.

'So!' said Abishek, appearing from a seat further up, grinning, his hair sticking out in tufts. 'The Virgin Veeru has just slept with a whole busload of girls.'

Sita hurled her book at him.

That night was Compulsory Chapel. It rolled round twice a semester and was deeply resented by most who weren't Christians and an embarrassment to most who were. This was largely down to Mrs Cornfoot's toe-curling solos, or Chaplain Park preaching for too long, or someone giving a testimony that reduced the teller to tears but half the students to sniggers. It was better when Mr Haskell led it, filling the hall with candles and music and his slides of India, but he was not in charge tonight. Indeed, he was barely speaking. He stood at the entrance to Benson Hall stone-faced, ticking off names on his clipboard.

The students arrived in clouds of scent and pheromones.

The girls wore dresses with shoulder pads and floppy bows, or shalwar kameez in jewel colours, or smartly tailored trousers, high-waisted and narrow at the ankle. Most had handbags, glossy hair-dos and lashings of makeup, and they twittered as they sat in the foyer to change from running shoes (for the trudge up the hill from the dorms) into high heels. The boys that hovered around them like moths had metamorphosed from their usual grubby jeans to a crisp display of pressed shirts, gelled hair and clean teeth. Although officially begrudged, Compulsory Chapel provided unique opportunities for mating rituals which were seized with enthusiasm.

As the flocks of hormone-charged teenagers settled into their seats and the first hymn struck up, Mr Haskell noted two names not ticked on his list.

Ruth and Manveer had met on the path up to Chapel and fell behind the others. He offered to carry her shoes. Dove grey with bows on top, their purchase had been the high point of Ruth's previous furlough in the States. She had hardly believed she was allowed them, but Ellen had just nodded and smiled and let her take all the time in the world choosing. As Ruth paraded up and down the shop, she'd seen her mother's gaze drifting to a pair of red kitten heels. She'd stroked the patent leather, but realising Ruth was watching, just laughed and put them back with a thump.

'Will you look at those! Ridiculous!'

Ruth's shoes were getting a bit tight and scuffed now and the rubber cap on one of the soles had fallen off so she made an uneven sound when she walked: *clomp, click, clomp, click.* But she knew there would be no new shoes till the next furlough – apart from Bata chappals and the frumpy things made by the *mochi* in the bazaar – so she treasured these. As did Manveer, it seemed, from the way he carried them. They walked slowly so as not to ruin the effects of intensive grooming.

Ruth had spent most of the day sleeping and fantasising about him. The danger he'd been in made him even more attractive to her, and in the afternoon she'd got up, thighs aching with desire, and gone to the toilet where she'd rubbed herself into a mouth-gaping spasm of pleasure. Flopped back against the wall, feeling the familiar rush of heat and guilt, she'd wiped her finger on a square of toilet paper and flushed.

After her shower – still dripping slightly under her frayed dressing gown – she'd stood before her open cupboard and agonised. Sita's advice was not as expansive as usual and she was preoccupied with threading her moustache. So Ruth set off, rubber chappals flapping, down the concrete corridors, from room to room, begging, rummaging, trying things on, taking suggestions, rejecting suggestions till finally, minutes before the dinner bell, her outfit was complete: her own grey cotton twills (bought the same day as the shoes, and a tad short now) with a white frilled blouse (made by Farooqi Tailors in the bazaar to copy the latest Laura Ashley), a scarlet cardigan (knitted by Grandma Leota) and an elegant charcoal coat (borrowed from Sita, as were the nylons, though she had seemed a little reluctant about the loans, stressing that the coat was new, pure wool and very expensive.) Ruth styled her hair into a soft, curly halo and (in long-established defiance of parental ban) applied dramatic make-up: green eye shadow, thick black lashes and lips glossed to a hot cherry. The finishing touch to her deviant glamour were the new nails, matching the red and gold bangles that had been bought specially for the part of Maya.

Now, with Manveer at her side, she was glad she'd made the effort. He shot her shy, approving looks and said she looked nice. In turn, she thought him more handsome than ever in black trousers and turban, a pale pink Oxford shirt and a down jacket.

'How you doin?' she asked. 'Must be pretty shaken up.'

'A bit. But I was so bushed and so relieved to be back I just crashed.'

'Me too,' she said. 'I had the weirdest dreams.'

'Like what?'

'I'm not saying.' She smiled.

'Why not? Come on, tell me.' He gave her arm a soft punch.

'No way, man. Too embarrassing.' She playfully pushed the hand back but let her fingers tangle in his.

'Oh, I bet I can guess.' He was still holding her hand. There was no one else on their stretch of path.

'What then?' she teased, stepping closer to him, her face lifted.

'I'm not telling.'

'Manveer!' She swatted him. 'Tell me!'

He tucked her shoes under his arm and captured her flailing hand.

'Ok, ok,' he grinned. 'After chapel. I'll walk you back. You tell me yours and I'll tell you mine.'

'No. Now.'

'We haven't got time.'

'Then ditch chapel.'

He looked shocked. 'It's compulsory.'

'I don't care.'

'But you're Christian!'

She took a breath. 'Not any more. I don't give a damn about that now. I just want to talk.'

'Could be big trouble,' he said, searching her face. She knew he was careful about rules. There were great expectations on him. Family savings, family reputation, family dreams.

'It's just skipping chapel,' she murmured. 'What's the worst thing that can happen?'

He continued up the hill, drawing her with him, walking in silence. As they came out of the trees at the school buildings they stopped to look south. The sun was a vivid ball with a train of fire-lit clouds. Below it lay the dusky ridge of the bazaar and the Winter Line, a belt of red and gold that stretched across the sky, dividing the light above from the well of black below.

He tugged on her hand. 'Where d'you want to go?'

In Benson Hall, as the final chords of the hymn faded, Mr Haskell leaned across a couple of stiffly coiffed girls and touched Sita on the arm. She turned to him, huge brown eyes cool in her sculpted face.

'Sita, do you know where Ruth is?'

She raised one eyebrow.

'Or Manveer?'

Her eyes narrowed. On the stage, Mr Park was tapping the microphone and starting to speak, so Mr Haskell dropped his voice to a whisper.

'Any idea where they might have gone?'

They moved quietly up the forest path, slipping like shadows through the trees. Behind them, the sun slid through the Winter Line and disappeared into the dark, leaving the sky gaping, haemorrhaging colour. Feeling their way with their feet as the light dimmed, they talked. About why she wasn't a Christian anymore and the fear on that bus trip and how sad it was about *The Gospel of Jyoti*. Manveer said he admired Mr Haskell's talent and passion and hoped the Oaklands performance would compensate for the loss of the Delhi ones, but Ruth just murmured yes and changed the subject. As they walked, they held hands like their lives depended on it.

It was a steep climb to the top of the hill and then long and dark round the back *chakkar*. They walked quickly past the graveyard, giggling as they recounted the stories (mainly Sita's) and felt their flesh prickle. When they got to Askival it was waiting, silent, and full of shadows. They stood on the south veranda looking down at the lights of Dehra Dun, a blaze of fallen stars on a black lake. The air was so cold and clear it brought a sharpness to everything: the silver rim of the moon, the smell of pine, the pure notes of an owl. Ruth shivered and he pulled her into the folds of his down jacket, her back against his chest. He smelt of freshly ironed clothes and a grown-up aftershave, although he never shaved. His beard tickled as she rested her head into his neck.

'Manveer,' she whispered.

'Mmm?' He tightened his arms around her, lowering his face so his cheek brushed hers, the folded edge of his turban against her ear.

'Show me your hair.'

For a moment he was perfectly still. Breath held. She

wondered if she had broken some rule. Were Sikh men not supposed to reveal their hair? Or not to women? Or not to non-Sikhs? Then she felt a rush of warm breath on her neck and a tight squeeze of his arms.

'Ok.' His voice was husky. 'Just don't laugh.'

She twisted round. 'I would never laugh at you, Manveer.'

He studied her face, then undid the pins on his turban and lifted it off. Underneath there was the cotton *patka* in a top knot, which he unravelled, revealing the dark coil of his hair, held in place by a small wooden comb. Ruth reached up and tugged the comb free.

'My *kanga*,' he whispered. 'Keep it safe.' She slipped it into her back pocket and unwound his hair till it fell in soft, curling sheaves down to his chest. As she teased out the tangles, he slipped his arms around her waist, eyes resting on her. She met his gaze, and drew back the hair from the sides of his face, breathing in the smell of shampoo and sandalwood. He pulled her closer, lowering his face as she lifted hers, till they closed their eyes and kissed. Just one, light and brushing, electric, kiss. Then another, and another. Gentle, soft-pressing kisses, faces stroking against each other, noses bumping and lips beginning to part. And then the deeper tasting, the stronger pressure, the hunger and giving and the flood of feeling in breasts, navel and thighs. Ruth had never felt anything like this. Anything so sweet and yearning and deep as Manveer's intoxicating mouth. Anything so thrilling as him whispering that he had never kissed a girl before, and he never wanted to stop.

So they did not stop. They kept kissing and holding and feeling, hands moving softly under the thick folds of jacket and coat. And they continued kissing as they tugged shirts up, slowly, inch by inch, and touched cold fingertips to warm skin. And they kept on kissing, as their hands slid like blue flame over liquored backs. And still they did not stop as he stroked over her bra and then under it, both of them moaning as he found her nipples. And there was certainly no stopping once she discovered the line of hair that led down from his navel.

They lay tangled together on the dirty floor of the living room, Sita's coat spread beneath them, his jacket above. They were still as tree roots. Just the breathing and the blinking of eyes, the soft fall of his hair across their skin. Outside, the pine trees were hushing and whispering in a light breeze. The moon was higher, brighter, a curved and gleaming blade against the black.

As a small gust of wind blew into the room, Ruth flinched and tucked her legs up under the jacket, pushing her icy feet between Manveer's thighs.

'Yow!!' He yelped and pulled back. 'You are frozen!'

'I know,' she laughed, tugging him close again. 'Aren't you?'

'No. I've never felt so warm.' He kissed her. 'But you should probably get some clothes on.'

They sat up and found their underwear, using it to wipe the sticky spillage from their thighs, then tossing it to the side. Sita's coat was a mess. Their trousers were cold, the fabric hard and unyielding as they tugged them on, shirts and socks gritty from the floor. Ruth brushed pine needles and dirt from Grandma Leota's cardigan and could feel it unravelling on one sleeve. She buttoned it up.

'Do you need help with your turban?'

Manveer was feeling around on the floor and didn't answer.

'I think you left it on the veranda.' She went out and found it, lying like an empty bowl beside a pillar. The *patka* was beside it. 'I've got a brush if you want,' she said, stepping back into the living room and reaching for her bag. She fumbled and searched, then tipped it out onto the floor, makeup, wallet and brush falling along with a crumpled hanky and a couple of dusty joints.

'Oops,' she giggled, but he didn't seem to have noticed. He was squatting beside the fireplace, holding something, his hair spilling over his shoulders like the delta of an inky river.

'What's that?'

'My *kirpan*.' He drew a small knife out of a leather sheath.

'A penknife?'

'No. Didn't you listen in RE?' he teased.

'Probably not.'

'The Five Ks?'

'Oh yeah, your long hair and stuff.'

'Exactly. The hair is *kesh*, *kanga's* in your pocket—'

'*Kara's* on your wrist,' she said, touching his steel bangle.

'*Kachha* is a mess,' he pointed to the wadded underwear on the floor and they both laughed. 'And this is *kirpan*.'

'Shit, I didn't know you had that on you all the time.'

'It was always just a ritual thing, you know, a habit, like combing my hair or putting on socks. I never really thought about it until today. After that bus trip and all. When I put it on, I felt so much anger... and hate.' The knife glinted as he turned it. 'I wanted to kill all those people who were killing my brothers. Who tried to kill me.'

Ruth watched him, uncertain. The breeze in the pines was picking up, like the rushing of waves.

'Are you going to do your turban?' she asked softly, holding it out to him.

He shook his head. 'No.'

'You going back to the dorm like that?'

'It doesn't matter how I go back, everything's changed now, hasn't it?' He raised his eyes to hers. 'It's nearly 9.30, Ruth. Check in was half an hour ago.'

'Oh, my god, I'm so sorry, Manveer. I've got you in trouble. I'm sorry, I—'

'No.' He put the kirpan on the mantelpiece and pulled her to him. The turban fell to the floor. 'I'm not sorry.'

'But your parents! The school will write and tell them and—'

'And your parents.'

'Mine have already had lots of letters, believe me, and I don't...' She felt the stinging of tears. 'I don't give a shit, anymore. They've given up on me.'

Manveer pressed her into the nest of his jacket. 'No, no,' he whispered, stroking her head. She was starting to cry. 'How could they not adore you? They must, they must.'

'They're never here!' she choked, scraping the spilled mascara from under her eyes. 'Always leaving me, pushing me away, working, working, working!'

'Mine are on the other side of the world! And my Mom doesn't even work.'

'But they want the best for you. That's why they sent you here.'

'The best for me or for them? All they want to know about is my grades, my exams, my college applications... then they show off to all the relatives.'

'But it's for *your* life. My life doesn't matter. It's all about

God.'

'Is it my life? I already know I have to do law, I have to get married to their choice, I have to make big bucks. No one asks if I want to or not. Better to lose your life to God than money.'

'I hate God.'

'Thought you didn't believe in Him.'

'It's the believing I hate.'

'All believing?'

'The believing that makes people kill in the name of God, that makes people cause harm and claim it's for good, that makes people save the whole world but sacrifice their children!'

Her crying rose like an earth tremor, shaking her, releasing sobs and gasping breath. Manveer held her, soothing and cradling, caressing the back of her hair where it was tangled and snagged with pine needles. When the crying had eased, he drew back gently.

'Will you wear this?' he asked and pulled the steel bracelet off his wrist.

'Your *kara*?'

'Yes.'

She looked at it, then up at him.

'Manveer, you can't do that.'

'I want you to have it.'

'Well... give me something else, then. Not this – it's sacred to you.'

'No. Love is sacred. That's all. Please wear it?'

She touched it softly. A long quiet.

'Ok. If you really want me to.' He pushed it onto her wrist and began kissing her. She wrapped her arms around him. 'I'll never take it off.'

They kissed for the longest time, bound to one another at mouth and breast and hip, till finally he drew back again and took her face in his hands.

'You are the most beautiful thing in the world.'

It was like lightning; a whip of fire down her spine; a shot of love.

She shook her head, a fresh tear spilling down one cheek. He released her and took the *kirpan* from the mantelpiece.

'I want you to cut my hair.'

She stared at him. He was perfectly still, the knife on his palm catching the moonlight. She shook her head again.

'Manveer...'

'Now. With this.'

'No Manveer.' Her breath was short. 'You can't cut your hair. It's the most important thing. And it would kill your parents...'

'I have to. I *want* to.'

Her face, lifted to him in the half-light, was pale as marble. 'Why?'

'Because I don't believe in it anymore.' She waited, searching him, not fathoming. 'My hair nearly got me killed. But worse – it made me want to kill.' He rolled the knife softly in his hand. 'What's the use of religion if it does that to you?'

She said nothing, barely breathing.

'You know, my parents still tell stories of their relatives killed at partition. And they are terrible stories and I always thought they were exaggerating... until now. But they don't talk about the Hindus and Muslims killed by Sikhs. And no-one talks about my Uncle Kushwant – a very proud Sikh – but he was in the troops that stormed the Golden Temple this year.' A soft hissing laugh like a puncture. 'Sikhs killing Sikhs! Should we just kill ourselves now? Like kamikaze pilots? It's mad. All mad, and I don't want it anymore.'

His hand gripped the knife, knuckles white and bulging.

'Manveer, Manveer... Don't say these things.'

'They're true! And you know it. You're saying the same things, you've given up on religion. You're right.'

'No—'

'Being here with you tonight I felt really alive for the first time, really happy, really me. I don't want to be a Sikh anymore, or a Singh, or a this or a that. I want to be me.'

'You *are* you, Manveer, and I love you—!'

He gripped her arm. 'What?'

'I love you.'

His voice was thick with feeling, his words slow. 'And I love you.'

They kissed again, sealing their lips and their fate as he pressed the handle of the *kirpan* into her hand.

The hair lay around them like a harvest of black wheat; above them, the sickle moon. The *kirpan* was sheathed and back on the mantelpiece, the *kara* on her wrist. It chinked against her glass bangles and bumped on his skull as she stroked his head, trying to smooth the choppy stubble that remained. He caught her hand and kissed it. Outside, the wind had died and, in the stillness, they could hear the octave owl's two sweet notes, and in their embrace they whispered the counts, waiting for the next two.

But they never came.

Just footsteps and the crashing door.

THIRTY-SIX

By the Monday in Kanpur, the attacks had subsided, but the city still smouldered with the burning of Sikh homes, and in the hospital, the morgue was overflowing. As James stepped out of the house that morning, the smoke stung his nose and eyes. He had barely slept and not touched breakfast – even his morning coffee made him sick – and though his hands had been scrubbed raw, he hadn't bathed fully in days. His hair was greasy, his mouth sour, body smelling of old sweat and disinfectant. And he could not stop the tremor in his hands.

Entering the ward he heard the furious cries of a baby, and then he saw her. She was sitting on the floor next to a woman who did not move, pulling on her hand, except that it was not a hand, it was a stump.

James bent to the baby and lifted her. She was screaming now, wet and soiled. He looked around for a nurse, but could see none.

'Nurse!' he shouted blindly into the crowd. 'Come now! *Jaldi!*' The entrance hall was teeming with people, with cries, with misery. He felt a sudden urge to roar, to scream, to smash things. At that moment a nurse came running and took the child.

Shaking and smeared with the baby's excrement, he turned to the next body on the corridor floor. A great felled tree of a man, beaten and burnt. James lifted a flap of turban that covered his face, the charred fabric disintegrating in his fingers.

It was his Senior Book-keeper, Gurpreet Singh.

THIRTY-SEVEN

When Ruth brought home her copy of the new Landour Community Cookbook, it caused something of a stir between her and Iqbal. James feigned disinterest, but was unsettled to hear Iqbal cry out and Ruth hush him. There was much page-turning and exclaiming, feverish whispering and scribbling of ingredients on shopping lists. Tonight, they told him, he was in for a treat. There was a gleam in Ruth's eye; in Iqbal's, a tear.

It was, indeed, no ordinary night, for a remarkable confluence of lunar and natal phenomena meant that James' 77th birthday coincided with Eid-ul-Fitr. What's more, the 139th anniversary of the Mahatma's birth was only the day after, making that midnight especially auspicious. Unimpressed by this extraordinary co-incidence and certainly not intending to stay up that late, James had insisted he wanted no personal celebration, but if Iqbal wished to mark the religious festival with one or two special dishes he would not object, so long as there were no fuss, no guests and no gifts.

Naturally, they ignored him. By seven-thirty, his living room bristled with gaudily wrapped presents and the voices of Reverend Paul Verghese, young Dr Lakshman and the rotund Mrs Puri. James hunkered in his chair, fighting the pain in his stomach and the faint nausea that rose from it like a swarm of flies. The others were in full swing with an argument.

'I tell you,' said Verghese, tapping the air with a peanut.

'If they don't get these Hindu fundamentalists under control they'll tear the country apart.'

Lakshman reached for his glass of squash. 'But don't you think the problem is not the Hindus but the fundamentalism? It's the same with Islam.'

'Yes, yes,' echoed Mrs Puri, popping peanuts with speed and perfect aim.

'And with Christianity,' said Ruth, from the kitchen end of the room, where she was working with Iqbal. Her glass bracelets – an Eid gift from him – jingled as she stirred a large pot on the stove. Under one of Ellen's aprons, she wore a green kurta churidar and a soft, filmy dupatta that fell from her neck to a casual loop in the middle of her back. It was a striking change from the grey and black she normally wore and was the first time James had seen her in Indian clothes since she'd left Oaklands. He could have done without the nose-ring and the sparkly bindi in the middle of her forehead, but otherwise, she was beautiful. Like Ellen. Yet so unlike Ellen. It hurt to look at her.

At her side, Iqbal hummed and swished around the kitchen in a voluminous shalwar kameez, salmon pink and embroidered at the neck and cuffs. Their work together was a kind of fluid dance: the bending and twisting, pouring, reaching, heads together for a moment then turning away. The plump old Asian man and the thin white woman, alike only in their curly hair and floral aprons. And – thought James wryly – their conspiratorial manner. They'd been like a pair of cackling witches all day, plotting and preparing, sprinkling powders, stirring dishes, as if their recipe book were a volume of spells and this meal a potion. He did not know what magic they hoped to pull off, but it filled him with unease.

He turned back to the conversation around him. Lakshman was thrusting his hands. 'India is a country where different religions have lived together peacefully for thousands of years. It works if everyone just follows their own beliefs and doesn't try to convert anyone else.'

'What about conquering them, hmm?' demanded Verghese. 'What about Aryans sweeping in and pushing the locals to the bottom of the country and the caste heap? Hey? Not tying to convert them, of course, just rendering them untouchable.'

Mrs Puri piped up, mouth full of peanuts. 'Or the Mughal invasions! Hindus were persecuted under them.'

'Or partition.' Verghese again. 'Nobody was trying to convert anybody. Just kill them.'

James pressed one hand into the other, knuckles straining.

'And after Mrs Gandhi's assassination, na?' said Mrs Puri, throwing up her hands. 'I was in Delhi that time and—'

'Supper ready!' Iqbal called, carrying a large pot and placing it in the centre of the table. The living room party stood and moved across. Reverend Verghese rubbed his fingertips together to dust off the salt, then smoothed his shiny hair with both hands. Mrs Puri, overflowing her dining chair in her red sari, put James in mind of a giant, glossy tomato.

'But that's exactly it,' Lakshman continued, taking his seat. Ruth leaned over him to put a platter of rice on the table and he was momentarily diverted by her fragrance and the fleeting pressure of her body, but pulled his thoughts back. 'When religion is used as a political tool it abuses people and distorts the very message at the heart of the faith.'

'But you can't divorce religion from politics!' Reverend Verghese replied, shaking open his fan-folded napkin. 'If the message of your faith is that some are born to be priests while others are destined to sweep latrines then that is how your society will be structured.'

'That is not the message of Hinduism!'

'Then what is its message, pray tell?'

Lakshman opened his mouth, then closed it again; wafted a hand. 'That is not a Hindu question.'

Reverend Verghese laughed. 'Sounds like a good way of *avoiding* the question. Are there any Hindu answers?'

'Sorry, what was the question?' asked Mrs Puri.

'Shall we pray?' asked James, as Ruth and Iqbal took their seats. Ruth shot him a warning look but James ignored her and nodded at Reverend Verghese. The man smiled beatifically and set his elegant hands together. Ruth's nostrils flared; all heads bowed.

It was a lengthy prayer. It extolled the virtues of the Lord and acknowledged with remorse the sins of the wicked, present company not excluded. It went on to give thanks for the Almighty's munificent blessings – elaborated at length – and in particular for the devoted life of God's faithful servant in whose honour the assembled company had gathered to render felicitations on the auspicious occasion of his anniversary. The prayer closed, at last, with a request that the repast so lovingly prepared by these precious souls be blessed unto them all, that they in turn might live as blessings unto the Lord and one another.

As they joined in the "Amen," James saw Iqbal's wide-eyed appreciation. He always spoke of the Reverend Verghese with the greatest of awe. Ruth, meanwhile, pressed her hand to the side of a dish.

'Shall I reheat the rice?' she asked.

'No, no,' whispered Iqbal. 'Everything is perfect. Go, go.' And he nudged her in the ribs. She lifted the lid of a pot, releasing a puff of steam like a genie.

'Tennessee Tandoori Chicken!' she cried. 'Recipe of Ellen Connor!'

James' stomach clenched. A chorus of *oohs* and *ahhs* around him, a little applause from Mrs Puri.

'How Tennessee?' asked Lakshman.

'Because she uses paprika instead of chilli powder and serves it with cornmeal naan.' Ruth extended the basket of golden breads.

'*Accha*,' he swayed his head, a gleam of understanding playing on lips and eyes.

'Found it in the book.' She jerked her thumb to the kitchen bench. 'It's got quite a few of Mom's recipes.'

James nodded, trying to pull his cheeks into a smile.

'What book?' asked Verghese, accepting a rice platter from Ruth.

'The Landour Community Cookbook, Pauly,' said Mrs Puri. 'We sell it down at the hospital to raise funds. Haven't you got one?'

'Never heard of it.'

'Second edition!' cried Iqbal. 'With all the latest recipes.'

'And some golden oldies,' added Ruth, smiling at him.

He winked back. 'Three generations of Connors!'

'And one—'

'Shhh!' he hissed, pressing his plump finger to his lips.

'Shhh!' she hissed back, and they both giggled.

James looked from one to the other, brow knotting.

'And this,' cried Iqbal, gesturing to the rice, 'is Biryani Birmingham by Marlene Lacey.'

'I think 'cause of the prunes,' added Ruth.

'Wow,' said Lakshman, heaping some onto his plate. 'This is fantastic. Thanks for inviting me to your birthday party, Dr James.'

James did not look up.

'So,' said Ruth quickly, taking the rice. 'If fundamentalism is the problem, Lakshman, what's the solution?'

'Oh god,' he groaned. 'That's the million-dollar question.'

'Might that be a Hindu question?' asked Verghese.

'A question for us all, surely,' said Lakshman.

'Beg pardon, but what—?' began Mrs Puri, but was distracted by the proffer of a serving dish. 'Oh my goodness! What have we here?'

'Shikampuri Kebab,' said Iqbal, grinning as he presented a set of chopsticks. 'Shanghai style!'

Mrs Puri erupted into bell-ring laughter. 'What is all this? Some kind of United Nations pot luck?!'

'No luck! Is very carefully planned.'

'Fusion Cuisine,' said Ruth. 'Mom's edition is full of it.'

'And she taught you!' Mrs Puri beamed.

Ruth tilted her head, glanced at James. His face was a yellowish pall, hooded eyes meeting hers briefly. 'I guess,' she said. 'Through the book and Iqbal. And we made some stuff up ourselves. This was my idea.' Ruth took the lid off the last dish on the table. 'Highland Haleem. Made with oats instead of wheat. A tribute to the Connor ancestral home.'

'And your now chosen home!' added Iqbal.

'My grotty flat in Glasgow? Hmmm... maybe not.'

'Well,' said Mrs Puri, helping herself to some of the rich curry, slick with oil and smelling of heaven. 'This is *divine!* Eid Mubarak everyone, and happy birthday James and Gandhi-ji!'

They all clasped their glasses of sharbat and lifted them, clinking and reaching across the table. *Happy Birthday! Eid Mubarak! Happy Birthday!*

'Do you remember James, we attended one of Gandhi-ji's prayer meetings,' Verghese said, delicately setting his glass down and wiping his moustache. 'Here in Mussoorie, no?'

James nodded, chewing slowly, painfully on Ellen's Tennessee Tandoori Chicken. Everyone waited but he said nothing; kept chewing.

Verghese cleared his throat. 'Bit of a nutter, I thought.'

Gasps, dropped cutlery, wide eyes. Except for James, who gave Verghese a penetrating look.

'Reverend!' cried Lakshman.

'He's not a god.' Verghese waved a warning finger.

'He is to some,' said Lakshman.

'Precisely the problem. Merely worshipping something does not make it a god – it makes it an idol. And idol worship is a kind of blindness. I tell you, Gandhi is one of the biggest holy cows in this country and until we can see past him to the truth of the conflicts in our midst we will not overcome them.'

'But that is exactly what Gandhi-ji was doing! Getting people to see beyond religious difference to our universal humanity. That is why he is revered.'

'Gandhi remained a Hindu—'

'And he was killed by a Hindu!'

'Was he?' asked Ruth.

'Oh yes,' said Lakshman. 'By extremists who did not like his tolerance of Muslims.'

'He was *just* like Jesus,' breathed Mrs Puri. 'Killed by his own people because of his teachings.'

Iqbal sighed, head shaking.

'He was *not* just like Jesus!' spluttered Verghese.

'But so much similar,' she appealed, spreading oily hands.

'Listen,' said Verghese, laying down his cutlery. 'When I was a young idealist, Gandhi was my hero, too. James can tell you.' They all looked at James but he remained silent, gaunt. 'My parents were in the freedom movement and supported him from the word go. They were thrown into jail for it! Yes, Gandhi *was* an extra-ordinary man, no doubt about it, and I do still love him. But now that I've lived in so called "free" India for sixty years my ideals and my heroes have taken a few knocks.' He took a small sip of sharbat.

'How?' asked Ruth.

'The problem, Ruthie, is that on the one hand,' he poked out his right like a policeman directing traffic, 'Gandhi taught that India could offer the world some kind of spiritual supremacy, but on the other,' his left shot forth, 'he kept faith with a religious system that was – and is – fundamentally oppressive and unjust.'

'Not fundamentally,' insisted Lakshman. 'Caste is not the essence of Hinduism.'

'What is?' demanded Verghese. 'Essence, message, answer – you are refusing to tell me.'

Lakshman nodded, lips working into a tight pucker, as he spooned raita onto his plate. 'Reverend Paul, you know

Hinduism is not about these things; it is culture and family and daily ritual.'

'Can you pass the lime chutney, please, James darling?' said Mrs Puri.

'It is not so much a belief system as a way of life.'

'Anybody is wanting more juice?' asked Iqbal. Lakshman's gaze flickered to him in irritation.

'Go on, Lakshman,' said Ruth. 'I'm very interested.'

'For example, you ask my grandmother what she believes and her mouth will fall open. Ask her what she cooks for Dusshera and she'll talk for hours.'

'Then I must meet her,' said Iqbal. 'Between cooks there is no divide.'

'What nonsense, Iqbal!' rebuked Verghese. 'You know perfectly well his grandmother would not open her kitchen to you nor eat anything from your hand.'

Iqbal's face fell.

'Do you know her?' Ruth asked the Reverend sweetly.

'Of course not, but I know the rules.'

'Actually, my grandmother is quite liberal. My uncle married a Sikh girl and there was no problem.'

'Was she rich?' Verghese asked, helping himself to the Haleem. In the slight pause that followed he turned his beetle gaze on Lakshman, eyes extra large, extra round, extra penetrating through his bottle-top specs.

Lakshman hesitated. 'Well... that's got nothing to do with it—'

Verghese roared with laughter.

'Oh no!' cried Mrs Puri, pressing a be-ringed hand on Lakshman's arm. 'It makes all the difference, *beta*, really. I'm sure your parents are looking for a girl with good assets also, because life is so much easier that way. Really, I'm telling you.'

'Mrs Puri! My parents know very well I will make that decision for myself.' A fleeting glance at Ruth. 'And I won't make it for money.'

'Well don't make it for love, sweetie,' Mrs Puri sighed. 'It doesn't last.'

'Then is not love,' said Iqbal.

For a moment all was quiet except for thoughtful chewing and the scrape of cutlery. James, who had said nothing since the unveiling of the Tennessee Tandoori, was struggling to eat. He had always delighted in this dish of Ellen's – which she'd reserved for special occasions like the girls' first night home from boarding – but tonight he could not stomach anything. Nor did he have the heart for sparring with Verghese.

Ruth broke the silence. 'Would you marry a non-Hindu, Lakshman?' Her bracelets tinkled as she cut through her kebabs.

'Oh yes!' he said, swinging his eager gaze to her, mouth full. 'Certainly, absolutely, definitely! If it is the right person, religion is irrelevant!'

'Poppycock,' said Verghese.

'Pauly, darling,' appealed Mrs Puri, scooping up a swathe of sari that was slipping from her shoulder. 'He's still young and idealistic. Let him have his dreams.'

'Fantasies, I'm afraid,' said Verghese, wiping his moustache with two measured sweeps.

'Are you saying there's no way people of different religions can get along?' asked Ruth.

'Of course I'm not! We're all here round this table getting

on famously! But what I'm saying is it won't happen by pretending religion is irrelevant or that they're all the same or that all ways lead to God and other such bunkum. Buddhists aren't even trying to get to God, for pity's sake!'

'But they're trying to attain salvation,' Ruth said.

'Yes, but their concept of it is entirely different to a theocentric view—'

'A what?' asked Mrs Puri.

'They are simply *not* trying to go to the same place.' He stabbed a finger on the tablecloth.

'Maybe not...' Ruth said.

'Absolutely not! What did they teach you here?'

'I guess I flunked 'O' Level.'

'Never mind, darling,' soothed Mrs Puri. 'You can always re-sit.'

'But my child,' said Verghese. 'Surely you had fellow students here at Oaklands who were Buddhist?'

'Yeah, there were a few, but that was a long time ago.' She scrunched her forehead and tugged on a curl. 'There was a girl, Pema, in my class... from Tibet, though we weren't that close and, to be honest, I don't think I ever asked her what she believed or where she was trying to go.' She grinned. 'But, I think it was America.'

They all laughed, from Iqbal's swelling drumbeat to Mrs Puri's birdy hoot. All except James, who managed only to curl a lip.

'Ah, the Promised Land,' Verghese chuckled, spearing a cucumber.

'And then there was Kashi,' said Ruth, thoughtfully. 'He was half-Buddhist, half-Hindu, half-I-don't-know-what.'

'Three halves?' asked Verghese.

'As many halves as you like. He seemed to believe it was all One, anyway.'

'He is Christian now, also,' nodded Iqbal.

'No way,' said Ruth.

'*Also?*' sneered Verghese. 'He might think you can collect religions like stamps but that is categorically *not* Christian.'

'Not collecting, I think,' said Iqbal. 'He is wanting to seek the face of God only. His path is art.' He pointed to the picture above the sofa. They all turned to look at the image of the blue-grey woman in her secret joy.

'Oh! That is a Kashi original?' cried Mrs Puri. 'We have one in the hospital foyer. So beautiful.'

'Yes,' murmured Ruth. 'I saw it.'

'And he is doing such good thing with *Kala Sangam*,' said Iqbal.

'What's that?' asked Lakshman.

'He is bringing the artists together from different religions to build the bridges. They are doing exhibitions and productions and what nots.'

'So sweet,' said Mrs Puri.

'Amazing.' Ruth said. 'What's it mean?'

Verghese lifted a finger. '*Kala* means art and *sangam* means coming together, or confluence – like rivers.'

'Yes,' chimed Iqbal. 'He is gathering everyone: painters, musicians, dancers, poets. Even wobbly old singers like me.'

'And all different beliefs?' asked Ruth.

'Right. But he is telling to me he does not believe in religion, he believes in... what is he saying...? Oh yes! In the One and Only whose Name is Love.'

Ruth stared and there was a quiet around the table.

Then Mrs Puri sighed, beaming, and set her fork on her empty plate.

'Food for the gods!' she declared.

'Please be having seconds!' Iqbal cried, gesturing to the food.

They indulged in the customary ritual of offers and refusals before she tilted her head coquettishly and relented.

'Just the smallest morsel, Iqbal-ji,' she said happily as he heaped food onto her plate.

'So, Reverend,' Ruth asked, passing the cornmeal naans to Mrs Puri. 'If pretending we're all the same isn't the answer... what is?'

'It depends on the question.'

'Ok then: how do we make peace?'

'Ah, but what is peace? Is it truth and freedom and the right of each individual to choose their own path, or is it everyone staying in their boxes and not upsetting the apple cart, as Dr Lakshman here would recommend?'

'I never—!'

'You did. Everything's fine so long as no-one converts.'

'No, it's the trying to convert *others* that is the problem. Going into a place where everybody's perfectly happy and messing it up – pulling families apart, spoiling culture, breaking down the whole way of life. *That* is what causes the backlash.'

'Yes, yes,' said Mrs Puri.

'Do you think India's 250 million Dalits are perfectly happy? Hmm? Untouchable, outcaste, oppressed? Do you think the young bride forced into marriage then tortured for the sake of more dowry is perfectly happy? What about the beggar whose karma renders him responsible for his own despair? Hey? And the savage violence in Orissa just now! Burning, raping, killing! Is this all part of your precious way of life, Lakshman? To be preserved at any cost?'

There was a terrible silence. No more chewing or tick-tack of cutlery. Lakshman and Verghese were locked eye-to-eye across the table, both motionless except for the twitching of a muscle in the doctor's jaw. Mrs Puri looked from one to the other, hand at her breast. Iqbal's face was a map of misery, James' lowered, masked. At last Ruth spoke softly, slowly.

'Sounds like... there are no easy answers. I'm sorry I asked.'

A slight breathing out of the tight air. A tilting of Iqbal's head.

'No, no,' Lakshman muttered. 'It's not you.'

James spoke, the sound of his long-absent voice a shock.

'You have to.'

All eyes turned; his remained on his hands, knobbled, gripping his knife and fork.

'Keep asking.' The voice was low, cracked. 'Keep... seeking.'

He looked up at Ruth, expecting at worst a face twisting with scorn, at best, a joke. Instead she was gazing at him, eyes bright, lips slightly apart, in a kind of alert wonder. It was the look on a wild animal's face when it has smelled something. That moment of waiting, of sensing, before the hunt closes in.

'I think we are needing dessert,' said Iqbal, leaping to his feet.

'Yes, yes,' agreed Mrs Puri, with a nervous giggle. 'When in doubt, eat dessert.'

Everyone started bustling. Scraping plates, passing plates,

stacking plates. The relief of chores. Ruth laid a hand on Lakshman's arm as they passed, to-ing and fro-ing from the kitchen area. His face flooded with gratitude but she moved on before he could speak. Then she landed a soft pat on Verghese's shoulder as she took his plate, and he looked up, startled, then busily folded his napkin. Leaning over James to pick up the jug of juice she hesitated for a moment, then rested her hand on his back. He did not move.

Iqbal was like a dervish, spinning from table to kitchen, tossing forks into the sink, scooping rice grains from the cloth. He kept running his hands down his apron, turning on the spot, humming frantic little snatches of song. Ruth smiled at him and winked. The smile he returned was shaky, quivering on the brim of joy and fear. At last, when the table was clean, she nodded at him and stood by the wall as he disappeared through the door to the store-room. There was scuffling and the striking of matches.

'Ready?' she called out.

'Ooh, what's happening?' said Mrs Puri, clasping her hands together.

'Ready!' yelled Iqbal.

Ruth snapped off the lights. Cries of *oh-my-god! what's this? hey?* and the store-room door banged open. A halo of candle-light wavered through the dark, casting a glow on Iqbal's chest and face.

'*Happy Birthday to you!*' Ruth sang, with cheerleading spirit. The others joined. '*Happy Birthday to you!*' Iqbal's voice was resonant, Verghese's a monotone, Lakshman's uncertain and Mrs Puri's like Bollywood's best. '*Happy Birthday dear Ja-ames.*' As the candles flickered closer, James could see they rose not from a conventional cake, but a strange white confection with lumps and pinnacles. It loomed from the shadows like an apparition. '*Happy Birthday to Yooooooooou!*' The singers were enjoying themselves now, hanging on to that last note like a herald's blast, ushering in an awesome personage. They burst into cheering and applause.

The ghost was upon him.

'Mogul Mango Meringue Pie!' cried Iqbal setting the sugared Taj Mahal at his place. More cheers. Iqbal held up his finger for silence, then with a voice brimming with emotion, cried out, 'From The Book, recipe of Mr Aziz Mohammed Hashim!'

James twisted, tried to push back the chair, but caught it on the rug and swung over. With a cry and a shooting pain up his side, he fell.

THIRTY-EIGHT

The last time James had been served Mogul Mango Meringue Pie was at Askival. Barely a week after, the pie's creator had sat huddled on his bed smelling of Dettol, with a tear-stained face, a mug of tea and a chocolate-chip muffin crumbling in his hands.

Outside, a mob of Sikhs.

At the sound of their arrival, Aziz leapt up, knocking cup and muffin plate to the floor and squeezed under the bed, shoving a guitar case and a tin trunk out of the way. James saw his legs sticking out, bleeding feet scrabbling against the floor, and it was absurdly funny and terrifying at the same time.

He turned to look again through the slit in the curtains and his stomach clenched. About half a dozen men were gathered at the foot of the veranda steps, burning torches in their hands and madness on their lips. They were shouting in a language James did not understand, but thought must be Punjabi. The light from the torches flickered over the high folds of their turbans and across their faces, sweating and contorted with passion. One of them came up to the door and pounded on it. His body bristled with a physical power James had never seen before and his eyes held the wild desperation of the hunted leopard, the charging boar. There was more banging and shouting and James felt his heart thumping as his head swarmed with images from Bunce's report and his father's letter: the burning and butchering in the Punjab, the hacking apart of two nations, the death trains.

It was then that he saw the *kirpans*. At each man's waist, tucked into a cummerbund, there rested a curved blade, glinting in the torchlight.

Fear possessed him. A vision of his father rose in his mind like a towering spirit, and he turned and picked up the gun that he'd dropped on the floor. Aziz had managed to tuck his legs under his body by then, though the trunk and the guitar case still jutted out at absurd angles, as if cruelly sign-posting his whereabouts. For the first time that evening, he was absolutely silent.

James returned to the window just in time to hear his mother unbolting the front door. 'No, no,' he breathed and heard a strangled gasp from under the bed. He watched in disbelief as Leota stepped out from the door and addressed the Sikhs.

'Brothers,' she began, in Hindi. She was trying to adopt the warm tones she used for leading Bible studies, but James could hear the tremor in her voice. There was a torrent of speech from the Sikhs, a fierce gesturing of hands, a raising of torches. Fighting the trembling in his fingers, James drew back the latch on the window. His mother was spreading her hands and tilting her head towards the men, trying to understand. He pulled gently on the window, opening it a crack, every hair on his body raised, heart racing. A man at the back of the group was screaming.

Leota tried again. 'Do you speak Hindi? I don't understand Punjabi.' The Bible Study voice was failing, though she still clung to a note of good will. James cocked the gun and lifted it to his shoulder, clenching his jaw to stop his shaking. The Sikh who had banged on the door took a step towards Leota, gesturing, repeating the same urgent phrase. James could not see his mother's expression, but he had the Sikh right in his sights. The man's face was jewelled with sweat, black with the beard that began high on his cheeks and curved into a roll under his chin. His brows were thickets, his eyes fierce, mouth trembling. Then the group surged forward and James fired.

The bullet hit the Sikh right in his heart, hurling him backwards down the steps onto the others. There was howling and a collision of bodies and a jet of blood.

James pulled back from the window and leaned against the wall, squeezing his eyes shut against the demonic din. The tremor in his hands spread through his body till he was shaking uncontrollably. He let the gun fall and pressed his hands over his ears, barely aware of someone next to him and a touch on his arm. Outside, the shouting and shrieking were borne away on the sound of pounding feet, leaving only a choked cry on the veranda.

He tore back the curtain and pushed the window wide, half falling out.

'Mom!'

She stood at the bottom of the steps, back to him, arms thrown out into the dark. As James stumbled towards her she whirled around, dress spattered with blood.

'What have you done?' she cried. '*What have you done?!*'

James stared at her, caught mid-stride, legs failing him. His mother was crying now and clutching herself with shaking arms.

'James!' she sobbed, her face crumpling. 'What in God's name—?'

'It was not James, Memsahib.'

They turned.

Silhouetted in the light of the window, stood Aziz, the gun in his hands.

In that moment, the world held its breath. They stared at him, the clear outline of his figure, the darkness of his face; how strange the gun looked held against him.

And then the world breathed out on a great rush and burst its veins. James sank to his knees and Leota flew to the window, bellowing at Aziz. It looked like she was going to hit him, but the cook took a step back, and her hands flayed the air.

Aziz shook his head, tears running into the creases round his eyes as he accepted her charges. Yes, he had been a terrible fool. No, he had not thought, Memsahib, not considered the consequences. Yes, unforgivable violence. And yes, Memsahib, worst of all, perhaps these Sikhs were not his attackers. Perhaps innocent men.

Yes! Leota cried. They had not come for harm but for help! One of their men was wounded and they were bringing him forward when the shot was fired.

James felt these words split him like an axe, the black night spilling into his head, his eyes, his heart. Huddled on the veranda, arms gripping himself, he watched his mother in horror. She was hoarse with ranting, hair pulled in tufts from her grey bun, face twisting as spit flew from her mouth. Under the beating of her anger, Aziz was bowed, head bobbing softly.

James wanted to speak, to tell the truth, but he could not say a word, or move, or stop the sirens in his head, nor the great rift opening up beneath him.

As Leota finally ran out of words, Aziz spoke, low and urgent.

'They will come back, Memsahib, with others, for revenge.' He was sniffing and slapping the tears off his cheeks. 'I will go raise the Gurkhas to guard the house. You go to Colonel Sahib. Go, go. I will fix everything.'

James saw Leota giving Aziz a pair of socks and his red basketball high-tops. They looked like clown's boots on the little man.

And then he was gone. Running down the path into the darkness, the shoes slap, slap, slapping.

He did not speak to James, and the boy said nothing to him.

He did not even see his face.

THIRTY-NINE

They left immediately for Colonel and Mrs Bunce's house on the back *chakkar* road. Once Leota delivered the story in a breathless rush on the doorstep, the Colonel donned his long black boots and strapped a revolver round his waist.

'Right then,' he said. 'Better find some Gurkhas and sort these buggers out.' And with a torch in one hand and a neatly furled umbrella (BUNCE 1) in the other, he strode off into the night.

Mrs Bunce ushered them into her living room where Leota went through the whole story again over mugs of cocoa. As James watched the skin form on the top of his drink, he listened to his mother solidifying what she believed – and what she needed to believe – into immutable fact. The women gasped together over the violence of these people and shook their heads.

Leota was given the guest bed and James a sleeping bag on the couch. He did not sleep, but spent the night staring at the window, flinching at every creak and rustle outside. Before dawn it began to rain, and the rain slowly washed the dark out of the sky, leaving a weak grey that seeped into the ground, the swollen walls of the house, the pith of his bones.

Then Colonel Bunce returned. James heard him stamping in the front porch and beating the rain off his umbrella. As he came into the living room, Leota appeared, wrapping a borrowed dressing gown around herself, hair hanging in greasy tendrils around her shoulders. Her face was pasty and drawn, eyebrows bunched with worry, mouth half open and gummy in the corners. James, sitting fully clothed in his sleeping bag, tucked his legs up to make space for her. He looked down at his hands, cold and white, veined with silent, sunken rivers.

The Colonel sat heavily in the armchair in the corner, pulling his trouser legs up to reveal startled black hairs above his socks.

'Well, it's all rather ghastly,' he said. 'I'm afraid the bastards got the poor fellow.'

A winded sound from Leota as her hand shot to her mouth. James could make no sound; he could barely breathe.

He kept his eyes on his hands as Bunce described how he and the Gurkhas had made straight for Mullingar Hotel where a crowd of Sikhs were refuged, but found only women, children and old men who refused to say a thing. How they'd moved up the mountain and met a triumphant throng coming down, with torches, knives and cries of victory. How they'd marched this lot down to Mullingar, removed their weapons and established a permanent guard at the place. How Bunce and a few of the Gurkhas had gone back up the mountain to scan for others. Which was when they'd found Aziz. Lying in the road, hacked and burned.

'His face was a ruin,' said Bunce, shaking his head, eyebrows arching. 'But I knew it had to be your chap because I recognised James' shoes. He was wearing your basketball boots, wasn't he, my boy?'

FORTY

Back at Askival, Leota's first act was to scrub the blood off the veranda steps. James watched her use the same basin and Dettol that last night had held Aziz' bare and bloodied feet. The feet that had slipped into James' shoes and run off into the dark. In his bedroom he took apart the rifle, piece by piece, cleaned it and put it away in the case and into the tin trunk that still jutted from under his bed. The black buck watched him. James would not meet its eyes. All the while he heard Leota scrubbing, and the faint huffing of her effort. She'd asked Colonel Bunce if they should leave everything at the house untouched so the police could inspect and take fingerprints.

'Oh, I shouldn't worry about that,' Bunce had said. 'The whole country's drowning in its own blood, the police won't care about one little servant in a sleepy hill station. I'll have a word with the Superintendent for you, but he won't be trotting up to Askival with a notebook, I can assure you. He's got all the other Mohammedans to get safely out of town and these hot-head Sikhs to settle. Quite enough for one afternoon.'

So Leota and James returned to Askival to clean up the evidence that no one cared about and to pack a bag for Salima. Leota put in her own best sari, some shampoo and soap, a small towel and a tub of Vaseline. James watched her. What can you give a woman in exchange for her husband? She fussed about trying to find something for the baby and eventually settled on a tin of condensed milk. James added his own small teddy bear.

He carried the backpack down the mountain, his mother beside him. He was silent. She could not stop talking: *They would send a telegram to Stanley. And Aziz' family in his home village would need to be notified. But that area of Kashmir – was it still in India or part of Pakistan now? Oh what a mess the whole thing was! If only they could live side by side in peace none of this would be happening.*

They reached the place where Aziz had died. The Gurkhas had put the charred remains of the body into a bag and left it at the hospital morgue, awaiting instructions. The rain had washed everything else away, leaving only a dark stain and the smell of wet smoke.

They stared at the shadow on the ground, Leota now unable to speak. She clasped her arms across her chest, gripping the flesh as if trying to hold the halves of herself together. She kept starting to say something, her mouth dropping open on a suck of breath, but then clamping shut again to stop the wobbling. At last she gave up. James heard her sobs, felt her hand gripping his arm and her body shuddering against his, but he did not look, or turn towards her. He could only stare at the inky patch of ground.

At Rampur House, a young Gurkha with a gentle smile ushered them through the main gates. A short, tree-lined drive led steeply upwards to the white mansion where women were spreading washing on the grass and children swarmed in giggling, bare-foot packs. Leota approached an old woman picking lice from a child's hair and asked for Salima. There was discussion amongst the women and a boy was sent.

James put down the pack, heavier now with food from the bazaar. He shoved one hand down his pocket and held onto his arm with the other, his sides running with sweat. The seven mile walk with a heavy bag in the cloying monsoon air was partial cause, but the imminent arrival of Salima was the most of it.

She appeared, Iqbal on her hip. They'd both been bathing and her long black hair dripped wet down her back and over her shoulders, plastering the thin cotton of her kameez to her skin. James tried not to look at the plump breasts with their nipples rising through the damp. He had been fourteen when Aziz proudly brought home this young wife, and her presence had become excruciating for the boy whose dreams both night and day were invaded by forbidden pleasures. The situation had only worsened when Iqbal was born and James could see her feeding him on the back lawn, a breast fleetingly exposed, swollen, wet nipple extended and glistening in the sun.

And here she was now, skin luminous and fragrant, beautiful face already puckered with the question that would be unbearable to answer. Baby Iqbal bounced on her hip, lighting up at the sight of them, his grin revealing two dimples and a perfect tooth. He threw his arms out to Leota and she took him, pressing a deep kiss into his curly head and squeezing him tight against her.

When Salima screamed and crumpled at their feet, James reached out to catch her, but in the moment his arms pressed around her body, he knew the depths of his error. Not meant to even touch a Muslim woman, far less embrace her, he was only adding shame to her torment. So he pulled back at once and let her fall, and watched miserably as Leota knelt and held her and cried with her, Iqbal between them, adding his infant wails to the terrible din.

Then James ran. He fled to the dense cluster of pines at the side of the house, to the dark cool between the trunks where it smelled of resin and the ground was thick with needles. There he threw himself down and wept.

FORTY-ONE

Nearly forty years later, in the Kanpur hospital corridor, James turned from Gurpreet's burnt body on the floor and ran again, a sour vomit rising inside him. As it erupted, dark spilled over his eyes and he heard the sounds of rushing feet and cries, like a flock of birds. Then hands were leading him, a chair, someone pressing his back forward, his head down. He felt the knobs of his knees, the floor spinning, his eyes pressing shut, an explosion of stars.

Slowly, someone drew his back up straight.

Strong hands, a glass of water.

Go home. Rest today.

He couldn't reply.

Opening his eyes, he saw the room swimming into place: the speed of things slowing down, the furniture returning, the floor flat. He wiped the back of a hand across his mouth: slime and cold sweat, the taste of sick. Someone extended a wad of toilet roll and he mopped at his damp face and the sticky corners of his lips. The wet wad was taken, a thud in a bin, and a mug of chai pressed into his hands. Whoever it was slipped out, and he sipped the tea, the sweet heat of it easing down his body, settling the visions and the shaking.

He didn't know how long he sat there, willing himself to get up, but failing to move. The tea was finished, the cup cold in his hand when there was a knock and the door opened.

Ellen. Her face white.

'I'm all right,' he said, but his voice was a croak.

She sank to her knees in front of him, took the mug and clutched his hands in hers.

'Oh, darling...' Something caught in her throat and she looked away sharply, but not before he saw the tears.

'I'm all right,' he repeated, lifting a hand to touch her head.

She started to cry. James lunged forward to embrace her, but his legs gave way. Instead of holding her, he fell onto her, knocking her backwards. They gasped and struggled, but he was like a marionette dropped and could not pull himself off. She pushed at the dead weight of him and rolled him to one side.

'Sorry,' he whispered. 'So sorry.'

She dragged her twisted leg out from underneath him and he slumped, cheek on the floor.

'James,' she said, gripping his shoulder. 'I have to go tonight.'

His eyes rolled up at her.

'It's Ruth. There's been a death.'

There came a sound from him.

A bird cry, a shot, a cracking of bone.

FORTY-TWO

When the door crashed open at Askival, Ruth and Manveer knew that what had just begun was already over.

She flinched. He held her closer.

It was Mr Haskell with a torch that ran across the underwear and the ruin of Sita's coat and the fallen hair. It ran up their bodies till it found their faces, Ruth's squinting into the harsh beam, Manveer's raw and strange with his butchered hair.

Mr Haskell's breath sucked in. 'What have you done?' He ran the light back down to the floor and over the long swathes of black hair, the empty turban, the *patka*. The beam fell across Ruth's handbag with its spilled contents, the brush and make-up, the joints. The circle of light halted there, damning.

'No!' she said, with sudden realisation. 'We didn't—'

He bent and picked them up. 'You stupid little idiots.'

'No, Mr Haskell,' Manveer tried, 'we didn't smoke—'

'Shut up!' he spat. 'What the hell are you doing? Have you got no idea—? *No* idea what's happening around you? Don't you give a shit about anybody else? What about your parents, Manveer? Yours, Ruth? The show?! You selfish, selfish, stupid *fucking* idiots!'

As he raged at them, Ruth felt the sting of tears and Manveer's hands tightening. At last, ramming the joints into his pocket, Mr Haskell barked at them to get moving and kicked open the door. They stumbled after him, Manveer grabbing his jacket, Ruth her bag and Sita's coat. The *kirpan* lay forgotten on the mantelpiece and the *kanga*, fallen from Ruth's pocket, lay beside the soiled *kachha* and the shorn *kesh*. Only the *kara* was with them, on her wrist.

Mr Haskell strode ahead, his torch light bobbing along the ruts of the *chakkar* road, his breath jagged as they followed in silence, gripping each other's hands. They passed the graveyard and old Morrison Church and an opening in the trees where they could see the ghost of the snows far to the north. When they got to the steep path dropping below the road, Mr Haskell did not look back at them or speak or offer any share of the light, but plunged straight down, his boots crashing and sending tiny stones skeetering down the *khud*. They slipped and staggered behind him, clinging to each other, erupting in small exclamations when they turned an ankle or stubbed a toe.

'Mr Haskell!' Ruth called, when they got to a bit that was treacherously narrow, and cut into a sheer slope. 'Please slow down – we can't – see—!'

But he ignored her and strode on, even faster than before.

Then there was a howl from Manveer as he tripped and knocked his knee against a boulder, all at once losing his balance, Ruth's hand and his footing. And then he fell. Right over the side, crashing through the trees into the darkness.

'Manveer!' Ruth yelled.

'What happened?' Mr Haskell spun round and sent his beam back up the path to where Ruth was kneeling at the edge.

'Manveer's fallen!' she yelled again. 'Manveer! Manveer!'

There was only silence.

The sickle moon watched, stunned, a veil of cloud drawn

over her mouth as the great trees swung and swayed in alarm. A hill barbet wailed and the night's breath was cold.

The *khud* below that stretch of path was so steep and overgrown that they could not navigate it, nor find Manveer in the desperate ray of the torch. Mr Haskell told Ruth to wait and keep calling while he ran for help.

On her hands and knees on the path she called and cried and shook with fear. Tears stinging her eyes, she flung herself onto the God of her childhood.

'Please, please, please God,' she cried. 'Save him. Let him be ok, let him live. I'm so sorry for everything I've done wrong, I'm so sorry, please don't let this be your punishment. Not Manveer, God, not Manveer. He doesn't deserve it. Punish ME, Lord, but not him! Please, God.' And then it hit her: a revelation, a sudden understanding of what this moment was for. 'Dear God, if you save Manveer, I will believe in you. I will live for you and love you and serve you with all of my heart for all of my life. If you are true, if you are love, then answer my prayer.'

When help came, it included Chaplain Park who joined the search, and Mrs Park, who led the shivering Ruth back to their house and put her straight to bed, where she fell in and out of sleep, the waking as bad as the nightmares.

They did not find Manveer till the grey dawn. He was hanging in a tree, twisted, his head bloody from where it had hit a rock in the fall. A pair of the school sweepers climbed the steep slope, lifted him into a sling and lowered him to the group of staff gathered on the clearing below. Mr Haskell took Manveer's body into his arms and sank to his knees, the boy stretched across him, a tangle of twigs and leaves caught in his hair.

Ruth was at the breakfast table in Mrs Park's pyjamas when Chaplain Park got back and broke the news. That day and night were a confusion of weeping and disbelief, of frantic talk and shocked silences, of hysteria and numbness. God vanished into the vortex, prayer and faith spinning after him, Ruth's whole self teetering on the edge. The only thing she could cling to was the news that her mother was coming. It was like a life-boat, plunging towards her through the storm, and she survived only on the vision of that embrace.

But when Ellen arrived at Oaklands she was taken straight to Principal Withers' office. He showed her the joints found beside Ruth's bag and relayed Mr Haskell's account of the sex and the smoking and how the teenagers had been so high they couldn't walk straight. Which was why Manveer had fallen. And probably why he'd allowed his hair to be cut. Because the terrible, tragic irony, Principal Withers pointed out, was that Manveer had been an exemplary student and a devout Sikh who had never broken a school rule, nor had a girlfriend nor touched alcohol, tobacco or drugs in his life. Till Ruth. Principal Withers had been obliged to break this appalling news to Manveer's parents and Ellen could only imagine, he was sure, how that had gone. Ruth, clearly, must be expelled.

By the time Ellen arrived at the Parks' house, she was white and trembling. Ruth saw only rage, as she did not recognise the heartbreak beneath it, nor did she know James was lying spent and unspeaking in his bed in Kanpur. Ellen was struggling to speak herself but managed, in terse, short sentences with eyes averted, to inform Ruth of her expulsion and their departure that afternoon. When Ruth cried out and reached for her, Ellen turned away.

Back in the dorm, as Ruth silently gathered her things, Ellen packed with brutal speed and none of her usual orderliness. Sheets were ripped off, blankets thrown in trunks, clothes, books and pens tossed in a jumble. Through it all, the pervading smell of mothballs rose from the trunks like a ghost. When Ellen tipped out a drawer of socks, a small paper bag tumbled with them. She ripped it open and five joints fell onto her palm. There was an awful quiet.

'How could you?' she hissed. 'How could you... *destroy* that poor boy?'

Ruth, who had not yet heard the official judgement, stared at her, not fathoming. Then the realisation dawned.

'What? What did they say?!' she cried. 'Mom, we didn't – I never—!'

'Mr Haskell *saw* you.'

'No, no, no – Mom!' Ruth tumbled over herself trying to tell what had really happened, but her mother merely shook her head.

'Believe me!' Ruth screamed.

'Believe *you*?' Ellen said, her face twisted with scorn. 'You disgust me.' And she slapped her. Hard.

Ruth fled to the bathroom. She tore off the false red nails and smashed her glass bangles against the sink, leaving cuts up both arms, blood on the ceramic, glass on the floor. Only the *kara* remained and she pressed it to her mouth as if needing it for breath. Looking up, she saw a face in the mirror so puffy and scratched and bruised she did not recognise it.

Two coolies carried her things to a taxi on the New Road and she watched, motionless, as her entire life at Oaklands was reduced to three tin boxes, a backpack and a bed roll. In all her dreaming of exodus, she had never imagined exile, nor how her yearning for freedom might become banishment.

She and Ellen sat at opposite ends of the back seat, a savage silence between them.

The taxi left while everyone was still in class.

No-one came to see Ruth.

No-one said good-bye.

FORTY-THREE

When James left India in December 1947 he was surrounded by well-wishers, but sick at heart. He stood on the deck of The Highland Queen as a small host of missionary friends waved and called from the quay side at the Calcutta port. The sea breeze tugged at him and filled his nose with the smells of salt and diesel and the brackish, dead-green water that slapped against the bow of the ship, frothing with rubbish. Seagulls skated the air and shrieked, flapping to land on the ship's rail then clawing up and down it and leaving their droppings like spits of contempt before taking off again. At his right, Leota was waving furiously and calling out, 'G'bye all, g'bye! We'll be back, we sure will! God bless you all! Bye!' Her voice was caught by the wind and tossed aside like a rag, as if the spirits of the air already knew its futility. At James' left, Stanley sat in his wheelchair and made no sound. His strong farmer's body was ravaged and shrivelled and he had finally accepted the Mission's demand that he return home.

To James, "home" was an absurd word for America. His only memory of the place was a year in Iowa when he was ten and had been tossed between the doting attentions of relatives and the remorseless persecution of schoolmates. The latter had laughed at everything about him: his clothes, his accent, his ignorance of the American way, (his scorn for it!) and his ineptitude on the football field. And they had pushed and tripped and kicked and beaten him. It was far worse than anything that had happened in boarding and he'd told his parents he would never go back. But now he had to, and despite his mother's avowals, he knew there was a finality about this trip. They were leaving India for good.

Working with the refugees in the Kurukshetra camp, Stanley had become host to a sinister cocktail of parasites, and despite long stretches in the Hillside Community Hospital, he was beaten. James now had to help Leota lift him from bed to chair and on and off the commode. This made him burn, to see his father's slack flesh and the way the bones pressed against the skin as if about to tear it. The smells of his sweat and his sewer breath and his streaming diarrhoea brought a pall of shame.

Yet his father had done nothing to deserve shame, James believed, or this suffering. As Bishop Lutz had said last night at their farewell service, Stanley was a giant of God, laid low in service and sacrifice, in his obedience to the Call and his taking up of the Cross.

Whereas James... His hands tightened on the rail in front of him. The weeks after Aziz' death had become increasingly unbearable for him. When he left Mussoorie he gave everything away – his guitar and books and binoculars, his hunting trophies and guns (which he had not touched since that September night), his collections of ferns and butterflies, even his beloved beetles. Leota had been shocked.

'We can take the beetles with us,' she'd said. 'That's the finest collection ever made up here.'

'Be good for the school to have it,' he muttered. He didn't explain the desperate need for penance. For punishment, even. How else could you expunge guilt? He had wanted to send as many possessions as possible to Pakistan for Salima and baby Iqbal, but Leota had refused. With the ongoing troubles across the border there was little chance of the goods arriving, she'd argued, and anyway, the Connors were making regular payments to them through the Mission headquarters in Lahore.

Payments. The word stung. How could you possibly, ever, *pay* for such a thing? For the first time in his life, he decided to study hard. He would get into medical school and after that, get whatever experience he needed to be of maximum use. Then he would return to India and lay down his life in atonement. He did not know if it would ever suffice, but of one thing he was certain: he would kill himself trying.

FORTY-FOUR

James was now sleeping on the camp cot in the living room, as he could no longer climb the stairs. Iqbal had carried him up and down for a while, but he so often fell asleep at odd times through the day, that it became easier not to move him. He no longer stood or walked. Ruth and Iqbal raised him to sitting and eased him down, plumped pillows, changed his clothes and his bed pan. He ate little, despite Iqbal's tireless array of mousses, juices, jellies and custards offered on small trays. Ruth sometimes held his glass and angled the straw to his cracked lips when his own arms were too slack.

Every day she read to him, choosing volumes from the dusty shelves in his bedroom. In a book on Himalayan flora she found the tree from the Peace Garden at Oaklands: *padam,* a wild cherry that bloomed both spring and fall. She had seen it the other day, covered in flowers, a shout of joy in the face of winter. There were only a handful of novels – cheap airport paperbacks and a mildewed Kipling – and one collection of poems. *Mountains: An Anthology of Silence.* These captured her, hung in the air, brought new notes to her voice.

> *What have these lonely mountains worth revealing?*
> *More glory and more grief than I can tell;*
> *The earth that wakes one human heart to feeling*
> *Can centre both the worlds of Heaven and Hell.*

For his sake, she also read from the Bible. His old King

James was almost indecipherable – so scored and scribbled by years of wrestling – but she chose it over the newer versions lying around. It was the language of his heart, but also of her childhood. Long-forgotten passages rose up like bees from a stirred hive, and they both stung and gave of their sweetness. While she almost choked at the stories of God's people ploughing a bloody trail into the Promised Land, she was moved by the beauty of the Psalms. And though the lists of laws and sins and punishments galled her, the mingled decadence and despair of Ecclesiastes brought surprise. She'd never realised such a book was included in the Scriptures. It had not featured in childhood devotions. *'Utterly meaningless! Everything is meaningless!'* the philosopher cried. It made her look further and deeper, and she took to reading on her own, in several versions and was troubled. The thorn-in-the-flesh prophets, the dancing for joy, the nightmares of kings, the songs of love. It was all there. All that was made and smeared, pure and profane, all who laboured and lost, who gave birth and took life, every place that blossomed or was burnt, every voice, every silence, every fall, every rise. All of it. And throughout it, from beginning to end, that wrathful, weeping, terrible, tender God.

When James listened, he said nothing, but his face lay open like a pool. It was bottomless and shadowed, the shape of his skull rising like a stone beneath the surface, the gap of his mouth revealing yellow teeth, jutting and crooked. Looking at him, she felt the burden of what lay unsaid between them and the fear that it was too late.

One evening she stood on the terrace with Dr Lakshman as dusk settled over the mountain. The lights in the bazaar were winking on and the sun was gathering the last colours of the day under wings of cloud.

'You need to be ready, Ruth,' he said. 'It's not long now.'

She nodded. 'Is he in pain?'

'He will be, but he hides it. I've given him morphine and I'll come back again in the morning. Call me in the night if he seems to get worse. I mean it – call me.' His eyes were like deep wells, drawing her in, drowning her. She broke his gaze.

'Thanks.'

He hesitated. 'Are you all right here with Iqbal?'

'Yeah, he's great. And the Rev visits a lot.' She jerked a thumb to the house, where Verghese was sitting with James.

'When's Hannah coming?'

'Saturday.'

'Five days. Ok. Let's hope...'

There was a pause.

'Are you ok, Ruthie?'

She looked back at him for a moment, knowing his concern was real, but also his desire.

'Yeah. Fine,' she said, and folded her arms, squinting across to the sunset. He sighed and took his leave. Once he had disappeared around the side of the hill, she rammed her hands in her pockets and turned up the higher path to the road, where she started to run.

By the time she got to Askival, she was crying. Panting for breath, her side splitting with cramp, she scrambled over the locked gate and up the path. At the veranda steps she grabbed a loose brick and hurled it at the front door. It smashed through the rotting wood and bounced down the hall, splitting open on the floor. She followed it, pushing through the house, crashing into doors, hitting walls, kicking anything that lay in her path. All that she had cleaned and scrubbed and painted she now spat upon.

When Iqbal found her she was a sobbing clot on the south veranda, a mess of dirt and scum and tears. He squatted and offered his handkerchief.

'He's leaving,' she said, shaking as she pressed the hanky to her nose.

'He's going home,' murmured Iqbal.

'Don't give me that. Don't give me any of that heaven, God, going home shit. I don't believe it!' There was a rage in her voice as if a fissure had opened and released a jet of fire.

'But he believes,' pleaded Iqbal.

'I know he does. And that's the problem. Always has been. God, God, God, God, GOD!'

Iqbal took her by the shoulders, shaking his head, shushing and clicking his tongue. 'No, no, no,' he hushed.

'Oh, yes! Everything – us – given up for God – sacrificed, thrown to the birds.'

Iqbal sucked in his breath. 'Never, never,' he breathed.

'Yes, ALWAYS. God took everything!' And she flung Iqbal's hands off her shoulders and curled up again, overcome by sobs.

By the time her cries had settled to occasional shudders, the night had become dark. She blew her nose and sat up, pulling her jacket close. Just off the edge of the veranda, Iqbal was building a small pyramid of sticks over dry leaves. There was a rattle of matches, a spark, then a tongue of flame. Iqbal fed it with tiny twigs until there was a crackle and spit and one of the bigger sticks flared.

Ruth felt another tear run down her cheek and brushed it roughly away, fumbling in her pocket for a cigarette. Lighting up, she leaned back against a pillar and cursed the trembling of her hands and the after-sobs that kept rising, unbidden. Iqbal did not look at her and it was a long time before he spoke.

'You have celebrated Eid-ul-Fitr with me.' He paused. 'But there is another Eid, coming soon. Eid-ul-Adha. I hope you will be here for that one also – it is very special.' The fire hissed, a burst of sparks. 'It remembers when God asked Ibrahim to lay his only beloved son on the altar.'

Ruth watched him, the way the firelight played over his face, alight, shining, etched with dark.

His voice held sadness. 'Because Ibrahim loved that child more than anything.'

Hers was a rasp. 'And God can't bear that.'

'God loved him even more. And he gave the sheep.'

'Not for me.' Or for Manveer, she thought.

Iqbal was quiet. Poked another stick in the fire.

'For you too. The Lamb of God.'

Ruth felt the heat of the fire on her face, the swelling of raw eyeballs, the cracks in her lips.

'But sometimes,' Iqbal went on, 'we keep our beloved on the altar because we have not seen the lamb.'

The pines above stirred in a soft breeze, a sighing chorus.

'Or,' he propped his elbows on his knees, hands dangling, 'because we cannot believe it is enough.'

She waited, but he was still.

'What d'you mean?'

For the first time since lighting the fire he looked at her, his gaze gentle yet penetrating; then he turned to the dark archway of the living room behind.

'Is very quiet for a house full of ghosts.'

Ruth followed his gaze, then looked back to his face.

'The poisoned British family,' he went on. 'The caste-breaking lovers, hmm? Perhaps my own father is sometimes visiting.'

A silence.

'And the other ghosts, Ruthie? Shall we let them go?'

She said nothing. Just smoked and kept her gaze on the fire.

'I read your letters, but they are stopping at the most interesting part. You are in Delhi, rehearsing for *Gospel of Jyoti*. But then? Nothing more.'

The breeze in the pines picked up, the fire whipped.

Her voice held a vast weariness. 'The end.'

'Please tell.'

'What do you already know?'

'Not much, I think. Not your side.'

She was quiet for the longest time, and then began, in a low, ragged voice, to tell the whole story, from assassination to lovers tryst, mob violence to haircut, Manveer's death to Mr Haskell's lie. How no-one believed her and she had been blamed. How, after her expulsion, she was not allowed to go home, but made to stay with another family in Kanpur because Ellen said her presence would make James worse. It seemed Ellen herself could not bear to be near her. How, when they packed for America a few weeks later, Ellen told her she would not be coming back. And how, at Hannah's wedding in Tennessee, just after they arrived, the bride was radiant but the rest of the family so destroyed they could barely speak. The day after, Ruth had got on a Greyhound bus and left.

'But the worst thing,' she said, 'was thinking about Manveer's parents. They had to come all the way from Canada to collect the body of their first born, their only son, their beloved. And what did they find, when they took him in their arms? His hair hacked off and no sacred comb. No shorts to guard his purity, no *kirpan* at his side, no *kara*. Not one of the Five Ks left. Nothing but a body that had broken the law of chastity and – so they were told – the law against addictive substances. Their son was not just dead, he was desecrated.'

She was quiet. Her voice, when it came, was a whisper. 'And all... because of me.'

There was a long silence, with only the hushing of the trees and the burning of the fire.

'You are carrying great burden,' Iqbal said at last. 'And this is why you are losing God.'

There was silence.

'No Iqbal,' she replied. 'God is why I lost everything.'

He shook his head softly and held a stick in the flames.

'Please,' he asked. 'May I also tell one story? Is not explaining all things, but maybe casting the light.'

Ruth nodded and moved closer to the fire.

The story Iqbal told was not his own, but the story of one who had been unable to speak it himself. The whole story, from a buck's head to a pair of burnt boots, from a widow's screams to a boy's silent pledge, from a father's cross to a daughter's fall.

FORTY-FIVE

James had often played with the baby Iqbal on the south veranda of Askival where the sun fell in slanting rectangles. When they returned to it over fifty years later, the house was quietly falling apart, a sheet of tin roof missing, windows long gone, walls crumbling. But on that late May day the sun was languid and soft, sweet with the sap of deodar and the warm fragrance of grass. Wild roses grew up the pillars and tangled with the broken guttering. Stands of purple cosmos filled the terraces, butterflies skittered. The two men sat in pools of light, sunshine warming their heads, and looked down to the spread of the bazaar and on to the gauzy blur of the plains. Crickets sang.

James did not need to tell the whole story – the truth at last – because Iqbal already knew it. In fact, Iqbal had told it to him the night before when James finally let him in. It was the night, three weeks after Ellen's death, when James had tried to cook Tuna Hash but ended on the sofa, sobbing.

Iqbal told the story just as Salima had told it to him: in quiet voice, with no one else around. Because she knew and had always known. Aziz feared guns and had never touched the Connors' weapons. Though he'd often accompanied them on their hunts, it was for the butchering and cooking, but never to shoot. And even if, in the terror of that night, he'd dared to lift the rifle, he would not have known what to do with it, how to aim, what to push or pull. Most likely he would have shot himself. What's more, Salima knew he wasn't wearing his glasses. The spares, for which he had returned to Askival, were tucked inside his shawl back at Rampur House. She'd found them the next day. But more than all of that, Salima knew because of James: his face when he arrived with Leota, his hands clawing at his sweaty underarms, his running away.

But she never breathed a word to anyone but Iqbal and swore him to secrecy. It was the Connors' missionary friends in Pakistan who employed them, the Connors' pension that sent Iqbal to school, the Connors' good name that guaranteed them work, shelter and a future, and the Connors' story, therefore, that must be maintained.

The truth, she told Iqbal, was that his father was noble and brave and good. He had taken no life, but had given his own for the love of others.

James acknowledged this truth like a leper unwrapping bandages. It was a truth so deeply buried beneath the accretions of guilt and shame, and such a threat to the family mythology, that he'd never been able to expose it. He'd never told anyone. Not even Ellen. He had come close, in the time after his breakdown when he was recovering in a retreat house in Arizona. It was run by Catholic monks and the very idea of it would have made his flesh crawl a few years earlier, but Ellen had pleaded and James was so deep in despair he was past caring where they put him. He was given a spiritual director who quietly walked him to meals and prayers and out into the desert each day. The Brother asked nothing and James said nothing. Silence. After the mountains of India and the crush of its plains, this place was empty. He could see nothing in it, hear nothing, smell nothing. Slowly, he realised the Brother was talking; just a little bit, now and again. Not about James' breakdown, or his past, or his faith. He was simply pointing out a cactus coming into flower, the cry of a bird, the colours in the rock. Then one day it rained. James stood in it, the silver needles sloping down and impaling him, the smell of the dirt rising up; it was like a ladder of angels descending and ascending into heaven.

That night, as he lay his head against the communion rail, the Brother told James that, whatever he'd done, God had forgiven him.

All James could tell Ellen was that they were going back to India.

What began through the Brother in the desert, and was nearly destroyed at Ellen's death, found new life in Iqbal. The man had not come to accuse, to avenge or to demand reparation. He had come to fulfil his father's heart.

James did not say much to Iqbal that day, but enough to ask and receive the forgiveness that was needed. As they closed the gate on Askival and walked home, the trees around were alive with birds.

FORTY-SIX

It was the final rehearsal in Benson Hall, the day before they squeezed into their bus and drove down to Delhi. Mr Haskell told them to give it all they had, like it was the real thing, a full-on performance with a packed house.

But because they did not know this rehearsal was all they would have – because they still believed in happy endings – it became something of a farce. People forgot their lines, costumes fell off, ankle bells went skidding across the stage. There was giggling and hi-jinks and so much fun in the dressing room that the Wedding at Kanpur scene began completely without guests. At which point, Mr Haskell threw down his script.

'Get out!' he yelled. 'Leave!' Everyone froze. 'I have worked myself to the *bone* on this show. For years.' His face was wild. 'I didn't force anyone to join me. *You* wanted to be a part of this. And all along I said it would be hard work and I didn't want half-hearts or lazy-bones or fools. All or nothing!'

There was a terrible silence.

'So go!' His voice was like a cry in the desert, his finger pointing to the door. 'Go now if you will not give me your best.' No one moved or made a sound. There was a glitter in Mr Haskell's eyes as he spun on his heel and walked up the long aisle alone. At the door he turned.

'I'm coming back in ten minutes. If you're still here, then you're promising to work your *butts* off.'

They were all there. And their butts did not disappoint. They worked like it was the real thing, and when they looked back they were glad of it, for in the end it was all they had.

Especially Ruth. She danced like her life depended on it; like it was her life. As she waited in the wings during the Feeding of the Five Thousand she felt a speeding of her heartbeat. The disciples were singing and passing chapattis around. Manveer was standing beside her, close enough that they nearly touched. Then Jesu was alone on the stage. He tore a last chapatti in his hands, lifted it to heaven and cried out, 'This is my body.' It was Ruth's cue.

'Break a leg,' Manveer whispered, his lips moving close to the sparkly scarf on her hair. She flashed him a smile and spun onto the stage. This was Maya Magdalen's most impressive scene: the exorcising of her demons. The cast had entered a lengthy discussion about what these demons might have been, as the original text is not specific, but Mr Haskell eventually settled on the Deadly Sins. Thus, the scene came to be called the Dance of the Seven Deadly Djinns, with the evil spirits represented by coloured scarves tucked into her waist.

Maya's first weapon of attack was Lust, the one by which she plied her trade and gained power over men. Mrs Banwarilal's original choreography was so potent, however, that a sweating Mr Haskell had been required to edit it. Jesu, of course, was unphased and whipped the offending red scarf from her waist the moment before she pinned him to the ground.

Maya spun into her Gluttony sequence, rolling her eyes and gnashing her teeth as if she would devour him on the spot. But just as she seized his chapatti, Jesu got her orange scarf and flung it to the corner of the stage. She surrendered the chapatti and he tore off a piece and offered it. She took, but did not eat.

It was Sloth next, though that was a little harder to dance. They'd tried a few approaches. In one, she had lain on the floor being bored and beautiful with Jesu trying to kick her into action. It made everyone laugh and him look impotent. Then there was the idea of her with a water pot that she was refusing to carry to the well, but it just made her appear petulant and alluring, and him... well, impotent again, so they cut it. It provoked a heated debate about the nature of Sloth. Was it merely a 'couldn't be bothered' Sunday afternoon feeling, and if so, was that such a sin? Or was it more? Dorcas raised the point about the sins of inaction. So, for Sloth, a stream of beggars, lepers and starving children passed across the stage as Maya pressed her hands over her mouth, her ears, and her eyes. Until Jesu yanked out the yellow scarf and she turned to see them.

Avarice was easy. She stole all the jewellery off the girls in the chorus line and gathered it into her blue scarf. Jesu hurled it into the wings where Kashi was supposed to catch it, but failed every time, occasioning a clattering of bangles and bells and a great deal of hissed swearing.

For Envy, Maya wound her green scarf around herself and then twisted and wrung it till finally it threatened to strangle her. Jesu removed it in the nick of time, stamping on its python head.

But was Maya Magdalen grateful? No indeed, she was furious. Seething. Like a wounded beast she roared her Wrath at Jesu, her feet pounding the stage, arms flailing. When he finally wrestled the black scarf from her hands, she spun helplessly to one side and stopped, crouching, with arms gripping herself. He let the scarf drop, stood panting and watching her, his bare chest a glistening sheen, eyes like burning coals. Then he offered his hand.

But did she take it? Was she thankful yet for all he had cast out? No! Of course not. She recoiled from him, drew herself up to her full height and turned her back. One demon remained. The last demon, most deeply rooted, for it was the first. The first sin, indeed, even before the Fall. The one that caused the fall before the Fall. The fall to end all falls, to start all falls, to set the Fall rolling, one might say.

Maya's back was like stone, her neck long and hard, arms clenched as if chained, breast cold. How can Jesu break Pride? How remove her purple scarf, now she has pulled it over her face? He seems to have given up. He picks up a broom and sweeps. He carries a clay pot and pours water into a blue plastic basin. Tying the scarf of Wrath around his waist, he kneels at Maya's feet, the basin at his side. She is still turned away, her face to the back wall. He sprinkles water on her ankles, her heels. Her head drops an inch. He lifts one foot; she trembles slightly, balancing on the other. He washes the foot, dries it with his scarf and sets it down. Her head is lower now, resting on her chest. He washes the other foot, this time with tears, and presses it into his hair. Her back is bent forward, her body shaking. Then he kisses her foot, and she falls. Free.

FORTY-SEVEN

In the days after Ruth and Iqbal swapped stories at Askival, she found herself sleeping long hours at night and falling into a doze through the day. It was a healing rest and she gave herself up to its deep work. In bed at night she read the letters sent to James on her mother's death, and with the familiar ache of loss, felt a swelling of love and pride.

Through the day, she stayed beside James and wondered how to begin. He slept even more than her and Ruth would watch him, fearing that this time he would not wake. She caught herself praying for time. For courage.

But Iqbal made her leave the house, sending her on small errands to Sisters Bazaar or the post box near Morrison Church. Just enough time to breathe and feel the sunshine and smell the quiet earth. It was late October and the rains were only a memory, the hillside lush and scrubbed clean, the blue skies clear as a bell.

'A new day!' Iqbal would say each morning. Did he know it had been Ellen's line, especially on mornings when the day before had been difficult or the day to come? Like the days they left for boarding, or the morning of Hannah's wedding.

Hannah would be with them at the end of the week and Ruth felt both eagerness and anxiety. She had always been welcomed at her sister's house, but the visits invariably caused mounting tension till Hannah was reduced to polite, strained sentences and Ruth to swearing. Then she would leave. They never got to the bottom of things; it was too far down.

On her errands, Ruth met people who asked after James and she found it in herself to be courteous, to answer and to listen. It was for him. He'd always had time to stop and be with people. It had annoyed her as a child, and she'd tugged on his legs and whined at him to keep going, but now that he could no longer do it himself, she felt she must. She was his embassy in the world and the knowledge of how poorly she had represented him brought shame.

It was the feeling that had dogged her since her teens, when her rebellion became wilful, rather than the mere product of personality or pain. She had tried to smother the shame with her sense of injustice, but it only deepened the wound, causing a kind of life-long internal bleeding. And now she was weary. There was no strength left for arguing half-truths or upholding well-worn defences. And strangely, letting them fall did not feel like defeat but a relieved surrender. She had drawn her battle lines in all the wrong places and misunderstood the enemy.

When she arrived home one day she saw Iqbal through the window, kneeling beside her father's bed, talking with him. He was holding James' hands and his face was intent and earnest, almost pleading. As Ruth walked in, he looked up, startled, and with a quick squeeze of James' hands, stood and started bustling with the shopping bags. James' gaze was on the forested ridges to the east, a rumpled blanket of fading greens beneath the wide sky. A great bird wheeled on the currents above Witches Hill and far off, a truck lumbered like a beetle on the Tehri road.

That night Iqbal and Ruth made chapattis and channa for

supper. Whenever Ruth looked across, James was watching her, completely still but for his eyes. They spread the food on the coffee table and sat on the sofa opposite his bed, bowing their heads for his prayer. It did not come and Ruth stole a glance. He looked asleep, hands folded in his lap, a soft rise and fall in his chest. Then his eyes suddenly flashed open, bright and steely as a hawk's, looking from her to Iqbal.

'Who will pray?' his voice rattled. Though faint, it sounded to Ruth like a prophet's cry. She blinked at him, then turned to Iqbal, who simply nudged her in the ribs and dropped his head.

'For what we are about to receive,' she mumbled, 'may the Lord make us truly thankful.'

Grandma Leota's prayer.

'Amen!' exclaimed Iqbal as James gave a small grunt.

Iqbal offered each dish to James, who shook his head and lifted a crabbed hand in refusal. As the other two ate, they talked about the Oaklands Activity Week. The students were all away on their projects: a hike to the source of the Ganga, a team to Mother Theresa's in Kolkata, an art tour of Rajasthan. Iqbal's Indian music pupils were performing in Delhi, though he had made his apologies in order to stay with James.

'Not as good as your *Gospel of Jyoti*,' he said, spooning dahi onto his plate, 'but we have done our best.' Ruth stopped chewing. Slipped her gaze to James. Since their long-ago phone call on the day of Mrs Gandhi's cremation, the production had never been mentioned. He looked at her and tilted his head the tiniest bit. Letting out a soft, whistling breath, he dropped his gaze to the chapattis.

'We sure were sorry to miss that show.'

She swallowed. 'It was understandable.'

'So sad it all went so wrong. A terrible time.'

The air pressed around her, pricking with the quietest of sounds: the faraway buzz of a motorbike, the hinges of a screen door, a distant child crying.

'The show was nothing,' she mumbled. 'You were going through much worse.'

'And you, Ruthie. Much worse than we knew.' His voice was slow, infinitely gentle. 'But we should have known.'

'No, no. How could you? You weren't there.'

'I know. I'm sorry.'

It caught her breath, held her. Then words came in stutters. 'But I know you couldn't be, with all the riots – I don't – I do understand—'

'No. Not then,' he said, and paused. 'All the other times.'

He reached for the chapattis, his bony hands trembling, and Iqbal quickly extended the plate. James took one, tore it in half and raised his eyes to Ruth.

'In the end, when you needed us, little *Piyari*, we were not there. I'm sorry.'

She could not speak or move.

He offered half the chapatti to Iqbal and half to Ruth.

'Take,' he said.

They held out their hands like beggars and he rested the pieces of chapatti in their palms. Iqbal lifted it to his forehead and then lowered it to his knees and gazed at it. Ruth was still.

'Eat,' James said. 'It is given for you.'

She understood. Keeping her eyes on the chapatti, she tore off a corner and ate it, slowly, the bread taking the longest time to soften and slip down, where it was a lump in her throat. She looked up at James and saw his eyes resting on her. It was the face she remembered from childhood. The searching intensity of his eyes, the looking right inside her but not fathoming; the knowing and the not knowing, the understanding and the questioning.

She moved around the table and knelt at the side of his bed. Tearing a fragment of chapatti, she laid it into his outstretched hands. He lifted them, shaking, and lowered his head till his cracked lips closed over the bread. With his face in his hands, he ate and she could see the effort as he swallowed. He reached for the cup of water on the table, spilling it over the rim. Iqbal leapt to help, but James turned it to him.

'Take,' he said. 'Drink.'

Iqbal knelt and sipped. James held out the shaking cup to Ruth and she drank, the water sloshing over the sides and down her chin. She wiped her mouth on her sleeve, took the cup and held it for him. He folded his hands over hers, which made the cup jerk and bump against his teeth. The water spilled over his lips, down his jaw and neck and onto his clothes. But he held it there till he had drunk and swallowed.

Her voice came in a whisper. 'I'm sorry.'

Iqbal took the cup and left them, Ruth kneeling beside James, her arms flung across him, face buried in his side.

FORTY-EIGHT

The next night, as the Friday prayer call pierced the dark outside, Ruth watched Iqbal set down his cloth at the kitchen bench, wash his hands and open the cupboard next to the sink. He drew out his rolled mat and cap and she knew his next move would be to get James' Bible from the bookshelf. But this time she took it down herself, lowering the ancient book to her father's lap like a sleeping bird. James was propped up on a dike of cushions and even lifting his head was a strain.

As Iqbal donned his white cap, Ruth sensed him waiting for her to go, as she always had done. But she returned to her chair in the corner and sat cross-legged, feet tucked in. He stared from her to her father, but James merely continued turning the pages of the Bible, which he could barely hold. The fragile paper shook. A rustling of words, a stirring of feathers. Iqbal finally took a seat opposite Ruth and clutched his mat.

In a faded, rattling voice James read:
Come let us worship and bow down,
let us kneel before the Lord our God,
our Maker.
There was silence. Waiting.

Ruth closed her eyes. The night was full of still, small voices: the notes of birds, the movement of deepdown things, the breathing of trees. They whispered of all that had passed the night before, in the mystery of bread and cup and the making of peace.

When she opened her eyes, Iqbal had unrolled his prayer mat in the middle of the room and was standing at one end with his hands at his sides. He lifted his hands above his shoulders, fingers open, tips just touching his ears, and began to sing in Arabic. It was ancient and strange but there were words she knew: *Allah – o – Akbar.* God is great. As his voice rose and wound itself like invisible ropes in the air, she watched the devotion playing across his face, the trembling of his cheeks and lips, the barely shielded light beneath his lids. He sang on, folding his hands across his chest, bowing, kneeling and dropping forward, nose to the floor.

Ruth looked at James. He was motionless, hands resting on the Bible, eyes closed. Something inside her took flight.

FORTY-NINE

On Saturday morning James lay on the camp bed, his limbs hanging like old leaves, ready for the slightest wind to tug them free. There was light in the room and song: an old recording of a *ghazal* singer lifting a cracked voice to heaven.

He watched Ruth through half-closed eyes: the gentle curve of her back as she stooped and stretched, the toss of curls, the fluid arms with their brown-backed hands that were never still. She was pouring hot water into a blue plastic basin, the steam rising around her in clouds. A squirt of bubble bath, a gush from the cold tap, a testing with her fingers. The water sloshing slightly, she carried it over to him and set it on the floor. Then she smiled.

Iqbal came with a towel and soap and squatted beside James.

'Ready ji?'

James gave the barest nod and felt Iqbal's plump hands slide beneath him. As they laid him on the couch, covered with a plastic sheet and towels, he felt the sunshine from the tall windows reach across him like a warm wing. Kneeling, Ruth unbuttoned his flannelette pyjama top and talked about the flowers blooming on the hillside: the cosmos and the wild dahlias and the small, bright things that clung to cliff and branch. He smiled. Iqbal draped a towel over his lap and reached underneath to tug his pyjama bottoms down. Gently, they stroked warm flannels over his body, Iqbal working below the waist, Ruth above. She told him she'd walked the back *chakkar* early that morning and heard the whistling thrush. He nodded and gave himself to the lifting and washing, body loose as an empty sack, head brimming. The snows were out, she went on, and in the sunrise they were lit up. Like angels.

He closed his eyes and felt her cradle his head in one hand as she poured water over the crown. She began to rub in shampoo, her *kara* bumping softly against him as the lather rose round his skull and gave off a long-forgotten fragrance. It filled him, humming notes of jasmine, of sun-dried washing, of Ellen.

At the other end of his body, Iqbal knelt and bathed his feet.

Then they dressed him in his soft, worn clothes, wrapped him in a thick shawl and carried him to a chair on the front terrace. The sky was an ocean of air, clear from its blue depths to its infinite shores, galleon clouds resting on its wide sweep. A light wind teased the clumps of wildflowers on the *khud* and trembled the deep green oaks. Then the wind turned and rushed up the slope, flipping the leaves and turning the hillside silver. Below him, the mountain fell away into the green swathe of the Dun valley where the twin sacred rivers coursed like ribbons of light.

And in the silence, he felt it.

A creature landing at his side, wings flashing in the sun.

And in its voice he heard it. At last.

The Hundredth and the Holy.

The Beautiful.

The Beloved.

FIFTY

Hannah arrived that night. Iqbal adored her at once and the pair worked in the kitchen together, chattering like old gossips about her children and how India had changed and the difference between chapattis and tortillas. Ruth stayed at James' side.

He drifted in and out of sleep, in and out of consciousness. Sometimes, in his faraway place, he smiled. Once, even, he laughed and they turned to look at him. His eyes were still closed, but he was saying something Ruth didn't understand. A strange tongue, whose name she didn't know. Sometimes his face was troubled, or his breathing fast and desperate. Even when his eyes opened they looked out on a different world.

The three laid out their bedding on the living room floor, though none of them slept much. A small lamp glowed in the corner of the room as they took it in turns to sit beside James.

When it was Hannah's shift, Ruth lay and watched her. Her long brown hair was drawn back into a bun at the nape of her neck, a few strands at the side of her face softening the severity. There were streaks of grey now, and Ruth knew Hannah wouldn't dye it, just as she never wore make-up or jewellery. The single gold band on her finger was her only adornment, as it had been for Ellen. Ruth had compensated for the family spurning of jewellery by piercing all the way up both ears, her nose and her navel and wearing rings on all her fingers, some on her toes, a tangle of necklaces and a shifting array of bands round her ankles. But she'd slowly shed them in her time in Mussoorie, lightening the load. Even the glass bracelets Iqbal had given at Eid were soon slipped off so as not to scrape James when she nursed him.

All that was left now was Manveer's *kara*.

It was hard against her skin as she lay with her hands folded under her cheek, watching Hannah, who sat so still, watching James. Ruth hadn't seen her for three years and was struck by the signs of age. Her forehead was creased and there were shadows under her eyes, made darker by the low light. Hannah's eldest two were away at college now and who could guess the anxiety for a mother who had hovered over them from birth.

Ruth had always wondered at it. Since marrying Derek in Tennessee at 21, Hannah had stayed in that same small town and never once been back to India. Never been out of America! She, who had graduated Valedictorian of her class and Best All Round Student, had neither finished her liberal arts degree nor ever had a job. She had home-schooled all seven children, made every curtain and cushion cover in the house and grown prize vegetables. As if she'd never had her Indian life. Or needed to counter it.

When it was Iqbal's shift, he could barely sit still. He was up and down to the kitchen getting damp cloths, dry cloths, a hot water bottle, a cup of ice, glasses of water and boxes of tissues. None were needed. He mopped James' brow, smoothed and tucked his blankets, and when he could think of nothing more to do, sat perched on the edge of the chair twisting his fingers and looking from James to the others in desperation.

Ruth felt for him in the void that lay ahead. James had already put Shanti Niwas into his name and made provision for his retirement, but Iqbal was a man made to pour himself out in love. For whom would he do that now? Then she remembered the mosaic of photos on his wall and the many Oaklands students who would learn from him a *ghazal* or a *sheesh kebab* or the wonder of grace. There would be no end.

At Ruth's turn, she just sat and held her father's hand. The dark outside seemed to deepen and spread, like an ink that was leaking into the house, into her aching limbs and all the spaces in her head. She did not know how long she'd been there, but woke to the rasping of his voice and a tug from his fingers. He was using that language again, barely a whisper. That unearthly river of sound, that seemed to come not so much from him, as through him. All she recognised in the spill of words was her name, leaping like a fish from the stream.

FIFTY-ONE

Paul Verghese conducted the funeral, eyes brimming behind his blocky spectacles, voice raised like a bugle. Ruth had expected a verbose and florid eulogy and a long sermon, but the Reverend was changed. Perhaps because of the threatening tides of emotion within him, or the standing-room-only crush of the church, or by dint of some other mysterious force, she did not know, but he lost all the usual rhetorical elaboration and wagging of fingers and spoke with a rare power.

James' life, he said, was a true story and a parable. He was Pilgrim, he was Everyman, he was Adam. And God's dealings with him were a picture of God's dealings with us all, should we only accept it. Verghese pushed his glasses up his nose and took hold of the pulpit with both hands. James did not want his praises sung, he said. He had forbidden it. He wanted one thing only: the truth.

And so the Reverend did his best to tell it, revealing the long-held secret and its legacy, drawing together James' tortuous journey to peace and Iqbal's testimony of love, the counterpoint memories of Hannah and Ruth, his own long friendship and the accounts of others. He knew the truth of a life was not an isolated narrative, but the confluence of all the stories it had created in the lives of others. So as he set out the tale, moving constantly from English to Hindi and back, the throng grew quiet, hearing about a man they treasured and a man they had barely known.

'Friends,' Verghese said at the end, 'I have no better way to finish the testimony of this man's life than in the words of his own choosing.' He unfolded three sheets of paper, crumpled, dog-eared and frayed. The typed text was much scored and hatched, the margins dense with notes. 'Months ago I asked Dr James to give the sermon one Sunday. He kept telling me he wasn't ready, was still working on it. The last time I saw him, he gave this to me and said, *It is finished.*'

Verghese smoothed the sheets on the pulpit.

'In the end, he crossed everything out.' He looked up and over the hundreds of heads before him. 'Months of work, years perhaps. A lifetime. On the last page, only this remained.'

An intense quiet; even the children stopped their scuffling.

'Dear friends, let us love one another, for love comes from God. Everyone who loves has been born of God and knows God. Whoever does not love does not know God, because God is love. This is how God showed his love among us—'

His voice began to crack.

'He sent his one and only Son into the world that we might live through him. This is love: not that we loved God –'

He paused, pressed his hand over his trembling chin. Took a breath.

'– but that he loved us and sent his Son as an atoning sacrifice for our sins. Dear friends, since God so loved us, we ought also to love one another.'

Verghese whipped off his glasses, face crumpling, tears splashing down his nose.

James was buried beside Ellen that bright October day, a gentle sunshine falling on bowed heads and damp faces. The deodars were a guard of honour, branches hushing an ancient requiem, sap a pungent balm for the dead. All around, the steep bank was velvety with moss and dotted with flowers, while at their feet, the open grave smelled of deepdown things, of the falling and dying of leaves, the rising of life.

Ruth and Hannah stood close, arms around each other's waist, leaning together and shaking as they wept. James' death had opened spaces between them and they had shared much, including Ruth's lost baby. Hannah had cried for her and gathered wildflowers which she now dropped into James' grave, whispering to Ruth, 'For our little David'. Iqbal was at their side, his hands twisted together, face a waterfall. He was meant to sing *Amazing Grace* at the end, but only got to the second verse when he broke down. Hannah and Ruth wrapped their arms around him as Mrs Puri took up the tune, bosom heaving, eyes closed.

Tis grace that brought me safe thus far,
And grace shall lead me home.

As the others made their way up the steep path to the road, the sisters stayed by the grave, their hands dirty from the earth they had thrown. When all was quiet Ruth knelt and pulled the *kara* from her wrist, touched it to her lips and let it fall onto the dark soil.

FIFTY-TWO

The next night, Ruth walked with Hannah and Iqbal into a sea of lights. It was Diwali. The walkways leading to the school Quad were lined with *dias,* oil lamps that flickered like fireflies, while above and around them, the balconies were festooned with bright coloured bulbs. Streamers criss-crossed the open space, and from every pillar and railing there was the gentle swinging of paper lanterns, foil stars and flowers.

'So lovely!' Ruth said, stopped in her tracks. At their feet was a geometric design made of coloured chalk with a *dia* in the middle. Further designs dotted the pavements, drawing them in and reminding her of the mandala Kashi had created the night before *Gospel* went to Delhi. Tonight she was in a sari for the first time since dancing Maya Magdalen. A deep, shimmering turquoise, it had been a gift from Mrs Puri. Hannah's was midnight blue, while Iqbal remained in mourning white.

They stood watching a troupe of elementary girls swirling in wide skirts, clapping and skipping their way through a Garhwali folk dance. After them, a long line of school servants dressed in lungis and turbans filed into the space and formed a circle. Their bare chests glistened in the lights and in their hands were brightly coloured sticks.

'Oho!' said Iqbal, 'The banghra! This is the best bit.'

'Yeah, I remember,' Ruth nodded, smiling, but before she could say more, the loud music had struck up and the men were off, circling and twisting, leaping and hitting their sticks together. These were wrapped with cap gun paper, making the whole performance a wild, fire-cracking whirl. Suddenly the dancers threw their sticks to the ground, broke rank and ran into the crowd, catching people and pulling them into the dance.

Ruth protested but Hannah grabbed her other hand and drew her in.

'Come on Ruthie!' she cried over the din. 'This one's for you!'

The music lifted and wailed and the circle took off, pounding around to the left, hopping and clapping, then stamping back round to the right. Inevitably, people collided, turned the wrong way, dug each other in the ribs and buttocks, tripped on saris and lost shoes. But all were laughing: hooting, squealing, rippling with laughter; even Ruth, who couldn't remember when she had laughed so hard. As the music went wild, she found herself stamping and sweeping like a dervish, and when it finally blasted to its triumphant close she threw herself into the roar of voices and applause, almost splitting her sari blouse as she gasped for breath.

Her head was wheeling, her sides aching, her feet on fire.

* * * * *

She returned to Askival alone. In the deep quiet of dawn she walked up the path and around the house to the rise behind it where the giant deodars stood. Beneath her to the south, the bazaar and the lower hills were sunk in darkness. The sky rose from it, seamless, blurring from black to inky blue to a humming indigo in the north-east. There, the long line of the

Himalayas was a silhouette, its ragged edge growing sharper against the lightening sky.

A touch of wind feathered the trees and she breathed in their cedar scent and the foretaste of winter. Rubbing herself to keep warm, she felt the empty space at her wrist where the kara had been, and the tenderness in her ribs from last night's dancing.

Askival sat hunched in the clearing below her with its face dark, shadows pooling on the veranda. She watched the slow coming of light over its broken roof and walls, its empty windows and lost doors. It would fall down, she knew. It would crumble, till the stones returned to the ground and the trees grew up through the floor and the birds came back to build their nests. And it would be beautiful again.

ACKNOWLEDGEMENTS

I am deeply grateful to so many people for their help in the writing of this book. Their number is legion, their kindness unbound.

Firstly, the many staff, alumni and associates of Woodstock School, India, who answered countless questions and shared with me their memories. It would take another volume to name them all, but special th anks to: Kavi Singh, for reading a draft and providing help, history and humour; Steve Alter, for support personally and through Mussoorie Writers; Deirdré Straughan, for gathering a treasure-trove of stories for the school's 150th; and to the late and much-loved Reverend Bob Alter, who was a rich store of information and encouragement. I am indebted to the memoirs of several from the Woodstock community, especially Steve Alter, Joseph Alter, Stanley Brush, Katharine Parker Riddle, and Marguerite Thoburn Watkins. Thanks also to Ganesh Saili, Ruskin Bond, Inder Prakash, Vinoo Bhagat, and the late Miss Edith Garlah for helpful information. And lastly, from the Woodstock stable, my love and thanks to Kathy Hoffmann, English teacher, mentor and dear friend, for reading many drafts and lending wise feedback and unflagging faith.

Others also gave generously of their time to read a draft and offer responses. Thanks to John Jebaseelan, Indrajit Ayer, Barbara Deutschmann, Anna Ghosh, Arun (Prabha) Mukherjee, Claire Anderson-Wheeler, and Sara Maitland, through Hi-Arts. In addition: Chris Powici, who also gave encouragement through Stirling Writers and Northwords Now; Kirsty Williams of BBC Scotland, who has been a stalwart champion; Fiona Thackeray, friend and writing buddy; Jo Falla, sage mentor; and the late and much-missed Gavin Wallace of Creative Scotland. Deep gratitude to Maria White of Booklink, who gave so much.

I acknowledge the support of key organisations in the writing of this book and extend my appreciation to: Creative Scotland for a generous bursary; Jan Rutherford and The Scottish Book Trust for granting me a mentorship; Peter Urpeth of Emergents (formerly Hi-Arts) for ongoing support; and the Arvon Foundation at Moniack Mhor for two weeks with inspirational fellow writers. Thanks also to the encouragement of those in the Society of Authors in Scotland and The Highland Literary Salon.

Deepest thanks to the team at Freight Books, especially Adrian Searle for believing in this, banking on it and being kind, and to Elizabeth Reeder, fine editor, for having the perfect balance of incision and respect.

This novel was begun on the dining table of soul friends Tony & Rosas Mitchell. To them and the many companions who have journeyed with me - sharing the bread of life, the water in the desert - my heartfelt thanks. We will be friends forever. And longer.

Immeasurable love and gratitude go to my family, both at the beginning and now. To Warren and Jessie, for raising me in Nepal, India and Pakistan and in the embrace of Love. To brother Mark, for being my oldest friend and for adding your fine ones to our tribe. To the Appleby Harpa tree, for grafting me in. To my precious two, Sam and Luke, for growing up under my ribs, listening to stories; to Alistair, kindred spirit, provider, beloved, for making this possible and for being my home.

GLOSSARY

accha – okay

ahimsa – non-violence

alu – potato

arè – an exclamation.
Arè yaar! equivalent to 'Hey, mate!'

ayah – nanny

babu – courtesy title for a man, like 'Mr'; also term for a clerk

bahot – very

bara – big

beta, beti – child (ending in 'a' for male and 'i' for female)

bidi – cigarette of tobacco rolled in a dried leaf

bistar – bedroll

brinjal – aubergine

chaan – cow shed, often also serving as temporary accommodation for herders

chakkar – circle road or path

chalo – 'Let's go!'

channa – chickpeas

chaprassi – junior office worker who carries messages; peon

chokra – young servant boy

chotta hazri – 'little breakfast', snack taken first thing in the morning,

chowkidar – watchman

chula – charcoal burning stove

churiwalla/churiwalli – bangle seller

darzi – tailor

dekchi – cooking pot

desi khana – Indian food, (literally, the food of this country)

dhobi – washerman

dia – small clay lamp

dudh-walla – milkman

Eid Mubarak – a congratulatory greeting: 'May your Eid Celebration be Blessed!'

garam – hot

ghazal – ancient poetic form, often sung

ghoral – mountain goat

gobi – cauliflower

gosht – meat, usually lamb or mutton

gur – dark brown sugar sold in a cake and melted to a syrup

hah – yes

harijan – 'child of God,' term used by Gandhi for the untouchables

jal – water

jaldi – quickly

jamadar – toilet cleaner

ji – honorific suffix added to name or title, or used alone

jyoti – light

kadai – bowl shaped dish with two handles for making curries

kachha – badly made

kala sangam – confluence, coming together
kanga – comb worn by Sikhs
kara – metal bracelet worn by Sikhs
kesh – term for Sikhs' uncut hair
khana – food
khansamma – cook
khud – steep drop down the side of a hill
khoon ka badla khoon – 'blood for blood'
kirpan – knife carried by Sikhs
koi bat nahi – 'It doesn't matter.'
idli – white, savoury cake from South India
machan – platform in tree built for a hunter
maf kijiye – forgive me
mali – gardener
mochi – cobbler
nahi chahiye – 'Not needed.'
namaaz – Muslim ritual prayer to be performed five times a day
namkin – savoury snack
paan – areca nut and spices wrapped in a betel leaf
padam – Himalayan wild cherry
paneer – curd cheese
patka – head-covering worn by Sikh men under the turban, or instead of the turban for boys
punkah – large swinging fan fixed to the ceiling and pulled by a servant
piyari – beloved
rat ki rani – night blooming climber with fragrant white flowers, 'queen of the night'
razai – cotton quilt
sadarni – Sikh woman

sag – edible greens
sahib – sir
sadhu – holy man
sani – little
samaan – luggage
satyagraha – truth force
sheesh kebab – meat or vegetables cooked on a skewer
shikar – hunting, game
shirvani – fitted, knee-length jacket worn by men
shukriya – thank you
swadeshi – of this country
tawa – flat cast iron cooking pan
theek hai – okay
thora – a little bit
topi – hat
yaar – friend

Iqbal's ditty on p99 means:
Add garam masala, coriander and cumin! Food for the queen must be yummy!